MAKER SPACE

MAKER SPACE

K.B. SPANGLER

A GIRL AND HER FED BOOKS
NORTH CAROLINA

For Dave, Cora, Tandy Rose, and Daphne Violet

ONE

Lovely. She had been lovely a twist of auburn hair pulled across her head like a princess, her white dress as crisp as the autumn morning. She had smiled at him before looking down and away, and had stepped lightly through the open door of a coffee shop.

His was a staircase wit and he realized, too late, that maybe he should have followed her. He caught himself before he turned back. Two blocks later, he found another coffee shop and went inside; something with ice to take the heat from him, and to purchase ten minutes of time at a seat by the front window. If he could arrange to bump into her again, good. If not, well, he was on his break anyhow.

He tugged at the knot of his tie as he watched for a slip of white in the crowd. She was gone, probably forever, but those who passed by were entertainment enough. The professionals in their tight suits. Tourists, overlarge bags weighing them down. Those sinister teenagers, killing time, pretending to smoke... He sipped his coffee and smiled; he had never looked like that, he was sure.

Some of those in the street suddenly stopped and turned to look back down the road in the direction of the woman in white.

He felt the tremor through his feet, a sharp but slow rumble that came up from the ground. He glanced around, then back out at the street. Earthquake? No, those outside had fallen but the ground beneath them was solid. A spray of dust flew over them, striking against their faces, their eyes...

He was out of the coffee shop before he knew it, helping one of the tourists regain her feet, pulling her back into the store as the rumbling clouds swept by. She was coughing, grabbing at his sleeve and begging for her husband. He pushed her into someone's open arms and went back outside, his face pressed into the crook of his arm to block the dust, searching for a man on the ground.

The glass caught him first, ripping up and over the left side of his body. It blew past him, shoved against him, went *through* him. He knew he was falling but he didn't know why; he tried to catch himself but his hands wouldn't move.

His chest struck flat against a lamppost, then the sidewalk. He rolled twice, a bundle of odd limbs, and came to rest against a shattered car. His right eye stared up at the burning husk of the coffee house and he thought he smelled barbecue.

The sound of a third explosion came from up the street.

TWO

The garden defied the laws of nature. Rachel Peng didn't know much about plants, but she knew tulips shouldn't bloom in mid-October. She was sure it should have taken the jasmine more than two months to be trained up the new trellises, or to spill down from the arbor in a cascade of white flowers. And she didn't even want to think about those roses.

Rachel ran a scan through her own front yard and saw the pansies by the mailbox were about to bloom. And, hiding behind the new hedge of hollies Santino had put in as a barrier between themselves and their next-door neighbor, Mrs. Wagner lay in wait.

Nope, Rachel thought.

She shifted her path mid-stride, moving smoothly from road to grass, and then down the rough gravel of the train embankment. This jogging path was a bit of a deathtrap. If the stones didn't kick out from under her, the perpetual unpredictability of Washington D.C.'s commuter rail might grind her shins to paste. The risk was worth it: she had nothing but scorn for those folks who plugged themselves into music or movies during their workouts. If you didn't enjoy something enough to experience it, why bother?

Still, there was a huge difference between being aware and being an idiot. Rachel threaded an autoscript through the warning devices on the nearby railroad crossings to give her a few miles' notice if a train came along.

She hopped up on one of the rails and ran along the bright metal for several hundred yards before her legs began to ache, then dropped back to the ground and pushed herself until she had to slow to a jog. It was getting easier. She was gradually beating her body back into its old Army shape, when she used to introduce new recruits to Afghanistan with a casual ten-mile sprint. Thirty, if they got mouthy.

Her implant flashed a warning from a railroad crossing to the east, and Rachel threw a casual scan towards the train coming up the tracks. It was moving slowly, and she had plenty of time to scramble down the embankment and over the security fence before it passed.

All trains had names. Rachel hadn't known this until she had found this jogging path and had learned to recognize each train as it flew by. The RFID tags on this one put it as the *Sweet Clementine* out of Glenmont Station, an older train, and one that somehow seemed a little proud of itself—

Rachel stomped on that thought, hard. Anthropomorphize a couple of fire trucks as a kid, and you found yourself doing the same damn thing as an adult once the trains started talking back.

She put in a few more miles to kill time, then looped around and retraced the tracks towards her house. As soon as she got within range, she threw another scan through her front yard, hoping to find an easy way home.

And Mrs. Wagner was still lurking behind the hedge.

The old woman had more stamina than Rachel, who swore bitterly before giving up and jogging towards her own front door. (Sneaking in the back way was not an option; the people who owned the house behind hers kept a bulldog, all jowls and teeth.) The moment Rachel came into view, Mrs. Wagner popped up, smiling.

This time, she had a casserole dish.

"Hi, Mrs. Wagner," Rachel said, stopping. Once, she had blown past her neighbor as fast as she could run, shouting and feigning a personal emergency. Mrs. Wagner had followed her up to Rachel's front porch, and then leaned on the doorbell for an hour straight. Contact meant conversation.

"Rachel, Rachel," Mrs. Wagner said, holding out the old Fiesta bakeware. Rachel had several formal titles, each of them unwieldy beasts in the mouth, and they all seemed to frighten her neighbor so Mrs. Wagner tended to just double down on her first name. "I was cooking, and I made a little something extra for you and your… For you and Officer Santino."

"Thank you." Rachel forced a smile. Mrs. Wagner's cookies weren't too bad, but anything that came in a casserole dish always tasted as though a cat had slept in it. The woman was also saturated in nervous yellows and oranges; if it weren't for the flashes of wine-dark red spotting her neighbor's conversational colors, Rachel would have scared the old woman off ages ago.

For a very brief period in early August, Rachel had been famous. Ten weeks later, only Mrs. Wagner seemed to remember her next-door neighbor had very nearly caught a couple of sociopaths. Microwave memory, Santino called it, that brief flash of public interest crisped quick and then discarded to make room for the next story in the news cycle.

Falling out of the public eye hadn't bothered Rachel in the slightest. As one of the three hundred and fifty-ish cybernetically-augmented humans employed by the U.S. government, Rachel valued whatever anonymity she could find. She was relieved—delighted, actually—when the media had moved on from her to obsess over drones, Edward Snowden, and the NSA. Cyborgs were on the verge of becoming yesterday's news.

She kept hoping Mrs. Wagner would forget about her, too. Rachel used to describe her relationship with her neighbor as "strained", a short, quick word which allowed her to gloss over the times when Mrs. Wagner had spray-painted slurs across her house, or assaulted her with a golf club. But when Rachel had briefly become a local hero, Mrs. Wagner had apologized for how she had treated Rachel, and had been doing a matronly version of heavy penance ever since.

Mrs. Wagner meant well. The woman was still scared to death of Rachel, but there was always some wine red within her conversational colors to show she was sincerely trying to make Rachel's life a little better.

Thus far, that wine red hue was the only thing that kept Rachel from outright strangling her.

Her neighbor pressed the casserole dish into Rachel's hands. "It's got butter in it. Make sure you eat it all," Mrs. Wagner said. "You're too thin."

Rachel started to reply with that old joke about never being too rich, when Santino cracked an upstairs window.

"Hey Rachel?" her partner shouted. "Where's the fire extinguisher?"

"I need to go," Rachel said as she took the old Fiestaware from her neighbor. "Thanks. I'll drop off the plate after I wash it."

Mrs. Wagner's conversational colors had shifted to the vivid orange of sudden apprehension. "I'll call the fire department."

"It's fine," Rachel said, backing away as quickly as she could. "We're cops. We'll take care of it."

She scooted through her front door and locked it behind her. When she turned, she found Raul Santino sprawled on the stairs, laughing in good-humored purples.

"I don't know which of you I should murder first," Rachel growled.

"It seemed like you needed an escape," he said.

"Yeah, but she threatened to call the—oh *God*," she sighed, as a plea to 911 sailed out from Mrs. Wagner's home line. "She actually called them."

"Put me through to the same operator," Santino said, holding up his cell. "I'll fix this."

Rachel followed the signal through the emergency router to its destination, and connected the operator's direct line to Santino's phone. "Done," she said. "I'll be in the shower. If the fire department is coming, tell them to pick up milk on the way."

Her partner, his phone pressed to his ear, nodded.

Rachel dropped the casserole dish beside him and pushed on up the stairs. She took a moment to enjoy the morning sunlight streaming through her bedroom windows; she had the master suite with its spacious private bathroom and southern exposure. When he had first moved in, Santino complained that his bedroom was all the way down the hall and offered no light for his plants. Rachel had told him to suck it up and start a garden if he wanted greenery so badly. He might pay rent, but it was her house, and they weren't switching just because he wanted more ferns. She was sure the new fairy kingdom barely disguised as landscaping was Santino's polite way of telling her to go fuck herself, but the joke was on him—the house had been reappraised the week before and had magically acquired an additional forty grand in equity.

And that was in spite of the ruin they had made of her kitchen.

She closed the bedroom door and made sure to set a privacy message before stripping off her jogging suit. An Agent forgot to set that message only once, and then never again. Every cyborg had a story of that single heart-stopping instant when, oh, for example, you were sitting naked on the toilet after an especially offensive five-bean salad, and someone from Accounting decided to pop in and ask whether you still needed that copy of last year's Form 1040A.

Not that they were still dropping in on each other without calling ahead, but hard-won lessons tended to stick. They had all done their fair share of hard learning over the past year as they adapted to their new lives.

Everything about the Agents was new.

Newish, really. By this point, the Agents were past the worst of the discovery phase, and anyone outside of the Program who cared to know about the Agents of the Office of Adaptive and Complementary Enhancement Technologies was familiar with their story. The Agents had decided to go public with the news that the U.S. government had turned them into cyborgs. Not the clankity-clank pneumatic gun-arm variety of cyborg, but the type that was otherwise completely human except for the tiny chip in their brain which allowed them to take control of any networked machine.

(If she had been given the option, Rachel probably would have chosen the gun arm, or the rocket legs, or any other heavy artillery to augment her own natural stopping power instead of the implant. But those were the stuff of science fiction; she had no idea how a piece of technology as complex as her implant could have been invented before the scientists perfected flamethrower fingers. Different priorities, she supposed. Still. Flamethrower fingers.)

The Agents had spent five long years in hiding before they had chosen to go public. Nearly nine months after that first press conference, Congress was still on the defensive, claiming the Agents were—well, not *wrong*, as such…perhaps *misinformed* was the better word—about certain details. Like the accusation that certain high-ranking politicians had decided that OACET was an unwanted headache, and that everything about the Program should disappear. Permanently.

There were nearly a hundred new graves at Arlington. The Agents had told Congress they were still trying to locate those missing fifty-odd bodies. It had been a rough five years.

Congress was on the defensive; the cyborgs were not. When asked, the Agents generally waved away the question of why they had waited so long to expose their top-secret organization. They said they had needed time to wrestle with the moral dilemma of whether it was better to follow orders and remain hidden as a top-secret government program, or to become whistleblowers and let the world know of the near-omniscient cyborgs in their midst.

It was a good answer. There was plenty of plausibility in it, and it established the Agents as people who struggled with outcomes in the eyes of the public. It showed how at least *some* people in this whole fiasco were aware of consequences, even if those people weren't exactly human any more.

Rachel hoped that answer wouldn't backfire on them in a big way.

Shower done, Rachel threw on old jeans and a worn Army sweatshirt, dragged her fingers through her short black hair, and called it done. Makeup required her to do funky things with her vision, and she couldn't be bothered on her day off.

She made her way downstairs. The hallway leading to the kitchen had been hurriedly painted white; streaks showed where a roller had been inexpertly run over the old wallpaper. The white paint was covered over in long chunky stripes of color, each of which looked suspiciously as though it had been applied with a finger.

The kitchen was a thousand times worse. What had once been her charming white country kitchen was now a vibrant canvas of paint swatches streaked across every available surface. Cabinets, appliances, even the ceiling, all had been peppered with blotches of color. Worse, there seemed to be no unifying pattern to the mess. Hunter green and dusty rose butted up against each other. Cedar red was offset by lime and ultramarine. It was a designer's headache come to life.

She and Santino had learned to ignore it.

Their guests were *appalled.*

Santino was standing over the trash can, staring at the contents of the casserole dish.

"What do you think?" she asked him.

"It's got fish in it," he replied. "Smells like it's gone over. You can eat some if you want to, but I'm not risking it."

Rachel nodded, and Santino knocked the dish against the side of the can until it was empty.

"Do we have any real food?" she asked, scanning the cupboards.

"Real food for normal humans, or real food for cyborgs who eat five times as much as I do?"

"Both," she said. "Unless we've just got the latter, in which case you are welcome to watch me eat."

He pointed towards the garbage.

"A-ha ha. Funny man."

"Rachel…" Phil's voice swept through her head.

"Hang on." Rachel laid her hand on the countertop for support. Conversations via the cyborgs' link were more intimate than using a phone, and she wasn't one of those Agents who could hold a long conversation in her head without tripping over herself. "Phil's calling."

Of the two Agents who worked with Rachel at the

Washington D.C. Metropolitan Police Department, Phil Netz was the one she liked. He was a clever ball of energy, slightly taller than herself and weighing just a few pounds more. His slight build was ideal for his work with the MPD's Explosive Ordnance Disposal Unit, where he was frequently required to slide in and out of spaces barely large enough to hide ticking cardboard boxes.

The bomb squad loved him. After Rachel herself, Phil was the Agent most skilled in perception. She had taught him what she could, and he had taken her training over to the bomb squad where he adapted it to machines. He didn't have her finesse at reading people or environments, but he had an innate understanding of the hidden nature of the digital and the mechanical.

"How's my favorite skinny blond?" Rachel greeted him.

"You and Santino are still at your house? Are you on your way?" Phil's voice in her head was dressed for business. Now that she was paying attention, she could feel his anxiety through the link.

"No, should we be?" Rachel began to speak aloud for Santino's benefit. Her partner's lack of an implant was a major inconvenience. "We were about to get some food."

"Holy shit, I can't believe nobody's called you! Turn on the television."

"What channel?" she asked, as the pit of her stomach turned to cold lead. When the news was bad, there was only one answer to that question.

"Any," Phil replied. *"Track me and meet me on the scene. Get over here as quick as you can. We need you to look for survivors."*

The small Agent broke the connection.

Rachel closed her eyes, flipped off visuals on her implant, and savored the last few moments of her day off.

"Suit time?" Santino asked.

She nodded, and ran back upstairs to change.

THREE

Once upon a time, back when she was in the Army and climbing the ranks as fast as she could, Rachel had been ambitious. She had lost that drive over the past five years—nothing quashed ambition quite like realizing your employers had screwed you—but she tended to think of it as a cancer, sometimes in remission, but never fully gone. Every time she walked down the administrative wing at First District Station and saw those shiny brass nametags, she would feel the distant tug of a General's star.

One day, she'd tell herself. *Maybe. If you get bored.*

Since the events of the previous August, she and Santino had been anything but bored. The two of them had recognized that playing cat-and-mouse with a maniac on the public stage had provided them with an opportunity that might never come again, and they had seized it. Their partnership at the Metropolitan Police Department might have started out as a publicity stunt to promote goodwill between OACET and local law enforcement, but they had kept the momentum going long enough to turn their temporary partnership into a formal unit within the MPD. When August came to an end, they found themselves with a budget, a supervisor, and business cards with fancy raised type.

Santino was thriving. Until Rachel had come along, the D.C. Police had neither a title nor a position for a nerd cop with multiple graduate degrees in computer engineering and information technologies. It was only after First MPD had agreed to take on a liaison from OACET that they had finally figured out what to do with him, and Santino had been given an office and told he could start wearing suits.

And Rachel, who had spent the last five years doing as close to nothing as could be arranged by the U.S. government, was working again. The ambition would probably return, but for the time being, she was content to hunt the bad guys and put them in jail.

Life's simple pleasures.

They were First MPD's new problem-solvers. Officially, she and Santino were specialized technicians that other MPD officers called when they ran into a technological wall. Unofficially, the two of them had become everything from repair guys to a portable diagnostics machine. After August, word of Rachel's abilities had gotten around, and Santino, who was so much better with technology than she would ever be, was the one who fixed what she couldn't.

He could not, however, see through walls. Which, on days like today, put him in the unenviable position of providing nothing but support.

Or, more precisely, a distraction which kept her from dwelling on the bad stuff under the debris.

They pulled up to the curb in silence. The first part of the drive had been filled with the babble of near-panicked reporters, every station turned over to cover the breaking story. When the news began to repeat itself, Rachel had flipped off the radio and immersed herself in the link to see if anyone else at OACET had inside information: they didn't; they were waiting on her to get down to the scene before they cranked up the gossip mill.

She had dropped out of the link and stared straight ahead, keeping her scan as narrow as possible as Santino, white-knuckled hands on the wheel, drove them through the checkpoints and barricades. They parked on a street cordoned off for law enforcement and first responders. Santino tucked his little car among the police vehicles, and took a breath; Rachel recognized it as his own private moment of peace before the storm broke.

A fighter jet screamed by overhead.

They opened the doors, and the chaos hit them.

Sirens, dozens of them. Camera crews and shouting reporters

followed Rachel and Santino as they stepped out of the car into a too-sunny autumn morning. Across the street, the public cried for answers. The D.C. Police pushed back against the press; a harried sergeant checked their credentials, and let them cross the final barrier.

They made an odd pair, her and Santino. A Chinese-American woman walking in step with a tall, dark Italian-American man didn't make much of a ripple in this day and age, but the two of them weren't exactly welcome here. If Rachel's abilities hadn't been needed, they would have been stuck on the sidelines with the civilians. The crowd parted for them, the police and EMTs pulling away. She noticed her partner was wearing dark glasses and a too-familiar stoic expression he had adopted from her own. Had circumstances been different, she would have teased him about trying to pass himself off as an Agent.

"How bad is it?" her partner asked.

"I'm running a tight scan," Rachel replied. "I see what you see."

He nodded.

"Phil's there," she said, pointing at a high-end shoe shop. "He's on the other side of this building." She was following the other Agent's GPS; Phil was too busy to give directions.

They followed the block to the end, then turned the corner onto what had once been a street.

"Oh," Santino breathed.

Rachel placed a firm hand on his elbow to steer him forward. She had seen worse, but not since the last time she was in a war zone.

The dust had settled. The asphalt was pitted and cracked where pieces had been blown out. The side of the block where the explosion had occurred was punctured by a broken hole. Signage was scattered across the street; Rachel recognized a distinctive green-and-white mermaid, and when she scanned the deepest regions of the crater, she found scraps of tables and the charred husk of a serving counter.

The other side of the block was almost pristine. In the bakery across from the coffee shop, the plate glass was broken but the bread behind it was still neatly stacked in thick loaves. The Halloween decorations were up in the neighboring drug store, cutouts of witches and cats strung alongside each other in black and orange.

She expanded her scan and sent it out across the ruins of the coffee shop, staying as shallow as possible. The upper layers of the debris were almost unrecognizable, garbage and metal ripped apart and thrown together without reason or meaning. A layer of broken glass was spread across the top, forming a scatter of sadly bright confetti. Figures in sealed uniforms carefully picked through the rubble to search for survivors, their surface colors dark and hopeless.

It looked like a battlefield after the survivors had fled, leaving dead and broken things beneath the wreckage. Rachel hadn't seen this level of destruction since Afghanistan, nearly six years before.

She dropped those frequencies which expanded her vision and restricted herself to simple radio waves; it cut her range of sight down to bumps and pulses, but there wasn't enough alcohol on the planet to blunt the sensation of her mind tripping and falling straight through a corpse.

"Holy shit," Santino whispered. He took a few hesitant steps towards the husk of the store before Rachel could grab his arm again.

"Don't." She shook her head and pointed at the third story. "It's unstable."

"You should warn them," Santino said, glancing towards the D.C. Police bomb squad combing through the rubble.

"Phil's with them," she said. "They already know."

The smallest of the uniformed figures broke from the others and jogged over to greet them. It pulled at a strap around its neck and the hood fell away. The Agent shook his head like a horse, his lanky blond hair whipping the sides of his face. His conversational colors were reds and grays, and she could barely see his bright silver core through the clouds.

"Hey guys," Phil said. He removed a glove to shake Santino's hand, looking intently at Rachel as he did. She nodded through the link and pulled up the memory of her morning jog, the simple rhythm of her feet on the bright metal of the train rail, and held that tight as Phil reached out to her under the pretense of politeness.

For Agents, skin contact was a curse or a gift, depending. She shut her eyes against his hard rush of feelings and hoped what he took from her could help.

"*That bad?*" she asked through their link.

"*Worst I've ever seen,*" he replied with a mental sigh. "*Don't go deep. You won't like what you find.*"

"*Yeah. Try low-frequency radar as your main and drop the others to secondary status. You still get the penetration, but you don't get the sensation.*"

"*Oh, Jesus, why didn't I think of that?*" Phil said, and his colors lost some of their grays as he shut part of himself down.

"What happened?" Santino asked him.

"Gayle Street's basically gone," Phil told them. Gayle Street was part of Washington D.C.'s shopping district, within easy walking distance of the monuments and heavily traveled by locals and tourists. "There's a fourteen-block stretch where a bomb was detonated almost every other block. Seven bombs in total. It was a coordinated attack. The bombs started down there," Phil said, pointing west. Over the arc of his finger were Capitol Hill and the White House, the first of which was barely a mile away. "The first one went off, then there was a small delay—we're thinking maybe two, three minutes, tops—before the second bomb was triggered. Sequential order going bomb, delay, bomb, delay, bomb, delay." Phil was a hand talker and pounded one fist against his palm to underscore those two hard words.

Rachel took a couple of steps backwards and swept her scans up and down the street. "Maximum confusion and damage?"

Phil nodded. "Looks that way. There's an explosion, people's first instinct is to take shelter. Nothing else happens, they get curious and go exploring."

"Or they turn into Good Samaritans and break cover to help the victims. Either way, they're just more fuel for the chaos."

In the nearby ruin of the store, a member of the bomb squad yelled at Phil to get his ass back over to them and help.

"Agent Peng's here!" he shouted to them. Their conversational colors brightened; Rachel was surprised. A lot of things had changed for her and Santino over the past few weeks, but it was still rare for anybody from the D.C. Police to be happy to see them.

"How can we help?" Santino asked.

"Rachel's Rachel," Phil replied. "We've filled up a dozen hospitals with the wounded, but there might be a few we haven't been able to locate. It'll be a while before the search dogs get here, and the rescue teams have to go slow because of the structural damage. Our best chance of finding survivors is if she and I start from here and work our way up and down either side of the street."

It was a good plan. Phil and another bomb technician headed east, while Rachel and Santino went west. Gayle Street was deserted except for the emergency crews, and the black body bags slowly beginning to line the center of the road. She had reactivated her full spectrum scans and was juggling multiple perspectives simultaneously. Her targeted scans penetrated the buildings on a straight line running perpendicular to her feet, hunting and pecking through the bomb sites for survivors. Distance scans came next, searching the rooftops for any sudden movement: first responders were a juicy secondary target.

She moved quickly across the debris, Santino stumbling as he tried to keep up.

"Step where I step," she told him, her implant helping her find the surest path when the rubble got thick.

The problem with sticking untested experimental technology in human beings is that human beings love to test and experiment. The implant was ostensibly for communication, its primary purpose to allow interaction between two or more Agents, or between Agents and machines. But wireless communications piggybacked on the electromagnetic spectrum, and you didn't really appreciate how big a role the electromagnetic spectrum plays in everyday life until you were suddenly able to perceive the whole damn thing. With some testing and experimentation, the Agents had learned they could do a lot more than talk to each other over distances. Every day, someone discovered a new trick or technique which looked suspiciously like a superpower.

Rachel had used her implant to develop and improve her perception. When a non-Agent asked her to describe what she could do, she'd shrug and say she could see through walls. If they wanted details, she'd put a name to it and call it her second sight or her sixth sense, but those terms were inaccurate in a whole bunch of ways, and she used them for no other reason than to keep her life simple. Everybody understood sight. They didn't understand vision entwined with touch, the sensations of light and dark, color and texture, blended together and running through her mind in the same way as if she had watched herself drag her hand across a warm, sunny carpet.

It was a complicated, confusing process, sorting out these crossed senses. Some days she thought she was finally getting the hang of it. Other days found her horribly motion-sick for no obvious reason, and she found her only recourse was to take a Tylenol and a nap.

Today was a very good day, perception-wise. She had no problems finding those frequencies which allowed her to see but not feel. Every detail of the street stood out crystal-clear in her head; she could penetrate fifty feet into the rubble, bumping into the debris of shops and businesses, running across what was left of the infrastructure beneath.

There were bodies throughout.

When she found them, she and Santino would stop and consult with the law enforcement presence at the scene. She would give what details she could, depth and location and similar, and they would move on, searching. Hoping.

There were no survivors.

Two blocks up, they consulted with the FBI bomb squad working the ruins of a drugstore. Eighteen bodies. No survivors.

Another block without a bomb. Rachel glared at the lone coffee shop that was still standing when all others had been blown to dust up and down the street, and idly wondered if its owner had finally hit on a way to eliminate the competition.

The next block was another bomb squad, this one on loan from Homeland Security. Three bodies, this time.

And no survivors.

Rachel had heard stories of search-and-rescue canine units, the dogs brought in after earthquakes or mudslides or whatever tragedy had swept a hundred souls beneath the earth. As the days wore on and the corpses started to outnumber the living, the dogs would become depressed, and would even begin to mourn the dead. She stifled a dark chuckle at the thought of Santino running a few blocks ahead and covering himself in debris, the handlers' trick to give their dogs the happy thrill of finally finding someone alive.

The next block up was different, somehow. It took Rachel a moment to puzzle out why: this bomb had just taken out the one store and left those to either side untouched.

Santino had seen it, too. "Smaller payload?"

"Or the explosives didn't detonate properly. Or they put the bomb in a stupid place... Could be a lot of things. Phil will know."

She turned away from the store and scanned the street, mostly to pretend to herself she was still working and not avoiding the inevitable body count.

Red pain burned fierce beneath a pile of rubble.

She paused, shocked, and stopped dead in her path.

Santino was watching the buildings instead of his feet, and ran straight into her back. "Sorry," he said instinctively.

Rachel was moving again, more slowly this time. "Shit," she whispered.

"What?"

Her stupor broke. She sprinted to the rubble and started hurling the top layer of broken bricks and granite aside.

"Help!" she shouted. "Medics! Help! We've got a live one!"

Santino swore and dropped to his knees beside her.

The victim had been protected by a scrap of corrugated sheet metal. Rachel thought it might be a scrap of a commercial awning, but didn't bother to flip her implant to reading mode to check the blurry text printed on one side. She and Santino scraped the debris away and tried to shake the metal loose. When it refused to budge, Santino removed his suit coat, wrapped it around his hands, then grabbed the awning by its sharp edges and hurled it away with a snarl.

The man—Rachel guessed it was a man from his build and his shoes—was conscious. His conversational colors brightened ever-so-slightly through his red pain, and he moaned.

Santino blanched. "Oh God," he said. "Look at him. There's barely any skin left… And his *eyes*…"

The victim's red pain darkened again, streaks of black and gray anxiety threading through it.

"Quiet!" Rachel hissed. "He can hear you."

The man on the ground tried to move.

"Stay down," Rachel told him. She knelt as close to his head as she could. He smelled of raw iron and cooked meat. "I'm Agent Peng, and this is Officer Santino. We're with the D.C. Police. There was an explosion. You were caught in it and it took us a little time to rescue you, but you're safe now."

The anxiety pulled away from the man's core: she was a strong believer that an informed victim was a calm victim, and it was gratifying to see she was right.

"…can't see…" His voice was thin and wet.

Rachel shushed him. "Don't talk. Stay still. You've got—" She paused, and ran a scan through his body. Her new medical diagnostic autoscript gave her an itemized injury report. "—fractured ribs, a diaphragmatic hernia, and serious damage to your brachial plexus."

Santino's eyebrows went up. Rachel wished the physician who

had written that autoscript had thought to add layman's terms; she was sure she had butchered the clinical pronunciations, and rather hoped Santino wouldn't ask her to explain the diagnosis.

The man coughed and then twisted, trying to protect his broken self. Santino tried to hold the man down by his shoulders, and he screamed at Santino's touch.

"I'm getting your wallet out," Rachel told the man, swatting Santino away. "We need to give your name and any medical information to the EMTs." She slipped her hand into what was left of the man's jacket. His wallet, thick brown leather, had survived. She drew it from his pocket as carefully as she could, and flipped it open.

"Jordan Meisner? Hey, Jordan," she said, handing his wallet to Santino. "You hear that? The truck driving up? That's your ambulance. You'll be resting on a morphine cloud before you know it."

The burned skin around Meisner's mouth twitched, his colors brightened ever so slightly. "Morphine," he whispered. "…heard good things…"

The EMTs arrived with shouting and shouldering, and Rachel and Santino were almost ten feet away from the victim before they knew it. They watched as an ambulance was let through the barricades, and then waited until the man was loaded inside before they turned back to the buildings.

"Aw hell," Santino muttered.

"What?"

He held up Meisner's wallet. "They took his license and insurance card. I didn't even think about it when the EMT handed the rest back to me."

Rachel opened her voluminous handbag and her partner tossed the wallet inside. "We can drop it off at the hospital. I'd like to follow up with that guy, anyhow, see if he's going to pull through. I'd like to think we saved one."

"We've still got another few blocks after this," Santino said.

Rachel nodded. They started walking again, their black mood wearing lighter.

"Do you know what you said back there? Because I sure don't."

"Shut up."

"No, really," Santino said, waving a hand as if searching for a thought. "I *think* you told him he's got soft tissue and nerve damage, but you might have been listing car models. It's hard to be sure."

"Not all of us are overeducated nerds, Santino."

"Obviously."

She casually stepped on the back of his shoe, then sped up ever so slightly so he'd have to shuffle behind her to fix his flat tire.

Good. His grays had taken on a very small tint of purple. She was sure hers had changed, too; she'd have to bring Phil up to speed on reading human emotions so he could check her own colors for her.

She was the only OACET Agent who could perceive the emotional spectrum. Jenny Davies, the physician who had developed the diagnostic autoscript, had a pet theory that moods had different wavelengths or frequencies, like color or sound, and that these were part of the electromagnetic spectrum. (Once, Jenny had asked Rachel to write down those emotions she could name—yellow for fright, blue for calm, and so on—and Rachel had invited Jenny over to see her kitchen. Jenny had taken Rachel up on her offer, and... Well. Jenny had let the subject drop after that.) But Rachel couldn't see her own colors, and sometimes grumbled over the circular irony of her own emotional state remaining inaccessible to herself.

The next block in the chain was the busiest. This had been the largest payload, and the buildings had sustained the greatest damage. But, happily, this was also the site of the fewest casualties; the firefighters were still trying to put out the blaze, but the paramedics were standing to either side, unneeded. She made a mental note to find out why.

"What was this place?" Rachel asked.

"Bookstore," Santino answered automatically. The purple

hue was gone. "They had a great gardening section."

"Was there a café, too?" She scanned the burning hull, unable to find anything other than hollow spaces where paper and wood had once been.

"Yeah."

She ran her mind up and down the street, foot tapping on the pavement.

"What?" her partner asked.

"You know Disneyland?"

The purples in his conversational colors returned. "I might have heard of it. Little place out in California, right?"

Rachel ignored him and pushed on. "Have you heard the story of how Walt Disney spaced out the refreshment stands?" She threw a scan over her shoulder and spaced the distance between the bookstore and where they had found Meisner. "He was having a business meeting in the park, right before it opened. He bought an ice cream cone at one stand, and he and his buddies walked along while he ate it…"

"…and when he had finished the cone, he told them, 'Put another refreshment stand right here,'" Santino finished for her. "I'm not sure if that really happened or if it's apocryphal."

"Small words, Santino," she said. "Normal human beings use small words."

"You don't get to lecture me on what's normal," he said, as he grinned at her. "Anyway. What's your point? That the bad guys dropped a bomb every time they finished an ice cream cone?"

"No," she said. "Maybe. Just a stray thought. They had to pick their targets somehow. If they were trying to do as much damage as possible, easy walking distance between those shops might figure into it."

"It's not our job to figure that out," he said.

"Oh, you wide-eyed innocent," she said as they moved towards the next site. "When bombs are involved, it's *everybody's* job."

FOUR

A bombing was like the murder of a family member: even if the two of you weren't exactly close, it still shut down your routine. When a bombing occurred, every schedule, every plan, got pushed aside, and the many clans of law enforcement would come together and put aside their differences to avenge the dead.

Rachel and Santino knew they were decidedly second cousins, at best. They had been allowed on site to search for the living, and once she confirmed all survivors had been located, they were told to leave. Politely, to be sure; Rachel's discovery of Meisner had led to friendly nods and high-fives all around, but now that their job was done, she and Santino were in the way. Santino passed out their new business cards, the FBI and Homeland and the rest promised to keep in touch, and each pretended they wouldn't immediately forget the other until the next time someone needed a favor.

"Lunch?" she asked her partner as they crossed the first checkpoint.

"After *that?*" Santino was horrified.

"They're dead. We're not." Rachel shrugged. "Life requires food."

"I used to shop at that bookstore," he said wearily.

There was nothing she could say to that.

As they walked back to his car, they saw Detectives Matt Hill and Jacob Zockinski waiting for them on the far side of the barricade. Their colors brightened when Rachel and Santino came into view, but they kept themselves to tight nods; homicide detectives were, by definition, too cool to wave.

"Got called in?" Santino asked them.

No," Zockinski said, shaking his head. "We were told..." he

said, and his voice dropped an octave to mimic that of Edward Sturtevant, their Chief of Detectives: "'Get down there, find the Agents, and make yourselves useful.'"

"Aw, that's so sweet," she said. "Sturtevant thinks we need you."

"Hey, he said *useful*. Maybe he meant we should arrest you before you make things worse."

"Not one word," she said to Santino, who pantomimed zipping his lips.

Zockinski and Hill had worked with them a couple of times since the four of them had gone hunting sociopaths back in August. Zockinski had seniority; he was older than Hill by a few years, and he had been with the MPD the longest of the four of them. Hill was an up-and-comer in Homicide, and Rachel considered him a distant relative; Hill had recently reunited with a cousin in OACET, which made him kin.

"What's the damage?" Hill asked her, nodding towards the far side of the street.

"Nothing you haven't seen before," she told him. Hill had served in Iraq and Afghanistan a few years before her. They never spoke about what they had done when they were over there, but she knew his unit had been one of the first on the ground and she had drawn her own conclusions. "But not stateside."

Hill's colors folded in on themselves in a purple-gray sigh. "This is going to change a lot of things around here."

The four of them turned towards the U.S. Capitol, not quite a mile away but hidden from sight by the city.

"Right on their doorstep," Santino said. "Coincidence? Anybody?"

No one bothered to answer.

"Are we using the T-word?" Rachel asked.

"Terrorism?" Zockinski snorted. "Of course. When was the last time we had an event like this and didn't call it terrorism?"

"When it was committed by a white guy?" Rachel replied, and Hill chuckled.

Santino and Zockinski, both white guys by way of different shores of the Mediterranean, ignored them. "Did anyone report a bomb threat?" Santino asked.

"No." Hill crossed his arms and tilted his head towards the Capitol. "Nothing, unless Homeland is playing it tight."

"They wouldn't," Rachel said, and shook her head. "Not with something like this, unless you believe the conspiracy theorists." Hill raised an eyebrow, so she added, "You know, the ones who say the War on Terror is finally winding down, so there'll be a staged attack to drum up renewed support, funding…"

Hill glanced back towards the street, then met Rachel's eyes. She shrugged to say: *That's not a conversation for today. There be dragons in it.*

"Who's taking credit?" Santino asked.

"So far? Everyone," Zockinski said. "If an organization has a black band on its file, they've claimed responsibility."

"Great," Rachel said. "They're going to make us flip this town upside down as payback."

"Who?" Zockinski asked. "Terrorists?"

Rachel pointed in the direction of Capitol Hill, and started walking the other way.

The three men followed her. Lucky for her, really. She had no idea what she was doing or where she was going, but with the others in tow she felt as though she had a sense of purpose.

She was not, however, fooling them; they had barely taken ten steps before they realized they were wandering aimlessly. A bomb scene on the other side of the buildings and they had no direction… *And isn't that annoyingly symbolic?* Rachel muttered to herself. *Let's just knock that off right now.*

"So," Zockinski said, as if reading her mind. "Do we head back to First?"

They all glanced back over their shoulders towards their cars, then the crowd, and down the street to where traffic was a thick smear of taillights. *Ah, logistics,* Rachel thought. First District Station was within walking distance but annoyingly so, and the Metro lines had been shut down due to the bombings.

"No, but let's not stand around here," Rachel said. Her stomach pinched a reminder, and she shot a cold glare at her partner. It would be so much easier if he had an implant. She had to rely on body language to communicate how if he didn't feed her soon, she would be forced to kill and eat him.

"We could," Santino said, "wait at that pizza place a few blocks over."

Oh thank God. Rachel sighed, as the others agreed.

She didn't know whether the restaurant would be empty or packed with tourists and ambulance chasers waiting for an opening. It was neither; most of the other patrons were in law enforcement themselves, killing time while the first responders finished the rescue and recovery phase. Once the last of the victims had been removed and the structural damage assessed, the scene would be turned over for evidence collection and processing. Until then, the forensics teams had little to do—at least, those who worked with buildings instead of bodies.

They snagged a booth near a window and pretended to talk about sports. Nobody's heart was in it, and their eyes kept wandering towards the street to watch the people walking by, the men and women too wide-eyed and alert, the couples holding each other a little too close.

Too much red or too much gray, and no joy anywhere: even on the rainiest day, there were always dots of happy yellow in the crowd. Rachel sighed and flipped off the emotional spectrum. It was a decision she regretted almost immediately, as no sooner did their food arrive than Edward Sturtevant walked in and headed straight for their table.

The men glared at her: she was almost always able to give them some warning before the Chief of Detectives dropped in on them. She gave a small one-shouldered shrug. *Sorry guys, dropped the ball.* Outside of OACET, only Santino knew she identified people by their core colors instead of their physical characteristics, and she rarely bothered to tell him when she turned off emotions.

Core colors were unique to each person. These formed the

center of their selves, and were almost always unchanging; when these cores did change, the change seemed to reflect a permanent change within the self. Sturtevant's core had been a dark burnished gold since the day she had met him; the color suited him. It was solid, official, and had earned a rough patina by rite of time and experience. She flipped the emotional spectrum on, and this dark gold core appeared, surrounded by a layer of what Rachel referred to as conversational colors. These floated just at the surface; conversational colors reflected a person's mood, and were thus always changing and in motion. Right now, Sturtevant's surface colors were so dark they were nearly black.

Rachel was still learning which mood was accompanied by which color, but she was pretty sure she had nailed down black.

Sturtevant stopped at the edge of the booth and looked down at them, and the three MPD officers scrambled to find him a chair.

Rachel stayed in her seat and gave him a jolly little wave.

"That thing you can do…" he told her. "Do it. But let them see us."

She usually hated ambiguous orders, but this time Sturtevant had his reasons. Rachel nodded, and flipped off visuals to concentrate. When it came to playing with frequencies, she was the best Agent in OACET by an enormous margin, but what the Chief was asking required a hell of a lot of concentration.

A bubble. A bubble large enough to seal the table away, to block any and all surveillance devices before they could record their conversation? Easy enough. But one which let them be seen and not heard, that was a trick and a half. Patrick Mulcahy, head of OACET, had shown her how to block frequencies by running what was essentially a series of scans, but his method was too crude, a shield built from scraps of stray frequencies and shoved into place to repel or scramble most of the major EMF frequencies before they could reach him.

No thank you. No generic all-purpose barriers for her. She had decided that if blocking frequencies was just another type of scan, she was going to master it.

She let her mind slip into the pizza parlor, gathering specific frequencies together like picking strands of woven silk from the air. Each time she did this, the frequencies needed to be different. There would always be radio—that was a given, there was almost never a time when she didn't use radio—but radio was a massive thing in and of itself. She had to pick out how and why radio should be used, and blend it into those other frequencies she selected to block, to counter, to screen...

Well. She was a cop. She loved puzzles.

An opaque silver sphere, invisible to everyone but her, wrapped around the table. She was smack dab in its middle, but that was mostly for convenience; trial and error had shown her that she could throw this sphere wherever she damn well pleased, and it would work just as well without her pretending to be the center of its universe.

Rachel opened her eyes and flipped on visuals.

"We good?" Sturtevant asked. She nodded. "Good," Sturtevant said, then turned to Zockinski. "How are the kids?"

They killed a few minutes discussing Zockinski's twin daughters until anyone who might be eavesdropping from the nearby tables would be thoroughly bored, and then Sturtevant said: "We've been expecting this for a while."

They all shut up, except Rachel. "Who's 'we'?"

"The MPD, the Feds, everybody. It's so fucking easy to walk into a coffee shop and blow it up," Sturtevant said, his conversational colors slipping into furious reds as he spoke. "It was just a matter of time."

Agreement all around; the four of them had sat through the preparedness scenarios and those endless repetitive drills.

"We were expecting an asshole with a backpack bomb," Sturtevant said. "Nobody expected a coordinated attack over a fourteen-block stretch in downtown D.C."

He was quiet for a few moments, lines of red snapping through the black like thin whips. "I don't like it," he finally said. "It doesn't play right. This isn't a bunch of idiot kids with pressure cookers, and there's been no chatter to suggest it's an organization. This is..."

"Surgical," said Hill.

"Yes," Sturtevant agreed. "Surgical. Good word. If an organization is behind this, it's a new phase in how they operate. If it's not an organization..."

"Oh, shit. Military," Rachel said, snapping upright. "You think this is military?"

"An attack by a foreign national on our soil?" Sturtevant said. "That's worst-case scenario. That's absolute worst-case scenario. And right now, it's an option."

"Can we not jump straight to the scenario that puts us in a war?" Santino said, "Just because this is the first time it's been big and clean doesn't mean a foreign power's behind it. There are zealots out there, and there are people who know how to build very good explosive devices. It was just a matter of time before those two came together."

"Everybody thinks they know how to build bombs," Rachel said around a mouthful of pizza. "Nobody does. Not the kind of bombs that can cause the damage we saw today. You can't even get the materials to do something like this, let alone get access to set those bombs in place unnoticed."

Santino shook his head. "You'd be surprised," he told her. "I know some people who could pull this off, no question. They wouldn't do it—they wouldn't even *think* about doing it—but they've got the skills, and they don't need much in the way of resources."

The rest of the table shrugged him off in a reddish-purple sigh. Outside of work and OACET, Santino's friends were usually nerds, and always functionally harmless. Her partner's colors dipped towards orange-yellow irritation, and she sent a quick text to his phone: *"Tell me more about them later."*

His phone buzzed and he slipped it beneath the table to surreptitiously check the message, then glared at her as his irritation darkened into red anger. Apparently, he was not in the mood for a sop.

"You two done?" Sturtevant asked them. "Okay. So. As of today, your cases have been reassigned or tabled. Yes," he said to Zockinski and Hill, "even that messy one. Sorry.

"You see what's out there?" he asked them, pointing out the window. "It's the biggest, friendliest law enforcement team-up we've had since September 11th. Bigger, probably, since we've been preparing for something like this for years."

"What do you want us to do?" Rachel asked.

"Nothing," Sturtevant said. "If the preparedness scenarios work as planned? You do absolutely nothing."

"What if things don't go as planned?" Zockinski asked.

Sturtevant pointed at him.

"You're worried about groupthink," Santino said.

"There're a lot of good things happening," Sturtevant said. "Law enforcement coming together, everybody focused on bringing the bad guys to justice. Should be perfect, right? We should be an efficient machine, each department playing its own part. We've got the resources, we've done the training. So, Agent Peng, tell me what's wrong with this picture."

She almost laughed. "That's the same reason Congress created OACET."

OACET was the bastard child of good intentions. It was sold to Congress by one of their own, a certain Senator Richard Hanlon, who claimed the technology finally existed to bridge those persistent territorial gaps between the different branches of government. They had good reason to believe him: Hanlon had come to office via the private sector and his company had developed the prototype of the cyborgs' implant. Congress had allocated hundreds of millions for the new Office of Adaptive and Complementary Enhancement Technologies, recruited five hundred young federal employees as test subjects, and tucked the whole thing away behind innocuous code words until the fledgling cyborgs were ready to return to their jobs. If things had gone as planned, Rachel would have been back in the Army by now, earning those General's stars as she coordinated military operations with the other members of OACET.

But things so rarely go as planned.

"Do I have to tell you why I'm worried something might go wrong?" Sturtevant asked her.

She shook her head and reached for the last slice of pizza.

"I know you can't serve two masters, Peng," Sturtevant said to her. "Tell me right now if this is a conflict of interest for you."

"What is it you want us to do?" she asked.

Sturtevant said nothing.

"Ah," she said, nodding. "No, I don't see why that should be a problem."

"Good," Sturtevant said as he stood to leave. "As of this moment on, you're working this bombing as part the MPD. I'll put your names on the clearance lists. If anyone tries to cut you out, have them call me."

Sturtevant stalked away from the table, his colors still lashing out in reds and blacks. The four of them watched him go.

"Yay, purpose," Rachel said once the door has shut behind him. She began to slowly unweave her barrier; the feedback gave her a hell of a headache if she let the frequencies crash in on themselves.

"Love it—*love* it!—when he gives us orders without giving us orders," complained Zockinski.

"I get the feeling he wants a team," Santino said. "You know. Guys he can rely on to get the hard stuff done."

"Hard? You have any idea how hard you have to work to make Detective?" Zockinski retorted, reds flaring over his core of autumn orange. "If I'd wanted to be somebody's hired goon, there are easier ways."

"Ways that pay better," added Hill.

"You ever play chess against Sturtevant?" Santino asked them. "Try it sometime. Cyborgs aren't the only ones who play a good long game." He shot another hard look at Rachel as he tossed a few bucks on the table and went outside to cool off.

"What's up with your work wife?" Zockinski asked her once Santino was gone.

"You know why Sturtevant came down here?" Rachel opened

her purse and fumbled around for her wallet. It was usually on the top layer of strata, but had somehow sunk deep enough for her to root around at the bottom of the bag. "Because he's worried that everybody involved is going to jump to the wrong conclusion. Anything the four of us find? It's not going to make a difference. It's not like we're going to trip over that one little piece of evidence the bomb squad missed, or that one bad guy the FBI didn't find... We're supposed to bear witness on the impending shitstorm. We're spectators, and when this is over, we're going to write some nice anonymous hundred-page report about what happened, and why everybody suddenly decided to gang up on, oh, let's say, Serbia. And if we do our jobs right, what we put in that report will let Sturtevant and the MPD prevent a repeat of mistakes in the future. So Sturtevant is counting on us to think outside the box, and the first thing we do is shoot Santino down because his idea didn't fit into what we already expect.

"Plus, he's tired of us thinking that nerds are as harmless as wet kittens," she added, finally locating some money for a tip. "Doesn't matter if they are or not," she said, interrupting Zockinski. "They're his people, and when we bust on them, we bust on him."

With that, they went outside. Santino had a classic Italian temper, quick to boil over but even quicker to cool off, and they found him talking on his cell. He hung up and rejoined them.

"Jason's got access to the video," he said. "Figured we can start there while we wait for Forensics to process the street."

"Which video?" Zockinski asked. "Security feeds, personal phones...?"

Santino grinned. "All of it."

Jason Atran was the other Agent working with the MPD. He was the one she *didn't* like. Much. He didn't like her either, but that was to be expected: Jason didn't like anybody. Rachel reached out through the link and found him in his office.

She tried to keep the contact feather-light, but he still felt her ping him. *"Rachel."*

"Hey, Jason," she said. They all had tricks to wipe themselves of emotion. Hers was to think of concrete. She didn't know why it worked; it just did. When things got really hairy, she thought of Madison Square Garden and it cleared her mind right up. Fortunately (or not), she had an entire ruined street less than a few blocks away which offered her plenty of distractions, and she held on to the image of a nearby broken building as he chitter-chattered in her head.

"Wait, what?" Jason had said something which yanked her attention back into his monologue. *"Say that again."*

He sighed in her mind, and she felt him roll his eyes. *"I said, I've got the facial recognition scans going and nobody has popped."*

"Bullshit," Rachel retorted. *"It's downtown Washington-freakin'-D.C. There's always a hit."*

"I've already run my scripts to analyze the past forty-eight hours. I've got the usual rogues' gallery of thugs and assholes, but there's nothing special about them. No terrorists. But there's no military brass, either."

*Okay, now **that's** weird*, Rachel though to herself.

Jason heard her. *"Yeah, thanks, that's why I mentioned it. There are the usual number of grunts and lower-ranking officers, but anyone with a Colonel's commission or higher? Normal population analytics put an average of thirty-one ranking officers per day on that street, but the last two days? Pas du tout."*

"Have you gone back any further?"

"No. The MPD's system can't keep up with my scripts. I'm only as fast as the processing power they give me."

"All right, thanks. See what you can complete by the time we get there." Rachel broke the connection before he could add another complaint, maybe one about how if his data analysis was so very important to this project, maybe they'd finally give him some better computers? Really, she didn't even have to hear what he said any more. She was already well-versed in his litany of complaints and criticisms.

(Deep down—very deep down, perhaps below the earth's crust or even the bottom of the Mariana Trench, she did like

Jason. He was OACET: she couldn't *not* like Jason. It was just that, as of August, she *had* to like Jason, and Rachel really would have appreciated the option to hate him, or, at the very least, think of him as that one brother who knew better than to sit next to her at family meals.)

She came up out of her conversation with Jason and found they had been retracing their path back to the cars. The others were nearly a block ahead of her. The men from the MPD had learned to leave her alone when she started chatting with another Agent; she had an unfortunate tendency to walk into the path of moving vehicles when she tried to carry on multiple conversations at once.

She had nearly caught up to them when Jonathan Dunstan fell into step beside her.

"No comment," she snapped at him.

Since she had moved to Washington, Rachel had been inundated with interesting trivia. She had learned that the U.S. Chamber of Commerce was not actually a branch of government, and that the summer squash at the Palisades Farmers Market was so astonishingly good that it was worth getting up before the sun to hold your place in line. And she had learned that every politician had a reporter to call upon: like a witch commanding their familiar, a senator could point their reporter towards a target and watch as their pet did their bidding.

Jonathan Dunstan belonged to Senator Hanlon. Rachel often fantasized about punching Dunstan dead in the center of his face.

"Agent Peng?" Dunstan wore a weasel's smile cut across his core of sky-dark aquamarine. She couldn't read his colors without thinking of a thunderstorm over a tropical island; the guy could ruin anything just by showing up. Dunstan was holding a notepad and a stubby pencil; his digital media was suspiciously error-prone around her. "Why were you and Officer Santino allowed on the scene before the FBI?"

"No comment," she said again. She scanned the block and

saw Santino had turned around, and was shouting to the others as he hurried back to join her.

"Is it true you found one of the victims?" Dunstan stepped in front of her and stopped to block her path. She darted around him, holding the arm nearest to Dunstan out as though she were offering him to grab it...

He didn't. The weasel had been well-trained.

"Agent Peng, is there any truth to the rumor that OACET is behind the bombings?"

"That is a patent lie designed to get me to stop walking and talk to you," she said as she caught up to Santino and the detectives. "Agent Glassman is OACET's media representative. Please direct all potential slander and libel to him."

That smile stayed plastered on Dunstan's face, but his surface colors blanched. He couldn't hold his own against handsome, charismatic Josh Glassman, and Dunstan knew it. Josh tended to end all interviews with Dunstan by offering the weasel a quiet place for a nap and a sippy cup full of apple juice.

"Also? No comment," Rachel told Dunstan. "Just in case you forgot."

"Agent Peng, are you blind?"

She should have kept walking, but her feet had carried her back to Dunstan before conscious thought intervened. "Am I *what?*" she hissed.

"Blind," he said.

"To what? Gender inequality? The overseas sweatshop industry responsible for my cheap polo shirts?" The part of her brain that handled these situations had finally caught up to her mouth. Santino grabbed her by the shoulder, but she shrugged him off. She lowered her voice and stood on her toes so she could stare directly into Dunstan's eyes. "Or if you're asking whether I'm blind to what Hanlon has done to OACET, *please.* You already know we're on to him."

Dunstan recoiled from her, then tried to recover by stepping so close their noses practically touched. It was a lovely dramatic gesture, except he was so scared he was awash in sick yellows.

"Physically blind," he said. "We have a source which puts you as sustaining irreparable damage to both eyes almost a year ago."

"Oh, *that*," Rachel said, rocking back on the flats of her feet. "Yes, of course I'm blind. I have an invisible guide dog named Boo who helps me load and aim my gun.

"What's that, Boo?" She cocked her head and pretended to listen to a voice coming from three feet above the ground. "No, we don't have to shoot him. He's just an unforgivably stupid excuse for a human being. Letting him live will be punishment enough.

"Boo says you are free to quote me on *that*," she said to Dunstan before she turned away.

Dunstan had lost the yellows when she was no longer close enough to slug him. Now, he was smug pink and determined to have the last word. "You can see through walls, Agent Peng. You used to be the only cyborg who could. Not too much of a stretch to think you taught yourself that trick to compensate for your loss of sight."

She spun back to face him. "Do your homework, Dunstan. *Every* Agent can do what I can. Hell, Agent Netz is working with the bomb squad right up the street."

"And Agent Atran said you were the one who taught the rest of them," Dunstan replied.

God ***damn*** it, Jason. She might never stop kicking him.

"You're fishing, Dunstan," she said. "You've got nothing, because there's nothing to it. Anyone who would buy this bullshit is the type of person who'd believe anything you threw at them. You want a good story? Look into the man who signs your paychecks. You know what he did to us, so…"

Rachel bit down on her next line, the one where Dunstan should leave Hanlon or plan to be taken down with him. It was a good line, but there was no reason for her to say it aloud; Dunstan already knew. Instead, she gave him a wide, toothy smile before she stalked off, the men from the MPD following in her wake.

She was so angry she could barely see. Her mind felt like it had been stuffed in a sock, and her scans couldn't penetrate. It was one firmly-placed foot in front of the other, all the way back to the car.

Medical records. It had to have been my medical records. So much for HIPAA, she snarled to herself. Somehow—honestly, it probably hadn't been that hard—Hanlon had gotten her information. She thought she had purged the details of that event from her medical history, but she must have left a trace somewhere. A pharmacist's note, maybe, or Hanlon could have tracked down the physicians who had treated her when Josh brought her to the hospital. Short of murdering everyone involved, there was no way she could have completely erased her stay in the intensive care unit.

Dunstan was wrong about one thing. It had been much less than a year since Josh had found her, lying flat on her back and staring straight up at the sun, awake but unaware of anything around her. When he finally slapped her back to sense, he had taken her straight to the hospital to treat the seeping blisters that covered her body. Those two days she had spent on her balcony were followed by two more days in the ICU, where she had fluids pumped into her while a dialysis unit took some of the load for her kidneys, just in case. The doctors said her body would be fine; even her skin wouldn't scar.

Her eyes… Well. One does not look at the sun for two days without consequences. The doctors had dire things to say about her eyes.

She had never bothered to ask Josh what he had told those doctors, what lie he had crafted to explain why or how she had suffered exposure on a balcony in southern California. Once she had gotten all of the good she could get from the hospital, he had talked the physicians into releasing her and had taken her home. She had never gone back to those doctors for a follow-up. By the time she needed treatment for her failing eyesight, the Agents had started to get their shit together and she was under the care of Jenny Davies.

But that last time they had examined her? She still had her

vision, but her eyes had already started to die. She was sure that's what Hanlon had found, someone who would testify that patients did not bounce back from the type of progressive macular degeneration she had at the time she left the hospital.

Rachel aimed a kick at a chunk of brick, just to prove to herself that she could. The brick skittered across the pavement and slammed into the curb, then bounced over and down the sidewalk until it plonged off of a dumpster.

Blind. Fuck Hanlon. She was *not* blind. Her eyes might not work, but she could see better than anyone else alive.

"Rachel?" The fury-fog was starting to lift. Rachel found Santino a few steps behind her. "Slow down. You're practically running."

She stopped. Zockinski and Hill had done the same, but a couple dozen feet out of earshot to give them time to talk. All partners had secrets; Hill probably knew things about Zockinski that even Zockinski's wife would never learn. They had probably guessed that Santino was privy to some of the inner workings of OACET, and they kept their distance.

"It's bullshit." She said it loud enough for Zockinski and Hill to overhear. "He's just fishing."

"Obviously." Santino was playing along. "But why would he ask if you were blind?"

She gave a forced sigh, and then walked back to rejoin Zockinski and Hill.

"I was in an accident, a few months before OACET went public," she told them. "There was a chance—a small chance— that I could lose my eyesight. Looks like a certain Senator got his hands on my medical records."

Zockinski and Hill exchanged a brief sidewise glance.

"Blind," Hill said. "That's…"

"…an easy accusation to disprove," Santino finished.

"Unless you're Rachel," Zockinski said. The three of them turned to look at him. "Dunstan had a point," Zockinski said, with a trace of brick-brown defensiveness. "I've seen you put on a blindfold and still put a full magazine dead center in the bull's-eye during target practice. It's not like you need your eyes."

"Yeah," Rachel agreed. "I don't. Not for target practice. That's point and shoot. But for everything else?" She threw up her hands to take in the street, the people, the vehicles, trees, the scraps of trash blowing by...

Hill nodded. To tell by his colors, this was an unnecessary conversation. Interesting, maybe, but the flecks of curious yellow were overpowered by a glaze of irritation. We have better things to do, folks. Move along. Nothing to see here—no pun intended.

"Sure," Zockinski said. His conversational colors were an uncertain orange, and there were dimples puckering his colors across shoulders and temples: he was lying.

God damn it all.

FIVE

When the sun reached the right place in the sky, the Consolidated Forensic Laboratory was a hard wall of light. Some architect had had the novel idea to run aluminum and brushed steel across blue-tinted glass; the goal was to get the MPD's new state-of-the-art forensics facility a coveted LEED Gold status by tossing extra heat away from the building, but the end result looked like a chicken coop. An expensive chicken coop, to be sure, but wire was wire and the whole place looked ready to cluck.

The MPD had given Jason Atran his own media lab on the third floor, and they had invested some hard cash to try to keep him happy. Jason might complain about the shoddy equipment, but that was his prerogative as its designer and primary user. Any other tech guy would have killed for the high-resolution monitors, the computers and their corresponding motion sensor input devices which he had programmed to track both his body and his mind. Jason was fully integrated into his system, and it bent and twisted at his will.

Rachel ground her teeth together as she entered the room. She hated visiting Jason at his office. The room wasn't hostile to her, not exactly, but there was a constant hard twang in her mind, like she had hit the wrong key on a piano in the middle of someone else's tune. She couldn't shake the impression that the room resented her presence: the Agents were welcome to Jason in his off-hours or when he was in the link, but when he was working, he belonged to his machines.

Settle down, she thought at nothing in particular. *Don't make me block you.*

The pressure eased ever so slightly; Rachel decided to pretend it was coincidence.

Jason was standing in the center of the room, digital media flying from screen to screen, and surrounding him in green. The green had nothing to do with emotions: invisible to anyone but an Agent, a baker's dozen of detailed life-sized three-dimensional recreations of human beings circled Jason like a human wall. Santino and the detectives walked through them, oblivious, but Rachel paused to inspect Jason's work. She pinged one to check the source of the signal and the computer pushed back. Jason might be creating the images, but the computer was running the program.

"Nice," Rachel said through the link, examining a rough-looking man taller than she was. He had a cell phone pressed to his ear and spiral tattoos creeping out from under his collar and shirt sleeves.

"Thanks," Jason replied. *"Those guys were all flagged in the RISC,"* he said, referring to the FBI's Repository for Individuals of Special Concern. *"But I doubt they're worth more than a follow-up interview."*

The green figures vanished with a pop, and the screens froze as Jason and the men from the MPD exchanged hellos. Zockinski passed Jason a bag with a couple of still-warm calzones, and the five of them sat on the floor and waited while the other Agent tore through a late lunch.

Zockinski and Hill were living proof that it was possible to get used to anything. If Rachel were to chart her eight-month history with the detectives on a calendar, the first six months would be solid black with harassment, the last month-plus a gradual easement from tolerance to genuine friendship. Not everybody (hell, almost nobody other than Santino) had welcomed Rachel to the MPD, and her early encounters with Zockinski had been absolute nightmares. Hill hadn't been as verbally vicious, but that was because he let his partner do most of the talking.

But hunting madmen was a great bonding experience, and Zockinski and Hill had learned that palling around with Agents had plenty of advantages. Agents were commodities:

they knew people. Yes, Jason could program Hill's new alarm system without bothering to drive over to his apartment, but he had also gotten Hill into one of the pickup basketball games at the congressional gym, and a city cop could always use good political contacts.

(Not to mention that Hill was single, and Agents knew how to party. The first time Rachel, Phil, and Jason had taken Hill out on the town, Rachel had warned him to dress for one part HazMat cleanup, three parts Freddie Mercury's 39th birthday party. Hill had shown up in jeans, a tight t-shirt, and an old leather jacket, and by morning these looked as though they had been dipped in acid and then run afoul of a Zamboni. Hill said it was totally worth it, and tagged along with them again the following Saturday night.)

When the calzones were done, Jason wiped the grease off on his pants and motioned them over to his main system console. There were chairs conveniently arranged around Jason, and as he gestured to them to sit, Rachel had no doubt that he had prepared to perform to an audience.

She stood behind Santino, arms crossed.

"You pissed at me?" Jason asked, as he went through a well-worn lecture with the officers about camera angles and video compression rates.

"Bumped into Dunstan on the way over," she replied, as she watched the data move through his systems. It meant nothing to her in this form, but she did appreciate how it ebbed and flowed. *"Been chatting about me?"*

"What are you talking about? I think I've said twelve words to him over the past six months," Jason said. *"And at least half of those were some version of 'go fuck yourself'."*

"Were the other half, 'Rachel taught us how to use different frequencies to see'? Because he's been digging, and he's got suspicions."

"Oh, shit." Jason's mental voice was small, and he faltered in his speech to Santino and the detectives.

"There are reasons it's policy to file a report whenever we have

a run-in with Hanlon's goons," she snapped. *"And one of those reasons is so they don't catch us blind—see what I did there?—and use what we've said against us."*

The men from the MPD were watching them with familiar bemused expressions. "You two need some time to talk privately?" Zockinski asked.

"Nope," Rachel said as she dropped in the empty chair beside Hill. "Just managing some administrivia."

"Mind if we get back to the dead people?" Hill said, pointing to the screens.

Rachel shrugged, and Jason resumed his lecture. By the time he was done with the briefing, she, Zockinski, and Hill were thoroughly educated in the methods he had used to survey the street and pick out each individual person and vehicle for analysis (and judging by Hill's colors, she could probably talk him into helping her strangle Jason). When Jason's seminar disbanded, the five of them clumped into smaller groups, asking questions and picking through pieces of data for something they could use. Jason's digital simulations reappeared in a burst of sudden green, and Rachel resumed her slow walk around the circle, peering into each face as though the hollow motes of light might hold an answer.

Off to one side, a sequence of faces began to run together in a vivid green blur. Rachel threw a quick scan through it to investigate, and found a separate digital construction that Jason had stuck in the unoccupied space. She waited until Santino and the detectives were quibbling over some bit of procedural minutiae, and then reached out to Jason in the link.

"What's this?"

Jason didn't bother to look up from his screens. *"Double-checking my work. I already ran the crowd through the MPD's standard facial recognition software and cross-referenced with the RISC."*

"Yeah, you mentioned."

"Well, this is my own program. It's a hybrid of our federal software and a few choice programs I ganked from China and

Germany. *Surveillance states write the best biometric snoopware.*"

"*Don't let Germany hear you call it that...*" Rachel said, throwing her scans towards the shifting green. She prodded the projection and felt resistance from Jason: he was running the program directly.

"*Whoa!*" She recoiled. "*Is that good for you, processing this much information yourself?*"

"*Hmm?*" he said, finally glancing towards her. "*I have to run it myself. I haven't gotten around to writing the program for the computer.*"

"*Jason, come on,*" Rachel said, wiping her palms against her pant legs. "*This can't be safe, this much raw data running through your brain.*"

"*I'm fine.*" Jason's face didn't change, but she felt him smile through the link. A nice smile, one with a hug in it; he never failed to surprise her. "*I use this program a dozen times a day. Have some faith, Peng. We're more resilient than you think.*"

She nodded, unconvinced, and broke their link. The green faces fluttered like wings.

As the men from First MPD prepared to leave, Jason called out: "Hey Rachel, stick around for a minute. I want to show you something."

She dropped back, motioning Santino to go ahead without her. Her partner nodded and followed the detectives out of the lab.

"Here," Jason said. He twisted his fingers and a projection appeared in the center of the room. It was a sheet of solid green, running the length of the room. "One-fifth scale," he told Rachel proudly. "Don't scan it until you're inside or it'll ruin the effect."

The green rectangle was taller than she was, but not by much. She bumped herself up on her toes to try and peer over it; she couldn't quite make it. She glanced at Jason, then stepped through it, noting as she passed that it was as thin as a mote of light.

"Damn," she said quietly.

The other side of the featureless rectangle was a fully-realized city street, etched in painstaking detail in shades of chartreuse and pine and lime green, complete with pedestrians and vehicles. As she watched, cars stopped for a traffic light. Individual figures scurried across the road to the beat of the WALK signs, opened tiny doors to shops and offices, chatted silently on cell phones...

"Holy shit," she said in a low voice. "You recreated Gayle Street?"

"Ten minutes prior to the bombings," Jason said. His conversational colors glowed with red pride. "Rendered the security feeds from every camera I could find, and compiled them into a single 3-D image. Don't worry," he said quickly, feeling her panic. "The computer is running the program. I'm just running the construct."

"This is incredible." The details were too much to take in at once. Rachel saw a little girl stumble, her father pause to help her up. Half a block ahead, the girl's brother scattered a flock of pigeons at a run. She felt like Gulliver among the Lilliputians, or—as she accidentally put her foot through a hot dog cart— Godzilla. "I've never seen a projection like this."

The twanging in her mind eased again. If Rachel didn't know better, she would swear Jason's machines enjoyed performing for an appreciative audience.

"I've got up to three days prior to the bombing in the queue," Jason said, kneeling down to inspect the miniature license plate on a windowless van. "It'll take time to render properly, and I'm not going to rush it. But this part's done, and it might be enough to give you guys a place to start."

"Has Phil seen this?" she asked him.

"Yeah."

"Good. Have you shown it to anyone else at First MPD?"

He sniffed. "Why? They couldn't see it if I did."

"You idiot," she said. The twanging pulsed, and she pushed back until it subsided. "Ever heard of Google Glass?"

Thirty minutes later, Santino had returned from his fast round trip to First District Station and was walking next to her along Jason's digital version of Gayle Street. They had moved the construct from Jason's office to the nearby hallway, where there was sufficient space to display the miniaturized version of the full fourteen blocks without the risk of the men from the MPD smashing face-first into the walls. They weren't alone: there was a crowd gathering in the open doorways all along the hall. Santino had offered to let one of the digital forensics specialists from the lab across from Jason's use his glasses, and the woman, amazed, had put the word out.

Santino had been one of those invited to participate in Google's smart glass trial, but he had opted out, choosing instead to build his own. Rachel didn't know where he had gotten the parts, but she thought his new girlfriend might have had something to do with it. Zia was an Agent; she had connections. He had made three sets, each pair an improvement on its predecessor. His most recent version was a slightly unwieldy copy of his usual reading glasses, with thick lenses and heavy frames, but Rachel knew he wouldn't be satisfied until he had a pair which passed as normal: his goal was to have a wearable computer which allowed him to see Agents' projections while also letting him read a McDonald's menu at fifty feet. For now, all three sets were more than adequate for the purpose of viewing Jason's reconstruction, although Zockinski was wearing the earliest prototype and was complaining about the heavy battery pack throwing heat against his chest.

With some prodding, Jason had fed his projection into the three mobile displays, and the men from the MPD were moving up and down the street, looking for details that might not appear in two dimensions. Jason's projection wasn't flawless. There were voids, as well as false renders; the cameras hadn't covered the entire street, and much of what was above the third story was supposition. Jason and his computers had worked to fill in the blanks, rendering these voids in a slightly transparent green. There were glitches when two or more cameras covered the same area; Jason had applied his master's craft of stitching images from different perspectives together, but not every camera filmed at the same rate or resolution, and the lines between these got a little muddy. And the entire digital construct had a habit of faltering when Jason lost concentration; the computer was doing the rendering, but Jason was keeping it active, and the street wavered with each female officer who dropped by to watch him work. But besides these relatively minor limitations, Rachel had to admit that Jason's digital projection of the scene was the best forensics tool she had ever used.

Not that it mattered. They had run the simulated timeline over and over, looking for something out of place. A single person running, maybe, or a car with a bomb-chucking madman behind the wheel. Thus far, nothing. They had covered the entire length of the fourteen-block incident until they knew the movements of the digitalized figures better than their own.

"Proves the explosions were on a timer," Hill said, his free hand on his watch as he checked the duration between each puff of green smoke at his feet. "Ninety seconds exactly."

"We knew that," Rachel sighed. Phil had been right; ninety seconds was exactly the right amount of time to create panic and bring people running, and then, boom. Chaos dominoes, all the way down the street. "Good to know the exact time frame, though."

She swept a foot through a bakery; the toe of her shoe disappeared into the green. Her cop's brain was ticking. She knelt by the side of the street where the bombings had occurred, and dipped her hand into a coffee shop the size of a dollhouse. *An **untouched** coffee shop the size of...*

"Can you make it life-sized?" Santino asked Jason, breaking her train of thought. His colors were gray. "I want to see it from a different perspective."

Rachel winced and stood. She had already lived through her fair share of bombings. She could bear her role as a witness when the figures were the size of toys; it would be impossible not to empathize with people who looked real enough to touch.

"Yeah," Jason said as he paused the scene. Everything—

traffic, pedestrians, pigeons—stopped in their last moments of normalcy, then grew to fill the hall. Rachel fell into parade rest and pretended not to notice the father and his two children a few feet away from her...

"Ready?" he asked. Rachel and Santino nodded.

Jason released the feed, and the first bomb went off.

He had slowed the scene down to half speed, but the first puff of green smoke still roared out of the nearest coffee shop. Green fragments—glass or dirt or stone, she couldn't tell, the cameras hadn't had a frame rate fast enough to capture the details—flew towards them. Zockinski unconsciously threw a hand up to protect his face, lowering it as the shrapnel passed harmlessly through him.

Rachel walked up the digital street, putting the father and his children behind her. No good; the problem with her vision was her vision, and she saw what happened to them as clearly as she saw her own two hands clasped tight at her lower back. She forced herself to stop and notice the details outside of the radius of the explosion: people turning, their eyes and mouths rounding in shock. Some dropped what they were carrying, while others crushed their bags or briefcases against their chests. The kinesthetic signs of terror were all around her, and she was absolutely grateful that Jason's construct didn't carry the emotional spectrum.

When the dust cloud hit, the entire scene went transparent. The security cameras above the explosion and on the far side of the street had captured everything, but the dust had obscured many of the details and the program had filled in the blanks as best it could. It wasn't an issue; the dust was a symptom, not a cause. They didn't expect to find anything that would point to the bomber in those moments of dust.

After the dust came the response. Nobody had to remind Rachel that human beings could be selfish pricks—OACET existed because of selfish pricks—but she knew the average person was genuinely decent, and usually compassionate. When she was in the Army, she had seen so much that was good. In times of crisis, whole communities would come together. She had been an outsider, she knew that, but she had still seen families reach out to strangers, entire towns pool those few resources they had to help each other rebuild. Altruism not only existed, but was embedded within the human experience.

(She couldn't understand the almost-universal decision to dismiss altruism, compassion, kindness of any type... These were treated as failings or, at best, a quirky human interest story good for nothing but a filler segment on the evening news. Sad, really, how people needed to believe the worst of themselves.)

Here, the explosions triggered the Good Samaritans. Green figures poured from the stores to help those in need. Nearby, a man in a business suit helped a tourist to stand, then escorted her into a coffee shop before returning outside to help...

The windows of the coffee shop exploded, and the man disappeared in a transparent chartreuse cloud. When the program was able to render the details again, he was gone.

She almost forgot him as she walked by—too much to take in, too many victims—but noticed a pile of broken bricks half-covering a metal awning.

"Jason?" she called out. "Could you back up sixty seconds and replay?"

"Sure." The green figures scurried backwards in time, then resumed their molasses-slow pace. They turned to look up the street, to shield themselves as the dust cloud swept over them. Some of the pedestrians fell to the ground, while others ran for cover. The man emerged from the coffee shop, helped the woman stand...

"Pause," Rachel said, and the scene froze. "Can the program track one person?"

"Not during this part," Jason replied as he walked over to join her. "There's too much data fragmentation because of the dust. What you see here is mostly an extrapolation of the scene built around the bits and pieces that were caught on camera."

"Okay," she said, and pointed to the green man in the suit. "Can it predict the most likely location for where this guy ended up? I think he's the one I rescued."

"Maybe," Jason said, his eyes losing focus as he spoke with his system. "Yes."

The city scene vanished, then rebuilt itself with the man in the suit at its center. The scope of the scene was tighter, a mere ten feet in all directions as the processing power shifted from playback to possibility.

"The computer removed the dust cloud," Jason said. "Same routine as before. If you can see through it, it's a rendered probability. If it's opaque, it was captured on a video."

The man, solidly green, pushed the woman into the coffee shop and returned to the street. When the explosion came, he faded instantly, occasional opaque spots painting him like a leopard. Rachel and the others watched as he was blown off of his feet, twisting in the concussive wave like a thing already dead. He caught a lamppost right above his waist, and fell and rolled in the wake until he washed up against an old Buick. Then came a second wave of debris, covering him from head to toe. The scene gradually became more solid as the dust settled and the cameras were able to resolve the details.

"Damn," Santino whispered. "Poor guy. He was stuck like that for nearly an hour before we found him."

"He's a witness." Hill stood rock-still like usual, but he was burning yellow-white with excitement. "He was in the shop just seconds before it blew."

"Hang on," Rachel said. She pushed her way through the crowd of MPD officers and forensic specialists who had taken over the hall, ducked back in Jason's office, and retrieved the victim's wallet from her purse. "Jordan Meisner," she said as she handed the wallet to Zockinski. "Thirty-two, lives over in Dupont Circle, so he's local."

Zockinski flipped through Meisner's wallet. "Where did you get that information?" he asked absently. "There's nothing but credit cards in here."

She tilted her head and blinked at him.

"Right, sorry," Zockinski said. "Did you find out where they took him?"

"No," she said. "There's no DMV database for hospitalizations. We'll have to do it the old-fashioned way and call around."

"I'll do that," Zockinski told her, and took out his cell as he left for the privacy of Jason's office.

"I feel terrible for this guy," Santino said, staring down at the pile of debris which had covered Meisner. He pushed at the bridge of his mobile display so it would sit solidly on his nose. "That must have been the worst hour of his entire life."

"We got him out," she reminded her partner. "And his injuries weren't life-threatening. If anybody can tell us what happened right before the explosion, it's probably going to be him."

"Yeah," Santino muttered, unable to look away from Meisner's digitized tomb. "I'm sure he'll think that makes it all totally worth it."

SIX

Old hospitals had hard faces. Jordan Meisner had been moved to one of the older buildings in the Washington Hospital Center complex, and while the building had been renovated a half-dozen times over the years, there was an unshakable sense of permanence within it. *Grumpy old man of a hospital*, Rachel thought to herself as Santino pulled into a parking space. *Seen and heard it all.*

They had left Zockinski and Hill with Jason, with the hope that the three men could find something of use as additional renders were completed by Jason's computer. She and Santino had dropped by the site of the bombings to pick up Phil for the Meisner interview. The nurse who took their call had told them Meisner was awake, and Phil would know exactly what to ask him.

Phil caught her looking at the hospital. *"Going to wait here?"* he asked.

She shook her head, took a deep breath, and kicked open the passenger's side door.

They went in through the main entrance, guessing it wouldn't be half as busy as the Emergency Department on a day like today. Wrong. There was a heavy line of visitors standing in front of the receptionist's desk.

"Stand in line or pull rank?" whispered Santino.

"Back of the line, like the good little doobies we are," Rachel whispered back. "And you're the lucky one who gets to stand in for all three of us while Phil and I go find our respective bathrooms."

"Nope."

"Yup," Rachel told Santino. "They might ask to see our badges, and we don't need to run into the OACET road block if they decide they don't want to deal with freaks roaming the halls."

Santino sighed and stepped into the queue.

She threw a quick scan through the ground floor until she pinged on the nearest vending machine, and she and Phil dove into the candy bars. At her urging, Phil bought a couple of extra bars for later; he tended to forget to eat when he was playing with explosives. (A few weeks ago, she had gone down to the basement of First District Station to check up on him after he had dropped out of the link unexpectedly, and found he had passed out while dissecting an old inactive landmine, his head pillowed on a spare pile of Semtex.)

They meandered back to the main hall to find Santino in a stalemate with one of the receptionists. Rachel guessed this receptionist was probably a lovely person on any day other than today, but the poor man had been running point for the victims' families, the press, anyone who needed information about the people caught in the explosion. It had worn on him, and he was spitting at Santino like a viper.

"Police. Officer." Santino had his badge out and was tapping it against the counter.

"You can go in," the receptionist said, pushing a stack of clipboards and a digital camera towards Santino. "Just as soon as you fill this out." He pointed at Rachel and Phil. "And if you're with him, I need a form from each of you, and I also have to get photos of you holding your official IDs. We've had too many bloggers pretending to be cops today."

"That's illegal," Phil said as he gathered up the clipboards.

"You are more than welcome to arrest them," the receptionist said, then forgot about them as he turned to the next person in the line.

Forms. **Handwritten** *forms.* She gritted her teeth and took the top clipboard from Phil. She hated filling out forms, especially when there were strangers close enough to watch her struggle with the words like a barely literate toddler. The three of them scurried off to an unoccupied corner so she could set her implant to reading mode and take her time.

"Made any progress with mixed frequencies?" Phil asked her through the link, as she scribbled her name and organizational information on the tight black lines. *"It's nuts how much effort you have to go through just to read and write."*

"No," she replied. *"You?"*

"No." He shook his shaggy head, guilt building in his conversational colors. *"But I'll be honest, it's not a priority for me like it is for you. Sorry, I should be doing more to help."*

"It's fine." Rachel said, and caught herself before she shrugged through the link. A pet peeve of hers was feeling another Agent's physical gestures in her own head, so she tried to avoid creating pot-kettle scenarios whenever she could. *"I'd like to be able to read a book again without giving myself a pounding headache, but it'll just take time to find the right combination of frequencies."*

"Got any spare time to practice this weekend?"

Rachel looped a scan through the dull, smoky grief of those waiting in line, the pulsing black of the receptionists... *"I think all of our spare time just got flushed down the toilet."*

Phil nodded, and left Rachel alone with her ballpoint pen.

Her scans were usually either short bursts as she pinged objects, or prolonged distribution of a penetrating wave. Reading was neither of these. The physician who had given Rachel the diagnostic autoscript had told her that the eye is a simple miracle, and that the frequencies which are found in light are only a small part of reading. When applied to reading, visual perception was a sum of many processes. She had learned about form consistency, and discrimination within a visual figure ground, and a hundred other individual terms and concepts she had never heard of, let alone knew existed. Rachel could duplicate many of these processes when she used a specialized visual mode made up of both pings and waves, but thus far it had proven impossible to blend this mode into her dominant set of environmental scans. Unless she was in reading mode, she could sometimes make out the forms of letters—

usually when these were printed bold and large—but reading and writing? No. Basic literacy was no longer an effortless part of her life.

It took her nearly five minutes to fill out the double-sided form. Both Santino and Phil knew better than to offer to help, but they were both an impatient yellow-orange by the time she was done.

When they returned to the front desk, they found that the rude receptionist had been replaced by an older woman who barely took a cursory look at Santino's badge before buzzing them through the security doors. Rachel tore her form from the clipboard and folded it up to stash in her purse, just in case, then dropped the clipboard in the nearest trash can.

They struggled through the hospital in the way of Theseus in the labyrinth. The hospital was undergoing yet another round of renovations, and many of the wings weren't where the wall maps claimed they would be. It was all the worse for her because she needed to continuously flip between reading and environmental modes to keep her place in the building. She wondered, briefly, if they should find some string.

The Agents learned a little too late that they could navigate the hospital by way of the RFID tags stuck to the medical equipment, and they had to backtrack across most of the building to reach the wing with the majority of the ICU codes. And even then, they found that they had been following an older generation of tags: they ended up outside of an equipment storage room on the third floor, swearing at the churn rate of information technology.

Santino was losing his patience. "We are intelligent people," he growled, staring up at another series of useless signs and arrows. "Why is this so hard?"

Rachel shrugged. Technically, the three of them were working and she wanted to judge the mood of those around her, so she had kept the emotional spectrum on. Today, though… It had already been a day full of negative emotions and the grief, anger, and loss coming from every direction of the hospital were beginning to overwhelm her. She didn't need more of the same coming off of her partner.

Phil reached over and laid his hand against her wrist. His usual good humor was muted, but it was still strong enough to break her out of her malaise.

She smiled at him and relaxed, ever so slightly, so he could carry some of the pressure.

They arrived at the main entrance to the intensive care unit a few minutes later. The windowless double doors to the wing were sealed, and the three of them shared a look before Rachel sighed and leaned over to push the call button. She looked through the doors to the ward beyond to check if the nurse was about to buzz them in, but found the nurse's stand empty, with aggressive knots of medical personnel rushing from room to room.

"What's the holdup?" Santino asked.

"The bombing victims," Phil replied. "The unit's over capacity."

Rachel reached out through her implant to unlock the doors, and the three of them entered as quietly as they could. It was wasted effort; she doubted if she could have made a dent in the noise if she had pulled her gun and fired into the ceiling. The unit was best described as a... Well, the word *cacophony* was so rarely put to good use.

And there, down the hall and standing within the thick of EMTs and paramedics, Rachel spotted the twisting kaleidoscope of colors that was Hope Blackwell.

"Hope's here," Rachel said.

Phil perked. He liked Hope.

Rachel *really* needed to teach him how to perceive the emotional spectrum.

Hope's surface colors were fireworks. She was always in motion, her moods shifting and popping as fast as light or thought. Her core was black at the edges and shifted towards a vivid cyan at its center. Hope's core did not violate the single-color rule of cores: the black and blue were not two colors joined together, but were part of the same whole. It reminded Rachel of colors on the surface of an oil spill, the blue always within the black but visible only when the black was burned away.

Hope noticed them almost as soon as they entered. She stepped away from the other paramedics and waved them over. "Hey guys," she said. "Lemme try and find us somewhere quiet." She checked the floor for some unoccupied space, then sighed and pulled them into the nearest bathroom. It was a single stall with a toilet, and built to accommodate a wheelchair; it would have been spacious for one person, but the four of them each had to pick a spot on the wall and stick to it.

"How is it out there?" Hope asked in a low voice. "They've got me moving some of the overflow patients to hospitals in Virginia. I haven't been able to keep up with the news."

"Not good," Phil said, shaking his head. "Total chaos, no big breaks. But we're here to see a patient who was at the scene. You know a Jordan Meisner?"

"The one Rachel found," Hope said, grinning at her.

"They told you that?" Rachel asked.

"They tell me anything that has to do with OACET," Hope said.

Rachel hadn't seen Hope since her wedding a couple of weeks back. The two of them were friendly in the way of shared secrets; Rachel worked for Patrick Mulcahy, Hope's new husband and head of OACET, and Hope was privy to all of OACET's inner workings.

All of them.

Nobody else, not even Santino, was as close to OACET without also being part of the collective.

(If pushed, Rachel *might* admit that Hope gave her the creeping willies. It's not that Hope wasn't trustworthy. As far as Rachel could tell, Hope would happily take what she knew about OACET with her to her own grave. But she'd also take whoever was stupid enough to try and kill her into the ground with her, probably with her teeth clenched around their throat and her hands dug into their sternum to wrap around their beating heart. She was dangerous, but not in any way Rachel could understand. Hope's wedding had been the most recent example of this—as part of OACET's administrative team, Rachel had been asked to stand with Mulcahy at his wedding. As a woman who loved pretty clothes, Rachel had been asked to help Hope get ready in the bridal preparation suite before the ceremony. After the last of Mulcahy's sisters had left, Hope turned towards Rachel, her surface colors bright and happy, but nearly lost within the light emanating from her blue-black core. This raven-haired beauty, a vision in her wedding dress, asked Rachel, "How do I look?" Rachel, without thinking, replied, "You look like Death." And this weird woman, a wide smile lit up her face before she gave Rachel a sweet kiss on the cheek and said, "Thank you.")

Today, Hope was just another paramedic. "Wait here for a sec," she said. "We don't need any extra bodies running around right now. I'll check and see if I can get you into his room." She opened the door and was gone.

They spent a few minutes talking sports and pretending they weren't stuck in a hospital bathroom, and then there was a quick knock and Hope let herself back in. "You guys wasted a trip," she said. "Meisner's doctor says he's incoherent. He's got some second-degree burns and is on a ton of pain meds, so he's gonna be out of it for a while."

"The nurse on the phone said he was fine," Phil complained.

"It's not exactly a normal day around here," Hope said. "It'd be easy to get some patients confused. Or he might have been conscious but took a turn. It happens."

"Can we see him?" Santino asked. "Rachel can usually get a read off of someone, even if they're unconscious."

"We don't need to clog the halls. I can check on him from here," Rachel said. "I just need to know which room he's in. I could go digging in the records, but—"

"But it's faster if you follow me," Hope finished.

Rachel nodded. Whatever she may have thought of Hope as a person, the woman knew her way around cyborgs.

Hope pulled a Bluetooth headset out of her shirt pocket and clipped it over her ear. "Testing."

"Received." Rachel replied through the headset.

"Okay," Hope said. "Give me a minute to walk to his location."

Hope left again, and this time Rachel looked around for a safe place to sit. The toilet was right out (no lid) and the floor was no better (it fluoresced under her equivalent of a black light), so she propped herself up in the tight gap between the sink and the wall.

"Going out-of-body?" Phil asked.

She nodded. "Always a good idea to get a feel for the physicals before you start poking around the psychologicals." And with that, she stepped out of herself.

Splitting her mind in two was getting easier, but it was still annoying as hell. There was the bumbling dual sensation of being in two different places at once, of course, but it was more that she liked having feet. When she went out-of-body, she projected herself as her own copy, a second Rachel, cut from the same bright green energy as Jason's digital constructs. This second Rachel had the ability to walk and talk—as well as pass through walls, fly, and whatever else could be expected from what was basically a sentient hologram—but something important was missing when the ground didn't push back.

Her second self breezed through the wall of the bathroom and hurried to catch up with Hope. Hope was familiar with the ICU and was able to circumvent some of the chaos, but like the rest of the hospital, the ICU was a rambling knot of identical rooms. Rachel kept a firm grip on her connection with the signal from Hope's headset to make sure the other woman didn't take a sharp corner and disappear.

She saw why Hope had stuck them in the bathroom. The deeper Hope took her into the ICU, the worse it got. Every single bed in the ICU had a patient in it, and most patients were covered in an extra layer of anxious friends and family. These spilled out into the halls, slowing down the medical teams. And here and there were the clusters of police officers or

Homeland Security representatives, demanding to speak with their witnesses… Her out-of-body self winced.

Luckily, she wasn't making things worse. As with Jason's projections, her out-of-body state didn't exist to anyone without an implant. It was easier to move through people and objects than take the time to go around them. And—

"…government set-up…"

—it was also shamefully easy to eavesdrop. Rachel usually went out of her way to maintain general expectations of privacy when she was scanning or traveling out-of-body, but the speaker was mid-rant and past caring who heard him.

"Fuckin' mark my words," the man said, as Rachel passed between him and a woman in scrubs. "This is the government's fault. Our own people killed them."

"Sir…"

Rachel sympathized with both the man and the nurse. She didn't need the emotional spectrum to see the man's heart was broken; the collar of his shirt was wet from tears. But he was also twice the size of the nurse, and he was mad enough to say or do anything.

"Hope?" Rachel called. *"You might want to circle back. I've got a full-blown conspiracy nut, and he's threatening a nurse."*

"Oh boy."

"Oh yeah, this is prime. Here," Rachel said, and started streaming audio to Hope's headset.

A small crowd had begun to gather around the man and the nurse. Several of them were trying to intervene, but the man wasn't budging. "My daughter!" he shouted at the nurse. "My *wife!* They could have stopped this, and they didn't! They *let* them die!"

Rachel felt a shoulder under her arm, a man's hand at her waist… She let her connection with her second self falter, and smelled Phil's shampoo as he hoisted her physical body to move her out of the bathroom. *"Phil,"* she said. *"Forget me. Get Santino over to help Hope. He's MPD. If anybody's going to calm this guy down…"*

She heard him say: "Right," then felt the bumpy texture of the fiberglass tile under her fingers as he lowered her to the floor.

The bathroom must be within earshot… Rachel thought. *"Hey, Hope?"* she said. *"I'm getting my body. Santino's on his way."*

She broke the connection and snapped back to her physical self. The first thing she noticed was the bathroom floor was unforgivably clean; she needed to spend some time working out the differences in fluorescent rates between the residue of sanitizing fluids versus biologicals.

The next thing she noticed was the bathroom door swinging shut. She rocked herself forward and into a sprint to catch up with Santino and Phil.

The three of them shot through the hallways in the direction of the shouting. They arrived at the same time as Hope, who shoved her way through the crowd to take a position slightly behind the man. Rachel grinned. Hope was a *Roku-dan* in judo, and if the man did decide to start swinging, he'd end up needing a doctor. He was in the right place for it, but still.

Santino came at the man from the front, his suit coat pulled back to expose the badge on his belt. "Sir?" he said. "People can hear you. Can we go somewhere to talk?"

The man stopped and blinked, then looked around. His colors crashed in on themselves, the fiery red of fury falling to the sickly reds and oranges of shame and grief. Gray appeared within the red; the asphalt gray of old roads and depression. He slumped to the floor, put his head in his hands, and wept.

Santino did the *move along* gesture and the crowd dispersed. Hope went with them, but returned a moment later with a box of tissues which she nudged towards the man.

"What's your name?" Santino asked him, kneeling beside him.

"Dalder. Ah, William Dalder," he said, scrubbing at his eyes. "I'm sorry, it's… It's been a hard day."

"We know," Rachel said. She sat on the floor next to Dalder. "We're with the MPD. We're part of the team working the scene on Gayle Street. Did we hear you say you lost your wife and daughter…?"

Dalder nodded. "They were meeting for lunch…" he began, but couldn't finish. She caught sight of his core colors beneath his grief, a sweet summer sky blue.

Meeting for lunch? Odd phrase to apply to a woman and her daughter. Rachel took a careful look at his face and found him to be older than she had assumed, probably closer to sixty than forty. Old enough to be a grandparent, maybe.

As if Dalder had read her mind, he said, "Joanna's husband's on his way. He's bringing the kids… Joanna…Joanna's my daughter…she was still alive when I told them to come. The doctors thought she'd pull through…"

"We're sorry for your loss," Rachel said. How she hated that hollow phrase: how she wished there was something better; how she regretted there wasn't. "Is there anything we can do for you now?"

Dalder rocked his head back and forth in a slow no.

"Guys?" Hope said, pointing down the hall. The river of health care workers had vanished, but only to avoid Dalder. Rachel followed the line of Hope's finger and found some of the other officers from the MPD were watching Dalder with lidded eyes. "We should move."

The man raised his head slightly and looked at Hope. His colors brightened in surprise.

Oh shit, Rachel thought. She had been briefly famous, but as Mulcahy's wife, Hope was on the cover of a magazine or was at the top of the news crawl at least once a week. And there was some heavy-level government conspiracy angst swimming around in the upper levels of Dalder's thoughts.

"Are you Hope Blackwell?" Dalder asked her.

Hope nodded.

Dalder was quiet for a moment. "Just…" he started, then said in a rush: "Thank your husband for me. He's one of the only honest people out there. What he's done, taking OACET public? If we had more people like him, maybe today…wouldn't…"

Dalder's conversational colors fell again; he had lost his will.

They helped him to stand, and the five of them moved into a nearby office too small to be good for anything other than temporary storage. Santino and Phil moved a few boxes of files and helped Dalder into the only chair, an old, overstuffed thing covered in cracked Naugahyde. It had heavy plastic arms, and Dalder bent almost in two so he could lay his head on one of these.

Rachel knelt beside Dalder. She glanced back at Santino: he was waiting for her in patient pinks and salmons. As were Hope and Phil… *Goddamnit,* she thought. *Thanks. Nothing better than being the default bad guy.*

"Mr. Dalder? William?" she asked. "Can I ask you a couple of questions? I know you weren't there, but anything you can tell us might help."

Dalder couldn't stop staring into space, but his conversational colors picked up a trace of Rachel's own southwestern turquoise core as he shifted part of his attention to her.

"I have to ask this, William, you understand? When you were in the hallway, you were talking about how the government was responsible for Gayle Street. Do you have any evidence?"

"Of course not," Dalder said in a flat, quiet voice. "I didn't know what I was saying. It was grief talking… It's… We put so much time and money into making this country safe, and things like this can still happen? It doesn't make sense."

"Ah, okay," Rachel said, checking his colors to learn if he was lying. Nothing: Dalder was clean.

"I'm not criticizing you," he added, glancing towards Santino. "The police, I mean. The police are different. You're… You're like us. There's no way in hell you guys would ever blow up a street."

"And the government would?" Rachel asked as gently as she could.

Dalder turned to face Hope. "I've heard the stories about what they did to your husband," he said. "They killed over a hundred Agents as part of the cover-up. What do you think?"

"I think you're grieving," Hope said. "And I think anything

you say today might not be how you felt yesterday."

"Yesterday?" A little red flame had rekindled in Dalder's conversational colors. "Yesterday, I had a *family*."

"Sir—"

"No, I want to understand this," Dalder said. He pushed himself out of the chair and loomed over her; Rachel realized she was kneeling at the perfect height to take a knee to the chin. "I want to understand how we can pay billions of dollars, let the NSA rip through our privacy, have fucking *drones* flying overhead, and my family is—"

Dalder's conversational colors suddenly lost their intensity, and Hope released her grip on his shoulders. "Sit down," she told him. "Slowly."

Dalder did as he was told, his eyes rolling back in his skull ever so slightly. His colors went purple, and he gave Rachel a happy grin.

"Do I want to ask?" Santino said to Hope.

"Vulcan neck pinch," she said.

"What?"

"Haloperidol-promethazine mix," Hope sighed. "Paramedic's little helper for agitated or violent patients. Not enough to knock them out, but enough to take the edge off."

"He's not a patient," Rachel said.

"He is now," Hope told her. "I'm checking him into the psych ward until I'm sure he's not a danger to anyone."

"Not a danger," Dalder said, his head lolling on the chair's backrest. "Rather die."

"Or a danger to himself," Hope said. She slid an arm under Dalder and helped him stand. "Santino? Got a few minutes?"

"Yeah," Santino said. He was roughly as tall as Dalder, and a much better fit to help him to the nearest wheelchair than Hope was. He wove his left arm under Dalder's right shoulder and the two of them half-carried Dalder into the hall.

"Hey, Hope?" Rachel called to her. "I'd still like to get a look at Meisner."

"Oh, right," Hope said. "Uh…" She glanced around to get her

bearings. "Room 3304—down the hall, right, right, left, and it'll be on your left."

After another long stretch of wandering and elbowing their way through the dense crowds jamming the hallways, Rachel and Phil eventually found Jordan Meisner's room. There were a goodly number of people on the other side of the glass doors. *Meisner's family,* Rachel guessed, judging from the similarities of their earthy core colors.

Phil pulled the chart out of the plastic sleeve by the door and paged through Meisner's medical status. "Looks good," he said. "He'll definitely make it. No serious damage other than the burns and…" His colors blanched white.

"What?" Rachel asked.

"Ah… He's lost both eyes."

"Right," Rachel said smoothly. "I thought that was likely. His face was a mess."

"Rachel…"

"Phil…" She mimicked his pleading mental tone as she turned away from him and pretended to peer through the glass at Meisner. *"Drugged,"* she said, as the man on the bed's conversational colors swirled like a liquid prism on a soap bubble. *"But conscious. Aren't you supposed to sedate patients with burns?"*

"I guess it depends on the case," Phil replied.

Rachel sent her scans through the nearest rooms within the ICU, briefly touching on each patient. Some of them were fully conscious, others were so far gone their cores seemed nearly drained, but many of them shared the same soap-bubble glimmer coming from Meisner. *"Bet you a dollar I could get something useful out of him,"* she said to Phil.

He chuckled. "If I thought you meant that… Come on, let's go find Santino."

"I'll catch up in a minute," Rachel told him. "I want to talk to Jenny."

"Sure," Phil said, nodding. "Do me a favor and tell her I'll have those results for her by next week. I keep forgetting."

"Hmm?" Rachel asked as she found an empty chair a few yards away from Meisner's room. "What results?"

"Nothing exciting. She asked me to log my workouts. Blood pressure, heart rate, just routine biometrics."

"That's strange," Rachel said, glancing down the hall. "She asked me to do the same thing."

Phil shrugged. "Probably more research," he said as he turned to walk away. "I never remember to reset my timer when I start, so it pooches the data."

"Yeah," Rachel agreed, glad they had stopped speaking through the link. She had an unpredictable and unfortunate tendency to vomit when trapped in a physician's office, and being in a hospital had already pushed her into feeling queasy. She was sure Phil would be able to feel that extra wave of nausea that had smashed into her at the mention of Jenny's data.

Rachel let the doors close behind Phil, and reached out through the link. *"Hey Jenny, are you busy?"*

Jenny Davies was one of twelve Agents who had medical degrees, but she was the most active in research. Over the past few months, Jenny had aggressively coerced Rachel to help her turn Rachel's perception scripts into a diagnostic instrument, and Rachel had spent most of that time suffering from what could have passed as persistent morning sickness. Jenny owed Rachel a very large favor.

"Rachel? Hi! No, I'm not busy. What's up?"

Rachel peered back into Meisner's room. The man's conversational colors were still there, but deeply muted; Meisner was doped out of his gourd.

"You know the bombings? I'm at the hospital with one of the victims."

"Medical question?" Rachel's mind was suddenly full of skulls, hundreds of them, and a laboratory-grade examination light over a table covered in loose papers: Jenny was in the OACET medical center.

"Yeah. The victim?" Rachel paused and steeled herself. *"He lost both eyes."*

Jenny was silent for a moment, and then said, *"Oh."*

"Is there anything I can tell him? I'd like to give him some hope."

"Without revealing yourself?"

"Yeah," Rachel said again. *"Got anything new? I'm sure you've been going over my data in your spare time."*

"What spare time?" Jenny laughed. *"Your data is fascinating, honey, but it's about halfway down the list."* The other woman must have felt Rachel's rush of hurt feelings, as she quickly added: *"Your abilities **are** a priority for me, Penguin. I just have a hundred other things that need to be taken care of first."*

Rachel sighed through the link. *"I know. Sorry."*

"I wish I had something for you. Maybe I can get someone else to help me with the research side of—Hey! That reminds me. Can you come home soon? There's something I need you to see."

For one shameful moment, Rachel thought Jenny had meant the house she shared with Santino.

"It's okay." Jenny had picked up on it. *"I'm trying to think of my condo as home, too. It's a good thing,"* she said, but sounded unconvinced.

"I'll ask Santino to drive me over there sometime this week," she told Jenny.

"All right, Penguin, see you soon."

Rachel felt Jenny's quick, strong hug before the woman broke their link.

She stood and walked back to Meisner's room, and paused right outside of his door. She nearly knocked and went in, but her subconscious knew better, and she found herself moving away from Meisner before she could intrude.

Santino had guessed her secret. No one else outside of OACET knew—they might suspect, they might be trying to find proof, but they didn't *know*.

She did not want to talk about it.

She did not want to *think* about it.

In Rachel's mind, blindness was a lack. Lack of sight, lack of ability. Rachel, who had both, had decided the term did not apply to her.

She *would* not think about it.

(Not even at night, in that space between the moment her implant was turned off and the moment she fell asleep, when her bedroom went from a magnificent multihued, multi-textured world to nothing. Those little stray thoughts she *did not have* that nudged at the outside edges of her consciousness, telling her it might be worse for her than for a blind person who did not have the sensory augmentation provided by her implant, that the blending of senses when her implant was *on* also made her world all that much smaller when it was *off*, and that if she ever woke up one morning and the implant refused to activate, she might spend the rest of her life in a dark, tiny box…)

She didn't think about it.

Which made it hard when there was someone who might need her help, just on the other side of a hospital door.

SEVEN

"This isn't the way to the house," Rachel told her partner.

"Very observant," Santino replied, turning down a narrow one-way street. They passed a Vietnamese import shop, followed by a posh after-hours bistro and a butcher's.

"There's a half of a pig in that window," Rachel said. "And I don't mean enough parts of a pig to add up to a half, or even a front-end-versus-back-end deal. That's the half of a pig you get when you have a whole pig, a bandsaw, and you want to see what happens when one meets the other."

"I saw it," he said. "I bet it's delicious. Find me a parking space."

She sighed and threw her scans down the road. "One block up, right side, behind the blue Toyota. Better hurry, there's a minivan coming from the other direction."

Santino swore and hit the gas. His tiny hybrid shot through the intersection and zipped into the space. They pretended not to notice the hand gestures from the family in the minivan with the Ohio plates.

Part of northeast D.C. used to be the warehouse district, and the neighborhood was partially gentrified in the way of persons young enough to work full days and still spend all night partying. Rachel felt the vibrations of heavy machinery beneath her feet; on the other side of the street, the air surrounding a nightclub was brightly blurred by the sound of a band warming up.

"If I'd known you wanted to go out, I would have changed," she said.

"I'm not taking you to a show," he said. "I'm taking you to school. You remember this morning, when I said I knew people who could make the types of bombs that could blow up an entire city street?"

"And we ignored you because that's total bosh, and you threw a tiny hissy fit? Yes. Vividly."

"Well," he said, his colors firmly set in a good-humored purple. "I've decided that wasn't your fault. You know that Sherlock Holmes quote, the one about eliminating the impossible?"

"*The Sign of the Four,* Chapter 6," Rachel said. An instructor in the Warrant Officer program had assigned that book as required reading. "Pedantic Holmes to Doormat Watson: 'How often have I said to you that when you have eliminated the impossible, whatever remains, however improbable, must be the truth?'"

"Well, my good Rachel," he said as he guided them down an alley. "How can you eliminate anything if you don't know what's possible?"

With that, he opened an old fire door and gestured for her to enter.

She stepped into a small lobby, beaten down by time and encrusted in filth. There was enough space for the narrow front door, a series of mailboxes embedded in the wall, a stairwell, and an ancient cage-lift elevator set behind a folding scissor door. A man in a proper business suit, his conversational colors a more intense version of the same anxious orange she had seen everywhere since Gayle Street, stepped out of the stairwell. His core color was that strange sort of yellow she associated with prescription medications, and he nodded at them as he went to open a mailbox. Rachel threw a scan towards the elevator, and decided that the man in the suit had the right idea.

"Nope," Santino said, heading her off before she could reach the stairs. "This way," he said, pulling the elevator gate to the side. The old metal shrieked; the man in the lobby glanced at them, eyes widening and colors fading in disbelief as he realized what she and Santino were about to do.

Rachel shared his opinion. As Santino stepped into the elevator, the entire contraption dropped under his weight. Santino didn't have to duck, not quite, but with barely four inches between the ceiling and the top of his head, it was a tight fit for him.

"Stairs." Rachel said, pointing over her shoulder. "Nice, safe, well-mannered stairs."

"Yeah, but you're a noob," he said. "It's policy for all newcomers to use the front door."

"Because they don't want us to come back?"

Santino ignored her and waited for her to step inside. She did, cautiously. The elevator smelled like stale crackers and burnt motor oil, and the cab dropped again as she joined her weight to his. As her partner pulled the steel security door shut, the man with the yellow core had a clear view of Rachel, and was staring at her in yellow-orange concern.

She winked and gave him a little wave, and his concern faded slightly.

Santino flipped the metal panel covering the buttons and jabbed the one for the top floor as hard as he could.

"Is something supposed to happen?" she asked after a few moments.

"It sticks. Give it a second." He bounced his thumb against the button until the elevator finally began to creak its way upwards.

She ran a scan through the elevator's mechanisms and found them to be… Well, the kindest description that came to mind was *antique,* but she was happy to substitute *ancient* or *frayed* or even *churning broken deathwheels* for accuracy's sake.

"You sure this is safe?" she asked her partner, wide-eyed.

"Oh yeah, definitely," he said, nodding. The car threw itself sideways; Rachel grunted and grabbed the metal cage to keep her balance, and Santino reached up with both hands to steady himself against the ceiling.

They watched four floors drop away without speaking, and then the rattling elevator jerked to a stop. Rachel ripped the gate aside, then wrestled with the security door until she could squirm through the gap.

"What the fuck is wrong with you?" she gasped. Santino

grinned in blues and purples as he took her by her shoulders, then spun her around.

"Wow," she heard herself say, her fallback phrase for when words failed her.

Rachel recognized that tunnel vision was more mental than physical; she had learned that when her stress levels amped up, her scans battened down. There was nothing which would have prevented her from seeing this from four stories down, except for the instinctual need to focus on the here-and-nowism of that death trap of an elevator. And now that the threat had faded, she could finally notice the door.

She knew it was a door because it couldn't be anything else. Two gas lamps, wrought iron twisted around bubbled glass spheres, were positioned to both sides of a metal sheet which began at the floor and stopped halfway up the wall. The lamps had been turned off, useless on a day like today when the door was bathed in autumn sunlight from the skylight overhead. The door itself was made from half a hundred pieces of metal, copper and bronze, tin, silver, maybe even gold…and yet looked nothing like patchwork. The artist—like the door itself, its creator could have been nothing other than what he or she was—had blended these different metals together into a whole. There were seams, of course, transitions between the elements, but these were to her mind like crossing from the grassy path to the stream; different, noticeably so, but nevertheless part of the same grand design.

The effect was only slightly spoiled by the plaque the artist had incorporated into the door at eye level, the one with *SPEAK, FRIEND, AND ENTER* picked out in raised text.

"Oh, nerds," she sighed.

"It's a combination lock," he said. "Takes a little bit of thinking to get in."

"Come on, even I've seen those movies," she said.

"Okay," Santino told her. "You're so smart, you open it."

Rachel stepped forward and steeled herself to quote Gandalf, but Santino was vividly purple, sure she was about to fail in a hilarious way. She shut her mouth and scanned the door instead. Six inches thick; hollow but still solid. Its workings were a mess of gears. There wasn't so much as a speck of digital machinery, but the right side of the frame and certain words within the plaque gleaming from otherwise unseen traces… *Ah!* Her old buddy, squalene.

Thank goodness for bodily secretions, she thought, and pressed her own fingertips against the *ENTER,* shining from where all of those who had come before her had touched it.

There was a small *click* at the edge of hearing, and the door swung open on hidden hinges.

Santino's colors drooped as she pushed the door wide. "So close."

She was about to nail him with a snitty response when she finally looked past the door to take in the room behind it.

It was an industrial loft the size of a football field. The west side of the room was baking from the late afternoon sun coming through the windows; the rest of it was comfortably warm. Brick and beaten wood formed the walls and floors, with iron peeking through the cracks. The ceiling might have been wood or plaster—she couldn't tell without running different frequencies—but it didn't matter which since it had been painted in a deep cobalt blue and dotted with white and yellow stars. She thought the artist who made the front door had likely had a hand in building this celestial temple, as planets cut and shaped from woven scraps of metal dropped from invisible cords in a rough mimicry of the solar system.

Tables lifted straight from a high school science lab were scattered across half of the loft in no apparent order. Their thick slate tops, scarred from dropped machinery and chemical burns, were barely visible beneath the tangle of equipment. She saw art supplies, welding tools, a stack of exotic woods, racks of colored liquids with handwritten labels she couldn't read…

There was no other furniture except a couch which would have been happier back out on the curb where it had been found, an industrial refrigerator humming in the corner, and a few old blackboards on rollers. These were positioned around the room; other than the odd arcane scrawl, these seemed to serve no other purpose than to hold receipts. The real body of written work was at the far end of the loft, where a computer lab was set apart from the main space by a glass divider running from floor to ceiling. It reminded Rachel of the conference room at First District Station, a fishbowl of a space, on display to the public but walled off by glass windows. There was writing on this glass, streaks which started three feet above the ground and ended at about head-height, and fluoresced in the telltale dust of dry-erase markers. She flipped to reading mode to try to understand what had been written there, but while she could make out the letters and the odd Greek symbol or two, she understood nothing.

She did, however, recognize Santino's handwriting.

"Come here often?" she asked him, starting into the room.

"When I can," he said. "I lease a table here. My landlord doesn't like it when I build robots."

"No, your landlord is fine with you building robots. It's the part where you nearly burned her house to the ground that got her worried," Rachel joked, but with half an ear. She was mesmerized by the others in the loft. As odd as the room was, it had nothing on the five people who stared at her and Santino as they walked through the front door. Four men—boys, really, the oldest couldn't have been too far into his twenties—looked up from their worktables and blinked at them, their conversational colors showing irritation at the interruption. Rachel did a double take at the boy closest to her: she was no stranger to the club scene and had seen plugs in ears wide enough to hold a garden hose, but this was the first time she had seen a 20mm taper sticking out of a stretched hole on the skin on either side of a human being's neck.

The fifth was a girl with her hair cut and colored in an emerald green bob. She was behind the glass wall at the end of the room, but she brightened in happy yellows and golds when she saw Santino. The girl banged on the glass and waved.

Santino led the way, weaving between tables and projects like a well-trained mouse in a familiar maze. He took Rachel to the computer lab and stopped in front of a silver arch in the glass. The two of them kept to the side as the girl hit some buttons on a keypad and a vacuum lock released the door.

"Santino!" The girl leapt at him and he swung her around. Rachel couldn't help but notice how the girl's clothes seemed to be made entirely of pieces of long unwoven string. She could never follow the Bohemian lifestyle herself: it would take her half of the day to put on the uniform.

"Hey, Silver Bell," Santino said, grinning.

"It's Bell. Just Bell," the girl said to Rachel as Santino set her down. "Unless you want to guess the day I was born. Helpful hint—you can shop for my birthday and Christmas presents on the same trip!"

"Hi Bell. I'm Rachel." She smiled at the girl as she peered through Bell's vivid surface colors to find a smooth gray core beneath. *Interesting,* Rachel thought. While gray surface colors were nearly always some flavor of sadness, gray cores almost always meant a sharp, focused mind.

"Where's Zia today?" Bell asked Santino.

Her partner's surface colors blushed bright red. "I didn't plan on coming," he said. "We were in the neighborhood, and I thought Rachel might want to see this place."

"All are welcome," Bell said automatically.

"She's welcome if she brought money!" shouted one of the men from across the loft. Two of the others snickered.

"*Agent* Peng might make a donation," Santino said, hitting her title a little too hard to be an accident. Rachel took the hint and let the flap on her suit coat slide over her hip. The bright green and gold of her OACET badge flashed out from beneath the wool.

"Jeez!" Bell's colors flashed orange-yellow in excitement. "Guys, she's an Agent!"

"Did the Agent bring money?" the same man quipped.

"Ignore him," Bell said, as Rachel laughed.

"It's fine. That's not the reaction I usually get," Rachel told the girl. The men's colors had barely flickered when they heard she was a cyborg. Anonymity was refreshing.

"Zia comes here a lot. They've busted their questions on her already."

"Ah, right," Rachel agreed. It went without saying that Zia—tall, blond, buxom, Zia—would have gotten their attention. (Zia got more attention than pretty much every other woman on the planet, and in Rachel's opinion, deservedly so.)

"What's your specialty?" Bell asked. The girl was standing high on her toes, her surface colors a bubbly curious yellow. Rachel felt a little like a live frog on the dissection table. "Zia does astrophysics. She's the one who aligned the planets."

Rachel blinked, then realized the girl was gesturing towards the metal solar system overhead. "Oh, right," she said. "My specialty's perception. I can see different electromagnetic fields."

"Really! Look!" Bell grabbed Rachel's hand and ran her left pinkie finger over Rachel's palm. "Look look look—Can you see that? Or feel it?"

Rachel shot a wry glare at Santino. "Depends," she told Bell. "What are you trying to do?"

"Parylene-coated neodymium magnet!" Bell said, holding up her pinkie. "I got an implant after OACET came out."

"Oh…" Rachel said limply. "So you can…wipe out credit cards?"

Bell's colors glazed over and she let go of Rachel's hand. "You're the Agent who works with Santino at the MPD, aren't you."

It hadn't been a question, but Rachel nodded anyway.

The girl's colors softened to a pitiful rose, and Rachel sent a quick message to Santino's phone to remind her to kill him when they got home.

"Hey," called one of the guys from his worktable halfway across the room. "Weren't you the Agent in that video? The one that went viral a few months ago?"

"Yup," Rachel answered.

"Did that really happen?" the kid asked. "Did Senator Hanlon pay those guys to murder somebody?"

"Yes," she said.

"Why isn't he in jail?"

Rachel laughed. "You know how hard it is to arrest a Senator? Even their red tape has its own lawyer."

"Sucks."

"Yeah," Rachel agreed as she walked over to his desk. The kid stunk. His hair was a nest, and she doubted he had showered in a year. He was also putting the finishing touches on the most incredible piece of marquetry she had ever seen outside of a museum.

"Holy Jesus, that is glorious," she said, flipping frequencies to take in its full beauty. The kid had carved pathways across the lid of a mahogany jewelry box, and inlaid those with exotic woods and mother-of-pearl. It reminded her of a Buddhist mandala, but made from polished slivers instead of paint or silk. "What is it?"

He stared at her blankly, then lifted the lid. "It's a box."

"Good job," she said, and went to rejoin Santino and Bell.

"He doesn't mean to be rude. Jake just gets lost in his work," Bell whispered apologetically. "He does art fabs. Tech doesn't do him."

Rachel smiled politely as she reached out through her link to the OACET server. The best course of action was to record the conversation, then have Santino translate it for her later.

"Do you want the tour?" Bell asked her. "I mean, Santino can show you around, but I've got a tour speech I give to potential donors."

"I'd like the tour," Rachel said. "If you've got time."

"Oh yeah, I've got at least another hour before my print is done," Bell said, looking over a bare shoulder towards the glass cage. "I'm trying out a new design so I need to get real-time data on it."

"What is it?" Santino asked her.

"Expandable choker with LED capacity," the girl said. "3D

jewelry is catching on in the clubs. There's a store downtown with a decent MakerBot, and they pay me for new designs. The club kittens pay crazy for a bracelet or necklace fresh from the printer, and if I can get it to light up... The store gets fifty bucks for a tenth of a spool, and I get twenty-five percent of each sale? Yeah, I'll take that."

"Nice!" Santino said. "That'll help with tuition."

The girl's colors faded almost immediately, and Rachel jabbed Santino in his side. Rachel had no idea what Bell was talking about, but it was clear the girl couldn't deal with the idea of tuition.

"You guys want something to drink?" Bell asked, and walked off before Rachel or Santino could reply.

"Don't bring up money," Rachel whispered to her partner. He nodded, and they followed the girl to the industrial fridge against the far wall.

Bell passed them a couple of cold cans of supermarket-brand soda and flopped on the couch in a tangle of string. A puff of particles rose around her; Rachel quickly adjusted her visual spectrum to compensate for the dust.

"Here, sit down," the girl said. "Plenty of room!"

"I'm good," Rachel said. "Thanks." She took a few casual steps away from the invisible cloud of industrial manufacturing and skin flakes which surrounded Bell, and went to investigate the long sequence of messages scrolling down the front of the fridge. The first two were professionally done in red enameled lettering over black metal, and had been secured to the door with a bolt driver. She flipped frequencies and began reading.

BIO EXPERIMENTS

WARNING: CONTENTS ARE NOT FOR
HUMAN CONSUMPTION

The rest of the messages meandered down the door on various shades of scrap paper and handwriting, and generally served to underscore the significance of the first two signs.

WE FUCKING MEAN IT

JESUS CHRIST PEOPLE STOP STORING FOOD
IN THIS FRIDGE

WE'LL PUT CHEESE IN YOUR FUCKING COMPUTER

WHICH ONE OF YOU ASSHOLES CUT OFF
THE PADLOCK?

FINE. **DIE.**

And so on. By the time Rachel had reached the messages at the bottom of the door, she was roaring with laughter and had gently placed her unopened can on top of the fridge.

"They don't *really* mean it," said Bell. "So far not a single person has died!" She and Santino were both richly purple.

Santino took down the can and handed it back to Rachel. "The biohackers moved out last month," he said. "Got themselves a clean lab. We bleached the fridge and left the signs for fun."

She checked his colors for white lies, and popped the tab when he checked out. "I'm going to be so pissed at you if I start to grow extra arms," she said after a cautious sip. It tasted like bubbly shoe polish, but this can of soda probably had that problem long before it was stored in a fridge of questionable intent.

"What is it you do here?" Rachel asked Bell.

"Me? I do tech hacks. Additive manufacturing, Arduinos…"

"Edwinos?" Rachel wasn't sure of the pronunciation; Bell sounded as though she had suddenly turned into a native Bostonian and was busy butchering first names.

"Arduinos. It's a programmable microcontroller. Like a computer designed to perform specific tasks, you know? You can stack multiple boards to increase functionality, but it's pretty amazing what a single board can do on its own."

"And additive manufacturing..." Rachel said, and ran a fast search through Wikipedia. "Oh. 3D printing. Yeah, I've heard about this. Somebody used it to print a gun?"

"We don't talk about the gun," shouted one of the men from his workbench on the far side of the loft. He was surrounded by pieces of curved plastic, and was trimming the edge of a Plexiglas sheet with a scalpel with an almost-microscopic blade. His surface colors had traces of her southwestern turquoise and Santino's cobalt core within them; he had been listening to their conversation.

"What?" Rachel asked him. "Why not?"

The man shrugged. "It's a gun. You've got one, Santino's got one... There's nothing special about guns."

"But you can't make a gun in your home," Rachel said. "If anybody with a 3D printer can make themselves a cheap plastic gun..."

The man finally looked up at her. "We *don't*," he said, "talk about the gun." He dropped his attention back to his workbench and his colors washed themselves of her turquoise: she was no longer worth his time.

Santino put a hand on her arm and tugged her aside. "They've got policies here," he said in a low voice. "They make things that help. They never make things that hurt."

"Uh-huh, sure. And how often does that distinction play out in real life?" Rachel whispered back. "The difference between whether a screwdriver is a tool or a weapon is the dude holding it."

"This isn't real life." Bell had overheard them. "This is a community with rules for participation. If you want to be here, you follow the rules. You *have* to," she added, "or the entire system would fall apart."

She gestured them to follow her, and started walking towards to the computer lab at the end of the loft. Rachel took the opportunity to glare at Santino: Bell's speech about following the rules was close to one of her own, the one about how

OACET was able to impose order and create sense in spite of their poorly-designed hive mind, and Santino had sworn he would never repeat it to another living soul. He stared back, eyebrows raised, then realized what she was implying and his mouth rounded in a silent *No! Never!*

His surface colors stayed clean; she nodded to apologize.

Bell left her soda on an old TV tray stationed outside of the silver archway. Santino did the same, and Rachel took one last gulp before she dropped her can beside theirs.

She stepped through the arch and entered the lab, and realized the room was singing.

The computers in Jason's office had felt like him, sleek and antagonistic, always ready for a fight. These machines were light but focused; they wanted to work, to *create*.

Rachel walked around the room, flipping through scans to take in the details. The computer lab had a glass roof: the glass wasn't for soundproofing, Rachel realized, but to keep out the airborne debris from the fabrication projects in the main room. The dusting on the roof above them was thick enough to look like a light layer of snow.

Unlike the ceiling, the interior and exterior of the glass walls appeared to be scrubbed clean on a regular basis. These walls were covered in colorful writing, much of it accessible to her scans because of the dry-erase markers. She flipped to reading mode, and saw how Santino's handwriting had taken over three panels of the exterior glass. A woman's handwriting ran parallel to his, sometimes joined in an obvious collaboration; Zia's penmanship was unmistakably Valley Girl, all loopy circles in unnecessary places. As time and the project went on, the two climbed and twisted together, shared thoughts that had grown into each other like twinned vines from separate plants. It was a passionate love letter between academics, and it told her more about Santino and Zia's relationship than her partner would ever put into words. She grinned up at him, and he smiled shyly and blushed deep rose.

"Nice place you've got here," she said to Bell.

"Thanks. What does it feel like to you?" Bell asked. "Zia likes my machines. She says they're friendly."

Rachel was surprised; Agents typically didn't describe their experiences with machines to normal human beings. "That's a good description. This is an amazing system. It must have cost a fortune."

"I wouldn't know. Terry Templeton paid for it," Bell said, her colors picking up a sweet earthy brown, as well as a pink that was close enough to smug to hint at bragging. "He bought most of our equipment. He owns this entire building, actually."

He was also the owner of a third of all information technology companies on the East Coast. Templeton Industries might not be a household name, but that was due to consumers' general unawareness of what made their households function. Crack the case on a desktop computer or a television's DVR, and you'd be staring at a logo for a company owned by Templeton Industries.

"He bought all of this for you?" Rachel asked. She didn't know the list price for this type of equipment, but no one, no matter how rich, would invest this much in one young woman without getting something in return. A slip of Ray Charles' velvet voice moved through her thoughts, singing about a woman way over town...

"Not just me," Bell said quickly, as if reading Rachel's mind. "I share them with four other hackers."

"Ah?"

"Doesn't mean the same thing it used to," Bell said. "We don't break into databases. We make some things, customize others...let me show you what I do."

The girl opened a locked steel box and took out a delicate white glove attached to a battery pack. "Here," she said to Rachel. "I used my own hand as the model for this, and your hand is about the same size as mine, so it'll work for you. Try it on and tell me how it feels."

"Plastic?" Rachel asked. Her scan showed that what appeared to be handmade lace was a knitted synthetic polymer, with thick boning hidden along the backs of each finger. *Stays in a corset*, she thought as she tugged the glove on and found that her fingers refused to bend.

Bell nodded. "This is something I'm working on for the V.A. Um…that's the Department of Veterans Affairs," she clarified. "So, imagine you're a soldier in the Middle East."

"Done," Rachel said as she glanced at Santino, who was purple and trying not to laugh.

"Say your hand gets injured and you have to go through physical therapy. Well, there are a lot of injured soldiers, and maybe not enough physical therapists, right? This is a therapy augmentation device. It won't replace therapy, but it'll supplement it by helping a soldier with mobility exercises when a therapist isn't available.

"You wanted to know about Arduinos?" Bell rummaged through the box and took out a second item, which she attached to the battery pack. "This is an Arduino with an extensor tendon therapy program."

The glove hummed to life. It began to warm itself as the miniaturized metal servos on the boning caught power, and then began to move. Her fingers extended and relaxed in slow repetitions, the extensions becoming slightly more pronounced each time.

"This program is adjustable and can be customized for individual patient needs. It monitors the user's physical responses, too, so the therapist can chart the patient's progress. The therapists at the VA think it'll really help vets with tendon damage. Since the glove'll do the stretching for them, it'll probably improve compliance."

"Nice work," Rachel said appreciatively.

"So, this is what I make," Bell said as she detached Rachel from the glove. "I've got grants from three different hospitals to develop different assistive devices. If we get the system working the way we want, each hospital will have a 3D printer. They'll scan a patient's biometrics to get the right size, print out a device that fits that patient perfectly, and a therapist'll design an individualized program for each patient."

"Just like that?"

"Well, money's always a problem," Bell said, relocking the glove in its metal box. "Even in a perfect world, these things'll still cost money to produce. But if we can show the benefits will offset the initial investment cost, the money will come, and this system will help a lot of people."

"Better living through technology," Rachel said, smiling.

"Damn right! I'm a transhumanist," Bell said, holding up her finger with its concealed magnet. "We've got so much potential, and we're just starting to discover the tools that'll let us realize it. Anything I can do to push us forward is worth it."

Transhumanism again. That term, at least, Rachel knew well. Not all of the anonymous letters OACET received were hate mail. Many of them were from self-proclaimed transhumanists, people who saw OACET as the next phase of human evolution. Sometimes these letters were more difficult to read than the hate mail. It was harder to ignore someone who, instead of assuming you were a staggering hellspawn stalking the earth, thought of you as a semi-divine being who needed some gentle prodding to recognize how you should begin using your powers for the greater good.

"So don't go getting hung up on the gun," Bell said, settling herself down on a brushed steel bench. "We don't do weapons here. This is where people like me build beautiful things. And since everybody's definition of beauty is different, we've got hardware, software, art... Me? I think the human body is beautiful. I want to help heal it when it's broken, or push it forward when it's not, and I think technology is the best way to achieve this."

"That's great. Really commendable." Rachel put her hand on the backrest of a wheeled desk chair and spun it around so she could sit facing Bell. "But Santino brought me here because he wanted to show me that whoever blew up downtown doesn't necessarily have to be on our Great and Ever-Growing Checklist of International Enemies."

"Not *me*," Bell said. "I couldn't have done that. I don't play with any hardware outside of computers."

"But the others? Are there other people who share this space who know how to make bombs?"

Bell's surface colors faded. "A bomb is just a fuel source and a fuse," she said defensively. "Those are everywhere."

"Complicated, complex bombs? Ones on timers?"

"Yeah," Bell grudgingly admitted. "Yeah, we could. And we know we could. But we've got a charter! We follow standard safety policies for what we can do, what we can make. If you want to hold a space here, you follow the charter. And anyone who violates it? They're out on their ass."

"They're really strict about it," Santino said. "All good Fab Labs have charters, and this is one of the best. Safety is a priority."

Rachel pointed at the industrial refrigerator and its layers of signs.

"That's a *joke!*" Bell exclaimed. "We had a mini fridge for food. Sometimes we stuck leftovers in there, but that was just to get the biohackers to move out. Their experiments always stunk up the loft."

"Bell," Rachel said, "Nobody knows better than OACET that it's not what you can do, it's what you choose to do. I'm not accusing you or anybody who comes here, but you have to understand that if the average person can do the kind of damage that happened on Gayle Street, we're all pretty much fucked.

"So," she continued, "what's your expert opinion? Can the average Joe build a bunch of big old bombs in his basement?"

"No." Bell was adamant. "There are three things all makers need: a plan, experience, and resources. Plans can be easy to find, but experience has to be earned, and resources are pretty much impossible to acquire.

"We are *broke*," Bell added. "I've got the experience, and I can make a plan, but I wouldn't have the resources to pull off something like Gayle Street. I might be able to build something small, like backpack bombs, but nothing big enough to take down an entire street!"

"What if someone rented space here, like Santino? Would they be able to make a bomb without your knowledge or consent?"

Bell pivoted to face the main section of the loft. "Hey, Landley!" she called out. "What do you think?"

"Unlikely," came the muted voice of the man who had asked Rachel about the video.

Bell glared at Rachel. "No one's crashing our space to use our tools. There's no such thing as a secret here."

"All right," Rachel said, holding up her hands in surrender. "All right, I'm convinced. Do you have a lawyer?"

The girl stared at her blankly, her colors a confused orange-yellow. "No?"

"Get one. Not for yourself, but to represent your community. And if any new applicants show up to rent space from you, make sure Santino and Zia are there when you interview them."

"Oh no." Santino closed his eyes, shifting to purple-gray in a silent sigh. "Bell, she's right. It's likely that law enforcement will try to infiltrate us."

"What? *Why?!*"

Rachel shrugged. "Same reason the FBI sticks their people in every organization they can, from anti-war groups to the KKK," she said. "You never know where the next threat will come from. But with an Agent and a cop sitting in, I don't think you'll have anything to worry about."

Bell's eyes traveled from Rachel to Santino before she could help herself, a sickly green washing over her.

"Not him," Rachel assured her. "He's not a spy. He's just a nerd."

"I really am," Santino told Bell. "But I'm a nerd who's a cop, and I've got connections to OACET. That'll be more than enough protection for you guys."

Bell's tension eased, the green weakening but not leaving her completely. Instead, a trace of red appeared, weaving itself into the green as she weighed anger against fear. "But we haven't done anything," she finally said. "Why would they waste their time on *us?*"

"Sorry, kid," Rachel said as she and Santino stood to leave. "It's just the way things are these days."

EIGHT

"Rachel? Got a moment?"

She didn't, actually. She was more than a little worried the floor beneath her was about to cave in; whatever Phil wanted would have to wait. She flipped up a privacy message and stretched her toes out as far as her boots would allow.

Fuckin' leather soles, she thought as she heard the support beam creak beneath her. *I'd stab someone for a pair of sneakers.*

Rachel had discovered that she and the fire department had very different perspectives on whether a fire-damaged building was safe to enter. The nice young firefighter had told her to keep to the walls where the support beams had sustained the least damage. The floor and subfloor were gone in the center of the room, and Rachel kept an active scan going to make sure she stood squarely on the joists. *They sure built them solid back in the day,* she thought, poking around the inside of the beams. *Hardwood, not pine. Oak or ash? Charred but solid. Very, very solid.*

She kept telling herself that as she walked the perimeter, hands clasped behind her so Zockinski wouldn't see how her nails bit into her own palms. She swept her sixth sense down and out, tracing each utility she could find. *Water line, sewer line, gas line, no power. Power must be aboveground in this neighborhood*—she glanced around and spotted a utility pole—*but they buried the cable? Strange.*

A full thirty-seven hours after the bombings and there was little progress in determining the Whos or Whys. They were all good on the What and the Where, obviously, and there was some rough progress on the How: the MPD and the FBI had combined their bomb squads and had found the gas line in each building had been rigged to blow. But who did the rigging, when they had access to the gas lines, and why they had decided to attack in the first place? Nothing.

The public was getting a tiny bit anxious.

The day after the bombing, she and Santino had gone with Zockinski and Hill to Gayle Street. The four of them bumped between teams, helping when they could. They had assumed they would be unwanted or underfoot, but every agency working the site was making the effort to collaborate and they welcomed the extra bodies.

And this odd quest that Sturtevant had set them on? None of them had expected to enjoy it. But (as Zockinski had confided over beers the night before) acting as witnesses? Quite liberating, really. They had no tasks to complete, no reports to fill out, no pressure to find the bad guys. They were free to watch—maybe even pass judgment—as their peers in law enforcement struggled to find answers.

She almost felt like a reporter.

The floor swayed beneath her and she instinctively reached out to grab what was left of a display stand; the scorched metal was cold against her raw palms.

"Hey Peng? Remember not to touch anything!"

"Thanks, Zockinski! You're such a blessing!"

Santino and Hill, both copious note-takers, had left to rotate through the many press conferences, leaving Rachel and Zockinski on Gayle Street. As this counted as a Mass Casualty Incident, the rescue-and-recovery phase had taken over a day and had ended the previous afternoon. The fire department had followed to assess the structural stability of the buildings: it had been safety first, evidence collection second, with Forensics permitted to enter only after the fire department had cleared the site for law enforcement.

Rachel and Zockinski had attached themselves to a forensics team from the FBI. They were friendly with some of them, having worked with them on the Glazer case. Rachel and Zockinski told themselves they knew better than to get in the way, but when the team had finished clearing a coffee shop,

Rachel had made the stupid off-hand comment that she'd like to see the inside of a bomb site for herself.

So, there she was, doing her best to pretend she was working instead of wondering if she could jump across the collapsing floor like Lara Croft if (no, *when*, definitely when) it finally gave way beneath her.

The store reminded her of a deer carcass shredded by trucks. Its bones had broken through its skin, and those windows that remained intact had a clouded, vacant stare. Her scans and her toes kept working the floor for anything whole, and when she found a spot that felt reasonably stable, she paused to run a full environmental search.

Rachel sent her scans down until she found earth instead of cement. The ground was hard but not frozen, and she slowly pulled her scans upward through the utilities. She saw nothing out of the ordinary. It wasn't uncommon to find an unused tunnel or cutoff, especially in communities which had suffered the brunt of early civil planning. This building and—she extended her range outward—the street didn't seem to have suffered from engineering growing pains. In fact, it looked as though some work had been done on Gayle Street within the last few years to clean up the outdated lines.

"How old is this neighborhood?" Rachel shouted.

"I don't know. Isn't it a good thing I have Google in my head?" Zockinski yelled back. "Oh wait."

"About 1870," said one of the firemen.

"See?" Rachel pointed, and regretted it as the floor swayed ever so slightly. "He's helping. Learn by example."

Always walk the crime scene, Rachel reminded herself. *You learned that last August. You can miss things when you rely on scans...Forensics has already been all over this floor and it didn't collapse under them. You will be fine. You will be fine...oh boy, there's a new noise, yep, I'm about to die.*

She walked forward on the beams, one foot placed carefully in front of the other as she probed the layers of debris. The fire had been out for more than a full day but everything was still damp, and there were large sections of the floor that were covered in broken chips of tile from what must have been a gorgeous porcelain floor. Not an easy place for a midmorning stroll. It reminded her of her jogging path along the train tracks, but smelling of burnt coffee instead of diesel fuel.

"Got anything?" Zockinski shouted.

"Hard to tell," Rachel replied. "Some asshole keeps yelling at me and breaking my concentration!"

The fire department and the last few members of the FBI's forensics team colored to blues and purples; Zockinski's surface colors quickly matched theirs as they all had a good laugh at his expense.

Good, she thought. *Different teams working happily togeth—*

The heel of her left boot cracked through the subfloor.

Quick as a cat, she threw herself to the right and landed a few feet away, squarely on top of another support beam.

"Peng?"

"I'm fine, Zockinski," she yelled. "Might have some strong language for the guy who cleared this building, though."

"I'm coming in," he told her.

"I'm coming *out*," she shot back. "This place barely holds my weight. It sure as hell isn't going to hold yours and mi—"

The joist beneath her groaned, and Rachel had just enough time to run another scan through it—*Solid! Burned but solid!*—before one end tipped out of its broken joint and rolled.

The floor shifted from the sudden loss of the joist, and Rachel fell and started a slow, helpless slide towards the hole in the middle of the room. Her nails dug into the wet wood, the shards of porcelain cutting her hands, as she tried to scramble on all fours towards the walls and the concrete sidewalks beyond.

There was another groan from the sinking floor. Rachel froze, hoping, praying… She instinctively looked to Zockinski; he was too far away to help, and was lit with the bright yellow-whites and sickly greens of helpless panic. And then her scans showed a rush of broken wood and tile as she fell.

There were a few stunned seconds where she knew she was

alive, but she was unable to do anything besides watch the floor (*ceiling?*) to see if the whole thing was about to crash down on top of her. Then she took a quick physical inventory; scrapes, nothing broken. She hadn't fallen very far, only five feet or so, and had landed on a stack of misshapen, melted plastic. The smell of burnt coffee was so strong it was almost an assault.

"Peng!" Zockinski's voice was muffled; she looked through the walls to see the firemen restraining him from entering the building.

"I'm fine!" she shouted.

"What?"

"I said I'm..." she began, then muttered: "Forget it," and called Zockinski's cell.

"Peng!"

His cell continued to ring. "Answer your damned *phone*, Zockinski!"

There was a pause, then Zockinski's voice resonated loud and clear in her head. "Peng?"

"Finally," she growled.

"Peng, are you okay?"

"Yeah, I'm fine. I can walk out of here. Let me talk to one of the firemen."

There was a pause and muttered conversation, and an unfamiliar voice said: "Agent Peng?"

"Yes, hello. To whom am I speaking?"

"Uh...Novak. Fire Lieutenant Novak?"

She scanned the cellar of what had once been a coffee shop. *"Don't come in after me,"* she told him. *"The floor joist I was on didn't break. One of its ends twisted out of its post. I can send images to Zockinski's phone if you want to see what I'm talking about. Now, I see three ways to get myself out of here. There's the hole I fell through, a back staircase, and the old skylight window set in the sidewalk. Which one is safest?"*

She was hoping it was the skylight. The foundation of the cellar extended past the upper stories of the building, and the side of the cellar closest to the road had been set with glass squares to let in the light. Rachel figured it would need a couple of good whacks with a sledgehammer, and then she could squirm her way to freedom without having to shuffle across that unstable floor or climb through what was left of the burned back room to reach the rear door.

More muffled conversation, and then Lieutenant Novak was back. "Um... Agent Peng? Take the back stairs."

"Are you sure?" she asked. *"I'm practically under the skylight."*

"Those things are stronger than they look. Anything we do to break it might shake the structure."

"I hear you. I'm not happy about trying to walk across that floor again. Can you get to me through the back door?"

"We don't think we need to. There's a window at the top of the stairs. Most of its glass is already broken. We think we can use a propylene torch to cut through the security bars and get you out that way."

"Okie-dokie," Rachel said cheerily, as the weight of the building seemed to settle on her shoulders.

"Agent Peng? We'll get you out of there as quickly as we can, but try not to move around, okay?"

"Not my first time stuck in a bombed-out basement," she told him. *"Take your time and do it right. I'll be here."*

She broke the connection with Zockinski's cell and started to pick out the small pieces of porcelain tile from her hands. That killed a few minutes, especially the twinned slivers that had skewered her left palm and wedged themselves in the muscle. She was wondering what else she could do to keep herself occupied when a green version of Phil appeared in the air beside her with a silent pop.

"Rachel!"

"Hey!" She grinned up at him. His vivid lime-green projection was fluffy and distorted. Phil wasn't good at going out-of-body. Rachel thought it might be because he never bothered to look in a mirror. Not that Phil was an untidy person: he simply didn't cotton to vanity, and Rachel guessed he didn't have enough experience with his own face to create a coherent visual image for others. "You're a sight for sore…me."

"Zockinski called," he said. "Are you okay?"

"Couple of scratches," she said, holding up her bloody hands. "I'll have Zockinski drive me home after this and get Jenny to stitch me up."

"I'll crack these idiots open for letting you come in here," Phil said. Out-of-body projections didn't carry the emotional spectrum, but she felt his anger through the link.

Oh. She suddenly felt a *lot* of things through the link; Phil had just spread the word that she had been in an accident. *"I'm fine,"* she told the collective. *"I'm not hurt, the fire department is going to get me out, and do **not** come running down here to get in their way. I mean that—the building is unstable enough as it is."*

She had added that last bit as more of an implied threat than anything else—Guys, if you all rush in here like a rampaging herd of wildebeests, I will *die!*—but she had found that a little bit of anger, a little bit of humor, those could cloud anxiety and keep it from the link. Nobody else needed to feel how close she was to screaming.

She hated bombs.

There was a second silent pop, and Josh Glassman's out-of-body avatar resolved himself on the stack of boxes beside her.

"Penguin," he said. "You promised you'd stay out of dirty holes."

"Look who's talking," she said. "You didn't need to come."

"I never *have* to come," he said, sitting back and stretching his legs out to rest on what had probably been a stack of plastic storage bins before the fire. Josh's avatar was rock-solid, and so intricately detailed she could see each fold of cloth in his trousers. Where Phil was fuzzy, Josh was crisp and polished, with his hair and clothing ever-so-slightly rumpled to prove he had more important things to care about than his appearance.

"Well, then, hail hail, the gang's all here," Rachel said. "Too bad we don't have beer."

A frosty green stein appeared in Josh's hand. It was as much an illusion as the rest of him, but he went through the gestures of drinking and settling it beside him, using the warped top of a box as his coffee table. Phil tried to copy him; his stein started out with a picture of Mickey Mouse on it, but its ears quickly melted as Phil lost his focus and the image got away from him.

Rachel laughed, and felt the weight of the building lift away. Phil and Josh smiled at her: apparently she hadn't been fooling anyone in the link.

"So," Josh said after about ten minutes of idle talk and playing with shapes of green light. "Phil, show us where this bomb went off."

"Oh no," Rachel said. "Oh no no *no*. I am staying right—" She realized what Josh was saying when he and Phil started laughing at her. "Shut up," she sighed, and slipped from her body to join them.

The three of them set out to explore, their green avatars easily climbing around and through the ruins of the basement. There was an impromptu game of tag, with Rachel and Phil ganging up on Josh as he flew gracefully through the broken building, eluding them with casual ease.

When they reached the back corner of the basement, Phil waved them over. "Here," he called out. Rachel and Josh drifted over to him. Phil was kneeling in the center of what might have been a crater if debris from the ceiling hadn't fallen and filled in most of the hole. Phil poked around until he found the edge of a pipe. "You guys want the full lecture on how we think this happened?"

"Yes," Rachel said, while Josh said, "No."

"Ignore him," Rachel said to Phil. "I want to hear this."

"All right," Phil said, pointing his finger at a small piece of metal sticking out of the wall. "This was probably part of the gas line, which we think was rigged to make a single-source explosion. Now, natural gas is actually really safe. There's safety equipment along each juncture, and it gets replaced on a regular basis to make sure it's kept up to code. In the United States, gas lines cause only about one explosion per day."

"Only?" Rachel asked.

"Mathematically speaking? Yes, only. There's about seventy-two million homes and businesses heated by natural gas, so we're talking a fraction of a percent. Really, we lose more buildings to space heater malfunctions."

"Okay," Rachel said. "So what happened here? I'm assuming Gayle Street didn't just happen to beat the odds?"

"Nope." Phil shook his head. "This is the weird part—this is how you know someone planned this. If Gayle Street were an accident, there'd be a single ignition point, followed by an explosion. That's pretty much the universal progression of an accidental natural gas explosion. Then, after ignition, the blast continues until the fuel source is exhausted. With the last generation of safety equipment, this usually happened when the utility company or the fire department closed down the gas line.

"Since this is a business district in downtown D.C.," Phil continued, "these gas lines have been updated with an auto-shutoff feature. Too much gas goes through within a certain period of time, and the main line supplying the block shuts down. That's the only reason the rest of the street is still standing, by the way. If PHMSA hadn't upgraded to that standard—"

"PHMSA?" Rachel asked.

"Sorry. Pipeline and Hazardous Materials Safety Administration. It's a subset of the Department of Transportation," Phil said. "I don't think we've got any PHMSA in OACET."

"You're right. We don't," Josh said. He knew the full roster of Agents like the back of his hand, and knew exactly who had been recruited from which government organization. "We've got one from DOT, but he specialized in civil engineering."

"Thought not," Phil said. "Anyway, whoever did this knew about the shutoff feature, so they front-loaded the gas line at each site."

"Front-loaded?" Rachel asked.

"Phil?" Josh's avatar was slouched against the wall, arms crossed. "Can you show us? It might be easier."

"Yeah…" Phil's voice trailed off as he stared at the half-full crater. A green pipe emerged from the wall, with a cylinder the size and shape of a large oxygen tank slowly materializing beneath it. Rachel noticed that while Phil had difficulty maintaining coffee mugs and his own face, he had no problem at all envisioning the fundamentals of a bomb. "Gas line," Phil said, pointing at the pipe, then pointed to the cylinder. "Storage tank. This tank is the main fuel source for the bomb."

He then pointed at the wall. "The shutoff is back there along the utility lines somewhere. There's only one per five blocks, which means there were three involved in this incident. I took a look at them yesterday, and they did exactly what they're supposed to do.

"We think somebody installed the gas storage tank down here a few months ago. They must have shut off the local gas line going into the building, installed the device, and then restarted the line. The storage tank then gradually drew on the line, so it would fill over time and wouldn't trigger the auto-shutoff. From the scrap we've collected, it looks like it could have stored fifty to seventy times the BTUs this building requires during peak operation."

"BTUs?" Rachel asked.

"Ah…British thermal units. Sorry, there's no easy volume conversion. It's basically calorie counting for household appliances."

"Fifty times the normal capacity doesn't sound like enough fuel to do the level of damage that happened here," she said.

"It's plenty," Phil said. "Natural gas is a cryogenic liquid. It's lighter than water and air, and it needs to be in a vapor state to ignite. You have no air? Then you have no fire. And if natural gas gets too diluted when it's in the air, that's a non-starter, too.

"But this," Phil said, indicating the cylinder, "is an extra reservoir that the local gas line wasn't designed to handle. Add that to the fuel that would still be coming down the main line before the blowback shutoff cut on, and you might be talking a hundred-plus times the average BTUs, depending on location.

The extra capacity was enough to turn a small, probably manageable explosion into one big enough to take out a store."

"That's why some of the explosions were smaller than the others," Rachel said. "They were at the end of the main line."

Phil nodded. "By the time the ones at the end of the line blew, the main line was exhausted. The smaller explosions had the reservoir tank and what was left in the local line, and that was all."

"Ingenious," Rachel said.

"Definitely," Phil said. "And royally screws up the investigation, too. The chemical composition of the explosive material is usually one of the strongest pieces of evidence in a bombing. This guy took away the chemical signature by using a fuel source that already existed on site."

"What triggered it?" Josh asked.

"We haven't figured that out yet," Phil said. "We know it had to have been on a timer, and it would have had to convert the reservoir to vapor, so there might have been a small explosion to detonate the canister first… We haven't seen something like this before, so we just don't know."

"I hate to say it," Josh said, "but this definitely sounds like something out of the abilities of your average backyard terrorist."

"That's what we're thinking," Phil said. "Some of the canister scraps we've collected have serial numbers on them. It's going to take Forensics some time to put the pieces together, but from what they've got now, they say it looks like military equipment."

"Maybe not," Rachel said. "On our way home yesterday, Santino took me to see a maker community. I get the feeling a lot more people can pull something like this off than you'd expect."

The downside of being out-of-body was the loss of the emotional spectrum, but she was fairly certain the look that the two men exchanged was the same eye-rolling reddish-purple sigh that she had shared with Zockinski and Hill over pizza the day before. She made a mental note to buy an enormous bottle of whiskey for Santino as an apology.

"All right, boys, let's try this again," she said. She fixed the image of the loft in her mind—the solar system, the rolling blackboards, the clever little machines, *Speak, Friend, and Enter!*—and brought that glorious room to life in the wreckage of the broken basement.

She kept the construct active long enough for Josh and Phil to gasp, then let it drop. *No wonder Jason sucked down two calzones*, she thought. *Maintaining something that size takes a hell of a lot of energy. Maybe it's easier if you're not also out-of-body when you're projecting it.*

"That was—" Phil started.

"I know," she said. "It's a playground. It's really… It's beautiful. I'll have to take you guys there after all of this is over. Just try and keep an open mind about what's possible, okay? These guys convinced me that a couple of not-so-average dudes could pull this off."

"Who was the woman?" Josh asked.

"What?" For a brief moment, Rachel had no idea what he was talking about, then realized she had imagined the loft with its occupants. He had spotted Bell. "Oh come on. I have that up for all of five seconds and the only thing you notice is her?"

"Not the only thing," he said. "But by the amount of detail you put into her, you noticed her, too."

"I'm a cop," Rachel said. "People are my job. Besides, I'm seeing someone."

"Oh?" Phil perked. "News to me. Who is she? How'd you meet her?"

"Hold that thought," she said as she heard her own name echoing through the basement. "I think I'm getting out of here."

She dropped her out-of-body self, but kept herself still while she counted backwards from ten. Disorientation was always a problem after spending a goodly bit of time outside of one's own skin. When she felt centered, she shouted back to Zockinski: "What?!?"

"I said, we're ready!" His voice came from the rear of the building instead of the front, and she brought up her scans to see him standing beside a window at the top of the back stairwell.

"I'm on my way!"

Rachel looked around for Phil and Josh. Phil had returned to his body, and she found him in the bomb squad's office at First District Station. But Josh was still floating beside her in greens.

"I'll be fine," she told him. "You can go."

He started to protest, then sighed and disappeared. She felt his quick hug through the link, and heard his voice in her mind: *"Just hurry."*

"No chance in hell. I'm taking this slow and steady, and then I'm never going into a coffee shop ever again."

Josh laughed, and she felt him ease back in the link without breaking the connection; she knew he'd stay with her in some way or another until she was safe outside.

She climbed down from the stack of melted plastic as carefully as she could, then made her way across the floor. Wet ash sucked at her feet and crept up her boots and the cuffs of her trousers. By the smell of it, she was shuffling through a swamp of scorched wood and coffee.

The back staircase was poured concrete and had survived the fire intact. She pulled herself out of the muck and crawled up the slippery staircase on all fours; she was keeping a firm scan on Zockinski and the others, and none of them were close enough to prioritize dignity over safety. As she reached the top, she stood and walked up the last two stairs, then turned the corner to step into the waiting arms of the firefighters.

They hauled her through the window. The sill had been covered in a firefighter's turnout coat to protect her from the glass and the newly-cut metal of the security bars. Rachel let herself fall forward as soon as her knees crested the sill, and as they caught her, they all shifted from bright reds and oranges to a deep relieved blue.

She was swimming in apologies: the firefighters were appalled they had put her at risk.

"Not your fault," she told them. "The floor was stable until I jumped up and down on it. If it's anybody's fault, it's mine."

There was an ambulance waiting for her. She let the EMTs clean and bandage her hands, then shouted them off when they tried to take her to the hospital.

"You should have gone with them," Zockinski told her as the ambulance pulled away. "You're a wreck."

"Huh," Rachel said, looking down and pretending to notice the state of her person for the first time; one did not crawl through a fire pit and emerge on the other side untarnished. She had kept a firefighter's emergency blanket and had draped it over her shoulders, but it was doing nothing to help either her appearance or her filthy, freezing feet. "You're right, I should have! Whoever drives me home is going to have a hell of a mess in their car."

Zockinski groaned.

The two of them moved to the center of the street. Rachel kicked a fallen lamp post to make sure that it, at least, wouldn't move out from under her, and then used it as a back rest as she sat cross-legged on the ground. She had reclaimed her purse from Zockinski, and groped around in the hidden pocket of her bag for a soda and an energy bar. Going out-of-body had left her famished.

"See anything down there?"

"Yeah," she said as she popped the tab on the can. "Phil and Josh came down to keep me company. Phil walked us through the crime scene."

"How—"

"Out-of-body, plus a bunch of projections like Jason showed us back in his lab," she said, but he was still slightly orange. "Just smile and nod," she sighed. "It's easier that way. Smiling and nodding is how I get through life."

Zockinski's colors shifted to a solid purple and he laughed. She found herself laughing along with him. Sometimes it was easier to laugh than fret about needing a shower. Or near-death experiences. And then, because she was a perpetual giggler once the danger was over and the pent-up stress had time to escape, she spent the next couple of minutes clinging to the lamp post so she wouldn't roll around on the ground in a small happy fit.

"You malfunctioning or something?" Zockinski asked her when she was sober again.

"Shut up," she said. "I'm dirty, I'm cold, and I just spent an hour in a basement wondering if I was sitting in my own tomb. I can damn well laugh about it if I want to."

"Fair enough." Zockinski shrugged. "Phil tell you anything interesting?"

"Yeah," she said, and told him about Phil's description of the bomb. When she had finished, Zockinski was quiet. It was such a change that she reached over and poked his leg.

He jumped. "What?"

"Hill's already mastered his role as the strong, silent cop. You're the belligerent comic relief. What are you thinking?"

"I'm not comic relief."

"You can tell yourself that if it makes you feel better."

He snorted. "All right. Here's what I'm thinking: I was working at the MPD when September 11 happened."

"Ugh, no," Rachel groaned. "Please, Esteemed Elder, do not treat me to a story from the Days of Yore."

"I'm five years older than you."

"Or ten. Maybe fifteen. Twenty? Honestly, I have problems counting that high."

"Want me to toss you back in that basement?"

"I'd like to see you try," Rachel said, grinning up at him. Zockinski had eight inches and eighty pounds on her, and neither of them had any illusions of who would win in a fight.

"All right, Agent Sass-Ass. You and Hill have the combat experience, and Santino's the academic, but I've been here longer than any of you children. I got my B.A. and joined First MPD," Zockinski said. "And not too long after that, we've got September 11."

"Right, right. The unthinkable has happened, the world has changed overnight, yada yada yada," Rachel said.

"Do me a favor and try not to reduce it to a yada yada yada," Zockinski said, the center of his conversational colors starting to glow red.

"Hey, I got turned into a machine thanks to the yada yada yada," Rachel said, parting her short black hair to show him the long white scar beneath. "There's a lot of stuff living and breathing and dying horrible deaths inside of the yada yada yada. As George Costanza said, it's a real timesaver."

Zockinski snorted and the red cracked into purples. "Okay," he said. "I'll give you that."

"So, O Ancient One…"

"So we've got September 11," he repeated, "and that became the model for our training and preparedness scenarios. We planned for big events, bombs that took out entire football stadiums, a nuke loose in the city, that level of attack. And we planned for single events, like a parked car in front of the J. Edgar Hoover Building, or a terrorist in a suicide vest getting inside the Capitol."

"Gayle Street counts as both," Rachel said. "A Mass Casualty Incident with multiple bombs, but basically a single big event."

Zockinski nodded. "Fits right into what we we've been expecting. But here's the thing—after the Boston Marathon? We realized all of this was probably bullshit. Training for single big events is probably not going to help us. We need to develop skills relevant to how terrorists might really fuck us up."

"Backpacks," Rachel said. "A big chunky purse, like mine. Hell, those stupid little fanny packs, or a big brown paper sack. Everyone's always got some sort of bag."

"Yeah," he said, nodding. "I forgot. You've been working with the MPD since last spring."

"That, and this is how we used to prepare in Afghanistan. None of this is new, Zockinski. It's just finally come home to the States, and *that's* new."

"I'd hoped it would never come here," he said, looking at what was left of Gayle Street. The purple left his conversational colors and the reds returned, but these weren't directed towards her.

They floated like a poisoned cloud at the edges of his core of autumn orange, anger with nowhere to go. "We told ourselves we'd be ready if it did, but now…"

"Yeah," Rachel agreed. "I've been with you guys on the drills. The new worst-case scenario is similar to what we've got here." She put the empty soda can on the ground and crushed it flat with her boot. "Upscale shopping district, but not too upscale; anyone can come and go without sticking out. Multiple stationary bombs with payloads bigger than what could fit in a backpack, but still small enough to hide in plain sight until the right time. Multiple casualties thanks to bombs timed *just right* so the first responders don't have the opportunity to figure out what's happening or break the pattern. We've got the perfect storm for three phases of maximum panic."

"Three phases?" Zockinski sat up and looked around. "You expecting another attack?"

"Nope. During, Epilogue, and Aftermath," Rachel said, ticking each point off on her fingers. "There was the big immediate panic of Phase One. That's when the bombs went off. But Phase One is done, and now we're stuck in Phase Two, the 'terrified public' phase. Have you seen anyone out and about over the last few days? Almost nobody, right? The roads are practically empty. I heard that First MPD had a huge number of people get stomach flu and call in sick yesterday and today, and there're rumors that cops are even starting to walk out on their shifts.

"But Phase Three's the worst. That happens about a week from now. That's when the public realizes they have to get back to their lives, but we still haven't caught the guy. And that's when people will start to panic again, but instead of being terrified of the guy who set the bombs, they're going to be cold and angry and mad at *us*. Because we're the ones who are supposed to prevent this from happening, and if we can't, and they lose confidence in us…"

"If we can't, they think they're alone," Zockinski finished.

"No," she said, shaking her head. "That's when they start to think that if they can't depend on us any more, they have nobody to depend on except each other. They'll band together. Forming groups. *Mobs.*

"And then," she finished, "we're going to see some *really* terrifying shit."

NINE

Rachel waved at Zockinski as he drove off down the long driveway. He had wanted to stay and make sure she had a ride home, but she told him she would work it out with one of the other Agents.

"Get a *car*," he had told her, scowling at the parts of his front seat that weren't covered by the fire blanket. Wet ash, thicker than mud, was everywhere. "Gonna have to get this detailed."

She had promised to look into insurance and start shopping around for a reliable two-door coupe. She wouldn't: the only place she didn't trust her scans more than eyesight was on the open road. Besides, it wasn't as though she had trashed Zockinski's family minivan. She and Santino might be stuck using Santino's personal car, but Zockinski and Hill tootled around town in their own unmarked MPD-issued sedan.

She ran up the sidewalk to the front door of the mansion. The path had become something of an obstacle course of late, as the Agents had carved pumpkins the previous weekend. As tradition demanded, they had left them to rot on the front steps until Halloween, at which time they would be set on fire and most likely burn the entire building down. The grounds would probably burn, too; there were three hundred and fifty Agents in the D.C. area, and even the front steps of a mansion couldn't accommodate every single pumpkin. The lawn had become a sea of grinning orange.

(OACET's first baby had arrived at the end of August, and everything had become a first. First Labor Day cookout, first apple picking, first Halloween... There was a first Thanksgiving coming up, with a first All-Purpose Exchange of Gifts Day after that—the plans for decorating the front hallway of the mansion included a Christmas tree and person-sized menorahs and kinaras on either side of the staircase. OACET was nothing if not diverse. The pumpkins had been carved in Avery's name, but the nuanced joy of an all-out pumpkin-innards war on the lawn had most likely been lost on the seven-week-old baby. This was a year of firsts for all of them, and Avery had become a joyous excuse for them to celebrate each one.)

She stepped over the threshold and the mansion welcomed her home.

Rachel was glad Santino wasn't with her. If he had been, she wouldn't have let herself slide down the closed double doors and sit splay-legged on the marble floor while she lived in the link.

There were different levels of connectivity for the Agents. The default setting was access, whole and complete access to all things capable of networked communication, including the Agents themselves. A lovely concept in theory, maybe, allowing the human brain unfettered access to peers and machines, but in practice it had driven them to the edge of screaming insanity. A single person split and made into five hundred? The pressure of holding those hundreds of minds within the body that had once been yours alone was a trauma; the realization that your mind was now split between five hundred different bodies an impossibility. Oh, it wasn't as though Phil could have possessed her and used her to prepare his mother's famous Spaghetti alla Foriana, but she could feel his expert touch on the pasta rake as he spooned out the servings with his own two hands.

Now, multiply that confusion times five hundred.

Madness.

Little wonder they had lost so many during those first years. Privacy was as much of a basic need as food, water, shelter, warmth… Deprived of privacy, the mind would struggle and die as surely as if the body had been left adrift on a scrap of wood in the middle of the sea.

But the mind could erect walls.

After the initial excitement had worn off, their gut response to being thrown into each others' minds was to retreat into their own. Barriers had been hastily cobbled together, like Ben nailing scrap wood and spare doors against the farmhouse walls to keep the zombies out. They had retreated within themselves, as far as they could go to avoid the chaos and confusion when they accidentally scraped against another mind, becoming catatonic souls within functioning bodies.

They had spent five years hiding from themselves. Coming out of shock was always more difficult than going in, and it had taken time to relearn how to be functioning human beings again. Over time, the Agents had trained themselves to reduce connectivity, to block themselves off and selectively interact with each other. Their barriers became polished, refined; they each had a single body again, and reaching out let them speak with a person, rather than the lump sum of the link.

And, once order had been established, they realized they missed the chaos. They were part of a whole now, a collective made from many; to pretend otherwise was to deny the loss they felt when the implant was turned off. Here, in their home, the walls could come down a little. Nobody wanted to throw themselves back into that soul-shattering rush of singularity, but they could relax, just a bit, and immerse themselves in the comfort of being one, within many, within one.

Today, after the slow waiting terror of the basement, Rachel took down her walls and let herself join with the link.

When they were home, many of the Agents chose to keep themselves open. Rachel felt a hundred minds take her into them, and she allowed them to enter her in turn. There was a mingled sense of will, of emotion. They were happy to see her safe and sound, and home. She lost track of time as she and the others shared themselves within the collective.

It didn't last long. She didn't have the endurance to lose herself for hours on end, the way some of the others could. When physical sensations began to intrude (*butt aching from cold marble floor, filth from ash caking skin, decorative rails on mahogany door jabbing into spine...*), Rachel began to rebuild her walls. She began to feel the physicality of the others; she

felt herself typing, talking on the phone, making a sandwich—
Oooh!

Rachel shook herself and pulled her mind back from the two Agents in the supply closet. She wished that some of the others would remember to close themselves down in the heat of the moment. The sensation of unexpected coupling—often outright *in flagrante delicto*—was something she had grown used to, but she didn't enjoy it.

She stood and headed towards the back stairs. Someone had been cleaning. The last time she had come home, the stairs had been a deathtrap of cardboard boxes and furniture. Now, nearly half of the boxes were gone; Rachel reached out and asked why she was able to walk downstairs without the danger of breaking an ankle, and was told the Federal Bureau of Prisons had finally gotten around to cleaning out their stuff.

Anyone without an implant would have sworn the mansion was haunted by the ghosts of seedy flea markets. OACET was part of the federal government, true, but if there really was a family tree, the cyborgs would be dangling all the way at the end of the branch with the redheaded stepchildren and the uncle who was never allowed near the good silver. As such, OACET had been assigned temporary headquarters in a mansion seized by the DEA at the height of the cocaine boom. The mansion had turned out to be unsellable, as the interior decorating choices of a drug kingpin were somewhat... unpalatable. As the drug raid had occurred in the 1980s and flipping properties upwards of twenty thousand square feet was not yet in fashion, the government had the options of spending millions of taxpayer dollars on renovations, or using the mansion as an overflow property warehouse for federal law enforcement. They chose the route that would look better during reelection, and crammed the mansion to its rafters with the assorted crap of broken lives and illicit trade.

The nice thing about working in a rundown mansion was that it was still a mansion. The size of the place was astonishing; they needed five industrial air conditioners just to make it livable during the summer. There was a solarium, a sauna, a full chef's kitchen, all looking like cover shots from outdated *Sunset* books but still more than adequate for the Agents' needs. They had repurposed what they could into offices, and stuffed the rest with junk: until she had been granted a desk at First District Station, she had done her typing in the trophy room, surrounded by animal heads with suspicious glassy eyes.

The not-so-nice thing about working in this particular mansion was the décor. Some rooms, like the kitchen, had simply been worn down by time and hard use. Others…well.

The massive wine cellar had become their medical lab. Like most wine cellars, the room was tucked away in the basement. This wine cellar was different, however, in that someone had decided to model the room and the adjacent hallway after the Catacombs of Paris. Plastic bones lined the walls from floor to ceiling, skulls dotting the bones throughout, all of which were meticulously hand-painted to show the bones in various stages of ripeness or decay.

Calling the whole mess "creepy as fuck" did not do it justice.

The mansion had tennis courts and a pool, and there was a decent-sized bathroom across from the plastic ossuary that the athletes had set aside as a locker room. Like many of the other Agents, Rachel kept an extra change of clothes in a nearby closet, just in case. She found her emergency suit and peeled off the sticky note she had painstakingly written out and stuck to the hanger (*If you need to use this, please dry-clean before returning or I will shoot you. Love, R.P.*), and walked her nice clean suit to the bathroom at arm's length.

She knew she was prudish by cyborg standards. Most of the others would have no problems asking for help getting out of their clothes, but she forced her skinned and burning hands to struggle with the fasteners on her ballistic vest. Same with the shampoo and soap in the shower; the hot water across the raw cuts was agony. But when it was over, she felt more relaxed than if she had shared the shower with someone else: privacy was sometimes as important for the body as it was for the soul.

When the last of the ashes and coffee grounds were sluicing down the mansion's drains and she was done struggling into her emergency suit, Rachel returned to the ossuary. She walked through the stacks of boxes that the Agents had piled against the walls to keep the bones at bay, then rapped on the glass door of the medical lab. *"Jenny?"*

The other Agent was in her office; Rachel had felt her in the link. But their mental walls were easier to maintain when everyone upheld the same myths.

"Hey, Rachel! C'mon in."

She gave the door a little shove and it glided open.

The medical lab was stunningly well-equipped. When the Agents designated the oversized wine cellar as their on-site hospital, they moved every piece of medical equipment they could find down to the catacombs. The era of institutionalized Medicare fraud had netted them some high-end items, and these were illuminated by the light from the glass-fronted refrigerators which stored the U.S. government's eclectic collection of top-shelf alcohol. The Agents kept the fridges padlocked shut, save for the one closest to the front entrance where Jenny Davies and the other physicians stored refrigerated medications on one bottom shelf, the crate of community vodka on the other.

A gaunt man with unkempt hair was sitting on the floor, assembling a jigsaw puzzle at a lightning-fast pace. He had been tucked into a corner and didn't look up when Rachel arrived; Shawn rarely noticed anyone unless they forced him to communicate with them. The glow from the nearest fridge put his face in shadow; he was smiling widely, with plenty of teeth, and looked as though he belonged among the skulls.

Rachel walked over and squatted down beside Shawn. His hands darted from the upturned pile of pieces to the slowly-growing rectangle in front of him, fitting piece after piece in their proper places.

"Hey, Shawn," she said. "How are you?"

There was no response. Shawn was immersed in his puzzle; Rachel flipped her implant to reading mode and saw he was assembling it upside down, with the unprinted cardboard backing facing up.

"*Shawn?*" she said through the link.

He stopped and looked up.

"*Rachel!*" Shawn smiled at her. "*Hello!*"

None of the OACET Agents had had an easy time of their transition. Rachel's had been so bad she had literally blinded herself, but Shawn's experience made hers seem as though she had spent those five years raising a slightly naughty puppy. Shawn had gone insane, and not in a happy-go-lucky-slightly-unhinged way. No, Shawn had gone insane in the way of clinical multi-tiered DSM-IV-TR diagnoses, where the all-purpose "insane" was replaced with specifics like "psychosis" and "severe disassociation disorder". After his implant was fully activated, Shawn had tried to kill himself, and when he had failed and been put on constant suicide watch, he had spent the next six months naked and screaming.

These days, Shawn was a different person, one who wore clothes and attempted conversation. He liked to hang out in the medical lab; he said all of the machines loved him and wanted him to get better, and the other Agents had decided not to argue since he was guaranteed continuous medical supervision. Under Jenny's care, he had begun to fill out; she had convinced him to ease off of the implant and not go out-of-body to the point of exhaustion, and his skeletal frame was finally keeping some calories to itself.

Rachel had never gotten a clear peek at Shawn's core. The Agent's conversational colors were deranged, a churning rainbow which ripped itself apart and rebuilt itself too quickly for her to detect patterns. Sparks of bright light swam around and through these colors, as well as passing through Shawn's body. Today, he was happy blues and purples, with a thick streak of out-of-place red lust.

Shawn was a headache. Rachel usually shut down the emotional spectrum when she was with Shawn to preserve her own sanity, and she did this now when she caught sight of his arousal. Not her business, not her concern.

"What's the picture on the puzzle, Shawn?" They spoke aloud to Shawn whenever they could, trying to make him talk outside of the link. He seemed more likely to retreat within himself when he forgot there were other ways to communicate.

He gave her a guileless stare. *"I don't know. It's not done yet. Want to help?"* His hands began to move back and forth between the puzzle and the stack of loose pieces again. Each new piece was fitted into position, or tossed into a separate pile; as Rachel watched, he went to the smaller pile, pulled out a certain piece, and plunked it down beside another he had just put in its proper place.

"Maybe later? Jenny said she wanted to show me something."

"Yes!" he said aloud, leaping to his feet. He took her hand before she could pull away, and she was bludgeoned with his joy, his longing—

He dropped her hand. *"You're scared of me?"*

"A little bit, Shawn," she replied. She never lied to other Agents. *Almost never.* "But not as much as I used to be. You're making a lot of progress."

Until recently, skin-to-skin contact with Shawn had been slightly less pleasant than drinking rubbing alcohol, but Rachel knew he wasn't the only one with baggage. She cleared her mind and held out her hand to him. He shied away, then reached out with his own, and grinned as she held an image of him wrapped in his purple joy.

"I'm...happy?"

She nodded. *"You're very happy."*

"Nice!" he shouted. He sounded like a teenager at the mall, and Rachel laughed.

They walked, hand in hand, to the open office door. Jenny Davies had been watching them.

"Rachel is here!"

"Thank you, Shawn," Jenny said. "Could you get ready? I want you to show her your special trick."

"Yes!" Shawn said again. He dropped Rachel's hand and

scurried away.

Jenny leaned back against the skulls. "What scans are you running now?" she asked Rachel.

Rachel had no clue where this conversation was going. "Full range, mostly," she said. "I don't have emotions up, if that's what you're asking."

"It is. Can you run them? I want you to monitor Shawn," Jenny said, then nodded to the gaunt man. "Go ahead, show her."

Shawn gave a tiny snort and hoisted himself up on the nearest examination table. He lay down, closed his eyes, and folded his arms across his chest as if responsible for preparing his own funeral. His colors flashed in purples and blues, sparks like liquid silver on the edge of a pinwheel within them.

Rachel waited, a finger tapping against her own forearm. "Guys…" she finally said.

"It's already happening. Give him a chance," Jenny whispered.

Rachel squashed a sigh and watched the little lights dart through Shawn's conversational colors, silver minnows within a rainbow lake. It was oddly soothing; when Shawn was calm, the little lights slowed and flowed close to his center.

She lost track of time. Shawn's little lights had started swimming in patterns, miniature glowing arcs which swept across the center of his body and then across his limbs. Then, gradually, the cacophony of his conversational colors began to thin and part, revealing Shawn's weak tea core.

Rachel realized he was asleep. Or, maybe not quite asleep… "Shawn?" Rachel asked aloud.

"Don't ping him," Jenny said. "It'll break him out of it. But go ahead and check his vitals."

Rachel took a couple of hesitant steps towards Shawn, then paused, her own hand hovering over Shawn's. She steeled herself, then slid two fingers beneath his collar and pressed them against his neck.

Nothing. No emotions, no pulse.

"Shawn!" Rachel shouted. She pulled back to slap him and Jenny grabbed her wrist; the physician was laughing silently, her good humor crossing over to Rachel.

"What's happening to him?"

"It's a deep meditative state," Jenny replied. "He's still breathing, he's still got a pulse. They're just suppressed. Here."

Jenny guided Rachel's hand back to Shawn's neck, where the two of them felt his shallow breathing and, every few slow seconds, a single heavy heartbeat.

"What the hell, Jenny?"

"You're still running emotions, right? What does he look like to you?"

Rachel removed her hand and stepped away from the exam table. "Like..." she started to say, then dropped down on her knees as though she needed a vantage point to peer inside his body. Shawn's conversational colors were almost non-existent; he was almost nothing but his weak tea core wrapped in slow translucent blues. He reminded her of those too-quiet rooms at the hospital, the silent minds within...

"...like he's in a coma," she finished.

Jenny shook her head. "It's not a coma. It's slow-wave non-REM sleep, or something very like it. He's let me measure his brain activity when he's like this. The EEG shows high delta wave activity, with little awareness of environmental stimuli. Those are hallmarks of this state of sleep.

"But," she added, "there's a huge difference between what Shawn's doing and normal deep sleep cycles."

Rachel felt Jenny reach out through the link to lightly ping him.

His eyes fluttered, then opened. Shawn sat up, a huge grin stretching across his face.

"Did it work?" he asked Jenny.

"Yes," the physician nodded. "Thank you, Shawn."

He dropped his legs over the side and began to swing them back and forth like a happy child. The table rocked furiously; Shawn used to be a large man.

"Shawn, honey, you're going to flip the table," Rachel said.

He stopped kicking and looked up at her with liquid brown

eyes. "Would you like to have sex?"

She blinked at Jenny, whose surface colors were fluttering in amusement.

"No thank you, Shawn."

"Are you sure? Jenny says I'm very good," he said, smiling sweetly as he swung off of the table and dropped lightly to the ground. Rachel caught a brief glimpse of the man he had once been, and mourned anew.

Jenny flushed. "Shawn?" she said. "I don't mind if you say that to the others, but I'd be very embarrassed if you bragged about you and me to anyone outside of OACET."

"Oh. Yes. Right." The little colored lights started churning around him again, and he backed away from the women and retreated to a corner of the lab. He sat on the floor and wrapped his arms around the base of the largest surgical microscope, then started humming in a tuneless monotone.

"Come on," Jenny said to Rachel. "He'll stay like that for hours. Let me look at your hands."

They left Shawn to croon to the machine, and walked into an offshoot of the catacombs adjacent to the lab. They had set this area up as a secret ICU, just in case. They had enough equipment for five patients, which was a concern: if they needed to hospitalize more than five, they'd have to go through normal medical channels, and nobody wanted that.

"You and Shawn?" Rachel whispered. "Jenny, *please.*"

Jenny raised an eyebrow. "He's mentally ill, not dead, and I'm neither his primary physician nor his therapist. Besides, he really is a good lover." She dragged a folding chair over to a stainless steel table, and gestured for Rachel to sit. "And he's getting better. He was scared at first, but he's started to get his confidence back. Over the last few days, he's been propositioning every woman who comes in here."

"I hope he didn't take my rejection too hard," Rachel said. "I don't want to be another setback."

"Nope." Jenny grinned over her shoulder as she rummaged through a cabinet full of small white plastic cases. "He's used to it; he gets shot down a lot. This is the first time he's used me as a reference, though, so he must like you."

"I told him he was happy."

"That would do it," Jenny said, nodding. "He's relearning emotions. It's a huge effort for him, to know the names of things but not how they relate to how he feels."

"Want me to work with him?"

"No. Well, maybe if you'd check in on him every so often and give him feedback, like you just did. Everybody wants to help him," Jenny sighed. She pulled one of the cases down from the cabinet and came over to the table. "But I can't tell if four hundred people in his head is beneficial or not."

"Is that why you asked me to come home?" Rachel said, glancing through the wall at Shawn. He hadn't moved, still clinging to the microscope.

"No, I wanted your opinion of his mental status when he was under. Was he conscious?"

"Definitely not." Rachel shook her head. "I was at the hospital a few days ago, and I passed a few coma patients while I was there. What Shawn was doing? His mind was almost identical to theirs."

"Identical, or *almost* identical?" Jenny asked, as she washed her hands and shook them dry.

"If I had known you needed this, I would have paid attention…" Rachel growled, thinking back to that hurried walk down the hallway. "Almost identical. Shawn had some blue to him."

"Blue meaning…"

"Calm. Rest. Um…" Rachel mulled it over: she rarely saw the emotion she was thinking of in anyone from OACET. Still… "Peace. He was at peace."

"Good," Jenny said. "That's what I hoped you'd say."

She took Rachel's left hand and removed the light bandages the EMTs had used to cover the injuries, and then inspected the deep cuts across the palm. There was no exchange of emotions or sensations at the contact; Jenny was a professional. Rachel had once asked her how she blocked out emotional transfer to her patients when she was working, and Jenny honestly couldn't answer: emotions didn't—couldn't—become part of the medical process.

"I see you did some bathroom surgery," Jenny said. She never spoke aloud around open wounds if she could help it.

"Bathroom surgery?" Rachel fought down her nausea as Jenny rolled her hand around in her own and applied a local anesthetic.

"Digging around on your own and making things worse," Jenny said. *"Did you use a nail file?"*

"Uh, no. My teeth."

"Oh, for—" Rachel felt the slightest shiver of annoyance from Jenny. *"Rachel, these cuts will most likely become infected. I hope you know this."*

Rachel laughed. "If you'd seen the state of that basement, you'd have used your teeth, too."

"Mhmm," Jenny said, nonplussed. She opened a suture packet and prepared a needle. *"This'll be hard to watch. You might want to turn away."*

Rachel grinned up at her, and Jenny squeezed her eyes shut. Embarrassment flooded Jenny's conversational colors and broke through her composure to run across Rachel's skin. *"Oh! Rachel, I'm so sorry!"*

"It's okay," Rachel assured her. "I'm happy you *can* forget. I'd hate it if it's the first thing that comes to mind when you think of me."

"Nobody thinks of you as blind."

"So this trick that Shawn does," Rachel said, changing the topic. "Why did you want to show it to me?"

Jenny looked up at Rachel, the slightest hue of orange-red frustration seeping into her colors before she clamped down on her emotions and started to stitch up Rachel's hand.

"Fine," Jenny said aloud. Rachel flipped off visuals and concentrated on Jenny's mental voice as the physician worked.

"Well, the first time I saw it, he did it in bed. To surprise me,

I guess. It scared the complete shit out of me. I came out of the shower and found him all but dead. I never thought to ping him—I just went straight into doctor mode. I did all of the same vital checks you just did, plus a few more. By the time he woke himself up, I was standing over him with a primed crash cart, ready to hit him with the pads."

"Did you scream?" Rachel asked.

"Like I was in a horror movie. I scared him worse than he scared me. It took him a few weeks before he felt secure enough to show it to me again."

"So what is it? What's he doing when he plays dead?"

"It's what I said. It's a deep meditative state, similar to slow-wave non-REM sleep. So far, it's also the best example of how the implant may be able to change us physically as well as mentally."

Rachel had to keep herself from yanking her hand away.

Jenny must have felt her sudden surge of anxiety, but her mental tone stayed calm and level. *"Keep in mind this is all pure theory at this point,"* she said. *"You've heard of biofeedback?"*

"Yeah," Rachel replied. "Enhancing mind-body relationships through machines. Plug a person into something that dings when his blood pressure goes up, and he can train himself to stay out of the danger zone."

"Right. Except for us, the machines are in our heads. Quantum organic computers, each one becoming more individualized through use. I'm working on the theory that our implants learn how we use our bodies, and then help us to use them more efficiently. Like how you trained yourself to make those insane trick shots of yours."

Rachel nodded. One of the first things she had done with her new senses was relearn how to use her gun. Compared to her, the best sharpshooter in the world looked like a kid with a leaky water pistol. "You're saying Shawn wrote an autoscript."

"Yes. He taught himself how to do this by accident. He was watching videos on meditation, how to keep calm under stress. He learned how to put himself into a… I guess you'd call it a trance? He kept finding a state of relaxation, then pushed himself deeper.

His implant learned to mimic the process. He can drop himself into it, any time he wants."

"Isn't that dangerous?"

"No. If someone doesn't ping him, he wakes up on his own. It's very close to a natural sleep state. He just uses a shortcut to reach it."

"Do you want him to stop?"

"No!" Jenny must have shaken her head, hard: Rachel winced slightly as the almost-unfelt thread tugged at her palm. *"Current thinking is the body does most of its repair work during slow-wave non-REM sleep, but we only experience it for thirty minutes at a time. Maybe forty, if we're lucky. Do you realize what it might mean from a medical perspective, if we could figure out how to trigger this at will?"*

"We could heal ourselves…" Rachel breathed. She flipped on visuals, then emotions, and looked through the wall towards Shawn. He hadn't moved from his spot on the floor, but his colors were blue and there wasn't a hint of gray in them. He still wasn't whole, but he was so much better… He was pushing himself to *get* better. "Jenny…"

"It's not just Shawn," Jenny said. Rachel turned her scans back to her; the other woman was burning yellow-white with excitement. *"You know how I've asked you and a couple of other Agents to keep track of your workouts? I need to run a few more tests—a shitload more tests, actually—but I think you're all writing autoscripts which improve your physical performance."*

"What?" Rachel arched an eyebrow to make sure the sarcasm landed.

Now that the wounds were closed, Jenny began to speak out loud. "Athletes injure themselves," she replied. "It's a fact of life. Athletes pull things, sprain things… But we have atypically low rates of injury. Like, practically non-existent. We've got martial artists, weight lifters, triathletes… I should be treating soft-tissue injuries or putting on a cast at least once a week. And I used to! I used to treat you guys all of the time! When we moved out here, I saw the usual number of exercise-induced injuries. Less than a year later, if I'm asked to treat anything, it's a pre-existing condition.

"Physical training is a form of biofeedback, where you continue to improve your performance through repetition, by teaching your body how to work more efficiently. My working hypothesis is the implant facilitates all biofeedback, including athleticism."

"Or we spent five years out of practice, and we're just getting back into the groove."

"Except not everybody was out of practice. Take Mulcahy, for example. He started lifting weights during the worst of it, and he still suffered sprains, muscle tears… After his implant was fully activated, these gradually stopped. And you've always jogged, right? When was the last time you twisted an ankle?"

The rhythm of feet on bright metal. Rachel shook her head. "Not that long," she said. "Couple of months?"

"You're going to lie to your doctor? I treated that ankle back in March. The only injuries you've had since then have been sustained in the line of duty."

"Jenny, I just fell through a *floor*. I'm not exactly a bionic commando."

Jenny glared at her, then tied off the suture with a deft twist of her fingers. "Biofeedback results in small changes," she said. "If the implant does facilitate biofeedback, you're never going to see yourself sprint at cheetah speed or jump entire buildings in a single bound. Your response time might be slightly faster and you may have increased stamina, but the implant is not going to magically morph your body into something other than basic human physiology."

"Aw," Rachel feigned a groan as Jenny clipped the thread. "And here I was all excited that I was about to turn into Wolverine."

"Sorry," Jenny said. "On that note, I'm using liquid bandages on you—which I *hate*—but I know you won't keep a proper wrapping on your hand. You'll show up every twenty-four hours so I can change it out and check for infection."

"Yes, mother."

"Don't you 'yes, mother' me," Jenny said, as she snipped the line and set Rachel free. "If I were your mother, I'd handcuff you to the wall until the risk of infection passed. We're entering the post-antibiotic era. Like it or not, we've each had brain surgery and a foreign object grafted inside of us, so we're at increased risk. I don't know about you, but I don't want to rely on biofeedback to keep myself healthy."

"I hear you," Rachel sighed. "I'll try to stay out of dank basements and septic tanks."

"That's all I ask," Jenny said.

"By the way," Rachel said, remembering. "I used your autoscript the other day. I found a victim at the bombing, and it gave me a diagnosis right at the scene."

"Really?" Jenny's colors brightened. "How did it work?"

"It was pretty accurate. I visited the same guy in the hospital, and the only thing the autoscript missed was part of his burn damage."

"Okay," Jenny said, nodding. "Improve the accuracy of the topical injury section. Thanks."

"Could you also add an English translation for those of us who aren't fluent in Medicalese?"

"Uh-oh," Jenny laughed. "Santino giving you shit again?"

Rachel sighed. "Nerds. Hand to God, there is nothing that man doesn't know."

"I'll work on it. It might take some time to get layman's terms in there. I don't think that way, so I'll have to figure out how to add a different language. Do you want to try a second one?"

For a moment, Rachel wasn't sure what Jenny was asking. Then she felt the back of her chair slam against the wall and realized her lizard brain had tried to escape, and had taken her body along with it. She took a slow breath before asking, "Shawn's autoscript?"

The other woman nodded. "It's safe," she said. "I'd like you to test it."

"More data?"

"Always," Jenny sighed. "It *is* safe, I promise."

Rachel slipped out of her suit coat and rolled up one of her shirt sleeves. "If I go stark raving mad, I'm taking you with me."

Jenny laughed and gently wrapped her hand around Rachel's wrist.

Autoscripts were passed from Agent to Agent via skin contact, and receiving a new script was far, far down at the bottom of Rachel's list of enjoyable afternoon activities. Her hard resolution to get through the next five seconds netted Rachel a smile and Jenny's best bedside manner. *"Shawn found the way,"* Jenny said gently. *"I've tamed it down. This script will feel like me, not him."*

The autoscript moved from Jenny to Rachel in a hot, slippery push of energy. Rachel's skin broke out in goosebumps, and she shut her eyes against the sudden pressure in her mind. The new autoscript held its form for a moment, then dissolved and blended into her in a rush of Jenny.

"How do I activate this?" Rachel asked, a little too loudly, as Jenny released her wrist. She scratched at her own arm until red welts appeared under her nails.

"It's just meditation," Jenny said, taking Rachel's hands in her own to keep Rachel from ripping herself apart. There was no autoscript this time: Jenny's warmth and confidence passed into her, and Rachel forced herself to relax. "Lie down somewhere quiet, then activate it. It'll be like you're falling asleep. You can set a timer or let yourself wake up naturally."

"You sure this isn't sleeping?" Rachel asked. The collective had strict rules against falling asleep with an active implant.

"Very sure," Jenny nodded. "In normal slow-wave non-REM sleep, the conscious mind isn't involved. You saw Shawn wake up when I pinged him. We're still alert when we do this. It's very, *very* deep meditation, but that's all."

"Okay," Rachel said. "I'll let you know how it works."

"Oh," the other woman added. "Don't forget to have someone there with you to monitor your vitals the first time you use it. Not Santino—it's got to be one of us, in case you need someone to ping you."

"Damn it, Jenny," Rachel sighed. "You said this was safe!"

"As your physician," Jenny said, "did you really expect me to let you leave without telling you the fine print?"

"Woman, I have a *gun!*"

TEN

Half a bottle of white wine in an old plastic cup had not had its intended effect. Rather, it had been too effective; she had poured half of the bottle in the largest glass she could find, and the wine had relaxed her to the point where she was almost asleep in her chair. Rachel was doing her best to stay alert as Santino and Josh shouted at the television, pretending she actually cared the Chicago Bears were about to lose their third game in a row. She usually enjoyed game night, but after that hour in the basement, all she wanted was to take a hot bath and then go straight to bed.

As neither Santino nor Rachel cooked, their formerly-formal dining room had been turned into an all-purpose media room. After Santino had moved in to her house, they had removed an old built-in china cabinet to make space for his new 70" high-definition television. Then they'd had a hell of a fight over what to call the room. Santino had said it should be the Man Cave; Rachel had replied she was not a man and the room was too open to be considered a cave. Santino had amended this to the Cyborg Café; Rachel had said that name was also wrong, as he was not a cyborg and besides, visitors might get the room confused with a certain bar uptown. This discussion had escalated until Santino had removed the set from the wall and hauled it upstairs to his room, threatening to keep it to himself until she apologized. He brought it back downstairs when he finally realized she had started the fight to get rid of the television until the World Series was over.

(Rachel, who was of the opinion that if baseball were any slower it would be called farming, was still trying to work out a way to escape the impending monotony of sixteen premium channels devoted to spring training.)

The doorbell rang. Santino and Josh stopped mid-expletive; Josh started grinning.

"It's Phil," she explained to Santino as she stood to answer the door. "Sorry, should have mentioned he was on his way. Mako's coming over, too."

"More the merrier," Santino said, not shifting his attention from the game. His conversational colors, a dark navy blue streaked with white-rimmed orange, didn't even bother to pick up Phil's silver-light core.

Rachel was halfway to the door before she realized Phil was deeply gray. She yanked the old farmer's door open, and he peered at her over two cases of beer. She moved to help him and he shook his head, stepping away so as to not touch her.

"What's wrong?"

"Oh, Rachel..." he began, and then shook his head again. *"In a minute. Right now, I don't want to do anything but put away as many of these as I can."*

She reached up and pulled down the top case, then covered Phil's hands with her own. He exhaled through his teeth as her languor passed to him; she had an image of scales balancing as his tension crossed over to her, and she was suddenly awake.

"Thanks," she said, reclaiming her case of beer and heading towards the kitchen. *"I needed that."*

*"**You** needed that? I've been humming at capacity since mid-afternoon."*

The beers were crammed into the empty crisper drawer, and she and Phil retreated to her study. This room was hers alone; Santino was not allowed in except to clean. The study was her favorite room in the house, lined with windows and long cubby shelves overflowing with her book collection. It was also the only room in the house without a single potted plant.

Phil closed the French doors and flopped in one of her over-stuffed leather armchairs. His beer frothed from the sudden drop. *"Damn it,"* he swore through their link, and took huge mouthfuls while she tried not to laugh.

"I can feel that," he said.

She pretended to be sympathetic. *"Are you okay?"* she asked when Phil was finally in control of the bubbling.

"No. Rachel..." Phil's mental voice trailed off. *"Those pieces of the canisters I told you about? The ones with the serial numbers on it? It was **our** military hardware. We traced it back to Homeland."*

"What?!" It was aloud and loud; bad news, that.

Phil nodded. *"There was a shipment stolen a few years back. The canisters were part of an aerosol fire suppression system. This guy I know over in Forensics? They found the supplier who works with Homeland, and got an intact canister from the same production line. They used the canister as a comparison, and the fragments we recovered are a match."*

"Man," Rachel said, tossing her feet up on her old pine coffee table. *"That won't go over well with Homeland."*

"You're not kidding," Phil said, shaking his head. "I'm glad I'm not in charge of this. Sergeant Andrews asked Homeland to explain. From what I hear, they tried to rip him apart. And Andrews gave as good as he got."

"Really?" she asked. She didn't quite believe him. Sergeant Andrews was in charge of First MPD's bomb squad, and Rachel had never seen him angry—in fact, after meeting Andrews, she was convinced that the primary job requirement for the head of a bomb squad was an innate inability to become angry.

"Yes. He—Penguin, he was all set to go to war with Homeland."

"Just because the canisters were registered to Homeland doesn't mean that Homeland is involved," Rachel replied. "The amount of stuff that goes 'missing' from the federal government? Government procurement services use the least efficient supply chains on the planet. They're a Gordian knot of subcontractors and institutionalized fraud."

"I know that, you know that, everybody knows that," Phil said, and took another drink. *"And it still looks really, really bad when it's the main story on the nightly news."*

"Yeah," Rachel agreed. "What did Homeland tell Andrews?"

"Short version? To get fucked," Phil sighed. "Long version is they'll look into it, that the information should be kept private until such a time as its release would not cause undue public alarm, blah blah blah, unspoken threat, and blah."

"And how do you know all of this?" Rachel asked. "I'm guessing Andrews didn't tell everybody in the bomb squad about the source of that serial number."

Phil shrugged. "OACET, of course. He implied it would be very convenient if I hopped into a few databases and tracked down exactly when and where that shipment went missing."

"Wow," she said. "That's bad. No, forget bad—that's *illegal*. Did he mean it, or was it just the rage talking?"

"He meant it," Phil said. "Illegal or not, he wants me to start poking around."

"But why? It's out of Andrews' hands," Rachel said. She didn't have to worry about misuse of power from Phil, but she hadn't expected that type of request from someone like Andrews. "The bomb squad figures out what went boom and how, and then the MPD investigates."

"Yeah, except Andrews is furious," Phil said. "When Homeland froze him out, he took it personally. This is his city, and Homeland's response is to deny and delay? Andrews isn't going to go rogue, but his report might be a little more extensive than Homeland wants."

"Huh. Sturtevant was worried that something would go wrong with the investigation. You think he expected this?"

"Who knows?" Phil said. "Do you think you can get me a warrant?"

She was stunned. "You're not actually thinking of doing what Andrews wants?"

"Rachel, I know the drill. If I do it at all, I'm doing it legally," Phil said. "But face facts. We need that information, and we shouldn't be blocked from it by a power play. This is what warrants are for."

She searched Phil's conversational colors; he was shifting towards the deep professional blue he wore at work. "Yeah," she relented. "I can't promise anything, but I'll call Judge Edwards and see what he can do."

"Thanks," Phil said. "We need help. We still don't know anything substantial about the bombs, other than they were tied into the gas lines."

Her cop brain kicked at her conscious mind again. *Gas lines...*she thought.

Phil glanced up as he felt her sudden change of mood. "What?"

The doorbell rang, and Rachel reached through the walls to see Mako on her porch, with Zockinski and Hill coming up the walk behind him. "Oh, *hell*," she snapped.

Phil followed her scans. "Shit," he agreed. "Did you tell Mako his cousin has never been to your house?"

"Nope," she replied. "But Josh is here." She pinged Josh and told him to keep the detectives out of her kitchen; she was not in the mood to spend her night doing damage control.

She opened her front door and was swept off her feet.

Mako Hill was enormous. Not just tall, like his cousin, but weightlifter-massive and broad enough to need to turn ever so slightly to fit his shoulders through the doorway. He was perpetually happy, and a hugger besides: he claimed to have been a hugger before the implant, and saw no reason to let the new issues posed by accidental skin contact change his habits. Nearly every time Rachel bumped into him, the first fifteen seconds of their meeting were like wrestling with a jovial bear.

"Hey, little thing," he said, setting her down. "Are you okay?"

She nodded, grinning. "Busy day," she told him.

*"But are you **okay?**"* he asked, and she felt his feather-light mental touch brush against the palms of her hands. She nodded and showed off Jenny's handiwork, and then escorted Mako and the detectives straight into the TV room and told them to stay put and enjoy the game.

"Let me play hostess," she told Zockinski and Hill. "I'd show you around, but the place is a disaster. Oh, and use one of the upstairs bathrooms. The one down here doesn't flush."

She shut certain doors, ordered pizza, and poured all of the ice in the house into a five-gallon bucket to make a cooler for the beer—anything to keep the detectives out of the kitchen. Once the men were settled and wearing their team colors (Zockinski was a closet Cheesehead, she noticed, the gold and green of Green Bay butting up against Chicago's blue and orange), she and Phil returned to the study.

"Think that'll do it?"

"Hell if I know," Rachel said, as she returned to her chair. *"They've got no reason to go to the back of the house, and Josh will block them if they try. If they do stumble into the kitchen, I'll…I'll make something up, I guess."*

There was a knock on the glass of the study doors, and Mako let himself in, the old brass doorknob disappearing under his hand.

"Thought you were watching the game," Rachel said to him.

"It's a slow one. I'm running scores and instant replays," he said, tapping his head. "If it gets interesting, I'll rejoin the menfolk."

"Hey!" Phil protested.

"Don't let him push your buttons," she said to Phil. "Once you let him start, he'll never stop."

Mako waggled his eyebrows at Phil, grinning lewdly. Phil resisted as long as he could, his colors a sturdy brick wall withstanding a wave of purple humor and Mako's core of forest green. The wall wavered and finally crumbled, as Phil shook his head and chuckled.

"So," Mako said to Rachel. "How was the cellar?"

"Dirty and smelly," she replied. "And I learned I don't like to sit on a pile of melted plastic for an hour."

"I learned Rachel's seeing someone," Phil told him.

"Lord, save me from gossips," she sighed.

"Oh *really?*" Mako cleared himself a seat by moving a stack of papers from one end of her old pine coffee table to the other. The coffee table creaked ominously under his weight. "Details, woman. When's my kid going to have another aunt?"

"All right, I'm busted," Rachel surrendered. "I'm not really seeing her. We've just gone out to dinner. We're going out again this week, so I'll see how that goes."

"Third date?" Mako used his eyebrow trick on her.

She snorted. "Second, thank you very much. And don't you dare say U-Haul lesbians."

Phil went ever-so-slightly yellow. "U-Haul lesbians?"

"You've never heard that one? What does a lesbian bring on a second date?"

Mako burst out laughing. "That's awful!"

Rachel shrugged. "Just a stereotype. World's full of them. She's made it clear she wants to take it slow."

"How slow is slow?"

"You know how the first date is mostly small talk? Work, pets, family stories, that sort of thing? Becca told me straight out that she doesn't talk about her job until the second date."

"Huh," Phil said. "That's ominous."

"Yeah. I'm fine with it," Rachel admitted. "It buys me more time. Women have walked out when I've told them I'm OACET. But…"

"But what's worse than OACET?"

"Yep." She returned her feet to her coffee table and ran a scan through her palms. The liquid bandage was still hugging the stitches. She started to pick at a loose flap until she realized Jenny might find out and slap her through the link.

"I still can't believe you want to date normals," Mako said. His wife, Carlota, was also an Agent. They had been one of the community's first marriages, and they were the ones who had had OACET's first baby a couple of months earlier. "That's un-*believ*ably boring!"

"Forgive me for wanting my relationships to exist outside of the collective," Rachel said.

"The sex alone!" Mako shrugged. "It's so…limited."

"I prefer to know where my genitals end and hers begin," Rachel said primly.

"No thank you." The large man shook his head. "Why be a

cyborg if it doesn't punch up your sex life?"

"Why have a sex life if it's essentially masturbation?"

Phil, who had been chuckling throughout their exchange, laughed so hard he squeaked. "She's got a point."

"Pft," Mako rolled his eyes. "Philistines. Once you go cyborg, you'll never...ugh."

"Still working on that one?"

"The only thing that rhymes with 'cyborg' is 'morgue'. Try and turn *that* into sexual innuendo!"

And then they heard Hill's voice from the kitchen, saying, "What the fuck did you people do in here?"

"Oh for shit's sake, Josh," Rachel muttered. "You had one job. Stay here," she told Mako and Phil, as she sprinted from her study.

Rachel pushed open the kitchen door to see Hill standing in the middle of the room, saturated in a flummoxed yellow. He turned when she came in and pointed to a particular kitchen cabinet. Its door was splashed with several dozen different colors, each with the name of one of their coworkers from First District Station written somewhere in the white space around it, with a little arrow to indicate which name corresponded to which stripe. Santino's name was linked to a streak of rich cobalt applied straight from the tube, with Rachel's own core color (a middling turquoise, not too light, not too dark) painted beside his. Below these came the hues of the MPD's police hierarchy: Sturtevant's was a strike of dark gold. Then came Zockinski, with his bright autumn orange, but once you hit on Hill's forest green, things got *complicated*, colors and arrows slapped up every which way, connections formed between persons and agencies and the offhand friend or relative who lived within more than one world.

The arrows were crucial. Nobody but Rachel would know what the colors meant without them.

She had finally carried out her threat to make a chart.

Right after Santino had moved in, they had the idea she could explain how she perceived emotions if she had the right visual aids. She had started with markers and copy paper, smearing the inks with her finger to try to get the right hues. Crayons came next, but even with sixty-four colors she soon ran out of combinations. Then came the acrylic paint sets, and the two of them had spent an entire weekend slopping around in pigment, Rachel blending, Santino pinning paper to the corkboard next to the refrigerator while the paint dried. When they ran out of room on the board, he started taping the paper to the cabinets, and when they ran out of paper, she had started on the walls. By late Sunday night, the kitchen looked as though a Pantone guide had exploded, a spectrum of colors coating every available surface and spilling into the hall.

Even the tile backsplash hadn't escaped. There was a strong chance liquor had been involved in that particular decision; Rachel knew she'd never get the paint out of the grout.

The tedious part had been the labels. Not for the core colors: those were easy. A core color was—with certain exceptions— simple and unchanging. It was the layers of color over that core that were the problem. Since no one else in OACET shared her abilities, there was no one to help her describe what she perceived. And, since what she saw was human emotion manifest as color, the naming process had devolved into the chaos of subjective linguistics. She and Santino had pitched battles over mixed emotions: how, for example, one person could be angry (Tuscan red, mixed with scarlet), horny (also red, but more of a crimson-carmine combination), and frustrated (red again, this time a rusty burgundy) simultaneously, and how the intensity and movement of these colors within a constantly changing surface layer revealed which emotions were driving the person at any given time.

Occasionally, their discussions on the nomenclature of emotions became so heated that Santino's temper would rise to match her own, the two of them shouting and hurling objects. He insisted she couldn't create terms for made-up emotions: she said that if she could see "lustafury", it was real enough to deserve a name of her choosing. Such fights usually ended when Rachel added another color combination under the hastily-scrawled heading: "Adult Male Temper Tantrum," and Santino would storm outside to plant something in spite.

"Why is my name here?" Hill asked, his palm pressed against the cabinet with the cores from First District Station. "Zockinski's, Sturtevant's—What's going on?"

Rachel had been trying so hard to keep the lying to a minimum. "Pet project of mine," she said. "I'm planning to do some major renovations to the house. Do you do any interior design?"

"What?"

"Personality color-matching! You design your home around colors you think your friends would like. I know I've got the magazine around here somewhere...you want to read it? The article's only about ten pages, and most of that is pictures."

Hill's colors went orange-yellow and then quickly glazed over; Rachel read some confusion, but mostly annoyance. "Maybe later."

"You sure? You can borrow it if you want."

"I'd rather see it when it's done." His shoulders were pockmarked; not just a white lie, but a full-on *Lord, save me.* Rachel covered her mouth to hide her smile. "You got any paper towels? I spilled some beer."

"Yeah," Rachel said. She retrieved a roll and the two of them returned to the den, where she chewed Josh out through the link. Nine yards on a first down was no excuse for him to slack off.

The pizza arrived at the same time Santino's phone rang. He stepped into the kitchen to duck the bill, and Rachel sighed and picked up the tab. Pretending to be a good hostess was expensive.

The next room over, Santino's conversational colors went white in shock.

"Take these," Rachel said to Mako, shoving the pizza boxes into his arms. She found Santino standing in the kitchen, staring at his phone, feet frozen to the floor.

"Hey," she said, tugging at his arm. "Santino? C'mon. You need to sit down."

He blinked, not seeing her, then shook himself slightly and looked down. "Rachel—"

"Come on," she said again, and led him back into the den. The men paused over the pizza boxes as they came in.

"Guys?" Santino said. "Got some bad news. Two cops over at Sixth? They just fished them and their car out of the Potomac. Looks like they were murdered."

The Agents and those from the MPD went white, then gray.

Mako, a computer science expert who had no involvement with law enforcement, recovered first. "Did you know them?"

"No," Santino said. This was echoed by everyone else in the room. "My friend says they were working security on Gayle Street."

Rachel and Zockinski exchanged a glance. There was some honest fear in his colors.

That third phase of panic, she thought. *So soon...I thought we had more time.*

"Shit," Hill said. He slumped over his knees. "Can this week get any worse?"

"Come on," Zockinski said, standing. He whacked Hill on his shoulder and moved to the front door. "It won't be our case, but we'll do what we can. If this ties in with Gayle Street, we need to know how."

There were some muttered goodbyes, and the two men left. *They're homicide detectives,* Rachel realized. *How did Sturtevant know we'd need homicide detectives on this?* She was reminded of Santino's comment about how Sturtevant played a good long game of chess. The Chief couldn't possibly have known how the Gayle Street case might turn, but...

Eh, maybe. Maybe not. Experience counted for a lot in Rachel's book, but so did preparation. Fill your roster with career cops, academics, ex-military, and cyborgs, and one of them would probably have the skills needed to deal with any given situation.

The television was muted, another round of beers came out. The death of one officer could wreck a good time, but when two or more were killed, it became a straight-out nightmare.

"You think people are gunning for us?" Santino asked.

"Thought had crossed my mind," Rachel replied. "Everybody wants closure. Vigilante justice is a goddamned stupid way to get it, but some people are goddamned stupid."

Over on the couch, Phil sighed. "Can you imagine how bad it'll get if people start to blame Homeland for this? There's going to be riots. Serious blood-in-the-street *riots*."

"Why would they blame Homeland?" Santino asked, his colors shifting to curious yellows.

"Oh. Um…" Phil looked around, realized there wasn't anyone he didn't trust, and described the serial numbers and the possible connection to Homeland.

"Oh fuck," Josh said, his grays growing to submerge his core, his head dropping into his hands. "Fuck fuck *fuck*."

"Josh?"

He rolled the bottom of his beer around his knee for a moment, then said, "I spend more time up on Capitol Hill than you guys do. We're at the point where it almost doesn't matter who bombed Gayle Street. All that matters is who the public *thinks* bombed Gayle Street! The climate is so—

"Okay," Josh said, as he organized his thoughts. "Imagine you're a politician, and the Manning scandal breaks. That's a problem, but it's manageable because some of the reporting methods are shoddy at best. It plays well with the conspiracy theorists and the liberals, but it doesn't hit in a big election year, and most of the voters forget about it before presidential election season begins.

"Then comes OACET. Your constituency suddenly learns their government has created cyborgs that can control any machine, anywhere in the world. This would be bad enough, but the government didn't make this fact public—OACET did. And the first thing the government does is to say we're lying, and when we prove we aren't, the second thing it does is to say it was all a big misunderstanding. Even though we can prove certain members of Congress had over a hundred Agents murdered to cover it up, but whatever. Mistakes happen. Nobody knows what anybody else is doing in a bureaucracy.

"Not too long after that? Drones attacking American citizens. And after *that*? Snowden, who's got an insane amount of evidence to prove that all of the things that Homeland and the NSA promised they won't do? Absolutely, totally doing.

"Politicians are *scared*. The only thing they've got going for them is the attention span of the average American. News fatigue is a politician's best weapon, because Americans have been whipped up into a frenzy over trivial bullshit so many times that it's hard to get them to pay attention when a real problem shows up. But they know that the country is getting close to a breaking point, because the average person is getting tired of being lied to and misled by their leaders.

"Finally? The extremes are looking for an excuse. Liberals hate conservatives, conservatives hate liberals, the rich and the poor loathe each other…it's an unsustainable system on the verge of collapse. We've reached a point where the only thing that's holding the country together is the people in the middle, those decent, average folks who recognize that nothing good will come of fighting each other.

"But if the middle tips to either extreme? The situation becomes unbalanced. The guys in the Capitol are terrified of hitting that tipping point, the one where the middle decides it's finally worth the cost to act."

Josh's anger had been amping up along with his speech. He looked red and ready to attack someone, the neck of his beer bottle seized in a death grip.

"If you're going to throw that, go outside," Rachel told him.

He closed his eyes and his reds slipped in intensity as he re-centered himself. "You guys do realize that if Homeland is in any way responsible for Gayle Street, we've probably hit that tipping point, right?"

"What?!?" Mako, the eternal optimist, couldn't consider the

possibility. "Why in the hell would we do this to ourselves?"

"Public pressure is powerful," Rachel told him. "If Homeland thought Gayle Street could be used to achieve a specific goal…"

"No," Santino said. "It doesn't matter what the goal might be. Nothing justifies Gayle Street."

Santino was unconvinced. So were Mako and Phil. *Must be nice to be innocent,* she thought. Rachel didn't know how any Agent could still have faith in their own government after what they had been through, but more power to those who did.

"I've got to go to work," Josh said, standing. "This might— God, I almost said *explode.* This might get bad."

"You're taking some food," Rachel said. It wasn't a request; Josh was as bad as Phil when it came to remembering to eat. She grabbed the nearest pizza box and brought it to the kitchen with her, then started scanning through the mess under the shelves for tinfoil wrap. The tinfoil was on the very bottom of the cabinet, covered with a hodgepodge of plastic to-go plates from restaurant carry-out meals.

We really need to start cooking, she thought. *Waste of money, eating out every*—Damn!" She yelped the last word as the rigid cutting edge on the side of the tinfoil box sliced the side of her finger open. She wrapped a clean paper towel around her hand before shoving the whole mess into the pocket of her sweat pants. "Damn," she said again, quietly this time. Nothing looked less professional than a cop with a big old Band-Aid, except maybe a cop with a Band-Aid and whose hands were already covered in scratches and transparent semi-permanent goop. She'd probably have to wear gloves for a month.

She yelled at Josh and told him to finish wrapping up his own stupid pizza, and retreated to the den. The mood was black; she curled up against Mako and the four of them pretended to watch the second quarter. Phil and Santino started passing a tablet back and forth, showing off their collection of recent Internet finds. Rachel and Mako quickly grew bored with clever macros, and Mako headed home to be with his wife and baby girl.

"Going to bed," Rachel announced to the room at large.

"Night," Santino replied. She got a quick wave and a distracted hug through the link from Phil.

She shut her bedroom door behind her and threw a casual scan around the room, noting how she had really let her house-keeping skills slide. Her sex life had been nonexistent over the last few months, so she had abandoned the pretext that the state of her bedroom might matter to anyone other than herself. It was part therapy, she reminded herself; she'd break that old Army habit of making the bed the moment her feet hit the floor if it killed her.

The tub, at least, was clean, but the urge to take a bath was gone. And she didn't want to sleep, and she couldn't get lost in a book, and watching television in her own lonely head was a step down from wearing nothing but purple and filling her house with pets—

"Fifty-seven thousand channels in your brain," she muttered to herself, "and nothin' on."

Deep in her pocket, her finger throbbed.

She reached out to Phil before she could think it through. *"Do me a favor?"*

"Sure, what?" he answered.

"Ping me in half an hour. If I don't answer, come and shake the shit out of me, and then call Jenny Davies."

"Wha—" Phil was hot with concern in her head. *"Are you okay?"*

"Yeah," she said, pressing her finger down into the wad of paper towels in her pocket. *"I'm about to try a new autoscript, and I'm not sure how well it'll work."*

"Ah, right," he replied, his concern fading. Autoscripts were a funny sort of thing. *"Do you want me to babysit while you play with it?"*

"Nah," she said, suppressing her anxiety from their link as best she could. *"Thanks, but I shouldn't have any problems."*

She procrastinated by spending a precious few of her allotted minutes tidying, then yanked the sheets flat to cover the bed, kicked off her shoes, and laid down with a sigh. She folded her arms as Shawn had done, then uncrossed them just as quickly; this was stressful enough without mimicking a corpse. Instead, she tucked her hands behind her head, crossed her ankles, and did her best to ignore how her heart was racing at NASCAR speeds.

She wondered if she was about to do something incredibly stupid. Patrick Mulcahy had told everyone that sleeping with the implant on could be dangerous. Rachel believed him; everyone believed him. The mischief a subconscious mind and an active implant could get up to? Nobody wanted to be the one who accidentally nuked Miami. The moment an Agent decided to go to bed, the implant was turned off.

Nobody but Shawn would have discovered this, Rachel realized. Shawn knew the rules and obeyed as best he could, but he did tend to forget. The others would consider meditating with the implant on to be dangerously close to sleeping, and would remember to turn it off, but Shawn might not be as careful.

She took a deep breath, checked her clock, and summoned the new autoscript.

It was a soft ball of wool in her mind, and she spent an awkward moment fighting it before taking several deep breaths and relenting. The autoscript wrapped itself around her. Jenny had been right: it didn't feel a thing like Shawn. It felt like Jenny, all confident and reassuring and safe.

Then, peace.

Her timer went off precisely fifteen minutes later. She woke, fully alert and able to see her bedroom upon waking since the first time since she had lost her eyes. She ran Jenny's diagnostic scan through her own body, bemused to find her blood alcohol content had dropped almost a full 0.06 percent. Agents metabolized alcohol at a fantastic rate, but even for her, that was fast. When she got to her hands, she pushed the scan as hard as she could, concentrating on the little details…

Well.

Rachel wasn't sure what she had expected to find. Her hands

were still a mess, the cuts and scratches still red and sore to the touch. But the older ones were no longer weeping pus, and when she unwound the paper towel from her finger, she saw the cut from the tinfoil box had stopped bleeding.

Could mean anything, she decided. *Could be you just stopped using your hands for fifteen minutes.*

She flipped off visuals and sat in the dark, running her thumb over the stitches on her left palm.

But...

Every cop the world over was aware their subconscious was just as smart as their conscious mind. It was what ticked away on the problems of the case even when the workday was over. It was what drove her to return to the scene again and again, to keep working the witnesses until they were past the point of breaking, until she found that one overlooked detail which locked the separate pieces of the crime together.

She used to be okay with this—she used to think it was normal. Hell, she had been told it was normal! During her early CID training, Rachel had suffered through long lectures from an officer who believed that Gardner's theory of multiple intelligences explained this division between the conscious and unconscious minds. The officer had turned every class into a discussion of how different people can excel at sports but can't carry a tune in a bucket, or could speak a dozen languages while mathematics left them cold.

Rachel took this a step further: there may have been different forms of intelligence, true, but she carried around the strengths and weaknesses of those intelligences with her in different parts of her own head.

And after she got the implant, she became absolutely convinced the damned thing was smarter than she was.

She processed information a little better these days. New information was a little easier to handle, routine tasks completed a little more quickly. She told herself she didn't have to like this new aspect of herself, she just had to like what it did *for* her, and it was definitely an improvement over Old Rachel, back when she was the only one inside her own head.

But...

But, oh, how she wished she could remember why she had stared at the sun.

She decided to chalk her hands up to the placebo effect and a good nap, and went back downstairs to catch the rest of the game.

ELEVEN

Of the many changes that had happened at First District Station over the last few months, the one she liked the most was her new desk. Prior to August, she'd had a lap desk, its bottom stuffed like a beanbag, tucked underneath a small chair in the corner. Now, she had a desk equal to Santino's own, one which held her computer monitor and keyboard, their shared printer, a large carved wooden owl, and nothing else; she had threatened to pistol-whip her partner if even so much as a dried leaf touched its worn laminate surface.

An extreme threat, yes, but well-deserved. If Rachel's house had become a tidy secret garden, their office at First District Station was Conrad's living heart of darkness. Santino had staked claim to the space with as many plants as he could cram into it, and then went up from there. Rachel had to untangle the Golden Pothos from her hair whenever she stood upright, and Santino walked hunched over to keep his head from crashing against the pots.

"Well?" he asked her as he crabbed his way towards his desk, the last of his lunch swinging from his hand in its plastic sack.

They had played this game before. "It all looks the same to me," she said, scanning the room. It was a wall of vegetation, the plants growing into each other in a curl of ozone and greenery, exactly the same as the day before.

Her implant did that nagging thing again. She let it work as she threw out her hand, and found herself pointing to something with dagger-shaped leaves and a spray of tiny purple flowers. "Wait. No. That one's new."

Santino was pleased in pinks. "Phalaenopsis," he said. "A Moth orchid. Nice job."

"Not entirely happy with you using me as a test subject," she said, as she pulled her own chair away from her desk and sat, facing him. Over the past month, he had been testing her response to environmental stimuli. Zia had been playing around with autoscripts that provided itemized inventories for objects she encountered during her daily routines, and it had inspired Santino to see if he could get Rachel to write a similar script independent of his girlfriend's. Rachel had agreed to the experiment before she learned it was also an excuse for him to buy more plants.

"Notices new objects?" he asked, leaning back and knitting his hands behind his head. They had been doing this on a daily basis, and he didn't need to consult his questionnaire any more.

"Check," she sighed. "I'm going to have to stage an intervention for you."

"Plant hoarding isn't a real thing," he said.

"It is. It so obviously is. You have a serious problem."

"Time taken to recognize new object?"

"Uh…" she consulted her internal clock. "Three centiseconds? That doesn't sound right."

"It probably is. You corrected yourself as you were talking, so it was working as fast as your mouth was."

She lobbed a cheese puff at him. He scooped it off of the carpet where it landed and deposited it in the trash: no floor food for him.

"Was any other object moved in the room?"

"Yes, uh…no," she decided. After she had started making progress, Santino had begun to rearrange the plants to throw her off. Except for the addition of the new orchid, it seemed as though he had left the room untouched since yesterday. "Been busy?"

He arched an eyebrow.

She chuckled and returned to her lunch. It *had* been a stupid question: she didn't know when he had found the time to buy a new plant. Additional proof he created them from raw aether, maybe.

There was a knock at the door.

"Jason," she said to Santino. "Irritated, angry verging on furious, but also pleased with himself."

"Six-pack of hard cider says he's done something he wants to brag about."

"You're on," she said. "I bet he's found something critical to the case, and wants to be praised."

"I can hear you," said the far side of the door.

"Come on in, Jason," Santino called out.

"You two are assholes," Jason said as he entered, pushing through the curtain of Pothos and spider plants.

Santino looked at Rachel, who said, "You didn't know? He's right. We're totally assholes."

"Here," Jason said, dropping a newspaper on Rachel's desk. "Thought you guys would want to see this."

She glared at Jason, then flipped her implant to reading mode and began to struggle with the text. She made out the name of the reporter and gave up: anything on the front page and with a byline by Jonathan Dunstan couldn't be good news. Rachel shoved the paper towards Santino and read the article by his colors. *Nope,* she thought as he went orange, red, and gray by turns. *Certainly not good news.*

"Dunstan broke the news of the connection between Homeland Security and Gayle Street," Santino said.

"What?! Is he trying to blow up the country?" she snarled.

"There's an unnamed source who confirmed this information," Jason said. "Apparently, this source sits on a Senate defense committee. Any guesses?"

"God *damn* him," she said, and kicked the back wall of her desk as hard as she could. The wooden owl rocked on its base and she lunged to steady it. "Josh was telling us just last night how every politician knows the country's starting to destabilize. That…that *person* will do literally anything to save his own skin."

She didn't have to use his name. Even if Dunstan hadn't written that article, the others would know who she was talking about. Senator Hanlon was never far from their minds.

"Is there anything we can do?" Santino asked.

"Nothing," she said. "Nothing that I can think of, anyhow. This is politics, not police work. I guess we just try to not get shot."

The three of them sobered. The officers who had been fished out of the Potomac had been family men, and the entire city was mourning. Rachel felt a new wave of anger towards Hanlon; he had just increased the pressure that every officer or federal agent was already feeling. If Hanlon had walked into the room that instant, she probably would have dug her fingernails into the thin line where his skin met his hair, and then peeled his face apart like an orange.

Or maybe she'd just wait a few days, and then feed him to his own mob.

Santino's phone rang. Rachel and Jason tensed.

"Do I want to answer this?" Santino asked.

"No," she said. "It's Sturtevant."

"Oh hell," Santino muttered, pressing the button.

It was a short call, and the cyborgs listened to every word of it. When Santino dropped the receiver, the three of them started their slow march to Sturtevant's office.

Rachel never visited the Gold Coast if she could help it. As First District Station had been renovated from an old public elementary school, she felt the sinking dread of visiting the principal's office every time she walked the long length of the hall. The MPD had set aside an entire wing for their supervisors, and she knew they were on display, Sturtevant's roving team of freaks and weirdos, marching past the brass and their staff.

She made sure to smile warmly at each and every one.

Sturtevant's secretary, a mousy gossip of a man whose name Rachel couldn't be bothered to learn, tried to make them wait in the hall. Santino cleared his throat, loudly. The phone chirped on the secretary's desk, and Sturtevant's voice crackled in the room. "Send them in."

Sturtevant's office was small, barely large enough for the four of them and the furniture. When Sturtevant motioned for Rachel to close the door, she gave the secretary a glare; the man made a habit of trying to listen in on their meetings.

"Why haven't you fired that guy yet?" Rachel asked, loudly, as she shut them in Sturtevant's office. Through the door, she saw the receptionist's colors blanch.

Sturtevant didn't bother to answer her. His conversational colors were hard browns and professional dark blues; he had called them down on business, his walls firmly in place.

"Sit," he told them. There were two chairs and she let Jason have the other, preferring to spend her mental energy on reading Sturtevant instead of sparring with him. She fell into parade rest and listened as Santino updated the Chief on what had happened over the past twenty-four hours.

"Agent Atran?" Sturtevant turned to Jason. "Have you made any additional progress on the video footage?"

Jason shrugged. "Yes. I haven't found anything that might be useful from the security cameras, but we might be getting somewhere on the facial recognition scans."

Rachel remembered the thirteen fully-rendered green statues that had greeted her in Jason's office, the rogues' gallery of felons who had been present on Gayle Street prior to the bombing. "Did one of the suspects pop?" she asked him.

"No, not them," Jason said to her. He turned to Sturtevant to explain. "One of the things I noticed when I ran population analytics was that ranking military officers had stopped coming down to Gayle Street. This seemed off to me, so I called around. Turns out that someone made an anonymous donation to a catering company. The last week? Gourmet meals and high-end coffee and desserts, free of charge for almost every military organization in downtown D.C. The company sent me copies of the menus; it was really good stuff. I wouldn't have gone looking for food, either."

"Didn't anyone think that was suspicious?" Santino asked.

Jason shook his head. "Happens all of the time," he said. "It's backdoor lobbying. An anonymous party supplies the food, then someone 'accidentally' lets the name of the donor slip out, usually before a decision on a grant or a contract. The catering service isn't usually a five-star affair, but Congress is planning a massive budget overhaul on the military next month. No one questioned it."

"We're trying to track down the donor?" Sturtevant asked.

"Of course."

"Good. And this?" Sturtevant said, moving aside his mug and an old piece of cardboard stained with multiple coffee rings. A newspaper had been under these; Rachel didn't bother to flip frequencies to check the headline.

"We didn't have any knowledge of that story," Santino said.

"I know," Sturtevant replied. "Neither did I—neither did any-body at MPD—and we should have had some warning. Usu-ally when someone up on Capitol Hill drags us into a situation, there's someone else ready to block them."

He drummed his fingers on the newspaper for a few seconds, and then pointed at Santino and Jason. "You two can leave."

Rachel and her partner exchanged a long look before the two men stood and saw themselves out of the office. Rachel settled herself in Santino's chair, and watched Sturtevant's colors weave in and out of each other, a professional blue over and through a mesh made up of yellows and her own turquoise core.

"Is there," Sturtevant said, "a particular health issue you'd like to tell me about?"

"I was not injured in the fall," Rachel said, her insides sud-denly plummeting as if she were back in Bell's rickety old eleva-tor. "Other than my hands, and they're healing well. Thank you for asking."

"We're doing this the hard way, then," Sturtevant said. "Agent Peng, are you blind?"

"Sir, would you like to go down to the shooting range with me?" Rachel said.

"Yes or no, Agent Peng? Are you blind?"

"No," she fired back. Short of a medical test, which the MPD was not authorized to perform on her, there was no way they could confirm the condition of her eyes. Besides, she was *not* blind.

"Agent Peng? Are you capable of processing visual data and interpreting it in a manner similar to myself?

"Actually, wait. Let me rephrase so there can be no possible misunderstanding," Sturtevant said. He leaned forward and wrapped his fingers together, his colors a focused, piercing blue. "Agent Peng, can you process and interpret visual data in a manner similar to the majority of persons within the general sighted population?"

"I don't know if I can answer that, sir," she said, almost sadly. "That's one of those trick questions, isn't it? How can I know if you and I perceive the same colors? I have no way of knowing what you experience when you see the color blue.

"Sir? Is this a test?" she added, as he glared at her.

Sturtevant closed his eyes. Rachel counted to ten, slowly. When she reached *ten Mississippi,* Sturtevant took a deep breath, then reopened his eyes and fixed them on her. "I can't protect you if you won't let me," he said.

"With all due respect, sir, I don't need your protection."

"If you work for me, you get it, whether you're on my payroll or not. Somebody out there hates you, Agent Peng, and when he's ready, he's going to try to destroy you. I would very much like to do what I can to prevent that from happening."

They sat, staring at each other. Rachel knew she needed to either blink or look away before he did—staring contests with her tended to end when the other person got the squirming sensation that something about her eyes was really, *really* off—and she wasn't about to do either of those. Instead, she said, "You remember last August? When I told you we needed to talk?"

"Vividly."

"Excuse me for a minute." Rachel stood and yanked the door open; Sturtevant's secretary was listening by the keyhole. "You are on a coffee break," she told him. "Starting now. Run."

As the mousy man raced off, and Rachel closed and locked the office door, she reached out through the link and told the head of OACET to come join her at First District Station. Then, she began wrapping frequencies into an invisible silver sphere around her and Sturtevant. When the weaves were secure, she expanded the sphere to encompass all of Sturtevant's office, just in case. "Your phones won't work until we're done," she warned him.

He glanced towards his computer monitor, where a notification had popped up to warn him that all network connections had dropped, and nodded.

"You are aware that a certain Senator is biased against my organization in general, and myself in particular," Rachel said.

"I am extremely aware," he said. "Did you know that Senator Hanlon has been trying to have me fired? That he has been whispering in certain ears that the MPD is corrupt and needs to go through a good housecleaning?"

She blinked. Sturtevant wasn't lying. "This is news to me, sir."

"You're not the only one who's got a target painted on them, Agent Peng. Now, what is it I need to know?"

So she told him. How Senator Hanlon's tech company had discovered the technology to build organic computers that weren't restricted by current security protocols. How this technology would only work if there was a sentient biological component integrated into its hardware. How Hanlon had recognized not only that donating this technology to Congress was safer than conducting illegal experiments on human beings, but that doing so would make the government eat the costs.

Sturtevant had heard all of this before, so he waited, fingers knit tightly together and hands resting motionless on his desk, until she reached the part of the story that was new to him. How Hanlon would only benefit from this plan if the human test subjects lost their sense, their reason, their ethics and morality—

How Hanlon didn't want people with consciences who could resist his instructions: he wanted machines who would do what they were told.

How Hanlon needed to purge them of their humanity.

This was the second time she had told this story to an outsider—the first had been Santino—and she was surprised that, yes, the second telling was actually much easier. Sitting there in front of Sturtevant, Rachel found she was able to gloss over the worst parts of those five lost years, from the moment when she received the implant to when it had been fully activated. She didn't use the word *brainwashed*; that word always left a bad taste in her mouth. She did say they had been conditioned through an insidious form of cognitive behavioral therapy to avoid introspection, compassion, any form of higher thinking or emotion...

Towards the end of her story, Sturtevant asked one question: "How did you snap out of it?"

She answered, truthfully, "We still don't know."

Patrick Mulcahy, who had been just another near-mindless cyborg back then, had saved them. Mulcahy said he didn't understand how he had broken free, not exactly, and Rachel knew he wasn't lying...not exactly.

(And as she heard herself disclose the collective's secrets to Sturtevant, her lizard brain squeaked and shivered with the knowledge that Mulcahy was going to lop off her head and stick it on a pike in the front yard of the OACET mansion, as the heads of traitors were displayed by the kings of old.)

When she was done, she realized she had unconsciously flipped off the emotional spectrum. She turned it back on, and Sturtevant was the deep wine rose of sympathy and weeping pity, shadowed at the edges with gray stress and a yellow-orange anxiety.

There were a few long moments where he didn't speak. "No wonder Hanlon wants you all dead," he finally said.

"Dead, discredited...Hanlon will settle for either. If he doesn't shut us up before the news of the brainwashing—" (*oh, God damn it*) "—gets out, he'll be ruined."

"I take it you have no hard evidence that he was personally responsible for any of this," Sturtevant said. "Otherwise he'd already be in jail."

Rachel stared up at the ceiling, pretending to find patterns in the constellations of dots in the acoustical ceiling tiles.

"Or," Sturtevant corrected himself, catching on. "You have plenty of evidence, but you can't use it without also incriminating Congress."

"They weren't happy with us, up on Capitol Hill," Rachel said. "OACET couldn't go public without suggesting there was a conspiracy to keep us hidden. We lost almost—ah, more than, actually—one out of five Agents to the cover-up. But it's better to be a dupe than a villain, and we're happy to let Congress claim they were innocent. Most of them *were* innocent, really; only a couple of them were directly involved with the... the culling. As long as Hanlon is held responsible, the others who helped him? They get a pass."

"And there is evidence of brainwashing?"

"Plenty," Rachel said, trying not to wince at that word. "Different set of doctors, different set of notes. Hanlon's fingerprints are all over those, metaphorically speaking. We've got proof he was directly involved in the development of the therapy program."

"You're going to leverage Congress," Sturtevant said. He reached into a desk drawer and removed a bottle of Scotch and two small glasses. He poured a thin finger into each glass, and pushed one towards Rachel.

She nodded, and took a sip of Sturtevant's bargain-basement Scotch. "They aren't stupid. They know we've got enough on their role in the cover-up to do some real damage. We choose to keep it to ourselves as a gesture of goodwill? Well, from that point on, they owe us. They know all we want is Hanlon."

"Was Hanlon the source of both sets of information?

"Yes."

Sturtevant's conversational colors went solidly gray as the pieces clicked. "If OACET can't use this evidence without incriminating Congress, Hanlon can use it as leverage *against* Congress. So they can't just sacrifice him or turn him over to you. It's a holding pattern."

"You got it." Rachel pushed her glass back towards Sturtevant for a refill. He obliged; work hours or not, this was a conversation in need of lubrication. "But this," she said, tapping a fingernail on the newspaper, "might resolve these problems for us."

His colors shifted to a curious yellow.

"How long have you lived in D.C.?" she asked him.

"Twenty years, give or take."

"I'm betting you've seen a lot of odd coincidences over the years. Like, oh, how unpopular politicians seem prone to dying in their sleep."

His colors were a sudden deep red, offset with his usual direct professional blue. "There are certain attitudes I don't sanction, Agent Peng."

She spread her hands, pure innocence. "Us, too. Hanlon is not in any physical danger from any member of OACET." Sturtevant didn't need to know about the fights, the screaming battles between those Agents who wanted immediate satisfaction versus those who wanted Hanlon to pay, and pay, and pay... Josh and Mulcahy had been very busy, that first month, keeping certain Agents from going for their guns.

Sturtevant stared at her over the rim of his glass. "But if...if someone else were to take care of Hanlon..."

"Kill him, you mean," she said. Sturtevant's colors blanched. "A rose by any other name still smells. Yeah, if someone else decided they were fed up with Hanlon and his baggage? We wouldn't shed a tear.

"But," she added, "OACET will only—*only!*—survive if we can prove we act within the confines of the law. Every Agent agreed to that before we went public. We have the capacity to do great, unbelievable harm, and the *only* way we won't be... How did you put it? 'Taken care of'? Since we don't want that to happen, we police ourselves."

Sturtevant grinned. "Who watches the watchmen?"

"The watchmen, obviously. Unless they can't be trusted, and if they can't, they shouldn't have been made watchmen in the first place."

"Point taken. So, how does this news article break the holding pattern?"

"It was utterly irresponsible of Hanlon to release that information," she said. "I don't have to tell you how the public has been demanding information. This is a national crisis, in a nation already on the edge, and Hanlon just dumped gasoline on the fire. Personally, I see no motivation for that, other than to shift attention from himself. Congress won't approve."

"Or he's playing to the public," Sturtevant said.

"Oh?"

"This isn't exactly an anonymous source; everybody knows who Dunstan really works for. If Hanlon's about to be shown as a lying, manipulative bastard, wouldn't he want to do something to pump up his credibility? And if he's already on Congress' naughty list, it seems like he won't do any additional harm to himself by bolstering that credibility with the general public."

Rachel snapped upright. *Nailed it,* she thought.

"And if anything happens to Hanlon after he—"

"He's just sealed himself in a nuclear bunker," she interrupted him. "Shit. *Shit.* Nobody can touch him now without turning him into a martyr. I bet Dunstan and Hanlon's lawyers have sealed copies of a letter that begins with the line, 'Should something happen to me...'"

She felt her palm burning and opened her left hand; she had clenched the shot glass so tightly she had popped a few stitches.

"Here," Sturtevant said, handing her a box of tissues.

"Shit," she said again, crushing the tissues in her fist to sop up the blood. "I thought we finally had him."

"Do you think Hanlon is behind Gayle Street? We already know he's not above that sort of thing, and we also know he can call the kind of people who can pull off something as complex as Gayle Street."

She was not yet ready to go all-in with Sturtevant—there was no reason for him to know the wheels-within-wheels of what had really happened in August—but there were other ways around that answer. "No," she said. "I don't think Hanlon would do this. He knows he won't bounce back from something like

Gayle Street if he gets caught. He'd capitalize on the opportunity, but it's not worth the risk to set it up."

Sturtevant nodded slowly. "Not sure you're right," he said. "Sounds good, but I'm not sure you're right."

"Look at it this way: our job is easier if he's not a suspect."

He almost laughed. "You can't be serious."

"Chief? If I thought Hanlon was responsible for Gayle Street, I would move heaven and earth to bring him down. But I don't, and that's hard for me to admit."

"All right," Sturtevant agreed. "So. What do we do now?"

"I go back to work, and you stay here and have a conversation with Patrick Mulcahy."

"Hmm?" His tone was easy, but professional blues snapped shut around him like armor.

Rachel wrapped the bloody shot glass in a tissue, and stuffed it in her handbag to wash it later. "What I've told you is confidential, but if it's to be of any use to you, or if you're going to be of any use to us, you need to talk to someone higher up in OACET's Administration than I am. That's either Josh Glassman or Mulcahy, and Mulcahy was available."

There was a knock at the door, and the head of OACET let himself in.

Rachel stood as he entered.

Patrick Mulcahy was a smaller man than Mako, but not by much; the top of his head barely cleared the lintel. He was built like a linebacker, but was light on his feet, and the only sound he made when entering the room was when he greeted Chief Sturtevant like an old acquaintance. His core of cerulean blue was covered by a curiously-pleasing combination of pink, purple, and orange; if Rachel didn't know better, she would have assumed the head of OACET was bemused by the whole thing.

Rachel noticed that Sturtevant was standing, too. "Agent Mulcahy," the Chief said. "Have a seat."

"Thank you. How are your kids?"

"They're doing well. Molly's just started her sophomore year at Brown. She's thinking law."

The small talk continued until Rachel wondered how the two men could stand it. Mulcahy played politics better than anyone she had ever met, while Sturtevant didn't play politics at all, yet they both managed to seem enthralled with the minutiae of each other's personal lives.

When the pleasantries were finally over, Mulcahy said, "Agent Peng tells me she disclosed some sensitive information."

Sturtevant nodded. "I'm sorry about what happened to you and your people. I understand why you need to keep something like that quiet."

Translated as: You can trust me. Don't worry about me spilling the beans, Rachel thought.

"Thank you," Mulcahy replied. "We know it will come out sooner rather than later, but it's best to control it before that happens."

Oh, nice one! A mild threat to Sturtevant, with a concise, "My Agent opened her big mouth ahead of schedule but this is the closest I'll come to shouting at her in public" in the same sentence. Well done!

"Is there anything I can do to help?"

Translated as: Is there anything... Huh. Sturtevant's sincere.

Mulcahy shook his head. "If you're willing to let Agent Peng stay active at the MPD, that alone would be a huge help to us. Although you'll probably catch some fallout if it comes out you knew about the mental conditioning and still kept her on your staff."

*Aaaaand fuck. Didn't think **that** would be the reason I'd be kicked out of the MPD—I figured it'd be because Mulcahy had me walled up in the ossuary and I stopped coming to work.*

Sturtevant weighed Rachel's turquoise core against the blues and golds of the MPD. "We work with more than thirty mental health professionals," he finally said. "If Agent Peng would consent to five separate evaluations, that would prove I did my due diligence after I found out."

Rachel forced herself to stay loose in her chair. If Sturtevant wanted to slip a physical in there, she wouldn't be able to dodge an eye examination. Not if she wanted to stay at the MPD. Sturtevant took a quick breath, as if he was about to add something, and the fingernails on Rachel's left hand bit into the wadded tissue.

Then Sturtevant let the moment pass.

"That sounds fair," Mulcahy said. "It would also help us to show that Agent Peng was independently vetted by the MPD, and found to be mentally stable. Could you make sure that Agents Atran and Netz receive the same evaluations?"

Sturtevant agreed. Rachel didn't, but she kept her mouth shut. Adding Jason into the mix was a bad idea. She could beat a psych evaluation without breaking a sweat, and Phil had nothing to hide. Jason, on the other hand, was a narcissistic mess; he might lack some of her more aggressive tendencies, but any good shrink would be able to draw him out.

"Agent Peng?"

Rachel turned to Mulcahy. "Sir?"

"Anything you'd like to add?"

"Chief Sturtevant may be too polite to mention it, but you should know that Senator Hanlon has decided he is also a target."

"Ah." Mulcahy nodded to the Chief. "I apologize for getting you caught up in our affairs."

"Don't worry about it," Sturtevant said. "We get very few opportunities in life to do lasting good. I'd consider it a privilege to help take someone like him out of public office."

"Thank you," Mulcahy said, standing. "I'll check to see what we can do to keep Hanlon off of your back."

"It would be appreciated."

"If she's free to go, I'd like to borrow Agent Peng for a few hours."

A southwestern turquoise flickered within Sturtevant's conversational colors, and was quickly submerged in yellow-orange trepidation. Nice to know that Sturtevant was worried about her. "She's yours," he said.

So much for being under Sturtevant's protection, she thought.

It was not as though Mulcahy was going to kill her for spilling OACET's secrets to Sturtevant (well, not *kill*-kill… probably), but she was sure he could make her crave the sweet peace of the grave ten times over.

Mulcahy held the door for her, and Rachel hastily unwove the silvery EMF barrier around Sturtevant's office. It was a rush job, and she felt the beginnings of a migraine as she let the ends of the weave collapse on top of them. Mulcahy's surface colors took on some red; he had felt the backlash, too.

She opened a link. *"Sorry."*

They both knew she meant her apology to cover more than a dropped barrier.

Mulcahy wasn't buying it. *"Jason says you read him the riot act for breaking the rules just a couple of days ago,"* he said. There was a little bit of red in his colors, but not nearly as much as she had expected. He was still mainly orange (irritated, probably at interrupting his workday to come down and bail her out), a small touch of purple (amusement), and pink. She had no idea what the pink meant, or why the purple was there at all.

"This was the kind of situation where I couldn't beg forgiveness after the fact," she said. *"If I was to continue to work with Sturtevant, I needed to prep him."* She didn't mention that while she might be begging for forgiveness herself, she hadn't needed to ask for permission. Mulcahy was the one who had promoted her to OACET's administrative team. If he didn't think she had the good sense required to manage their allies, he shouldn't have promoted her.

At first, Mulcahy didn't reply. She felt slow anger in his head, but he was more annoyed than anything else. After a few moments, he said, *"I know."*

"Where are we going?"

"Home," he told her. *"So Jenny can take care of your hand."*

Oh goody, she thought. *Now everyone can be in a passive-aggressive huff with me today.*

Picking up on private thoughts was a side effect of a casual link. Mulcahy heard her: she saw it, the strong flash of purple as he suppressed his grin, and knew she'd be fine.

"What'd you drive?" she asked aloud.

"The Goat," he said.

A little thrill ran up her spine. Mulcahy had a weak spot for classic muscle cars, and his 1967 Pontiac GTO was a favorite of hers. The thing was a beast. If she still trusted herself to drive, she would have stolen it out from under him.

They took a side door and stepped into the late morning sunlight. First District Station's garage was still being repaired, and they had to walk several blocks to where Mulcahy had parked. Rachel refused to run after her boss like a small child, so she slowed her pace until he remembered how he covered nearly twice the distance with a single step. He shortened his stride, his reds rising as he dealt with this newest irritation.

The best defense was a solid offense. *"I thought you'd be furious,"* she said.

He looked down at her; it was a long, long way up to meet his eyes. *"I am."*

"No, you're angry, not furious. Furious is a burning red. You're just on a slow boil."

The strange combination of purple-orange bemusement grew stronger. *"This wasn't the first unauthorized disclosure I've managed,"* he admitted. *"After you showed Santino could be trusted, there's been something of a rush on confessions."*

"Really?" Rachel was honestly shocked. She hadn't heard a word about this, and Agents were awful with secrets.

"We're up to at least three a day," he said. *"Mostly family members. I've actually been waiting for your call to let me know you spoke to Sturtevant."*

Mulcahy must have felt her sudden anger; he went yellow-white in mild surprise. *"What?"*

"You do realize if you had told me full disclosure is now an acceptable policy, I could have arranged a formal meeting? Maybe not stressed myself stupid about it?"

He stopped walking. *"It's **not** acceptable,"* he said, the red anger flaring. *"We put ourselves first. **Always.** You're Administra-*

tion—*you know this!*—*and yet here I am.*"

Rachel wasn't about to back down, and pushed her words at him as hard as she could. *"Bringing Sturtevant in? That* **was** *putting us first. He's a good ally. He's smart, he's connected, and he knows if he helps us, we'll help him."*

Mulcahy nodded. *"I know,"* he said. *"That's why he and I arranged for you to come to the MPD in the first place."*

She gaped at him.

"Sturtevant never told you he was the one who wanted an alliance between the MPD and OACET?"

Rachel closed her eyes and flipped off visuals. She had known someone at the MPD had insisted on working with OACET, but Sturtevant?

Well…

It would explain why the Chief of Detectives had attached himself to her and Santino. And why he had appointed himself as their supervisor at the MPD. And why he had allowed her to bring in Phil and Jason… And had increased Santino's budget… And made sure she got a desk… And those fancy business cards, and…

And Rachel felt very stupid.

And now she was the one who was furious.

They crossed a four-lane road. Anger had shut her visual control down to almost nothing; all she could see was black, and her feet within the crosswalk. A horn blared and a man's voice shouted something cruel; Mulcahy had been spotted.

They ignored the shouted threats and kept on walking.

"Did you ever ask yourself," she said to him, after the tunnel vision had started to recede. *"if I might have made faster progress at the MPD if you had told me Sturtevant could be trusted?"*

"No." His answer came almost before she had finished with her question. *"I put you there to fight and win. Your purpose was to build new alliances, not develop those we already had.*

"And you've done that, Penguin," he added in a softer tone, his red anger shifting towards pride. *"Faster—better—than I thought was possible."*

She flipped off the emotional spectrum: it was nearly impossible to be angry with someone when they held positive thoughts about you, and at that moment, she wanted to be angry at Mulcahy. *"I don't like being used."*

He shrugged through their link; she shuddered at the sensation. *"I know,"* he said. *"I wish it could be different."*

"Yeah," Rachel said aloud. She didn't need to see his colors to know he was carrying guilt. None of the Agents had wanted to be in their current situation—Mulcahy certainly hadn't woken up one morning and decided to crown himself the Cyborg King. Sometimes you just had to play the hand you were dealt, even if that hand was nothing but the two of clubs and a bunch of venomous spiders.

They reached Mulcahy's car, gleaming black and riding low against the curb. She felt him reach out to ping it, and the Goat's engine turned over, purring; some purists would consider a remote starter on a classic car an act of desecration, but they weren't cyborgs.

She slipped into the passenger's side and settled down in the leather bucket seat, ready for a long and silent ride to the mansion.

Mulcahy surprised her. After a few quiet minutes, he asked, "You trust Sturtevant?"

She flipped emotions back on. *Yellow and blue. Curious, mostly. Professional blue...aw hell.* Every single conversation with Mulcahy turned into a performance evaluation. "I didn't say that," she said. "I don't think I implied it, either. But it's... interesting...that you trust him."

"I didn't say that," he said. "Or imply it, either." A flash of purple flipped over his surface colors like a wink.

"Oh my God," she sighed. Testing her *and* playing games. "Why hasn't your wife strangled you in your sleep?"

"She says I make her laugh."

Rachel blinked at him, then broke down in a mild case of giggles. "You can be a real jerk, Mulcahy."

"So I've heard." This time, he actually cracked a grin.

She wondered, just for a moment, what he had been like before the implant.

"I used to sing."

"What?"

"I used to sing. Before." He must have noticed her expression. "Sorry. You were loud."

Damn. Rachel looped her scans through the road running under them, seizing on the strength of concrete. "Better?"

"Yes." He turned onto the highway and steered them out of the city. "Your conversation with Sturtevant? I assume you were running emotions. How did it go?"

She told him. When she had finished, she glanced up at Mulcahy. Curious yellows has replaced the last of the blues. "What?" she asked.

"There's usually some psychological stress when we do full disclosure."

"Oh, there was plenty of pity. He just didn't show it. And I think he's more vested in what we do next than what happened in the past—as long as we're mentally stable now, what they did to us isn't relevant to our role at the MPD."

A wisp of gray spun through his colors. "Could be."

"I think it's a good sign," she decided. They hadn't been sure how the general public would react when they learned how the cyborgs had been victimized. "If Sturtevant doesn't think we're an inherent risk, maybe it means that the other normals we work with will vouch for us when the brainwa—uh, *that*—hits the press."

"Probably not," he said. "Josh and I work with Congress, remember?"

"I meant people who mattered."

This time, Mulcahy laughed, and the gray in his conversational colors blew apart like smoke.

"You should have let me know that others are doing full disclosure," she told him. "It would have helped me plan my strategies."

"That's why I didn't," he said. "It shouldn't be an option. If we don't control what others know about us, they'll have control over us."

"Except now Sturtevant understands what we went through, and he's probably going to be a better ally because of it."

He tapped his index fingers against the steering wheel, orange-yellow annoyance beginning to appear as she pushed him. "Did you tell him about Shawn?"

"What? No!"

"And are you still going to hide your calorie consumption from him? Did you tell him about the missing fifty?"

She didn't answer. She didn't have to; Mulcahy already knew.

"We have to keep control," he said. "It's the only way we can survive."

Rachel nodded and muttered something agreeable. It was easier than fighting with him; Mulcahy didn't even realize he was lying.

TWELVE

Rachel slammed the Goat's door with a satisfying thump. Mulcahy wasn't staying; he said he needed to get back to the Capitol. It was a half-truth at best: neither of them wanted to spend any more time in each other's company for at least the next few days.

Her skin twitched in the autumn air as she walked up the cracked sidewalk to the front doors of the mansion. The car had been nicely toasty, and her suit coat was not thick enough to keep the chill away. *Jacket,* she told herself. *Remember to start carrying a jacket.* She was from Texas, born and (on her father's side) bred, and she had expected winters in the D.C. temperate zone to be a little more temperate. Still, winter here was nothing compared to Afghanistan. She was sure she had been one rotation away from losing toes.

The mansion's grounds were going dormant. Santino wasn't the only crazed gardener in her life: OACET had at least a dozen dedicated hobbyists who had cut and slashed the overgrown landscaping back into some semblance of domesticity. They were working from a five-year plan, replacing the dead plants with new hedges and perennials to complement the mansion's traditional French cottage exterior. Mulcahy had told them they would have moved to their permanent headquarters before those five years were up, but the gardeners just laughed and kept digging. The collective was a technological marvel at least a generation ahead of their time, yes, but they were also employed by the federal government. No one expected their new offices to be finished within the next decade.

In the meantime, the gardeners were planting for pollinators. Rachel had been subject to many a passionate lecture on how humanity was on the verge of starvation, damning itself to an empty produce section by killing off bee colonies for the sake of aphid-free roses. The gardeners had built beehives from untreated cypress stumps, and were refusing to bag any fallen leaves until the moth larvae beneath them had a chance to mature.

It was a work day, and most of the Agents in the mansion were at their desks. Rachel knew she was one of the lucky ones: thanks to Mulcahy (and Sturtevant, apparently), she had an actual job that put her back in the field. The others were still waiting for placement. Not every federal department had an opening for a cyborg, or was willing to take one on, or wouldn't abuse said cyborg in the name of convenience or some nebulous Greater Good. It left some of the most powerful people on the planet to waste their days doing data entry.

Rachel went in through the back. The solarium was empty, her footsteps muffled by layer upon layer of antique carpets. There were occasional conversations as she passed Agents on her way downstairs, but she was more likely to get a wave or a brief mental greeting; she hadn't fallen into a basement today.

The medical lab was empty. Rachel felt a twinge of mild astonishment—Jenny practically lived there. Rachel searched for Jenny's signal and found her doctor hurrying downstairs from the kitchen.

"Sorry, Penguin." Jenny's mental voice was slightly shaky. *"I just got back from a food run. Everyone's converging on the kitchen."*

"I'm in the lab. Can you bring some lunch down for me?"

Jenny's horror that food was about to enter her precious quasi-sterile environment was palpable, and she calmed down only after she felt Rachel laughing at her through the link. *"Oh, very funny,"* the doctor said. *"And your wounds are open again. Swear to God, Rachel—"*

They bickered pleasantly until Jenny entered the lab, and then the two of them reenacted the previous afternoon: Jenny, taking down the little white case and numbing Rachel's hand before stitching up her palm; Rachel, doing her best to not throw up all over Jenny.

"Have you used Shawn's autoscript yet?" Jenny asked.

"A few times. Have my mutant healing powers kicked in yet?"

Jenny laughed through the link. *"Nope,"* she said. *"Your hands are still a mess. You're lucky I can restitch these cuts, but if you do this again, you're going to have to wear a full bandage over your left hand. How did the script work for you?"*

"You were right, it felt like going to sleep. Actually," she added, mulling it over, *"it felt like the best power nap I've ever had."*

The other woman nodded as she finished the last row of stitches. "Even if we get nothing else out of that script, that'll be useful. Now," Jenny said, standing, "I'm going to give you a half-assed physical, because I cannot trust you to have the good sense to take care of yourself."

"Right," Rachel said. Jenny was all about spontaneous physicals: the woman seemed convinced they were all on the verge of complete systems failure. "Ballistics vest on or off?"

"You can leave it on. I'm just checking for signs of infection," Jenny said, coming at Rachel with an otoscope and a tongue depressor. *"Say Ah."*

"Ah." Rachel grinned.

"Out loud, wiseass," Jenny said, prodding Rachel with the butt end of the otoscope.

Rachel obliged. The other woman studied the inside of Rachel's mouth, then tossed a few quick notes to Rachel's digital medical file. The rest of the physical was quick and painless, with nothing more involved than a quick squeeze with the blood pressure cuff. All perfectly routine, and Rachel wouldn't have thought anything was wrong if she had turned off the emotional spectrum. As it was active, she couldn't help but notice how Jenny was slowly feeding a deep internal anxiety, and that this anxiety was woven into thin strands of Rachel's turquoise core.

Not good. Definitely not good.

"What's the prognosis, doc?" Rachel asked.

"Your hands will be fine. Again," Jenny replied, busying herself in Rachel's charts. "No signs of infection. You're completely healthy."

"Then why the orange?"

"What?"

"Orange," Rachel hopped off of the exam table. "Sort of a yellowish-orange, like marmalade. You're two parts anxiety, one part curiosity. And it's related to me; it popped when I asked how I'm doing. So…" Rachel trailed off.

"Oh. No, I'm just—I have something for you," Jenny said in a rush. The anxious oranges overwhelmed her surface colors. "Promise me you won't tear it up and throw it into the trash?"

"What a weird thing to ask."

"Promise? I want to you keep it for at least a week. What you do with it after then is your business."

"Fine," Rachel said, smiling. "I promise. Now, what equipment do I have to drag around for an entire week?"

Jenny pressed a business card into Rachel's right hand. She felt the raised bumps of Braille—*Oh shit, Jenny, no!*—beneath her thumb, then flipped to reading mode to see an elegant Roman font, a company's name…

Visual Cybernetics Incorporated.

Rachel crushed the card into a ball. "Jenny, what the fuck?"

"Hear me out," Jenny said. "Please. That's Dr. Gillion's number. He's one of the leading researchers in visual prostheses—ah, you'd call them bionic eye implants. I'm not telling you to call him, Rachel, but if you ever do want to work with a specialist to help the visually impaired, Dr. Gillion is the one you should talk to."

"I don't want to work with a specialist." Rachel kept her voice as flat as possible. No whining in front of friends or doctors.

"I know, Rachel, but…Penguin, I'm *dying* here," Jenny said. Rachel snapped her head up and searched deep within Jenny's colors; underneath Jenny's anxiety, almost close enough to touch her core, was a strong streak of worn-out gray. "I'm working on a dozen different projects, any one of which might revolutionize medicine in ways that we haven't seen since the discovery of penicillin. Do you understand what I'm saying? What you can do might literally help the blind to see, and it's still not at the top of my list!"

The hard wad of paper pressed against the half-healed scrapes on Rachel's palm. "Does he know?"

"What—*No*." Jenny was offended. "I would never do that to you."

"Yeah." Rachel nodded. "Yeah, I know. It just came out."

"It's not just about my workload," Jenny said in a softer tone. "A specialist has the training and connections within their field. If you and I worked together, we'd be starting from the ground floor. Gillion is already occupying the penthouse suite."

"I hear you," Rachel said. She reached for her purse and made sure Jenny was watching as she shoved the crumpled ball of paper in its hidden pocket. "One week," she told Jenny.

The woman's anxiety eased. "Just think about it," she said. "And keep in mind that Gillion would be bound by patient confidentiality, so if he publishes anything, it could be done anonymously."

"Jenny? Not a good time to argue the merits of patient confidentiality with me," Rachel said.

Jenny winced. "Oh, right. I heard about that."

"Don't," Rachel said.

"Don't what?"

"This is usually when you try to convince me that I should get ahead of the problems and out myself."

"Rachel! I'd never—"

"Not *you*-you. That was more of a universal 'you,'" Rachel clarified. "I have this conversation a lot."

Jenny's conversational colors vanished into the almost-off-white of lab coats; Rachel assumed this was Jenny's version of professional blues. "Not from me," Jenny said. "And if you have this conversation with your therapist, I need to have a talk with him."

"No, the two of you are the exception," Rachel said. "Everybody else is the rule."

Jenny started to reply, then reached out and grabbed Rachel's right hand, a trace of alarm flicking across her surface colors.

"What?" Rachel asked.

Jenny turned Rachel's hand over to show her the thin layer of blood across her palm. The edges of the crumpled business card had aggravated some of her injuries. *"Honest to God, Rachel,"* Jenny said with a mental sigh, as she stood to fetch another little white case. *"It's a wonder you're alive."*

"Jenny, you're the greatest."

The other woman glanced up at her in curious yellows.

"Well," Rachel explained. "Everyone else thinks I'm going to die in a knife fight, but you're worried about microbes."

*"**Please** ask me to cite the statistics on leading causes of death. Knife fights don't even make the list. And a long, agonizing death in a hospital bed is nowhere near as glamorous."*

Rachel tensed as she remembered an item on her to-do list.

"What?" Jenny asked aloud.

"Do you have time to drive me somewhere?"

Thirty minutes later, Jenny pulled up to the main entrance of Washington Hospital Center. Rachel froze in the passenger's seat as her body relived that first visit to see Jordan Meisner, her initial reluctance to leave the car and confront the almost-overwhelming emotions within the hospital.

"Will you be okay?" Jenny asked her.

"Of course!" Rachel said brightly. She popped the door and waved goodbye to Jenny, and let the hospital take her.

Poetry had been Rachel's first love. As a teenager, she had hidden herself away with whisper-thin folios and great gasping tomes, and had, very gradually, come to realize that some poems were perhaps not as good as others. In those worst offenders, Death was reduced to stilted phrases. Skin, with its inescapable waxy pallor, was always cold and unyielding. Last breaths never failed to rattle in the chest, and there was always one, then another, and another, as the speaker tried to pace out the moments between worlds.

Rachel had never read a good poem about a hospital. She had

searched, but everything she found was overly fond of those waxy pallors and clocks where the hands had stopped turning. It had frustrated her: back then, Rachel had thought only the best of hospitals, and couldn't understand why her poets hadn't shared this opinion. When you were sick, if you were injured, you turned to the hospital. Yes, people died there, but people died everywhere, and you never heard of anyone who had been healed by that four-way intersection with the hill and the curvy blind drive.

And then she had received her implant, and the emotional spectrum had transformed hospitals into a completely different environment. The moods which ran through a hospital were a river of extremes: there were small sunny shallows, like the maternity ward, but most of it was the dark depths of the oncology wing, or the hard and fast rapids of the Emergency Department. She felt it was still worthy of poetry—more so, perhaps!—as now it was exhausting and heartbreaking and exhilarating, all at once.

The problem was, it stripped her nerves raw. Too bad she was working. If she hadn't wanted to assess how the workers were coping with D.C.'s first significant act of terrorism since the attack on the Pentagon, she would have turned emotions off and gone skipping down the halls.

A receptionist told her that Meisner had been moved from the ICU to a newer wing of the hospital. Rachel muttered horrible profanities under her breath; she had been hoping to retrace her steps from her earlier visit, but was now resigned to wandering the labyrinth again. She decided to start in the gift shop and work her way out from there, until she realized the RFID tags that were always scratching at the edge of her awareness were trying to be helpful. She dropped her screens and let them talk to her; they told her how they were installed in each door card, each sign plastered throughout the hallways, and she followed them like a trail of breadcrumbs.

Freakin' adore these updated tags! she thought, remembering how she and Phil had gotten lost by following old and misplaced signals, and wondered if there was someone on the hospital's design team who would be interested in ergonomics from a cyborg's point of view.

This new route through the hospital took her up four flights, and across a covered walkway which connected two wings of the hospital. She paused in the center of the walkway, leaning heavily against the brushed steel railing as she pretended to look down.

Rachel loved heights. This was a fairly new development in her personality: she had never actively disliked heights, but loving them, wanting to experience them? Definitely new. Up here, her perception scans stripped the floor away, and she could feel the electromagnetic spectrum humming all around her. It was like going out-of-body, with the added benefit of having feet.

On a whim, Rachel scanned the area. The walkway was empty, and nobody was coming towards her. She froze the feed to the security cameras, and then flopped down on the linoleum and kicked her legs above her head to rest her feet on a windowsill. With a snap, she shut off emotions, then the visual spectrum, and finally let her scans filter down and away.

It was almost vertigo, this seeing-without-seeing, this spinning rush of sensations which filled the holes where her sight had been. The implant had given her an acute case of synesthesia: even when she removed any frequency which would give her visual feedback, she could still feel the shape of things around her. Her mind rolled, expanding through the space below her, voids and solids forming as she brushed against girders or fell through empty air.

Flashes of vivid blue lurked in pockets throughout the hospital, a color so unmistakably like Hope's core that Rachel had to double-check to make sure the emotional spectrum was still turned off. It was: the blue existed independent of any one person or machine. Rachel watched the blue as it flitted around: it had no form, no obvious purpose. Stray bursts of energy, or resonance within the spectra, maybe. She wasn't a scientist, and was left to guess at what they might be.

Up here, the digital ecosystem was quiet. Not gone—she'd have to travel past the Moon to escape it—but muted, with fewer frequencies finding her in the middle of the walkway. The more her senses spread out, the louder it got: the entire hospital hummed to itself, a tune made up of machines designed to perform hard tasks. She listened, trying to pick out an underlying melody, but couldn't find one. Bell's and Jason's systems had each functioned as a single unit, but the hospital's machines weren't tuned to a shared purpose. Each kept to its own, concentrating on single jobs.

But maybe, just maybe, there was a different kind of music within those parts—

"Ma'am?"

Rachel opened her eyes, and flipped visuals and emotions on. An orderly was standing over her, confused in orange-yellow.

"I'm fine," she said, standing and brushing herself off. "My doctor says to lie down when I start to feel dizzy. Sorry to bother you."

"Do you need me to call someone? Your doctor?"

"No, I'm fine," she said, walking away with a wave. "Thanks."

Behind her, she saw the orderly watch her leave in a bemused orange-purple, and then turn his attention to jiggling the wires on the security cameras. She winced, and released the feed.

She found Meisner's room soon after that, a private suite on a floor set aside for the victims of Gayle Street. The curtains were closed against the viewing window, a second set wrapped tight around the bed. Rachel tapped on the door. The lone figure on the other side of the curtains glowed a mixed orange-yellow, both apprehensive and curious, and Rachel let herself in.

"Hey," she said. "You're looking better than the last time I saw you."

Jordan Meisner's core colors were a warm woody brown. There was some red pain in his surface colors, but this was briefly chased aside by his purple-gray sigh. "Are you Andrea's replacement? I thought she said it'd be another hour before she went off-shift."

"Oh. No, I'm not your nurse," Rachel said, realizing his eyes and much of his upper face were bandaged. "I'm Agent Peng. I'm the one who found you after the bombings."

"Hey!" he said. He struggled to sit upright, but gave up as the red bloomed anew. "Thank you. Thanks so much," he said. "I'd stand, but—"

"Don't worry," she said, grinning. "I'm not fancy. I just wanted to check in and make sure you were doing okay, maybe ask you a few questions if you feel up for it."

"Yeah," Meisner said, tucking the sheets up under his chin. "They say I'll be fine. Internal injuries, mostly, except for…" His voice trailed off as he swept a hand up towards his face, the grays becoming more pronounced.

"I spoke with your doctors. They said the facial damage wasn't too bad," Rachel tried.

"Yeah," he said as he forced a chuckle. "They're going to take some skin off of my butt to patch the holes. Looks like my little sister was right about me."

Rachel laughed. "Use that one much?"

"The last couple of days? All the time."

She moved a pile of magazines from the room's only chair and sat down. "I checked in on you earlier, but you were asleep. You had a lot of family here."

"We're local," Meisner said. "You should have come in. They've been buying drinks for everyone that was on the rescue team."

He kept his head pointed away from her. She recognized his body language; she was familiar with the instinctive need to hide a set of ruined eyes. She shuffled the pages of the magazine for the sound of moving paper, then said, sadly, "Oh."

"Hmm?"

"Just…your medical file," she said. "I'm sorry."

His surface colors fell, leaving him almost wholly gray. "I got out of there with my life," he said, and a small streak of intense blue shot through the gray. "That's more than almost everybody else who was on Gayle Street can say."

"Well, aren't you a happy little Pollyanna."

"What?" He hadn't expected that.

"You lost your vision. That would…that would *enrage* me! Especially if it happened because some asshole decided you were collateral damage in their terrorist plot."

Red anger flared, complementing his pain. "Thanks for the compassion."

"What?" Rachel said, stretching out in the chair. "I'm not your shrink. I'm the person who's working to catch the fuckers who did this to you and punish the absolute shit out of them."

She had found profanity to be a useful tool in interviews. Profanity conveyed a sense of plainspoken honesty, especially when used in a setting where it shouldn't be. It could nudge the listener out of their comfort zone, force them to pay attention, maybe recognize the speaker was also actively involved in their situation. Sure, sometimes it caused things to escalate, with both parties hurling words like pointed rocks, but when that happened, Rachel dug in her heels and went hunting for information hidden in the harsh language.

Here, Meisner took it as honesty, and his red anger eased. "Thanks," he said after a long moment.

She counted to five, slowly, then feigned a sigh. "You know how I found you?" she asked.

"They told me you're an Agent," Meisner replied, yellows coming through the gray.

"Yeah," Rachel said, as she leaned forward. "But do you want to know *how* I found you? I specialize in perception. I can see pretty much everything in this hospital, whether I'm looking at it or not."

When he didn't reply, she pushed on. "I'm saying there are alternatives. Yeah, your eyes are gone, but the technology's out there to replace them. And trust me, Meisner, once you start seeing the world through those alternatives, you'll never want to go back."

He was quiet, and then said, "With all due respect? Not the same thing. You've still got your eyesight, and I don't have your options."

She couldn't reply to that, so she waited a few moments before she changed the subject. "All right," she said. "I know everyone has been asking you the same questions, but I'd like to go over what happened one more time."

"Yeah," he said. The reds eased, and his core of woody brown started to come through. "I don't know what else I can tell you..."

"I actually saw what you did. You were caught on camera," Rachel said to prod him. "Helping that woman after the explosion? Pretty impressive."

"Thanks," Meisner said. "But I wasn't thinking. It just...it just happened."

"Yeah, maybe. Seems pretty cool, though, to have proof."

"Proof of what?"

"Most of us never get tested like that. You've got proof that, deep down, you're not an asshole."

He laughed, a quick barking noise that stopped as soon as the pain seized him again. "And I'm not dead," he said when he could breathe. "The police said that if I'd been in the store when the bomb went off, I'd probably have been killed. So, you know. Small favors." Gray storm clouds rolled in over his core as he lost himself in regrets.

"Let's start at the beginning," Rachel said. "Why were you in the coffee shop in the first place?"

"For coffee. No, sorry. There was a woman," he said, and his colors brightened through the gray.

"She must have been pretty," Rachel said, smiling.

"Yeah, she was gorgeous. She went into a different coffee shop, somewhere up the street, and...I should have followed her, but I didn't. I had some time to kill before a meeting, so I thought I'd hang out, maybe see if I could bump into her if she walked by me again.

"I've been worried about her," he admitted. "If she was still on Gayle Street... Can you check into it if I give you a description?"

"Do you really want to know?" she asked him. "If it helps, tell yourself she bought a coffee to go, and was off of the street before the bombs went off."

"The one who got away," he grinned. "Literally."

"Exactly."

"I want to know," he said, his surface colors taking on a stony resolution. "I don't think I can let it go—it's one of those things that'll eat at me."

"I'll do what I can," Rachel promised. "Maybe she was in one of the coffee shops that wasn't bombed out."

Meisner's colors shifted to a confused orange-yellow. "Weren't all of the shops on that part of Gayle Street destroyed?"

"Most of them. He missed a few."

"Huh," Meisner said, sinking back into the bed. "I wonder why he didn't hit those."

THIRTEEN

"You sure you want to go in here?"

"No," Rachel replied, forcing herself to not peek inside the coffee shop from the other side of its locked front door. "Pretty sure I don't, actually."

It was still three hours from sunrise, and the buildings on the west end of Gayle Street were cast in black shadows. The fourteen blocks that had been affected by the bombings were still closed to traffic, pedestrian and otherwise, but these had been end-capped by two additional blocks: explosions weren't clean, and debris and damage tended to travel. There was a single coffee shop which fell in this dead zone. It stood on the far side of Santino's ruined bookstore, untouched by the bombs but still abandoned.

Hope Blackwell stood at Rachel's back, her face turned towards the street as if she was expecting them to be attacked from behind, while Phil struggled with the front door. With the exception of the city cops standing watch down the road, they were the only living things in sight. The Forensics teams were still concentrated along the east end of the incident, and the paparazzi and other ghouls who haunted the crowd control barriers were down where the action was. That part of Gayle Street had portable generators and high-intensity floodlights. The three of them had a single portable scene lamp with a dying battery. Rachel tried to keep the light steady for Phil, as he jammed key after key into the security lock.

"Damn!" Phil snarled, dropping another key back on the ring.

"The lock's a Schlage," Hope said. "Are you trying just the Schlage keys, or all of them?"

Phil's colors glazed over and he glared at Hope. "They're copies of copies of copies," he said, rattling the heavy ring at her. "The MPD got the originals from the store owners in case we needed to enter a building, and they've been handing the copies out like candy. I don't know if any of these keys actually work."

"Right," Rachel said. She handed the lamp to Hope, then picked up a good-sized chunk of broken pavement and chucked it at the store's front window. The window collapsed in on itself in a crash.

"It was already cracked," she said to them as she kicked out the remaining glass from the bottom of the panel. "And I'm perfectly fine standing around in the dark, but if you guys want to run down the battery while you play with your keys."

"We're good," Phil said.

Rachel shimmied through the opening and let the others in through the front door.

"Don't move around too much," she told them. "I need to scan the floor."

"Stinks," Phil said, covering his nose.

"Five-plus days of curdled milk," Hope said. "Power's been out."

Five-plus days of dust, Rachel thought as she knelt by the entrance. *Fourteen blocks, but three gas main shutoffs... I hope I'm not wrong about this. We're running out of ideas.*

Her lizard brain had scratched her awake at two in the morning, funneling numbers into her head. The math hadn't added up. If each gas line was loaded for five blocks, why had only fourteen been affected? Shouldn't the explosions have covered the full fifteen?

She had threatened her lizard brain with everything from whiskey to a hundred milligrams of diphenhydramine, but the math kept coming. In fact, new numbers started to wedge themselves into the equations. The two murdered officers, dead for nearly three days before they were found...

And then came the question Meisner had asked in the hospital—a simple *"I wonder why"*—and Rachel found herself unable to go back to sleep because those shops were left standing. She had finally dragged herself from her nice warm bed and started making calls.

Santino was nowhere to be found (and Zia had a privacy notice up), so she had left a message for him to meet her at the west end of Gayle Street as soon as possible. Then a call to Sturtevant; the Chief of Detectives might have been used to phone calls in the witching hours, but he had been excruciatingly clear about how he felt about being woken on a hunch. Still, he had arranged for a member of the bomb squad and a paramedic to join her, just in case. Phil dropped by her house to pick her up within five minutes, and neither of them were surprised when the paramedic turned out to be Hope.

Rachel walked into the middle of the coffee shop. She had decided not to explore the space until she was standing inside of it; she missed too much when she relied on her scans instead of walking the scene in her own body.

The air inside the store was stale and autumn-cold, and also somehow empty. The power was off, the only working electronics the odd battery-operated flashlight, the abandoned radio on a shelf in the back room. The digital ecosystem that defined her waking hours had been shaken to its roots; she needed to throw her mind a full block to the south before she pinged off of the nearest working streetlight.

She traced the gas lines from the front of the shop to the rear of the building. These lines were different from those in the building where she had fallen through the floor. There, the lines had entered through the basement; here, they came in through the back wall.

Rachel moved her sixth sense away from the utilities and into the room. Her scans caught on a trash can, full of flies and mold, and churning with life. She winced and shifted her attention to the floor. *Nothing. Could have sworn...*

Her scans caught on the light tracing of footsteps through the dust behind the counter.

Bingo.

"Phil? You're sure nobody's been in this building since Gayle

Street was locked down?"

"You saw that key ring. Of course I'm not sure," he said. "But my best guess? Yeah, we're the first ones in here. This store isn't a priority site. It's out of the blast zone but within the lockdown, and no one's had the time to check for structural integrity yet."

"Okay," she said, kneeling. "Might want to call for a Forensics team, then. Someone else has been in here within the past five days."

"Let's hold off on that," Phil said. "If we are dealing with a potential bomb site, I'll have to secure it first anyhow."

"I can tell when you're lying," Rachel said, grinning at him to show no harm done.

Phil blushed pink. "It's a wild goose chase, Penguin."

"Yeah," she said. "Maybe. But try to walk where I walk, just in case."

The three of them crept through the store to the back room in a single line. "There," Rachel said. "What do you see?"

Hope crouched low. "More dust?"

"Drywall dust," Phil said, his colors beginning to brighten. "Someone's busted up an interior wall."

"Recently, too," Rachel said, noting how the white layer of drywall dust had fallen on top of the ashy residue that had covered all of Gayle Street since the bombing.

The source of some of the dust was a roundish indentation about five feet above the floor. "This was caused by hard contact with someone's head," Hope said.

Rachel, who had seen Hope in a fight, didn't question what she considered to be a professional opinion. Instead, she kept walking towards the back of the store where a trail of dried liquid droplets fluoresced as organic.

"Hope?" she called. "Can you take a look at this?"

"Oh, man." The other woman knelt a second time, and brought the light as close as she could to the droplets without touching them. "Blood. Mostly skeletonized around the edges. Whatever injury caused this probably happened at least two or three days ago."

"There's a piece of pipe against the wall," Rachel said, pointing. "There's more blood on it, plus some hair."

"Yummy," Phil said. "I think I'll call Forensics now."

Phil stepped outside to make the call in peace; the Agents had learned it was harder to ignore distractions without an actual phone. Somehow, an object pressed against the ear helped ground the conversation.

"Some spatter up the wall," Hope said, following the spray of blood with the light of the lamp. "And by the back door... Rachel, is that *blood?*"

Rachel nodded. A black stain had spread, thick and noxious, across the floor and towards the drain in the center of the room. Neither of them felt the need to mention that whoever had lost that much blood was undoubtedly dead. Someone had walked through the pool, leaving a crisp trail of footprints across the back of the room.

"What happened here?" Hope asked softly.

"I think this is where the two cops were killed," Rachel told her. "The timeline's right."

"Why would they be in this store?" Hope asked as she set the lamp on top of a nearby rack of old pastries. A swarm of flies rose in protest, and she waved them aside. "This block wasn't part of the bombing."

"Yeah," Rachel said, following the gas lines again. "But it *should* have been...hah! C'mere," she said to Hope. "Take a look at this."

Hope tilted the head of the lamp towards Rachel, and joined her at a utility panel large enough to be a good-sized doggy door. "What am I looking at?"

Rachel removed a pen from her suit coat pocket, and used it to swing the panel door open. A faint smell of gas wafted out. Inside was a cluster of utility junctions. One of these, a copper tube only slightly thicker than the pen itself, had its two exposed ends hanging free in midair where it had been cut in the center.

"See?" Rachel pointed to the open ends of the copper tube

with the pen. "The gas line was pinched and cut, probably with a pair of heavy-duty pliers. Whoever did this was working in a hell of a hurry. I'd bet they were removing one of those gas storage cylinders."

"Oh shit," Hope whispered.

"Your guess that the blood's a few days old seems right," Rachel said. "Gas dissipates pretty quickly. I think any major leakage would have taken about that long to clear out if he had locked the room up behind him."

"Why didn't he blow this place, too?" Hope said.

"I don't know," Rachel said. "If it were me, I would have punctured the canister and chucked a lit cigarette at it on my way out of the door. Maybe there was equipment failure. Maybe the cops interrupted him, he killed them, and then he panicked."

"Or maybe he knew that if the bodies were found here, they'd pick the place apart."

"Interesting theory," Rachel said, sweeping her scans out again. "But now that we know what happened, it'll be picked apart anyhow."

She went over the bloody footprints, her mind lightly brushing over the ridges which separated the dried blood from the dust. In and out, over and through, a pattern she had seen before—

God damn it.

"What's wrong?" Hope asked her.

Rachel glanced up at her; she didn't realize she had spoken aloud. "Shoes."

"The footprints?"

"No, the whole… Okay, sorry, this might be wordy but I need to talk it out."

"Shoot."

"Here's the thing about shoes," Rachel said to Hope. "In the early days of forensics, shoes were a pretty useful tool. You could tell a lot about a person based on the type of shoe they wore, how they wore it… Sometimes you could break a case if you matched a print to a wear pattern.

"These days?" she said, casting her scans to retrace the light holes in the dust. "Basically you've either got very poor people who wear their shoes until the soles fall off, or not-very-poor people with closets full of them. Manufacturing methods help—most makers will stamp their brand into everything, and it's become so cheap to innovate and produce a rubber sole they can make a new design for every shoe—but there's a tradeoff to that because mass manufacturing means *mass manufacturing*. Cheap to buy, cheaper to ditch, especially if your average murderer has turned on a television set in the last fifteen years and realizes his blood-covered shoes are a one-way ticket to the needle."

"Your Texas is showing," Hope said, grinning.

"No, we'd still hang them in Texas if we could," Rachel said. "But my point is that shoes are nearly useless in an investigation, unless…"

"Unless?"

Rachel was quiet for a moment. "Unless the person wearing them got them from the military."

"Oh hell," Hope muttered, her kaleidoscope of colors catching gray along the edges.

"It gets worse," Rachel told her. "Did you know there's no such thing as standard military-issued footwear these days? Or," she amended. "I should say instead that you always get something when you go through boot camp, but the days of every soldier wearing the same style of shoe are over. The military's got multiple suppliers, multiple types of footwear. Soldiers like me from hoity-toity suburban families never bothered with military issue, either. Our parents usually shipped us something nice which matched our ballistics vests each Christmas."

"So these footprints aren't…I'm not following you." Hope said, staring down at what she couldn't see.

"Well," Rachel said. "There's an exception to every rule. With the military and shoes, it's Special Forces uniforms."

"Oh shit."

"Yup. Everybody's supposed to match when they go on missions. Part of their outfit is a pair of top-of-the-line combat boots. Anybody can buy them, but only a very few people outside of Special Forces wear them. Unless they're civilians with dreams of grandeur," she corrected herself. "Military guys know better. They strut around in those boots, and they're treated as though they're pretending they've earned them. Usually doesn't end well."

"So we're hoping these footprints were left by a civilian?"

"That, and we're also hoping the bullet stuck in the cinderblock doesn't match Special Forces issue," Rachel said, pointing to the far wall.

Hope tilted the light to shine on the pocked hole. "There's no blood around the hole," she said.

Rachel nodded. "Looks like a stray. I don't know why they didn't bother to dig it out of the wall when they left; cinderblock can wreck a bullet, but Forensics will still be able to get something from it."

"I don't like this place," Hope said, glancing warily around the room like a rabbit in an open meadow. "Something is *not* right here."

"I'm with you," Rachel said. The hairs on the back of her neck were itching. "I think we should wait outside."

They left the room as quickly as possible, backtracking through the shop until Hope could close the front door behind them. They kept walking until they found themselves standing in front of the stationery store across the street, as far from the coffee shop as they could get.

"I hate bombs," Hope muttered under her breath. "Cannot stand the ticky things."

Rachel grinned at her. "Me too."

"You're both nuts," Phil said as he rejoined them. "A bomb is more predictable than a person. I'd take an unstable bomb over an unstable psychopath any day."

"What about unstable psychopaths wearing combat boots?" Rachel asked, and told him her theory.

Phil's colors brightened and dimmed in turns. "This is the

best lead we've had yet," he said. "But..."

Rachel shook her head. "It wasn't us."

"Rachel—"

"It's not," she insisted. "The evidence can point wherever the hell it wants. There is no motive big enough for us to do this to ourselves."

A major advantage of finding a smaller crime scene within a larger one was the response time. The nearest Forensics unit arrived within minutes, a team from the FBI that had just finished processing a site three blocks up. Rachel caught sight of a familiar core color from within their group. "Stay here for a sec," she said to the others, and jogged back across the road.

"Campbell," she called to the man with the pea green core. "Got a minute?"

His conversational colors brightened when he saw her. "Peng? They said an Agent had found the site. You?"

"Yeah," she said. She and Santino had assisted Special Agent Campbell on a bank robbery a few weeks back. He was a good man, and the Forensics team he led was solid and thorough. His voice reminded her of Laurence Olivier's; Campbell tended to ramble, and she didn't mind at all. "I came down here on a hunch. If I had thought it was a real lead that would pan out, I probably would have waited until morning."

"No," Campbell chuckled. "We're thrilled. We needed some real evidence."

She nodded. Everyone working the Gayle Street scene was wearing the same gray across their uniform blues, but Campbell's team had shaken most of it off. Phil had been right: everyone had needed a new lead. Desperately.

"Do you need our help?" Rachel said, indicating Phil and Hope across the street. OACET had the authority to freeze Campbell out, but Rachel was well aware Campbell and his team were more qualified to process the scene.

"It's better if we work it alone," Campbell hedged, his colors going a slightly-sick green as he thought about them clomping through his near-pristine crime scene. "Unless you want to watch?"

"That's not necessary," Rachel said, shaking her head. "A note that OACET found it would be nice. For the record, I was the one who broke the front window, and the paramedic and I walked into the back room to check if anyone was injured."

Campbell smirked at her white lie. A certain level of intrusion was to be expected, but it still looked bad on the paperwork. Nobody could raise a fuss if someone entered a site in the best interests of possible victims. "Sounds about right," he said. "I'll make sure you get credit for the find."

"Thanks, Campbell," she said. "I mean that."

She crossed Gayle Street to rejoin Hope and Phil, and the three of them stood around, chatting idly as they waited for Campbell's team to process the scene. Now that the adrenaline was fading, Rachel could feel the cold starting to creep through her suit; she checked Hope's colors and found her shivering.

Ten minutes later, they had invaded the nearest all-hours diner. The three of them had spread out in a booth large enough to seat eight, and were halfway through a platter of hash browns. The hash browns had arrived on a diner-dirty plate, with small scraps of previous meals baked onto its surface by countless trips through a dying dishwasher. The three of them couldn't care less; Hope used a thumbnail to chip off a sliver of old tomato, but it was more for science than sanitation, as she inspected it for a full five seconds before flicking it into a basket of lukewarm creamers.

Rachel used to be picky about food. Well, "picky" was a stretch. Maybe "selective" was a better way to look at it. In the old days, she probably would have sent the hash browns back and demanded a salad on a paper plate. Now, she slathered ketchup on her share and wondered if she could talk the others into adding some ranch dressing.

(Once in a while, she caught herself remembering how it used to be, back in high school and in her easier Army postings, when almost every conversation she had with other women revolved around food. Calories, specifically—one friendship-

ending conversation in particular had caused Rachel to imple-
ment a policy to never discuss dieting, or dessert shaming, or
any personal weight-related topic with anyone outside of the
medical profession, ever. It had been a minor epiphany, really,
when she finally recognized that eating with other women led
to endless rehashes on the consequences of food. And did those
same topics come up when she ate with men? No, never. It was
ridiculous, she had thought at the time, how much energy
women spend resenting energy. But stick a chip in her brain
and fast-forward five years, and food had reasserted its rightful
place as a commodity instead of a liability. Jenny Davies believed the implant consumed anywhere between thirty to fifty
percent of an Agent's daily intake of calories; less for smaller
women than larger men, certainly, but Rachel hated how she
was now as obsessed with food consumption as a supermodel.
It was poor comfort that she was no longer trying to consume
too little, but rather worrying about whether she was consum-
ing *enough.* Food had value again, and she supposed that was
how it should be, but oh, how she loathed the reason why.)

And then she caught a glimpse of a smooth gray core hurrying past the window. "Hey!"

"What's up?" Phil mumbled around a mouthful of fried po-
tatoes.

"Spotted someone I know," she told them. "Be right back."

She pushed open the door to the diner and got hit with a
blast of cold air; the wind had picked up. The person's size and
core colors were a match, so she called out: "Bell?

The girl stopped dead in her tracks, her colors snapping tight
around her to protect her. She half-turned towards Rachel, and
the armor fell away in recognition. "Agent Peng. Hey!"

"What brings you out at this hour?" Rachel asked.

Bell sighed and shook her head. "I lost track of time and the
buses stopped running. I'm just trying to get to a working Metro line before I get mugged."

Whoa, Rachel thought. Washington D.C. wasn't the biggest
city out there, but if Bell was coming from the makers' loft, she

must have already walked more than a mile. At night. And she was wearing another bohemian outfit, more holes than wholes, and was thoroughly chilled in icy blues. Rachel could already hear Santino shouting.

"We can give you a ride home," Rachel said, "if you don't mind sitting through an early breakfast with us."

Bell's conversational colors flared with a gnawing red at her midsection: the girl was starving. A money-green hue suppressed the red. "Thanks, but I should get going," she said after a long moment.

Rachel was not personally acquainted with the starving artist phase of young adulthood, but she had seen it often enough to recognize it in others. "My treat, I insist," she said. "Santino isn't here, but there's another Agent. Phil Netz? He works with the MPD's bomb unit."

The reds of hunger and pride wove through each other as Bell fought with herself. Rachel sighed—she really didn't have the patience to see which of Bell's drives would win—and played her trump card. "Oh, and Hope Blackwell is here, too," she added. "So if you're still looking for donors, this might be a good chance to get to know her."

Bell's mouth fell open and her surface colors went white. "Blackwell?"

"Yeah," Rachel said as casually as she could. Hope's husband might be the reason she was famous, but she was the reason Patrick Mulcahy was rich: Hope was apparently a literal genius when it came to day trading. The woman's net worth was somewhere upwards of fifty million dollars and climbing. She worked as a paramedic because, in her words, she got bored easily and there were fewer fights at home after a twelve-hour shift.

Guaranteed food and the possibility of money? Bell couldn't resist. "If you're sure they won't mind?"

"I promise," Rachel said. "Come on, you'll like them."

Phil's colors lit in blue recognition when Bell came over to the table.

"You've met her?" Rachel asked him while Bell introduced herself.

"Only in your construct," he said. *"I didn't realize her hair was actually green."*

Interesting, Rachel thought to herself. She had been sure she didn't pay attention to faces. If Phil could recognize Bell from nothing but Rachel's image of the loft, then maybe she was better at visualizing people than she had assumed—

"Sorry, no. I didn't recognize her from her face," Phil cut in. *"You nailed her movements and build perfectly, though."*

Rachel snapped their connection shut with a mental snarl. She wasn't sure if she was mad at Phil or herself, so she took it out on the hash browns.

It took Bell a few minutes to adjust to warmth, food, and strangers. She kept her hands wrapped tight around a thick cafeteria mug until she had drunk three cups of coffee so light they were mostly sugar and cream. Phil drew her out; by the time her omelet arrived, the two of them were happily discussing the pros and cons of six-speed manual transmissions.

"So," Rachel finally interrupted when the car talk had reached soporific proportions for her and Hope. "When I was at the loft, Bell showed me this incredible project she's working on for military vets."

Bell nodded. "It's a physical therapy device. It'll take some time to get the system in place, but the potential is crazy."

"Oh?" Hope said.

That was all the opportunity Bell needed. She launched into the same presentation she had given to Rachel, minus the visual aids and with as much medical terminology as she could cram into it; Hope was in her paramedic's uniform, and Bell was tailoring her pitch to her audience.

"That's amazing," Hope said when Bell had finished. "How did you get started with this project?"

"Oh, God, it's so sad," Bell said. "The guy who owns the loft? Terry Templeton? His son was killed in Iraq. He offers free workspace to qualified candidates—students, mostly—and when he interviewed me, we got to talking about medical uses for 3D printers. He's the one who put me in touch with the V.A. hospital so I could get funding."

"*Some* funding." Bell corrected herself as quickly as she could. "I've won a few government grants, but those don't go nearly as far as they did before the recession."

"The economy's starting to come back," Phil said. "It might not be too long before the grants pick up, too."

"Doubt it. The government's screwing researchers," Bell said, squeezing a generous helping of ketchup across the top of her omelet. "It takes years for the science and service sectors to get funding, and when that funding's pulled, it's almost never replaced. Drives me crazy, how the politicians and the military gets everything they want—Congress even gets their gym renovated!—but the science side gets screwed over. Seems like we're the only ones who are trying to do good, but the government's just interested in the bottom line."

"'Government'...I *hate* that word," Hope said. "Such a shitty catch-all."

Bell went bright red in embarrassment. "I'm sorry!" she said. "I didn't even think—"

"No, no," Hope said, waving the girl's concern away. "It's not what you said. I just hate that term in general. I mean, my husband? And Phil and Rachel here? They're with the government, but they've got nothing to do with science or funding."

"No kidding," Phil said. "Every time Congress goes up for a vote, I walk around telling strangers I'm not with those guys. I'd fund your projects over a new military base any day, Bell."

Rachel, who used to wear thick rubber-soled shoes in the shower to keep from being electrocuted by the current running through the metal floors of Afghanistan's repurposed Soviet-era bathrooms, kept her mouth firmly shut. Like most former grunts, she had learned long ago that there was the military, and there was the idea of the military, and these could not coexist within the same mind without a hell of a fight breaking out. She dumped more eggs on her plate, and let the others decide how to run the country.

"But…" Bell was struggling to say exactly what she thought Hope wanted to hear, her surface colors thick with Hope's pulsing blue-black core and wrapped tight within the color of dollar bills. "…if we don't call the government—well, the *government!*—what should we call it?"

"There's nothing else you can call it!" Hope said. "Not without breaking each department down, and that's just not gonna fly in everyday conversation. But to call it 'government'… No. That term's just *wrong*. It groups every person who works in a government office into a single thing, and they *aren't*. The government's not even a hydra with a hundred heads. It's…it's a bunch of poor dudes stuck in the same clown car, 'cause that's the only way they can get to work."

"That's about right," Phil said. "And half of the time, you've got to wonder who's driving the thing!"

Bell laughed, a light, happy sound, and Phil smiled at her. He was slowly shifting from casual blues to a more intense purple, with a thread of red lust. The lust was hard to place; Rachel couldn't remember the last time she had seen it in him.

Phil caught Rachel looking. *"What?"*

"Little young, isn't she?"

"Half your age plus seven," he replied.

"And how old would that be, again?"

"I don't want to ask her," he sighed across their link. *"If she's old enough to vote, I'm just barely safe."*

Rachel tried not to wince. They had lost five years to the Program, and she couldn't quite wrap her head around how she had woken up one morning and had chronologically aged out of her prime dating years. These days, women who should have been attractive had become…girls. Bell was smart and cute, but she was exhaustingly young. Rachel wished Phil luck.

"If you want to see a part of the government that's actually working, I'll take you on a tour of the MPD's Consolidated Forensic Laboratory," Phil said to Bell. "There's an Agent who works there, and he's got the most impressive video setup you'll ever see."

Bad move, Phil, Rachel thought to herself. Phil was cute in his own way, but Jason was haughty and model-sleek, and Bell was still young enough to find arrogance an attractive trait. Best for Phil to keep her away from Jason's lab complet—

There was a sudden thin tremble in the air.

Everyone at the table stopped talking.

"Earthquake?" Bell said, when the shaking had stopped.

"I don't think so," Rachel said, throwing her scans back towards Gayle Street, two blocks over. She hoped she was wrong.

She wasn't.

She felt Phil's scans pulse beside her own. *"Penguin,"* he said, his mental voice almost broken. *"Did we cause this?"*

The coffee shop they had explored barely an hour earlier was gone. She searched the space where it had stood, her scans not finding anything but a fresh rolling cloud of smoke and debris. *"No,"* she told him. *"We absolutely did not cause this. We weren't the ones who booby-trapped the store."*

She didn't mention that it was absolutely their fault for not finding the trap, and broke their link, hard, before Phil could pick the guilt out of her mind.

"Phil, take care of Bell." Rachel dropped her long-distance scans and stood.

"They need me—"

"No." She came down on him with her full mental weight. *"You will see Bell home safely, and then call Sergeant Andrews and tell him to join us at First District Station for debriefing. You will **not** talk to anyone else. Do you understand?"*

There was a moment when she thought Phil would fight her. It passed, and Phil looked down and away. *"Yeah,"* he said. *"I'll take her home."*

"Thank you." Rachel turned away from the other Agent. "Hope? You good to run?"

"Shit. Yeah." Hope threw her paramedic's bag over her shoulder, and the two of them were out the door before Bell could ask what had happened.

They sprinted back to Gayle Street. The moment they turned the corner, Hope froze.

"Oh my God," she whispered. "That could have been us."

"It wasn't." Rachel grabbed Hope's arm, maybe a little too roughly, and pushed her towards the group of law enforcement officers clustered around three men sitting on the ground. Hope stumbled forward, then launched herself into paramedic mode and went to do what she could for the injured.

Rachel turned to the nearest person shouting orders, and waited until he was done before asking, "What happened here?"

"Agent Peng?" Special Agent Campbell seemed to barely recognize her. He had his left arm up and his coat sleeve pressed against his forehead to staunch the blood from a cut on his forehead. "We don't know for sure. We were processing the scene when the back room blew. Did you... You didn't see anything when you were back there to suggest there was a second bomb?"

"No. I scanned that building from top to bottom. There was nothing live in the entire place that could have been a—*oh*. Oh *no*," she said, finally realizing what she and Phil had missed.

"What?"

"There was a battery-operated radio on a shelf, and a big emergency flashlight on a charger. Both of those still had power."

Special Agent Campbell's colors shifted towards reds; her turquoise core appeared within the middle of his anger. "Agent Peng—"

"I know what you're thinking," she interrupted him. "But there was no way I could have known if either of those had a bomb in it. I'm not omniscient. I can tell when a radio has power, and I can look inside of it, but if I don't know what the interior is supposed to look like, it could be filled with plastic explosives shaped to mimic speakers and I'd never know the difference. I wasn't even thinking of looking for traps. After I realized it was a murder scene, I got out of there and called it in."

Rachel intentionally left Phil out of the discussion. Phil did know what a bomb secreted inside of an electronic device would look like, but he had been the one who had gone outside to call for backup. She needed to keep the focus off of him.

Special Agent Campbell weighed her words, then nodded, reds fading at the edges. His own team had been trained to spot hidden explosives: there was plenty of blame to go around. "Do you think someone remote-activated the bomb?"

"I don't know," Rachel said, shaking her head. "If it was hidden in the radio, maybe. I would have noticed if the flashlight could talk back to me, but the purpose of a radio is to pick up radio waves. If it was wired for remote detonation, I wouldn't have noticed anything wrong."

"So it was in the radio."

Rachel turned to look at the speaker, an MPD officer she didn't recognize by either his voice or his core. She pinged the RFID tags in his badge and got his name and credentials: Officer Kerry, out of Fourth District Station. "I didn't say that," she told him. "What I said was that I wouldn't notice if it was. As far as I know, this could have been caused by a landmine on a trip-wire. I went in, saw it was a probable murder scene, and got out.

"I have the ability to talk to machines," Rachel said, hitting Officer Kerry with the cold, soulless gaze that was only possible when the other person had no idea they were looking into the eyes of a blind woman. Almost everyone she met assumed her eyes worked; this assumption, coupled with her long experience in dealing with problems that didn't want to be solved, gave her an unbeatable competitive edge in staring contests. The officer took a step back and turned away, but she kept the pressure on him, moving forward and leaning in as close as she could. "But none of the machines in the store told me they were bombs. I did not presume to check for explosives. I did not think to bring a bomb-sniffing dog. Please tell me what you would have done differently if you were in my place."

And please, she silently begged any higher power listening in, *don't let them remember that a man who works with their own bomb squad was the other Agent with me.*

Kerry finally relented. "Yeah," he muttered. "Sorry."

"All right, then." She took a breath to steady herself. "How many were killed?"

"No one," Campbell said.

Relief smashed into her so hard that she nearly bent in half. "Seriously injured?"

He grinned at her and pointed to his forehead with his free hand. "You're looking at the worst of it."

"Campbell?" she said when she could trust herself to not punch him. "Never do that to me again."

"Try and find the bomb next time, okay, Peng?"

"Come with me," she said, and dragged Campbell over to where Hope Blackwell was patching up his team. She left Hope with firm instructions on how to treat Campbell ("Don't be gentle, and anything you've got that burns like acid in an open wound? Double up on that."), and stepped away from the group to call Phil.

Their connection opened, but he didn't greet her. Instead, she felt a steering wheel under her hands, one foot on the brake, the other on the gas... *"Phil?"*

"I'm taking Bell home," he said.

Rachel wasn't sure if he had meant to add *"Like you ordered,"* but she had heard that thought nonetheless; Phil was furious.

"No one was hurt," she told him. *"Couple of scratches, at worst."*

Phil's sense of relief was stronger than hers had been. Rachel had to reach out and steady herself on a nearby mailbox until the surge of his emotion passed. *"Thanks for telling me,"* he said after a moment.

"Phil—"

"Not right now, Rachel."

She threw some authority into their link. *"Yes, now. How do you think it would have looked for OACET if their resident bomb expert got an FBI forensics team killed?"*

"I know!" he shouted. *"I know the collective comes first! But you think I want to walk away and let you take the blame?"*

"*Chain of command, Phil. Doesn't matter what you do when I'm the one who's responsible. If there was any fault here, it was mine. I should have been the one to go outside and make the call, not you. But no, I was too busy thinking about shoes.*"

Phil's raw anger filled her, and he broke their link without answering.

"Rachel?"

"What?!"

Hope and Campbell each took a step away from her when she snapped at them, but Hope started grinning. "Brain fight?" she asked.

Rachel nodded. To Campbell, she said, "Walk me through what happened before the bomb went off."

"Uh," Campbell said, mildly orange and uncertain. "Everything was business as usual, and then the back room went up. We were all outside at the time, so—"

"Wait." Rachel threw up a hand to interrupt him. "Was *anyone* in the store?"

Campbell shook his head.

"Shit!" Rachel whispered as she turned to face the bulk of Gayle Street. She threw her wide scans out and ran them up and down any building with a direct line of sight on the coffee shop.

Campbell picked up on her thinking almost immediately. "Shit!" he agreed, and moved to rejoin his team.

"What?" Hope asked Rachel. "What's happening?"

"If the bomb wasn't on a tripwire or was activated manually—"

"Oh!" Hope looked up and around. "Remote...uh, detonation?"

"Yeah," Rachel said. "So unless the bomb was on a timer—which I doubt, because I would have noticed a timer—someone had enough control to decide when to set it off."

"You think he waited until everybody was out of the building?"

Shit, Rachel thought to herself. "Hey Campbell!" she shouted to the FBI. "I'll be right back." She snatched Hope's medical bag off of the pavement and started walking. "Come on," she whispered to Hope. "I have to get you out of here."

"I can't leave the scene," Hope said. "You think cops are the only ones who have to deal with paperwork?"

"I think the guy who set off the bomb didn't want to hurt anyone in law enforcement," Rachel said in a low voice as she grabbed Hope's arm and pulled her into a jog. "And you're the only person here who isn't part of that club."

She had expected the other woman's colors to go white, but Hope pulled away from Rachel, electric blue with intent and purpose. "No," she said, searching the street. "I'd *know*—"

Hope's colors shifted to greens, an odd combination of sage and an odd almost-orange lime. Rachel had no idea what those colors meant, and she didn't care; Hope finally relented. "Yeah," she said. "You're right. Let's get out of here."

Rachel nodded, and the two of them fled into the dark.

FOURTEEN

"Ever seen a dead body before?"

Santino's conversational colors glazed over in irritation. "I was a beat cop in downtown D.C. There were very few days when I didn't see a dead body."

"Liar."

"Exaggerator," he clarified. "The guys at the morgue said we went out to collect the garbage every Tuesday and Thursday."

"That's morbid."

"Yup."

Rachel was trying to ignore the elevator. Until today, she hadn't appreciated how the elevators at the Consolidated Forensics Laboratory whispered to her. She usually got out on Jason's floor, but the new autopsy suite was on the fifth; the cab had paused on its way up, asking her without words if she was *sure* she didn't want to get out on the third floor?

She wasn't sure if the elevator had recognized her or if she had unconsciously written a half-assed navigational autoscript for her own convenience, but she was not happy being second-guessed by a machine.

Next-generation technology, she thought. *A few extra processors, and it starts getting a high opinion of itself.*

The cab did not drop sharply to punish her; she was secretly grateful. She didn't know what she would do if an elevator suddenly developed sentience. Or a sense of humor.

Or maybe it just has good manners, that little voice in the back of her head chimed in. She pretended to cough and shook her head, hard, to silence it.

The doors pulled apart and they exited on the fifth floor. The Office of the Chief Medical Examiner had relocated from its old building before Rachel had been sent to the MPD, and Santino assured her the new autopsy suites were spectacular. Almost as good as those in the movies.

Zockinski and Hill were waiting for them at the receptionist's desk, Hill slightly green around the gills. Rachel was surprised; out of the two detectives, she had assumed that Zockinski would be the one who couldn't stomach a corpse.

"Are we late?" she asked Hill.

"Right on time," he said. She smelled mint on his breath, lots of it: Hill had been crunching Altoids to ward off his nausea.

The autopsies had already been conducted on the two officers who were killed on Gayle Street. Zockinski and Hill hadn't caught their case, but Hill knew the detectives who did and had called in a favor. They had made sure Hill could sit in on a second walkthrough of the findings, with both of the late officers putting in an appearance.

Rachel was the only one of their small group who hadn't yet attended an official MPD autopsy, so she had to run the usual gauntlet of forms and explaining to the receptionist that yes, she really was with OACET and no, she couldn't adjust his bank account and make him a billionaire, oh so *very* funny! She would have enjoyed poking the receptionist apart, but he was her excuse for taking far too long to fill out a simple access request. Instead, she played nice and pretended to flirt while scribbling with Santino's gel pen.

Ten minutes later, they were following a harried intern across one of the gross pathology rooms towards the autopsy suites. Rachel spotted a flock of visitors passing the windowed wall of the gross room, peering around and over each other to get a glimpse of the pathologist fiddling with the spot laser settings on a microscope. She was mildly shocked: she had known the MPD offered limited tours of the Consolidated Forensics Laboratory to the general public, but she had assumed that these did not include the autopsy suites because, well...*autopsies*. Rachel poked Santino, and tilted her head towards the tourists.

"Yeah," he said in a low voice. "You can thank television for turning autopsies into a spectator sport."

She was relieved to find that only the smallest of the gross pathology rooms was on display, with the real meat of the organization (so to speak) hidden from view behind a steel-reinforced wall. Rachel sent a deep scan through the wing, and found a long hallway, with rooms off to either side. Most of these were large and spacious, with multiple tables in each. The showpiece was the medical examiners' operating theater, a large semi-circular room with a few levels of stadium seating on three sides. Out of all of the rooms in this suite, only the autopsy table in the operating theater was unoccupied: it was nearly a week after the bombings and the casualties of Gayle Street were still keeping the medical examiners busy. Rachel half-expected the intern to veer off and deposit them in the theater, but no such luck. He knocked on a door near the end of the hall, and then turned and left as quickly as he could.

The reason for the intern's quick escape opened the door, a tall woman wearing a layer of antagonistic reds over a deep red core the color of fresh candied apples. The woman saw Zockinski, and her surface colors glazed over and faded to a muted yellow, with the detective's core of autumn orange wrapped up in a tight ball of red. Even without those cues, Rachel could tell she wanted to be anywhere else but here; the woman slumped in on herself, fingers flicking back and forth against her smartphone as she pretended to have better things to do.

Rachel knew first-hand that Zockinski and Hill could be bullies, but she had assumed they had taken the sum of their anger out on her. It had never crossed her mind that they could have also gone after other coworkers.

"Meet Dr. Kowalski," Zockinski said, his conversational colors moving towards the piercing blues of directed intent, with a point of bright red light aimed at the medical examiner. "She's an old buddy of ours, aren't you, Kowalski?"

Rachel put one shoulder under Zockinski's arm and shoved him out of the way, fullback-style. Zockinski blinked white in mild astonishment as she held out her hand to the medical examiner. "Pleasure to meet you," she said to the woman, trying to put as much sincerity into her words as she could.

"Yeah, right," Kowalski snapped, as she left Rachel with her hand dangling in mid-air. "Let's get this over with."

"See?" Santino stage-whispered to Rachel. "We're not the only ones who can be assholes."

The woman sighed, long and loud, and slid her phone into the back pocket of her pants. "Listen," she said. "I don't mean to be cold, but we're helping the FBI with the Gayle Street victims. It's been six days and we're still backlogged. This is a huge waste of my time—it's not like Officers McElroy and Reeves haven't already been autopsied. This is going to be a lecture, not a discovery process. If you want something better than that, the original autopsies were conducted in the operating theater and you can watch the videos in high-def."

"I was on the team that found the crime scene last night," Rachel said. "I walked the room. I may be able to contribute something."

The woman's jaw dropped, OACET's eye-searing greens and golds surging in her conversational colors; Kowalski might not have recognized Rachel, but she had heard about the discovery. "You're an Agent?"

Rachel nodded.

Now she held out her hand. "Erin Kowalski, Medical Examiner, Forensic Pathology Unit. It's a pleasure to meet you."

"Agent Peng," she replied as she took Kowalski's hand. She expected it to be sweaty and limp, but it was rock-hard from a very specialized type of labor. Kowalski was in her mid-thirties, and Rachel had expected the small frown lines at the corners of her eyes, but not the tattoos that shone across the insides of her wrists and wound their way under her lab coat.

Kowalski's mood was starting to brighten. "I've met the other Agent who works here at the CFL a couple of times. Agent Jason Atran, right? Listen, any chance you can get him to come down here and sit in on an autopsy? I'm got some digital imaging ideas I want to run by him, but he never seems to have the time."

Bonus points for Jason, Rachel thought to herself, but said, "Maybe you can show me how you run your autopsies first?"

"That's fair," Kowalski said, smiling at her. Apparently Santino and the detectives had ceased to matter. "Is this your first autopsy?"

"Stateside?" Rachel replied. "Yes."

"Ah, I see," Kowalski said, glancing at the detectives. Hill's core of forest green was wrapped within a seasick green and an ugly orange Rachel associated with scorn. If context had anything to do with that combination, she'd guess that Hill had tossed his lunch during one of Kowalski's autopsies. Maybe their mutual antagonism had started there.

Or maybe not. Interpreting conversational colors to learn about a person's past was about as accurate as astrology, and the pictures weren't nearly as pretty.

"Faster we get started, faster this gets done," Zockinski said.

Kowalski colored red again. "Follow me," she said to no one in particular, and led them at a brisk walk into the warren of pathology rooms. She stopped before a bright blue door to hand out disposable respirator masks. While the others were fiddling with the straps, Kowalski leaned in towards Rachel. "Just so you know," she said to Rachel in a low voice, "women who have experience with autopsies but who are pregnant may still vomit."

Rachel nodded. Vomiting might actually be a real concern for her. Not because of a chance pregnancy, but because of her weak stomach when in a doctor's office. Autopsies in Afghanistan had been quick and dirty; she had never been in a formal autopsy suite before, and the clinical setting might send her scurrying for the sink.

Kowalski told them to enter single-file and find space along the back wall. Her directions were followed to the letter, as the room was barely big enough for the two pedestal tables and their occupants, let alone five living persons. Despite her best efforts, Rachel felt a sharp pain against her hip as she slammed into the edge of one of the stainless steel tables; Hill must have spotted the body on the table move when the table jerked, as he turned an entirely new shade of green and swallowed hard.

"Don't be scared," Kowalski told Rachel. "They were in the water for nearly two days and they're not pretty, but they can't hurt you."

The two officers were lying naked, one to a table. Kowalski was right: two days in the water hadn't done them any favors. They had been sealed in their car, true, but those small things which lived in water were infinitely cunning. The eyes were almost always the first to go.

Rachel fell into parade rest and moved her scans up and down the two men on the tables. This was her first autopsy as a cyborg, and it was...

It was *fascinating!*

Jenny's diagnostic script had not been designed for use on patients who were already dead. The list of physiological errors kept growing, almost-familiar words forming like a wizard's spell in her mind. *Soft tissue injury occurring in the epidermis, basement membrane, dermis, hypodermis...*

She reluctantly turned the diagnostic script off and went back to her environmental scans. The man on the table closest to her was piecemeal from the neck up. He had no face, no top to his skull, and Rachel assumed that it was his brain floating in the jar of preservative beside him. There was a strip of thick black cord running up the center of his sternum, a rough lacing to hide the damage of his autopsy. He had been shot twice, once at close range to the chest, once at *really* close range to the back. The entry wound on his chest looked like a delicate polka dot next to the cavern of the exit wound beside it. Rachel traced the track of that massive wound through the victim's body, her mind brushing against cold meat and bone until it found the tabletop beneath.

The man on the far table had been shot in the neck. Cause of death had likely been from blood loss; his jugular might as well have been removed with an ice cream scoop. Other than that, the damage caused by his own autopsy, and the nibblings of those oh-so-finicky fish, the officer might as well have been asleep.

"Officer Reeves," Kowalski said, standing over the far table. Her conversational colors were wearing her own version of Jenny's professional whites. "Cause of death, gunshot wound to the throat. No other external injuries that predate immersion in the Potomac. Very straightforward case.

"Now," Kowalski continued, snapping on a pair of surgical gloves. "Officer McElroy is more complex. He has severe cranial cerebral trauma." Kowalski indicated the shattered pieces of the officer's skull. "Injury is consistent with a baseball bat or a similar instrument."

"There was a piece of pipe at the scene," Rachel said.

"That might do it. The head wound would have killed him eventually, but he didn't get the opportunity to die slowly. He was shot twice. I'm reasonably confident the first shot was front to back," Kowalski said, indicating the polka dot. "It was a through-and-through. Perforation of the right lung was the most serious damage caused by this first shot.

Kowalski paused, her colors taking on a slight hue of rain-damp gray. "The second shot was back to front. Based on this second gunshot, the shooter would have needed to be standing over him and aiming down, at approximately a sixty-degree angle. I'm guessing that Officer McElroy was pushing himself up from the ground on his hands.

"This was a man who went down fighting," Kowalski said, almost sadly.

The five of them pushed through a moment of silence, and then Hill said, "A pro didn't do this."

Kowalski snorted. "Are you kidding? These murders are the textbook definition of amateur. Your guy had never fired a gun at another human being before."

"So," Zockinski said. "The officers find our guy in the coffee shop. They interrupt him in whatever he's doing, but he takes down Reeves with a lucky shot to the neck, and then fights with McElroy..." He trailed off as he realized that scenario didn't quite fit.

"Where's the head wound come in?" Santino asked.

"Our guy was waiting for them," Hill said. "Come on."

Hill practically shoved them out of the autopsy room, then took up a position in the hallway on the other side of the door. "You're McElroy and you're Reeves," he said, pointing at Zockinski first, Rachel next. "Go back inside and come out again."

They did, Zockinski leading. As Zockinski came through the door, Hill pretended to swing at his head with an invisible pipe. "McElroy gets hit and goes down," Hill said. "Reeves sees what's happened but doesn't shoot. Maybe can't get in the room fast enough to get a clear shot, maybe he does something dumb and goes to help his partner first.

"Bang," Hill said, pointing an imaginary gun at Rachel. "You're dead."

She obliged by clutching her neck and sitting down on the ground to watch the rest of Hill's performance play out.

"You're up again," Hill said to Zockinski. "Probably reaching for your gun. I shoot you once," Hill said, pulling the imaginary trigger, "and you're down."

Zockinski dropped to the floor, then began to push himself up on his hands. Hill stood over him, his imaginary gun aimed down.

"And bang," Hill said. Zockinski flopped face-down on the linoleum, then held up his hand. Hill took it in a soldier's grip and hauled his partner to his feet.

"That works," Kowalski said, nodding. "Everything fits."

"How'd he switch from a pipe to a gun?" Santino asked. "It couldn't have been that long between when he put McElroy on the ground and when Reeves entered the room."

"There was all kinds of storage in that room," Rachel replied. "If he was waiting for them, he could have had the gun lying on a nearby shelf."

"Then why use the pipe at all?" Santino had started to pace. "Why risk having two angry cops in the same room with you?"

"Because he needed to get them both to come into the room with him," Rachel realized. "He was trying to immobilize the first man who came in, but make sure the second would have time to enter."

"But why?" Santino asked.

"Because…" Rachel mulled it over. When the answer hit her, she gasped. "Because he was already planning to blow the crime scene!"

"What?!" Zockinski and Santino asked together.

She pushed herself to her feet. "He wanted…I don't know what he wanted. But he needed to kill them in that room. He couldn't shoot them out on the street."

Santino shook his head. "He wanted to blow the scene, he didn't want to shoot them on the street… Then why go to the bother of dragging them to their car and dumping them in the river? If he was worried about getting caught, why not just leave their bodies in the store and blow the whole thing?"

Nobody could answer him.

They were preparing to leave when a woman ran down the hall towards them. She had a vibrant core of orchid purple, and had a large Visitor's badge affixed to her lapel.

"You're Sturtevant's team?" the woman asked, huffing slightly. "Good, I was worried I'd missed you." She began the handshake rounds, starting with Zockinski and Hill. "You two are the detectives, right? I'm Elissa Smith, from the Firearms and Toolmarks Unit," he said.

The name of her unit wasn't familiar. Rachel pinged her badge. "FBI?"

Smith nodded. "They brought me in to consult," she said. "The MPD has their own ballistics experts, but since this might be connected to Gayle Street…"

"Right." Rachel understood. There would be less chance of the media calling out conflict of interest over the findings. (Of course, by this same logic, the autopsies should have been performed by one of the FBI's own medical examiners, but people were complicated, bureaucracies infinitely more so, and nobody in their right mind wanted to drive to Quantico for meetings if they could possibly avoid it. But if they were willing to come to D.C.? Speak, friend, and enter, indeed.)

Smith had reached Santino, and started pumping his hand in a vise grip. "I've wanted to meet an Agent for*ever*," Smith said. "Is it true that you can reach the Curiosity rover on Mars?"

"Yes," Rachel said. "But it gives me a hell of a headache."

The woman's conversational colors plummeted. "Oh my God," she said. "I am so sorry—"

"No problem. We get it all the time," Rachel said, grinning to show she harbored no ill will. She didn't: she picked her battles. As long as Smith didn't make the same mistake again, she'd let it go.

"I'm really very sorry," Smith said again. "Wait, are you... You're Agent Peng!?"

Rachel nodded.

"Oh, I have *got* to talk to you after we're done. Did I miss the autopsy walkthrough?"

"We just finished," Kowalski replied.

"Oh," Smith said. Then she asked, "The FTU has some new evidence that might help you look for the shooter. Mind if we go over your findings again?"

Hill froze in yellow-grays and greens, and Kowalski's conversational colors rolled over themselves in an ugly orange when the rest of them replied no, certainly not, any little bit of information would help. They shuffled themselves back into Kowalski's autopsy room, picking out their same places against the wall and then squeezing tight to accommodate Smith.

The FBI's ballistics expert wore a combination of professional blues and curious yellows as she knelt to inspect Reeves. "This is my first time seeing the victims myself," she explained, peering into the cavity where the front of Reeves' neck used to be. "The MPD sent me high-res videos, but there's nothing like a first-hand inspection.

"Your killer was standing so close that the bullets were through-and-throughs," Smith said, her white mask bobbing up and down as she spoke. "Agent Peng, did you see any fragments or bullet casings at the scene?"

Rachel shook her head. "Nothing, but I did see some disturbances in the dust. He must have cleaned up after himself. There was a bullet stuck in a cinderblock wall, though."

"They didn't get a chance to retrieve it," Smith said. "It was lost in last night's explosion. They might find it during processing, but I'm not holding my breath."

Damn. She had hoped that Special Agent Campbell had managed to get the bullet out of the wall before the store was blown.

"So you've got no way to determine the make or model of the gun," Zockinski said.

"Not exactly—Well, okay, yes. Speaking from the perspective of expert testimony? You are correct. There is no way to determine the make or model of the gun. But if the bullet hit the bone, as occurred with McElroy's shoulder—"

"Oh lord," Santino sighed, as his colors began to drop into orange annoyance. "Reversed striations are fiction."

"You're right, you're absolutely right," Smith said quickly. "But we've made some progress with metallurgic engineering and imaging."

"Guys?" Rachel said, her right hand pressed against her forehead.

"Right right right." Smith thought for a moment, and then tried again. "Have you seen those procedural dramas where the bullet is missing, but the scientists take the impression the bullet left against the bone and reverse it to create a computer model of the bullet?"

"That's a real thing?" Zockinski asked.

"No, it's an excuse to use CGI. The science is total bullshit," Santino said.

"It's not total bullshit!" Smith protested. "It's *almost* total bullshit. There's enough of a difference to make it useful, even though I'd never stake my reputation to the findings."

"Are you saying..." Rachel started, then gave up. "What are you saying?"

"She's claiming that if a bullet comes in contact with bone, it'll leave an impression which is clear enough to show the mirror image of the bullet."

"No," Smith corrected Santino. "I'm saying the impression will look like it's been pressed in Silly Putty, stretched, distorted, and then chopped up to take out random pieces. What's left after that can be useful."

Santino's conversational colors had become an unpleasant mix of oranges; Rachel had the impression that her partner was full of rotting citrus. Santino's opinion was not lost on Smith, who sighed, pulled out her smartphone, and called up an image. "Here," Smith said, handing the phone to Santino. "The shot to McElroy's back passed through his left shoulder. We took a high-res *in situ* image of a particular aspect of McElroy's scapula."

The others gathered around Santino, leaning over to see for themselves. Rachel picked the image off of the phone, turning it around in her mind as she tried to find why Smith thought it was significant. It meant nothing to her, a goopy smear of red with fragments of white inside.

Smith seemed especially excited about one specific grouping of pixels. "There!" she said, pointing. "You see that?"

Zockinski glanced over at her. "Peng?"

"Got it." The monitor mounted to the wall above them fizzed in static, then jumped into clarity as Rachel connected Smith's smartphone to it.

"Oh," Smith said. "Okay. Okay, that's better. Okay, you see here?" she said, pointing at the monitor. To Rachel, it looked no different than anything else in the image, but that was specialization for you: education and experience could redefine the entire world. "The size of the wound means this was definitely caused by a .45 caliber. The size and shape of the injuries, in addition to the trace left behind, makes me reasonably confident that the bullets were copper total metal jackets.

"As for applying reversed striations… Well, we didn't find anything clean. The bullet was traveling too fast to leave any significant imprint. That in and of itself is telling—almost every .45 leaves some kind of reversed mark."

"Except the marks might as well be made by sandpaper traveling at a thousand miles an hour. While spinning." Santino said. "It's useless."

"In a court of law? Yeah, definitely. But I'm going to tell you to look for someone carrying a relatively new M1911, one that's been fired about five hundred to a thousand times. That'll be the model of .45 with enough wear in the barrel to rub down some of the factory striations, but one that hasn't been professionally cleaned and permanently rescratched yet. It's the only .45 that comes out of production with a barrel that smooth."

"Fuck," Rachel and Hill both said.

"What?" Zockinski asked.

"The Marines recently switched over to the Close Quarter Battle Pistol for its elite units. It's a custom version of the 1911," Rachel explained. "It's gotten really popular with other Special Forces units, too, so the 1911s have gotten a bump in demand."

"And civilians like it," Smith said. "So it might not be a newly-manufactured gun. It could be a collector's piece. The basic design of the 1911 hasn't changed too much in the past hundred years.

"Or," she added as an afterthought, "it might be an older gun with the barrel swapped out. It's highly customizable."

Santino looked ready to choke her. "So we're looking for a .45 caliber gun, which is probably one of the most popular models out there, and it could be new, but it also could be a century old?"

Rachel jabbed her partner in his side. "Take a walk, dear."

"None of that is science!" he hissed at her. He glowered at Smith, his colors churning as he tried to find a polite response, then stormed out of the room without another word.

Smith took it in stride. "Forensic ballistics is as much about proving negatives as positives," she said. "Drives the purists absolutely nuts. Just don't rub it in that I helped you narrow down all of the handguns in the D.C. area to a specific category of M1911s."

Rachel laughed. "He'll figure that out as soon as he calms

down."

They left Kowalski's autopsy room in a small pack. Kowalski guided them back the way they had come, and left without saying goodbye.

"We're headed to First," Zockinski said to her at the elevator. "Now that we have the general manner of death for McElroy and Reeves, we're gonna see if they need us to help with some real policework."

"Then you better hurry," Rachel replied. "You need to find some real police before you get there."

Zockinski laughed as the elevator door closed on him and Hill.

"Hey, Agent Peng?"

Rachel glanced at Smith as she pushed the *down* button with her thumb.

"I studied the video, the one where you pulled off those incredible trick shots," Smith said. "I've never seen anything like it. Would you be interested in doing a demonstration for the Firearms and Toolmarks Unit? I think we need to update the books because of you."

"As soon as we wrap up Gayle Street, sure," Rachel replied. The doors to the second elevator opened, and she waved goodbye to Smith as it whisked her down to the third floor. It wasn't the first time she had been asked to show off her shooting abilities, and she had expected this sort of request when Smith had wanted to speak with her. Rachel had been at the MPD for less than a year, and she was already renowned for her skill with a gun.

(And for the subsequent frivolous lawsuits. After the video of her shooting a bad guy had gone viral, OACET was inundated with civil suits against Rachel for setting a bad example for idiots with guns. After discussing the first of these suits with Josh, she had let him handle the rest; every time a new one came in, his conversational colors brightened in sheer joy and anticipation. Typically, a single ten-minute call to the plaintiff's lawyer would resolve the situation and leave Josh in a good mood for the rest of the day. The tears of shysters, he said, were mother's milk to him.)

She stepped out on the third floor and followed Santino's cell phone to Jason's lab. The two of them were dissecting a pair of Santino's optical smart glasses, and were deep in an amicable argument over how to improve the design. Jason's computers pressed in on her mind; she swatted them off, in no mood to deal with their half-imagined antagonism, and fell into Jason's desk chair to wait for the men to finish.

Paper crinkled under her elbow; she scanned the desk and found a copy of the *Washington Post*. "A newspaper?" she said, interrupting them. "Jason, please. You're a cyborg."

"Some of us still like to read," he snapped at her without bothering to look up. Santino smacked him lightly across the top of his head; Jason's colors went red and orange, then turned into a mortified blush. "Oh. Rachel, I'm...I didn't mean—"

She grinned and blew him a raspberry, then flipped her implant to reading mode to check out the headline. Gayle Street was still front-page news, but it was nearly a week after the bombings: with no new leads, the story had dropped below the fold. At the top was a news article of an upcoming budget hearing, the subhead declaring that they were about to enter a new era of military funding.

Rachel forced herself to read the first few paragraphs; she felt she owed the Army that much. She had hoped for a puff piece but the article was heavy on statistics. Apparently, a series of Congressional hearings were to take place over the following month to evaluate the current status of the military. The reporter was using that new-old argument, the one where the United States was fighting a new type of war with an outdated military infrastructure, and the country was poised on a showdown between what was familiar and what was needed.

No shit, Sherlock, she thought. She wasn't sure of the exact dollar value of the chip in her head, but she was sure it was a good bit less than an *Ohio*-class submarine. And, unlike the average submarine, it was actually applicable to a cyberwarfare scenario. As soon as the scientists found a way to remove the need for that pesky human element, the technology used to make her implant would revolutionize the military power structure all over again.

Every once in a while, she was glad the collective had decided to go public.

Rachel dropped the newspaper on Jason's desk and went to nag the men about lunch.

The three of them hit a sandwich shop. The women behind the counters knew Jason by sight: the younger ones smiled at him. Santino was halfway through his third-rate meatball sub when the conversation turned to Smith's reverse ballistics analysis. "I can't believe that woman's an expert," he said. "Using distorted data to eliminate possibilities, prove what she wants to prove…*God!* That's the *worst* kind of science snake oil."

Jason put down his sandwich in mid-bite. "What are you, fucking stupid? You and I, we do that all of the time."

"Bullshit." Santino scowled.

"Christ, man. You play with computers and this is news to you? Almost every time I process an image, I build new content around existing data."

"Yeah, but you don't distort—"

"Of *course* I distort the data!" Jason sneered. "Half of the time, it's distorted when I get it, and I've got to twist it around again just to figure out what it's supposed to mean.

"Data's corrupted," he added. "Data's *always* corrupted to some degree… sometimes by context, sometimes by manipulation. When I'm working on a render, the best method is to look at the results and work my way backwards to see how the pieces fit."

"You gonna help me out here?" Santino asked Rachel.

"And crash your ass-kicking party?"

"Okay," Jason said, moving past his orange scorn. "Remember my construct of Gayle Street? That was my end product. I got there by taking pieces of data and extrapolating the rest of the render around it. I'd never take it to fucking *court*, though—

there's no way I could justify some of the details the computer and I generated! But if you're involved in the process, and you understand the pieces, you can build a whole picture out of those parts."

Rachel couldn't resist. "It's not your fault if you don't get it," she said to Santino. "It's not as if you're in a profession where you have to *police* a scene, or *detect* small pieces of data—clues, perhaps?—and then put those together to learn the *motive* for certain events... Maybe use those clues or that motive to find the person who caused those events?"

"Fuck you both very much."

After lunch, she and Santino said goodbye to Jason and returned to their office at First District Station. There was a plastic penguin on her desk. She ran a light scan across it to take in the details; this one was wearing an excessive amount of safety gear and riding a skateboard. Rachel pulled open her top drawer and dropped it inside. Something squeaked as it landed on a pile of its toy brethren; Zockinski's work, she was sure. Ever since he had learned her nickname, a new penguin appeared on her desk at least twice a week.

Rachel had no idea what to do with them. What would probably happen was she'd fill a garbage bag and leave them on the checkout counter of the local Goodwill without saying a word, but that seemed a tremendous waste. She was playing with the idea of waiting until Christmas and conscripting as many uniformed officers as she could find into her formal escort, and marching them in parade formation to the local mall. Then, she would walk up to Santa, present him with a sack full of penguins, and order him in her best drill sergeant voice to *"Give these to the little children!"*

Really, when you had a desk full of penguins, the opportunities were endless.

Her subconscious nudged her away from the toys as she spotted something out of the corner of her mind. An almost-familiar core of tropical storm clouds split by lightning jostled its way down the hall.

"What on—" Rachel sent her scans through the walls. *Yup*, she thought.

"Hmm?"

"Unless I'm very wrong—and I hope I am—Jonathan Dunstan is coming to visit us."

"No shit?" Santino quickly moved his sandwich to the bottom drawer on his desk. Rachel followed his example and started cleaning at hummingbird speed. Even Madeline was shoved behind the curtains for safekeeping. By the time Dunstan was readying himself to knock on their door, the room had been stripped of personality; the only information Dunstan could carry back to Hanlon would be that one of them really liked plants.

"What do you want, Dunstan?" Rachel shouted as the reporter raised his hand to knock.

"I… Can I come in?"

Rachel and Santino exchanged a nasty look. "Sure," Santino said. "Be our guest."

Dunstan's conversational colors were slightly gray as he entered: he wasn't happy about being there. She noted he wasn't surprised by Santino's pocket jungle, and she was instantly furious—anyone who hadn't been warned about such an impossibly stupid number of plants in one small office couldn't *not* be surprised! Someone from First MPD had been keeping tabs on them for Hanlon.

"What do you want?" Rachel asked him a second time, and reached out to the OACET community server to record the conversation.

"This is hard for me," Dunstan said. "I… You know who I… Occasionally, I do some work with—"

"You're Hanlon's lapdog," she snapped. "We know."

Dunstan tried to pace the length of the office as he arranged his words. Rachel watched her core of southwestern turquoise and Santino's cobalt blue trip over themselves within a complicated tangle of colors.

"It's okay," she said to Dunstan in her best false-honeyed

voice. "Just take your time and you'll remember what he told you to say."

He flashed yellow-white in surprise. "I came here on my own!" he snapped.

Liar, she thought, as the pockmarks appeared across Dunstan's shoulders and temples.

"Fine. What is it you want us to know?" Santino asked.

"Nice phrasing!" she said appreciatively.

"Thank you."

Dunstan's colors started to roll with red loathing. "I'm here because I've got proof that Homeland's responsible for Gayle Street," he said. "If you don't want to hear it—"

"No no," Rachel said, launching to her feet. "Sit. Please."

She let Dunstan take her chair, and she and Santino fawned over him for a minute or two before her partner asked, "What proof?"

"I can't just hand it over," Dunstan said. "You know that's not how this works. But…Agent Peng? You know how you told me to think about what side I wanted to be on? Well—"

"Some things you can't ignore," she said, shaking her head sadly.

"Right. We need to bring those who destroyed Gayle Street to justice. So…let's say I got a hot tip about when and how those canisters went missing, and I've got the documentation to prove it. If OACET is willing to commit to going after Homeland—"

Rachel cut Dunstan off. "Don't say anything else," she told him. "Not right now. Not until I've had a chance to talk to Administration."

"But…"

"No," she said, shooing Dunstan out of the room. "Mulcahy or Glassman will be in touch, I promise. This is simply over my head."

"But I just got here!" Dunstan stuttered in protest, as Rachel shut the door in his face.

Santino hummed the *Jeopardy!* theme, exactly thirty seconds long, while Rachel watched Dunstan slither his way down the hall.

"Lying?" Santino asked her when his countdown ended.

"Like a rug made of pants on fire," Rachel said. "I chased him out of here because he was wasting our time."

"Yeah," Santino sighed, his colors a wistful purple-gray. Rachel felt the same: if it had been a normal day, they would have played with Dunstan like cats given a half-dead mouse. "Why the hell does he want OACET to go chasing after Homeland?"

"To discredit OACET, maybe break our alliance with the MPD as a bonus," she said. It was becoming a familiar refrain: she was almost relieved to learn that Hanlon was a one-trick pony. "You and I go screaming after the government, Hanlon wrings his hands and says '*I told you those people were nuts…*' God, what a bastard he is, trying to use something like Gayle Street to his advantage."

"Does that mean Hanlon knows who did it?"

Rachel weighed that idea, then said, "Probably not. Except he doesn't have evidence which might incriminate Homeland—there's no way Hanlon would give us a lead that would actually benefit us."

"What if he's got the opposite? What if he's got evidence which clears Homeland? Think he'd use that?"

"Oh yeah, definitely. Set OACET up to look like idiots, then drop the evidence to clear Homeland? One-two punch for him."

She recovered Madeline and returned the owl to its place of honor in the center of her desk. It was too large for the space, but Rachel had developed a habit of touching it when she was thinking. She reached out to stroke the time-worn wood of Madeline's beak. It had been polished by time and casual hands, and she wondered how many people before her had petted the owl for comfort.

"Did we make any progress today?" she asked Santino.

He shrugged. "We know how McElroy and Reeves died," he said. "And, thanks to Dunstan, we know Homeland isn't responsible, but we can't prove it."

"And we know our guy was an amateur."

"At using a gun? Definitely. But he did manage to blow up an entire street and get away clean. You can't call someone like that an amateur."

Different types of intelligence, Rachel thought, running her thumb over the owl's carved feathers. A person smart enough to set up a bomb, but not skilled enough to pull off the other parts of a successful crime. She mulled that over, then said, "That's what I don't understand—why did he go back to the coffee shop? We had already pieced together enough about the bombs from fragments to know how they worked and where the source material came from. There was no reason for him to recover that canister."

She sighed. "If we don't catch a huge break soon, he'll have not only pulled off one of the top three deadliest terrorist attacks on American soil, but got away clean after the fact."

"Oklahoma City, September 11... What about the Boston Marathon?"

"The Boston Marathon bombings killed three people. *Three.* Yeah, a couple hundred were injured and it shut the city down for a week, but that was the best those schmucks could do with some pressure cookers. Gayle Street is... It was a huge and incredibly efficient bombing, but everything since then has been sloppy. I mean, he couldn't even dump a car in a river properly."

"Additional proof that one guy did this," Santino said. "Just one guy. Someone who was great at building and hiding bombs, and lousy at everything else."

Hearing Santino say it aloud sealed it as fact; Rachel's relief was so intense she sighed and slumped forward on her desk. *I knew this was another set-up. I just **knew** it. I think—*

"Oh shit," she said aloud, as she snapped upright in her chair. "Did what happened in August cause Gayle Street?"

"What?"

"Hidden bombs, set-ups, conspiracies..."

"No," Santino said, digging through his desk drawers as he restored their office to normal. "That's one thing we can be sure of—nobody's come forward to say they noticed a dude from the gas company installing weird equipment in their stores. Those canisters had to have been in place since the last time the gas lines were refitted in that part of town, and that was around two years ago."

"Maybe everyone who knew a different story died in the explosions."

"Maybe. Unlikely, though."

They both trailed off, poking at their own ideas. Rachel dropped her head on top of her desk again, and sighed.

Why is this never easy? she thought. She rested her chin on her closed fist and pulled Madeline towards her with her bad hand. *One guy. Just one. He can blow up a street like a pro, but he can't kill when he's face-to-face with his victims.*

She stared into the owl's eyes, resisting the urge to flick the rest of the yellow paint from its irises with her thumbnail. The paint had been there for fifty years, easy; she had no right to hurry the owl along into entropy.

Entropy... Nothing...

We have no motive. And because of that...

Because of that, their most likely suspect was Homeland.

Or was it? She knew it wasn't Homeland; so did Santino. So did Hanlon. And so did everyone else working the case, really. Even Sergeant Andrews, angry as he might be, didn't consider Homeland to be a suspect as much as an institutionalized barrier to the investigation.

Because we're so fucking egotistical that we think the only one clever enough to pull something like this off is our own government.

"Santino?" She shoved Madeline away from her. "Who benefits from chaos?"

"Hmm?"

"Say Josh is right and Gayle Street becomes the tipping point for the middle class. Who would benefit from the change in the status quo?"

"Oh jeez. Politicians, anarchists, the upper and lower classes, the military... I can give you a historical background and rationale for each of those—"

"Please don't."

"—but it really comes down to anyone who hates the existing system, and thinks it needs to be shaken up if it's to be changed."

"That's what I was afraid of," Rachel said, as she pushed Madeline away from her and reached for Santino's desk phone. "It's time to call my golfing buddy."

FIFTEEN

"How are you doing?"

Santino took a deep breath, and replied with a whispered, "Interesting place you feds have here."

"Don't blame me for this. I would have commandeered a high school gym."

Santino forced a chuckle. He was doing his best to pretend he was Anywhere Else, his hands buried deep in his pockets, his conversational colors firmly set in the crisp window-cleaner blue that meant he was powering through his OCD. As for herself, Rachel was glad her new boots came up to slightly below her knees: judging from the graffiti on the walls and the somewhat sticky stains slopped across the floor, the Department of Homeland Security had leased this site from the local teenage potheads.

In the movies, when law enforcement needed more space for their investigations, they moved to an airport hangar or the floor of the local coliseum. As a staging element, this made nothing but sense: the camera loved the drama of those little specks of character far, far below.

The reality was much less poetic. Law enforcement got what was available. Abandoned big-box stores usually made the top of the list: the rent was dirt-cheap and the size was almost on par with that of the mythical airport hangar—you didn't appreciate how big the physical space of a building could be until the mess inside of it had been removed—even if it didn't come with the same level of visual romance. Judging by the pile of broken crockery swept against a nearby support post, Rachel was fairly sure they was standing where the housewares section used to be.

Brown plastic tarps covered the cracked linoleum floors,

held down at the edges with long strips of silvery duct tape. The residue of Gayle Street had been spread out on the tarps; each site was defined by its address, all materials that might be related to the bombing placed on the corresponding tarps for processing. When a specialist found an overlooked item that might be part of the bombs, it was dropped into a sterile plastic box and whisked away to safety. The rest of the mess was all fragments and stray pieces of what might have been evidence but was most likely garbage: what was left of the barista counters rearranged to show the direction of the blast; the scraps of tabletops and chairs laid out in a parody of seating; the personal effects of the victims.

Too many of those, Rachel thought, her scans brushing across the charred cover of a Hello Kitty day planner. She reminded herself that young children have no need for day planners, and kept walking.

Her golfing buddy had come through. As soon as she had arrived at work that morning, Judge Edwards' office had called her and let her know that the warrant had been issued. Homeland Security was required to turn over all documentation that might help the MPD locate how, when, and where the canisters used to make the bombs had gone astray. When the paperwork had failed to arrive by lunchtime, Rachel had placed a call to a disgruntled security chief over at Homeland. The chief had done some stonewalling, and then done some yelling, adding more than a few veiled threats against the MPD and OACET, and finally ended with several specific insults leveled at Rachel herself. Receiving a warrant was one thing, complying with it was another, and the security chief expressed several interesting strategies she could use to dispose of a warrant issued by a lowly D.C. Circuit Court judge.

After she had placed Santino's desk phone back in its cradle, Rachel started reaching out to every person and organization she knew who was directly involved in Gayle Street. She quickly learned that Homeland had been doing quite a lot of stonewalling: even Special Agent Campbell said his team hadn't received clearance to the site where the evidence had been stored.

(That news had sent shivers down her spine. Campbell worked with the Joint Terrorism Task Force; as such his team was integrated into the Department of Homeland Security. When she had spoken with Campbell the previous evening, she had assumed that he already had everything Homeland had on Gayle Street. Learning that the FBI was as thoroughly locked out as the MPD had caused her to doubt—just for a moment—her conviction that Homeland wasn't behind the attacks. And then Rachel had remembered how the government worked, the closet bickering and in-fighting and territoriality that locked the system into an unmoving lump of frozen parts, and she felt both better and worse about the entire mess.)

Rachel had no problem playing by the rules. If Homeland was going to use perfectly legal tactics to keep the MPD from making progress, she would be happy to waste an hour or two to show them that turnabout was unfair play. By the time she and Santino had arrived at what had once been a booming strip mall, a caravan of forty police cars, black SUVs, and specialist vans were making their way through the back streets of D.C.'s rougher suburbs to join them.

She had marched in through the sliding doors, her new boots drumming a military march against the water-stained floor, Santino beside her, and several other members of the MPD bringing up the rear. The armed guards stationed at the entrance had tried to block them, but the green and gold badge at her waist had its advantages: in the extended family of the U.S. government, OACET was accountable to no one.

She had signed herself into the roster as *Agent Rachel Peng, OACET, plus guests.* At last count, more than a hundred people in all walks of law enforcement had used her to gain access to the site, and more were arriving by the minute.

Now, Rachel and Santino were taking themselves on a slow tour of the building while they waited for a ranking official from Homeland to show up and yell at her.

For once, she didn't feel alone against the world. There was

Santino at her side, of course, but two other Agents were picking through the mess in different corners of the building. Phil was there with Sergeant Andrews and several other members of the MPD's bomb unit, as was one of the Agents serving as a temporary liaison to the FBI.

"Rachel?"

"Phil wants us," she told Santino, and they began to creep around the various teams to reach him.

She was thrilled to see the pops of joyous yellow among those combing through the debris. Whatever had motivated Homeland to seal off access to the evidence had done more than slow down the investigation; it had also broken the camaraderie that had united the different law enforcement teams who were working Gayle Street. Rachel had known the investigation had stalled, but she hadn't realized that the primary reason was Homeland itself.

Sturtevant couldn't have known, she thought to herself. *Just coincidence, how I'd be needed to come in here and break the stalemate. Really.*

Rachel decided to bring the Chief of Detectives a good bottle of Scotch, for no reason. Really.

They crossed the length of the old store to reach Phil. The MPD's bomb unit had taken a position near the front of the building, picking through pieces laid out across multiple tarps. She flipped her implant to reading mode and saw that each tarp in Phil's section had the same address from Gayle Street scrawled across the linoleum beside it in black permanent marker.

"Well, that's not coming off," she muttered under her breath.

"That's okay." Santino had heard her. "I'll remind Homeland to burn this place behind them when they move out."

The men from the MPD's bomb unit greeted them, and Phil nodded curtly at her as she and Santino reached him. He hadn't worked through his anger from the previous night, but Phil was a professional; his conversational colors showed her turquoise core wrapped tight in reds, set aside to deal with later. He was also yellow-white with excitement as he knelt by the edge of a tarp, a thin metal probe in his hand.

"What's up?" Rachel asked Phil as she dropped to the ground beside him.

"Check this out," he said, using the probe to carefully nudge a scrap of melted plastic aside. Beneath this were two sections of small bronze rings, a scorched face plate sandwiched between these. The rings were still bolted to a badly damaged segment of pipe. Rachel scanned the bronze rings and found a layer of broken glass above the face plate, like the protective glass bubble which shielded the face of a clock.

"What was this?" she asked.

"We've seen pieces of these at a couple of the other sites, but this one is the best example so far," he said. "We think it was part of a velocity water meter."

"And?"

"Gayle Street uses external displacement water meters at utility junctions. This type of meter is designed for a private residence. There's no reason for something like this to have been inside of a building."

Rachel stood up so quickly she heard the blood rush in her ears. Behind her, she heard Santino say, "Whoa."

"Yeah," Phil said. "And if we're right and this was part of the bomb, it was probably the arming device. Take a peek inside," he said to Rachel.

She did. Her scans found traces of copper and gold, with the residue of plastic and solder burned to a coarse residue around the interior of the bronze ring. "Electronics?"

Phil nodded. "There was something digital in here. I don't think we'll be able to reconstruct it—there's not enough of it left—but it could have been a receiver, maybe an old cell phone… Something simple, with a power supply. It released the gas in the line, primed the reservoir, and sparked the explosion."

"All of that with this?" Rachel tapped the tarp next to the bronze rings with the toe of her boot. The rings were small enough to vanish under her foot.

Santino shrugged. "The largest component would be the power supply. The rest of the mechanism would take up practically no room at all."

"Batteries aren't that big," Rachel said.

"Batteries are too unreliable," Santino said. "Two-plus years in an active device might drain them dry. They'd need a long-term power source, and those would take up space."

"Right," Phil agreed. "Rachel, when we found the murder scene last night, did you notice anything that looked like a water meter?"

"No," she said, thinking back to the smooth dusting of drywall and ash which had covered the floor. "All I found was the blood and those footprints."

"That's it?" Phil sounded surprised. "No drag marks, no impressions to show where a canister had been set down?"

"No, nothing," Rachel said.

"That's weird," Phil said. "You'd think he would have put the canister on the floor when the cops interrupted him."

"I might have missed it," Rachel admitted. "Hope and I didn't stay there too long."

Phil stifled a yawn. "That, and it was *really* late."

"I miss all of the good stuff," Santino said, half-joking.

Rachel wasn't sure if there was a proper name for the glare that your friends gave you when you reminded them in an offhand way that you were sleeping with the most beautiful woman on the planet—the Germans might have had one, she didn't know—but this was probably one of those times when words weren't needed anyhow. Santino took a step backwards and pretended to fend them off with an open hand.

"Hey, Rachel?"

Rachel tossed a quick scan over to the Hardware section. Joie Young, one of the Agents on loan to the FBI, waved to her. Joie's conversational colors were slowly churning in antagonistic reds and oranges across her core of rich scarlet. *"Bad news?"* Rachel asked her.

"A friend of mine over at the NSA just let me know that Homeland's sending Bryce Knudson."

Exhilaration and adrenaline swept through Rachel. Five hundred feet away, Joie burst out laughing. *"I thought you hated that guy,"* Joie said.

"I do," Rachel replied. *"Oh, I do. This'll be fun."*

Like most things in her professional life, antagonizing Homeland Security had been a calculated risk. OACET came first—OACET *always* came first—little else mattered except the welfare of the collective. Rachel's duties at First MPD had been to make alliances, to bind the police to OACET as closely as she could. She had made rapid progress within that community, and now she was slowly expanding her reach outward to encompass the other law enforcement organizations which worked with the MPD.

The Department of Homeland Security didn't fall within her scope. Not yet, at least. In August, Rachel had fallen deep in the stink over at Homeland, and she hadn't found a good opportunity to pull herself out of it. Today, she had decided to go with the odds: since Homeland had alienated its brethren, she'd use that to OACET's advantage. And, hell, if throwing OACET's weight around could help solve Gayle Street before the country burned itself down? So much the better. They would *all* remember that, even Homeland.

Especially Homeland. If she could get the Gayle Street investigation rolling again, Homeland would have to realize that OACET made a better friend than an enemy.

(No matter the outcome, she did not expect to smooth things over with Bryce Knudson. Even if Rachel and Homeland resolved their bumpy patches, she was sure Knudson would keep her on his personal shit list. She was fine with this; she'd never forgive him, either. That one time they had worked together, Knudson had tried to coerce her into breaking the law in a way that would have most likely cracked OACET wide open, and when she refused to take the bait, he had told the press that she and the rest of OACET were child-killing machines. After things had settled down, Santino had asked her if she was going to have Knudson fired, and she had laughed and said she was looking forward to working with Knudson for years and years and years.)

Rachel and Santino walked to the front of the store, where a catering company had set up a few coffee machines on a folding table. There were some mismatched chairs nearby, but judging by their condition they predated the occupation; when Rachel suggested they should have a seat and wait for Knudson, Santino shivered and his colors ran a sickly green. Instead, they stood around and chatted with the various officers and agents who found their way to the coffee.

The automatic doors squealed open a few minutes later, and Bryce Knudson pushed his way towards her.

If she could still see, Rachel was sure that her conversations with Knudson would have been especially awkward. His head was shaved to the scalp, and Santino assured her that light reflected off of it in a truly spectacular fashion. Her encounters with Knudson usually occurred when he had reached the point of rage, and to her, his head glowed as though it was lit from within. Had she the use of her eyes, she would have surely lost control of their arguments by trying to make his bald dome pop like a tick.

He was bright red now, and shining as though he had been polished. Rachel covered her mouth to hide a smile.

"Agent Peng!" Knudson's low bellow made her think of a bull who had learned to talk.

"Hello, Knudson," she said as she topped off her Styrofoam cup of coffee, her voice all syrupy sweetness. "Can I help you with something?"

Laughter rolled towards them from all corners of the room. Knudson's head snapped around, his conversational colors whipping with reds and blacks, as he realized he was in the center of a group of heavily-armed people who did not think kindly of him.

"Come with me," he snapped, and then turned and walked

away from her, heading towards an empty doorway cut in the nearest wall.

"You coming?" she whispered to Santino.

He shook his head. "If I do, I drag the MPD into a federal fight."

"Yeah," she sighed. "I'll try and keep you out of it."

She went after Knudson, the sound of their feet the only noise within the suddenly silent building. Rachel passed a quick scan through the doorway and found a flight of stairs that led to what must have been a manager's office. The stairwell was dark, the lights busted out years ago. Knudson might have been hoping she'd trip and fall, but the joke was on him.

(Or maybe it was on her—sometimes it was hard to tell.)

At the top was a wreck of a room. Graffiti covered the walls and ceiling. A one-way mirrored window had been smashed out years before Homeland had taken control of the building. It took Rachel a moment to realize why Knudson had brought her up here, until she realized that the pile of trash which covered the floor had been swept aside to make a small clearing near the missing window. In that clearing was a folding table and a matching chair set up like a desk, a desktop computer surrounded by fast food wrappers, a portable clip lamp gripping the edge of the table like a miserable bird… This was Homeland's on-site office.

Beneath them was the whole of the store with its audience of more than a hundred law enforcement officers, all of whom were pretending they couldn't see Rachel and Knudson on what was, for all practical purposes, a balcony.

This idiot wants to feel like he's in control of the situation, so he goes and puts us on a stage? Rachel thought. *How delightful.*

Knudson rounded on her, black and red rolling within a dark storm-cloud gray. "Agent Peng, you had no—"

"Let me stop you there," she said, putting herself into an unmovable parade rest as he came at her and tried to use his size to force her backwards. "I had every right to come here and bring my team and our support staff to assist. We've already made some terrific progress—members of the MPD's bomb unit think they found part of a detonator—and we will share this information with you.

"Because *that*," she said as she took a fast step towards him, "is what we are all supposed to be doing. Collaborating to find those responsible and bring them to justice. Or am I misquoting the rhetoric?"

"You want rhetoric?" Knudson snapped. "Try watching the nightly news. The last few days, Homeland's been tried in the media. They've decided we're responsible for Gayle Street."

"And you think this is going to help?" Rachel gestured towards the floor below. "How is shutting the rest of us out supposed to improve anything? The purpose of Homeland was to promote collaboration, not more territoriality and infighting."

"I don't know most of these people," Knudson said. "I can't keep track of what they're bringing in or taking out. Homeland is vulnerable, Peng. The public doesn't understand what we're supposed to do, and the only time we make the news is when they're screaming about how we've fucked up. If Homeland doesn't control who has access to our information, it could be used against us."

She suppressed the sudden urge to smack her forehead: at least when she had this argument with Mulcahy, her frustration was usually offset by the novelty of riding in a classic sports car. "If you do control access—especially like this, like you've got something to hide!—the media, the general public, they're going to assume the worst. If you collaborate, you've shown how the police and the other federal agencies will back you up. If the media is dumping on you, Knudson, spread the blame around!"

"Because that's worked so well for the NSA," Knudson said, the sarcasm so thick within his conversational colors that the reds and blacks literally dripped. "Let's all thank Edward Snowden for this brave new world of transparency and accountability, and the NSA is finally the super-villain we all knew it was."

"Snowden is full of shit," Rachel heard herself say.

"Don't you fucking *dare!*" Knudson snapped. "OACET is *worse* than Snowden! Every single one of you should be tried for treason!"

"We didn't—" Rachel started, but caught herself even before she saw the burst of anxiety from both Phil and Joie, fifteen feet below. She quickly sent her argument down a safer path. "We came out with as much information as we thought the public could bear at one time, and we were open about what we chose to share, and why. The way Snowden disclosed information, like he was teasing the highlights of a movie? It turned the issues, intent, and methods into the same shitty mess."

"He was one employee. No, not even that. Snowden was a *contractor.*" Knudson barked a laugh. "OACET is a federal agency. At least one of you things should have remembered your oaths."

"You've got to be joking," Rachel said. "When we volunteered to join OACET, we didn't know what they would do to us. Before they stuck all kinds of ungodly crap in our heads, each of us swore to uphold the Constitution. After we learned what they wanted us to be, we realized there was no way to keep our oaths without going public."

"I've heard that story before," Knudson said. "And Manning gave a better press conference."

"Okay, try this: when you have a misinformed public, you get a misinformed response. Can you imagine what might have happened if the press found out what Homeland's been doing here?"

Knudson leaned towards her. "Is that a threat?"

"No, Knudson, but you should ask yourself why you think it could be one." Rachel decided to give him one last chance. "Listen," she said, as calmly as she could manage. "Try and see what's going on here from my perspective. What do you think would have happened if the public found out about OACET through a news site? If they learned about OACET any other way, it could have destroyed the country—it *would* have destroyed America's reputation. Once we found out that we had been lied to about our purpose, we came out to put the record straight. Not because we couldn't have stayed in hiding, but because the consequences of being caught were too high.

"I'm saying the same type of thing is happening here, now. In this building. By suppressing information, you're creating conditions where the outcome will be a hundred times worse than if you were open from the start."

"*If* that information gets out, maybe," Knudson snapped. "But if it's locked down, then *everybody* benefits. The atomic age is over. A bomb is just a fucking bomb—nuke Manhattan and maybe twenty million people get sick and die—but in the digital age, information is power.

"You don't get it," he said, and now his underlying rant was beginning to emerge. "OACET was supposed to be the next generation of weaponry. We could have had decades to establish a competitive edge. But thanks to you, every enemy we have is trying to develop their own versions of OACET, and you know they aren't going follow your false moral code."

"False?" Rachel arched an eyebrow. She had wondered why Knudson hated the Agents, and now she knew. "I am the living embodiment of the surveillance state, and I'm sick of hearing how that means I should have no say in how I use my own technology. Ask any Agent—we're scared shitless of what we could do, so we all make sure we don't do it! It's pretty fucking simple!"

"Don't you dare pretend to take the high ground with me!" Knudson shouted, all cold blue ice. "If OACET had stayed undercover, we could have monitored you. But you know how this works—you know that once the technology is out there, we start getting sloppy about how we use it. OACET may pretend to be all moral today, but it's just a matter of time before you lose that fake edge of yours. Come back in a couple of years, Peng, once everybody is used to you and you think you can get away with doing whatever you want. *Then* tell me how you've never once abused your powers."

"Thank you," she said to him.

"What?" His colors froze; he hadn't expected that.

"I couldn't figure out why you had forced Homeland to close the others out of the evidence," Rachel said. "That *was* you, right? You were the one who made that decision? I couldn't understand why you'd force Homeland to do something that stupidly self-involved. But what you just said told me more about your personal philosophy than anything else."

The anger flared within his colors, so bright she nearly recoiled. Instead, she stepped forward, coming up on her toes to break through his personal space. She lowered her voice so the crowd below couldn't hear her as she pushed him. "You're a coward, Knudson. Worse, you're a coward who's got power, and you're incapable of seeing that other people with power aren't afraid to do the hard thing—the *right* thing!—and reach out and help. Not hide in a hole and cover their own asses."

When she could think again, the first word in her mind was *centiseconds.* That must have been all of the time she needed for her conscious and unconscious selves to go to war, because she very clearly remembered making the tactical decision to take the hit. Instead, she found herself rolling away so Knudson's heavy fist grazed her right shoulder instead of landing on her face.

And that extra momentum tipped her straight through the open hole where the windows should have been.

Rachel reached behind her and grabbed the metal sill with her left hand. Distantly, she heard two separate cries of pain: Phil and Joie were riding her body, and they felt the edge of the broken glass stuck in the sill pierce her palm.

Knudson was standing over her, red and orange and yellow as he tried to decide what to do.

"I am not a problem that will go away because of a fifteen-foot drop," she hissed at him.

He grabbed her arm and hauled her up.

They stared at each other for several long seconds; Knudson looked away first, the professional blue in his colors slowly fading as he realized what he had done. This was a career-ender.

They both knew it. You did not attack another federal agent, no matter how she provoked you, no matter if the agency she represented was unpopular. No matter if she wasn't technically human.

Rachel used her good hand to unbutton her suit coat, and then pressed her other hand against her hip to keep her blood from pooling on the floor. Jenny Davies would never stop shouting at her.

"I used to be a soldier," she said, when she had finally decided what to do with Knudson.

He didn't bother to look at her.

"You want to know why you're wrong? Ask the soldiers. Better yet, go find a commanding officer in the Army and ask them if social networking has changed how they operate. They'll bite your damn head off."

A trace of curious yellow appeared in Knudson's reds, and he turned towards her.

"Soldiers have a voice, Knudson. Do you realize how incredible this is? One soldier asks a question, it gets picked up by others, and soon it's a big thing and our commanding officers have to give us an answer. They have to give us a good answer, one that'll stand up if we beat on it to check if it's true.

"And if they don't? If they ignore a problem and pretend it's no longer an issue? The soldiers won't forget. We remember— we keep it *alive*. It becomes a part of us.

"This has never happened before," Rachel continued, as she tried to ignore the hot red stain spreading up her dress shirt. "There have been armies as long as there have been civilizations, and this is the first time that soldiers have access to some of the same information that their officers use to send them off to war. Yeah, it's a huge pain in the ass for the officers, but ask a soldier if they want to go back to how things used to be, when they went off to die without knowing why.

"You're right. Information is control. It's *power*. But that's not always a bad thing. It's a brave new world, Knudson, for better or for worse, depending on how you look at it. We're all trying to find our way."

She started towards the stairwell. Somewhere down there, someone had some Band-Aids, or a clean sock, or anything, really: she was losing a lot of blood. There was a tampon in her purse if nothing else turned up, but talk about an undignified solution, that stupid little string dangling from her fist…

"Peng?" Knudson said quietly.

Rachel froze. Knudson's tone of voice suggested he was about to apologize; his emotions showed he would shoot her dead if he could get away with it. She looked over her shoulder at him, playing along with the niceties.

"Never lecture me again."

"That better be a request," she said without bothering to turn around. "Because it's not an order. Not coming from you. They didn't just give OACET access to new technology—they gave us the authority to back it up. I walked in here and took over Homeland's precious little playground, and you can't do shit about it, Knudson. If I exist because Congress thought that cyborgs were the only way to force the kids in the federal government to share their toys, then by God and country, I'm going to do my job."

She walked off, telling herself that Knudson wouldn't be stupid enough to take a shot at her when her back was turned, and besides, she'd be able to see it coming anyhow so it was *not* an issue and she was *not* getting woozy from blood loss and…

The hand rail is right beside you if you need it, Rachel told herself, her new boots ringing on the aluminum stair treads as she descended. *But you don't need it now, and you will not fall down once you reach the bottom. Yup, you're perfectly fine.*

The steadiness of the main floor was a blessing; she barely even noticed how the anxious orange of the crowd eased when her feet hit solid ground. Still, she needed to finish the job.

"I tripped and fell out of the window," she said, as loudly as she could without crossing over into a shout. "If I hear any other version of that story, I will deny it, and I'll have some strong words for the person responsible for that rumor."

Above her, Knudson's conversational colors shifted. Not towards the blues, as she had hoped, but deeper into the reds and blacks. He was not about to accept any favors, not from her.

So be it.

SIXTEEN

Santino was waiting for her at the bottom of the stairwell. The two of them began a slow circuit of the room, stopping to chat with each team they passed. It took less time than she had anticipated. Everybody was pretending to be engrossed in their work—there was a lot of awkward orange as they realized they had no idea how to talk to Rachel as if a showdown between OACET and Homeland hadn't just occurred—and she and Santino were able to walk the store in no more time than it would have taken to run in and buy a gallon of milk.

When every person in the room had gone back to their jobs, he slipped her a wad of paper towels.

"Thanks," she whispered.

"Are you okay?" he asked.

"My shoulder is killing me, and I've lost some of the feeling in the fingers on my left hand," she replied.

"Shit."

"No kidding. One more time around the building to prove to Knudson that he didn't scare me off, and then I need to get this looked at."

She made them take another couple of laps, just to be sure, and then they left the building.

"Think Knudson will try to throw everybody out?" she asked Santino as they reached his car.

"Not with Phil and Joie here," he said. "They might not be as rude as you are, but they're still Agents. He's not going to try and pull rank with OACET so soon after you slapped him down."

"Aw, you're so sweet."

"Don't mention it."

She pulled the paper towels away from her skin and prodded

the bloody mess that used to be her left palm. Santino hissed through his teeth at the sight. "That's the worst your hand has been all week," he said.

"Google Maps says there's a walk-in clinic a few miles down the road," Rachel said. "They'll put me right."

"Don't you want to go to the mansion?"

"I can't," Rachel sighed. "Jenny swore that if she had to stitch me up again, she'd dope me up and tie me down until I was healed."

"I know," Santino said, grinning at nothing in particular.

"I'm serious!" Rachel said. "Don't you dare take me to the mansion!"

"I won't," Santino said. "I promise."

"Thank you," she said, and snapped off her implant to nurse a growing headache in peace.

They drove for all of five minutes before she felt Santino pull over. Rachel flipped her implant on and found they were in a run-down gas station, with Jenny's personal GPS waiting a mere ten feet away.

"I will kill you," Rachel said to her partner.

"I know."

She kicked open the door of the car and walked over to where Jenny was waiting. The other woman was sitting in the back of her SUV, with yet another one of those little white plastic medical kits on the floor beside her.

"What happened to trying to keep a sterile environment?" Rachel asked, using her good hand to pull herself into the SUV. The engine was running and the cab was comfortably cozy.

Jenny glared at her through a cloud of heavily-irritated orange. "Don't you try and pull that with me," she said. "Take off your coat. You're going to be here a while."

This time, Jenny was not as gentle when she cleaned Rachel's hand, or maybe the cuts were that much worse. Whichever the case, Rachel had to flip her implant off to keep the pain from jumping from her to Jenny until the anesthetic finally took effect. Then came the now-familiar half-felt tug of thread across her palm as the new wounds were closed, the stitches across the older ones inspected and tightened.

Jenny paused before snipping the last thread, and Rachel felt the quick rush of heat from rising steam. She turned her implant on to see Jenny dump the contents of a large vacuum flask in a metal pan.

"Jenny?"

"Hold out your hand," Jenny said, a no-nonsense shade of earthy brown thick within her conversational colors of doctor's whites. Rachel did as ordered, and Jenny slipped a thick cotton sleeve over Rachel's hand.

Then Jenny returned to the box and took out a roll of powder blue tape.

"Jenny, no, I can't do a cast. I need to use my hands."

"Thermoplastic," Jenny said. *"Used to make casts with variable rigidity. I'm putting you in a light casing of flexible plastic, like a thick fingerless glove. You get to keep mobility in your fingers and thumb, but your palm is going under wraps for at least ten days."*

"Jenny—"

"This is the compromise," Jenny said as she shook the roll of tape at Rachel. *"Your other option is to spend the next seventy-two hours under sedation in the mansion. Your choice."*

"Fine," Rachel sighed. "Although you might want to brush up on the definition of patient consent."

If Jenny was prone to swearing, Rachel was sure she would have learned some new words. As it was, Jenny bit down on her response as she dunked strips of tape in the hot water and wrapped Rachel's hand in warm flexible plastic.

"That's an awful lot of tape," Rachel said as Jenny ended the cast halfway up her forearm and sealed the edges. Her fingers and thumb poked out from under the blue.

"Pretend it's broken," Jenny told her. "That'll keep you from moving it too much. But if you really—and I mean *really*—have to use your wrist or your hand, the cast will bend to compensate.

"Now," her doctor said, as she settled back against the wheel well, "tell me why the nice man threw you through the window."

"Lots of things wrong with that sentence," Rachel replied. "Technically, he isn't a nice man, and that window was already gone, and…"

Jenny felt Rachel's mood fall. "And what?"

"And, technically, he didn't," Rachel said. She let her fingertips explore the new weight on her arm. The cast had plenty of give to it: she felt as though she was wearing an extra-thick sock. "I think I threw myself out of it."

"You think? Isn't that something you'd know?"

"That's the problem…" Rachel started, and found herself unable to go on. Jenny reached over and laid her hand on Rachel's exposed fingers. There was warmth and concern, and quite a bit of love. Rachel sighed, then scooted across the SUV to snuggle up against Jenny. "You remember last summer, when Mulcahy let that congressman punch him? Because it would play better in the news if Mulcahy took the hit and shrugged it off, instead of flattening the congressman into a pancake? I knew Knudson—the not-nice guy from Homeland's name is Bryce Knudson, by the way—was getting ready to take a swing at me, so I told myself to take the hit. And at the last second, I dodged."

"Good for you."

Rachel didn't answer.

"Rachel?"

"I didn't want to dodge, Jenny. I knew it would hurt, and I was okay with that, so it wasn't the threat of pain that got me to move. It was just… One second I knew how things were going to play out, and the next, I had turned to take it on the shoulder, and that extra momentum tipped me out of the window."

Jenny's colors went yellow-orange in confusion. "I don't understand."

"I know. No offense, but you're not a fighter. Think of it like chess, where sometimes you have to take a beating to win, but…but today I couldn't."

Jenny wrapped her hands around her knees. "I see."

"I don't know if you do. When I'm in a fight, I need to trust myself. *All* of myself."

"Oh. Oh!" Jenny said, finally understanding. "You think your implant drove you to move?"

Rachel nodded, picking at the edge of the blue tape covering her knuckles. "In the Army, they say that success in physical combat is the outcome of instinct and training. If something is overriding my training—if something *inside* of me is overriding my training…"

Jenny propped her chin on her knees, and her conversational colors weighed themselves against each other as she evaluated what Rachel had said. "How big is Knudson?" she asked.

"Huge. Not Mako-huge, but he's over six feet and probably weighs in at 225 or more."

"Okay," Jenny said. "There's a difference between a 65-year-old congressman and a combat-trained Homeland agent. And there's also a significant size difference between you and Mulcahy. He was much less likely to get hurt than you were, no matter who punched him. Agreed?"

"Agreed."

"Now, let me see that shoulder."

There was no escape; Jenny had already seen the tissue damage. Rachel pulled down the neck of her dress shirt until her right shoulder poked out. Jenny pressed down on Rachel's skin with the ball of her thumb, then watched the blood move through Rachel's flesh with a clinical eye.

"So?" Rachel asked.

"If I didn't know better, I'd have said you were hit with a sixteen-pound bowling ball," Jenny said. "What on earth did you say to him?"

"Little of this and that."

"Right. Well," Jenny said, "if you want my advice—and you should, because I'm the most brilliant physician you'll ever meet—your last-second escape kept you from taking a punch that could very well have killed you. If this was caused by a glancing blow to the shoulder, I can't even imagine what type of brain damage you might have sustained from a direct one to the head."

Rachel's heart sank. She found herself staring through the floor of the SUV at the asphalt below.

Jenny caught her mood. "What's wrong?"

"The implant protected itself."

"What? No. Don't jump to conclusions. There are several reasons why you're probably wrong. First, you're assuming you lack common sense, and while recent events might prove you right," Jenny said, poking Rachel's new cast, "I'd still put good money on the likelihood you changed your mind about playing the martyr when the big, angry man took a swing at you.

"Next, I've been working on my biofeedback research for months. I have terabytes of data on how the implant affects physicality, and I have found nothing to suggest that it can take control of our bodies. Help us improve how we use them? Yes. Take control of them? Absolutely not.

"Finally? There's nothing in that data to suggest the implant can think for itself. Even if it did give you that last mental nudge you needed to make you move out of the way—and I strongly doubt that happened—you had probably already come to that same decision subconsciously. Yeah, 'you' may be plural there, but that's what we are, now. Plurals. In a symbiotic relationship, there is nothing selfish about keeping the both of you alive and well."

"Except when it's in conflict with what I have to do," Rachel said aloud, and then opened a link with Jenny as their conversation turned to the inner workings of the collective. *You think I enjoy slicing myself up? My job's not a nice one—I go up against some hard people, and I have to do it in a way which makes OACET look good. I* **wanted** *Knudson to hit me. I was antagonizing him so he'd slug me in front of a hundred witnesses, and they'd all go back to their respective departments and spread the story that the big bad man from Homeland was beating up on the tiny woman from OACET.*

"Isn't that what happened?"

"Say again?"

"Is anybody in that room going to tell a different story? I mean, didn't he hit you so hard you fell out of a window?"

Shit, Rachel realized. *That's exactly what happened.* She flipped off her implant, and in her mind there was nothing but the sun.

"Penguin?" Jenny said softly. "Where did you go?"

Rachel took a deep, slow breath. She was going to break her vow about whining in front of her doctor, she just knew it… She pulled herself together and reactivated her implant, and Jenny flooded back into her head.

"What's wrong?"

She tried to look at Jenny and couldn't. Her vision was like breathing, really; it worked when she didn't think about it, but if she concentrated on how, and when, and why? That left her gasping.

Rachel shied away from Jenny as she held out her hands.

"I can't," she said aloud.

"You can," Jenny told her, and took Rachel's injured hands in her own.

There was an almost-familiar tug of emotion as Jenny drew her out. Their walls might be different, but everyone in OACET had experience in building them…and in taking them apart. The presence in her mind that was Jenny stepped into Rachel, just a little bit, just enough to learn if she was welcome to enter Rachel in something more intimate than a conversational link.

She was.

"Do you remember how I damaged my eyes?" Rachel asked her.

Jenny nodded; Rachel felt the motion as if she had been the one to move, and had to steady herself. *"Yes,"* Jenny said. *"But you never told me the reason why you—"*

*"Why I decided to stare at the sun for two days? I couldn't tell you, because I don't remember why. It just happened. Like dodging Knudson—it just **happened**!"* Her mental voice broke on the last word. She wasn't crying; she was long past mourning what had been lost. But she was terrified of what else she might lose,

and went willingly into Jenny's arms as she rocked Rachel like a child.

"*I don't remember!*" Rachel's voice floated in their shared space. "*I crippled myself, and I can't even remember why! I can't live like this. There's me, and then there's this thing in me, and if it's what's driving me...*"

"*...then what else might it make you do?*" Jenny finished for her.

Rachel nodded, her worst fear sounding somehow more real as the other woman gave it life. She was shaking so hard her teeth rattled together, and every time she tried to pull away, Jenny hugged her close and blanketed her mind in her warmth and strong waves of positive emotions—*safety, belonging, love*—as she let Rachel's panic attack burn itself out.

It didn't take long. This particular fear had left a well-worn track in Rachel's mind, and she had nearly a year's worth of practice in wrestling it to the ground. It took a few minutes for the tremors to stop, to push away from Jenny and give her an embarrassed half-smile. "Sorry."

"*Stop that,*" the other woman said. "*Come here.*" Jenny reached out and gathered Rachel to her again. There was a long moment of tension, and then Rachel let herself relax.

Her nose was running, she noticed; Jenny was good enough to not mention the shiny wet spots Rachel had left on the knees of her jeans. Rachel grabbed the bloody towel off of the floor and smeared her face across it, like a toddler rubbing her nose on her favorite stuffed animal. "God, I'm such a wreck."

"*If it makes you feel better,*" Jenny replied, "*you lost your eyesight before your implant was fully activated. It's what I was telling you about when the physical changes from biofeedback started. They occurred after full activation, not before—the implant had nothing to do with your going blind.*"

Rachel laughed so hard she nearly started crying. "*How is that better?*" she asked Jenny. "*How could that possibly be better if it means I went blind because of* **me**?"

"*Because the implant can't be removed,*" Jenny said, brushing

Rachel's short hair back from her forehead. *"Not without killing us, which means if it causes us any problems, we're stuck with those forever."*

"But if the problem is…if it's me…" Rachel started, but couldn't find a way to end that thought. There was relief within it, but also the closing of a door she had wanted to keep open.

Jenny shut it for her, gently. *"If it's you, the problem can be diagnosed and managed. It'll take time, and you'll have to live with the knowledge that you screwed up your own eyesight, but this is something that is within your control."*

"Jenny, this is so far from something I can control—"

"It feels hopeless," Jenny whispered. *"I know."*

If they hadn't been linked, it would have been a throwaway comment—*I know*—two words used so often, so carelessly, they could stand as a period at the end of a sentence. But in a link, they were as true a thought as Rachel had ever heard.

And then Jenny let down her walls.

They were no longer neophytes at this: Jenny didn't allow Rachel to plunge into her own mind, nor did Rachel step into Jenny unaware. The two of them shared a long measured moment on the periphery of her being, and then they both entered the eternal sense of self that was the core of Jenny Davies.

Fear, hidden deep below Jenny's professional whites, flooded her. She—Jenny and Rachel, one person, at least for the time being—was lost within *potential*. Not just people, not even the newness of energy and semi-sentience coming from machines. No, the first she could manage through her education and training, while the second would require time and experimentation. But the balance of the unknowable, that soft space that took her mind from her, like looking up at the stars, like floating weightless in an infinite ocean… *That* was beyond her ability to understand. It tipped in on itself and blew her away… It would be better had she been nothing, meaningless, but no, she existed. Those things that were, they weighed her worth, and found her valid.

Valid, but small. Small in the way of atoms, molecules—

Did cells deserve names?

(God help her—God, please let her escape from all of it—there's too much of it—please)

She was standing in the medical lab. The collective was upstairs and all around her, and here, in this room, she was safe. Here, that humming that was infinity was almost silenced, and these new senses which let her feel the constant churn of things living and dying were sated by the data. Here was where she let the raw materials of her research run through her mind. Data was clean. Data could be unlocked. She could find the patterns within it, she could put those patterns to use, and then, finally, she might learn what she was—what *they* were—becoming.

"*I barely sleep any more,*" Jenny said. Rachel heard her from a distance, still lost in Jenny's memories of the struggle to understand that which was completely familiar and unimaginably alien, all at once. "*Every day, I learn more about what we might be able to do and it terrifies me, because I don't know if we have enough capacity to go along with this much ability. I can barely talk to anyone outside of the collective, because when I'm not at the mansion, I can't stop thinking about the size of it all...*

"*But I do know this,*" Jenny said, her mental voice absolute. "*I do know that my obsessions aren't caused by the implant. They're how my mind has decided to cope with what they did to us. Trauma—years of trauma—doesn't go away overnight. And I think a good way to go crazy is to start blaming the implant for the after effects of abuse. It's stuck in our heads, and it's not coming out. We have to learn how to live with it, not use it as an excuse for problems that we'd still need to deal with if we didn't have it.*"

They pulled apart, body and mind, and Rachel scrubbed her fingertips against the carpeted floor of Jenny's SUV to ground herself. She felt the gritty residue from feet and food buried within the rough weave, the hidden pebbles of grit which climbed up under her nails...

"I'm so sorry," Jenny said in a hoarse voice, as she wiped away her tears with the collar of her blouse. Guilt was starting to run through her surface colors, like drops of blood in water. "My therapist told me I needed to drop most of my projects. Yours—your vision—it was one of them. I had to triage… So I dropped those that weren't related to everybody's health, and…"

"I know," Rachel said. The concrete under the car was ancient and worn, lacquered over by layer after layer of thin rubber. "I know."

Jenny's hard sadness clung to Rachel; she kicked herself for not realizing why Jenny was always at the mansion when she dropped by. Jenny was always available—Jenny was always *there*. And Rachel was so self-centered she has assumed that was how things should be. It was her turn to reach out, to take Jenny into a hug, and entwine the fingers of her good hand through both of hers.

"Who's your therapist?" she asked Jenny.

"Margaret."

"How'd she finally get you to stop pushing yourself to exhaustion?"

Jenny sighed. *"It was easy. She came down to the lab and said she wanted to monitor my work day. After sixteen hours, I started nagging her to go home and go to bed. I finally caught on when she started suffering from sleep deprivation."*

They sat, holding each other and their shared emotions. Their walls were back up, but there was no need to talk, so their link was mostly images, with scraps of thought blowing around and occasionally brushing against their shared consciousness.

"You want to know what gives me hope?" Jenny finally asked.

"Sure."

"The collective. You, me…everybody. **Us.** *We can all share each other, and be part of each other, and we know beyond any doubt whatsoever that everyone else in the collective is completely screwed up. And I still can't tell when I'm doing something self-destructive. Not until it's too late.*

"That," Jenny sighed, *"is such a perfectly normal human failing, I know I'll be okay."*

Rachel roared with laughter.

Later, she stepped down from Jenny's SUV and rejoined Santino in his tiny hybrid. She was feeling better than she had in a long, long time.

As soon as she closed the door behind her, Santino broke her good mood apart. "Good news," he said. "They found the gun that killed McElroy and Reeves. Fished it out of a storm drain a block away from Gayle Street."

"The hell?" Rachel was dumbfounded. Anyone with common sense and a television knew better than to toss their gun down a storm drain.

"I know, right?"

"Model?"

"M1911," he muttered. "So...yeah." Santino started the car and began to pull into traffic. He jammed on the brakes as he finally noticed her face, his conversational colors going wine red in sympathy as he read what had happened in the SUV.

"Do you want to talk about it?" he asked.

"No," she said, and then remembered that she was with Santino. "Yes."

She started at the point in the story where Knudson swung at her, and then gave an abbreviated version of what Jenny had said to her about their implants. Not about Jenny's own situation, of course; that story wasn't hers to tell. But Rachel did mention, in an almost off-hand way, that she had been worried about Santino finding her cold body in the garden one morning, her gun or a bottle of pills beside her and no note anywhere in the house.

"It's not that I *want* to," she said, trying to reassure him, knowing she couldn't. "I'm not even considering it, and I'm... I'm actually happy with my life right now," she realized. "I just don't know if I can trust myself. Not completely."

Santino's colors were weaving in and out of themselves as he finally turned the car into the street. She saw her turquoise core bound within the separate reds of worry and love, as he tried to find something to offer her.

"Zia has nightmares," he said.

She looked over at him.

"Screaming nightmares," he added. "I think it's night terrors. Every time I stay the night, she'll wake up and have no idea where she is, or who I am. She thinks it's three years ago, and she's still living in her apartment in California.

"And when she finally remembers me, she can't stop crying. Her heart beats so fast, I don't know why it hasn't given out."

"You shouldn't be telling me this. If Zia wanted me—"

"She's getting better," Santino said, his words riding over Rachel's. "She still wakes up screaming, but it's getting easier to calm her down. After I do, she can go back to sleep. That's new—she used to spend the rest of the night awake, pacing."

"Santino—"

"You guys are making progress. If, deep down, you're headed towards putting a bullet through your own brain, then why did you bother to throw yourself out of the way of Knudson's punch?"

She slumped to the side and pressed her forehead against the window.

"I'm waiting."

"Shut up." She was exhausted: for once, she almost meant it.

"See, it's that level of maturity that's gotten you to where you are today."

"Swear to God, Santino…"

"All I'm saying is, you should trust your instincts a little more." He looked over at her and grinned. "You're the only one who doesn't."

SEVENTEEN

"What do you see?" Santino asked in her head.

Her scans pinged on red. Angry, frothing red.

"Nothing good," she replied.

Jonathan Dunstan's byline was getting a lot of mileage over the past week, and this morning's news article was his most incendiary thus far. The reporter had gone live with a story quoting a certain anonymous someone who was active in Congress, and who claimed that evidence implicating U.S. Special Forces had been recovered from the scene where the two officers had been killed. That same someone had then indicated the Department of Homeland Security had intentionally locked local and federal law enforcement out of the investigation. Dunstan's article had concluded with a statement from a certain anonymous someone, who had suggested a large spontaneous gathering on the lawn of the National Mall would be proof of the unbreakable spirit of the American public in the face of government oppression.

Rachel hoped that a certain anonymous someone would die in a fire.

She supposed she was undercover, wearing a white windbreaker with a huge marinara sauce stain across one arm, and her rattiest pair of jeans. Fifty feet away from her, Santino was in a Caltech sweatshirt old enough to date back to the first time he had done his own laundry. Zockinski and Hill were similarly dressed, and Rachel thought that anybody watching for undercover cops would just have to look for the slobs.

When Sturtevant had heard about the demonstration, he ordered them to get down to the Mall and see what they could learn. They were each working the crowd in their own way, trying to get a read on the city's rising tension. Rachel was looking for happy people. Not the rich purples of general happiness or those rare sun-bright bursts of pure yellow joy, but the smug pink of things going according to plan. (Her search was not going well: if she struck up one more conversation with someone who wanted her to convert her bank account to gold or bitcoins, she was going to have to find a place to dump a body.) She was keeping a firm lock on Santino's smartphone, just in case—she did not like all of the red around her, the traces of hard black surrounding it...Rachel had been in more than her fair share of riots, but this was going to be her first as a cyborg. When she turned off the emotional spectrum, the crowd was scary but familiar; with the emotional spectrum on, it was *terrifying*. Red whipped from person to person, a shared aura that fed on itself, growing ever stronger.

All it would take was one rock.

She would have pulled the men out if they hadn't been with the MPD. The hero worship that came and went for city cops was at an all-time high; the two murdered officers had convinced the crowd that there was Homeland, and then there was everyone else. If they had known this before they had come down to the Mall, they would have been wearing uniforms like armor. As it was, Santino, Zockinski, and Hill wore their badges on thin ribbed chains around their necks like talismans, and told anyone who asked that they were off-duty and were here to show their support.

Her own badge was tucked beneath her windbreaker. OACET wasn't part of Homeland, but she didn't want to explain the fundamentals of federal agency alignments to strangers while they tried to stomp her skull open.

She was relatively close to the Reflecting Pool, but too far from the Lincoln Memorial to hear the speaker: Homeland had gotten news of the flash mob and had decided to turn it into a public relations event. On the steps of the Memorial, a spokesman from Homeland was sharing the podium with politicians, policymakers, and the odd and angry representative from the MPD. When Rachel rode the signals coming from the news crews, she could hear the speaker from Homeland reassuring the crowd that despite all evidence to the contrary, they were not responsible for the tragedy on Gayle Street.

Nobody was buying it.

The noise bothered her: there should have been more of it. Not that the crowd was silent, but this far back from the podium, most of them had their eyes and ears buried in their smartphones. Easier to watch the live feed from the local news stations than to elbow their way into ringside seats.

Rachel had seen many a freaky thing over the years, but she had bumped some of them down the list to make room for a mob mentality taking place on variable delays: some of the news feeds were instantaneous, others had a one-, two-, or three-second pause, and the flares of red within the crowd went up like timed explosions. It was eerie, and she was pretty sure that being hooked into a live feed couldn't help but make a bad situation worse.

"Hey."

The word was aimed at her, and Rachel sent a fast scan around to locate the speaker. He was a man with a core of white lilac and surface colors picked out in red (of course), but with red lust stampeding its way across the anger. *Terrific*, she thought. *Trust me to attract the perverts.*

"What?" Santino asked.

Rachel winced; she had forgotten she was maintaining an open connection to Santino's phone. *"Nothing,"* she told her partner. *"Some dude's decided an impending riot is a great way to pick up chicks."*

"Well, yeah. That's how my parents met," Santino replied. "Call me back."

Their connection broke as Santino hung up. Rachel ran the man's features and came away with a man in his mid-twenties with little in the way of a chin.

"Hey," she replied, pretending to notice him.

"Lost in thought?" he said, grinning.

"Just…" Rachel swept out her left hand, palm up, to take in

the crowd. "It's so scary, you know?"

He took the bait. "Oh man," he said, seeing her cast. "What happened to you?"

She quickly pressed the palm of her cast against her chest and dropped her eyes to the ground.

"Gayle Street?" he asked quietly.

When she nodded, his colors turned over, the lust dipping into the wine reds of sympathy and empathy. "I'm sorry," he said. "Are you okay?"

Fuck, she thought. It was always harder to play them when there was a nice guy under the pickup artist: her guilt got in the way.

Harder, but not impossible. "Yeah, I'm okay," she whispered, letting her shoulders and the tilt of her head tell him she was not okay, no, she was not okay at all.

He reached out to try to catch her in a hug. "I'm sorry," Rachel said in a wet sniff, stepping out of reach. "I just… I can't. Not right now." *Not when you're sure to notice my vest and gun.*

He took a step back, nodding. "Are you here alone?" he asked.

Rachel's Texas accent was always right under her tongue. "I'm in town on business," she said, letting her drawl run through her words. "I didn't expect to be here this long, but the police want anyone who was on Gayle Street to stay close."

"And you decided to come to the rally?"

She looked down, not allowing her body language to cue him in to what she was thinking: no point in reading the crowd if the crowd just regurgitated what you wanted to hear.

"Come with me," he said. He made a path for them through the crowd, using his elbows to nudge aside those immersed in their phones. Rachel followed him to the edge of the Reflecting Pool, where he found some unoccupied space along the concrete coping. He sat, and patted the ground beside him.

Good choice, she admitted. During a stampede, sitting was only slightly better than lying down, but her new buddy had put them in a location with a variable wall. True, they might get a little wet if they had to retreat into the Pool, but she'd rather be damp than dead.

She settled herself beside him and looked around. "Is something about to happen?" she asked, as if she were slightly slow.

"They're pissed," he said. "Just look at them."

Interesting. She supposed nobody liked to think of themselves as part of a mob, but he seemed to embrace the difference; his conversational colors were slowly leaking reds as he picked up traces of her turquoise core.

"They're tired of the same shit," he said. "This is new. This is totally new."

"What do you mean?"

He shrugged. "I live in D.C. We've got a different protest or political rally every other day. My friends and I play a game, where we guess the cause based on the people. Old white guys? Republicans or Tea Partiers. Kids in a drum circle are usually Occupy Wall Street or some liberal shit like that. But…" he said, craning his neck to look up and around them, "…this is different. This is *everybody!*

"I'm Jamie," he added.

She gave him a weak smile. "Phyllis."

"Really?"

"Really." Rachel didn't have to feign her sigh: Phyllis was her much-hated middle name. "Why is this different?"

The angry reds in Jamie's conversational colors returned; he began to blend in with the rest of the crowd again. "We're sick of it! Aren't you?"

"Sick of what?"

"The *lies!* Don't you watch the news? Homeland bombed Gayle Street! We need to do something. We can't let them manipulate us like this!"

And now he's decided he's part of the general American public again. This guy's a mental mess, and I think he could represent the entire freakin' status quo.

As Jamie rambled on, Rachel pretended to inspect her hands. Behind her, the crowd was reaching a fever pitch; she wished she was capable of splitting her attention between the speaker and dear Jamie, but she was one of those Agents who had to pick her target. Her cop's brain was telling her to stick with Jamie, who was spewing public opinion like he was hooked up to a garden hose.

"What do you think we should do?"

She had spoken so softly that Jamie nearly missed it. When he realized what she had said, he replied, "Anything! Don't you think that anything is better than this?"

Spoken like an asshole who's never seen war outside of a screen, she thought, but said nothing.

"Listen," Jamie said, leaning towards her. "Aren't you sick of this shit? Every week, we learn how they're fucking us over in new and exciting ways. They're spying on us, they built fucking cyborgs that can take control of any machine we own… That was bad. That was really bad. But now… You were on Gayle Street. They did that. They did that to you. They tried to *kill* you, Phyllis! Don't you understand? We have to draw the line, 'cause if we don't, they'll know they can get away with anything.

"You see these people?" Jamie pointed. "Someone sent out a tweet three hours ago and said we should flash the Mall. And how many people showed up? A thousand? Five thousand? We let it go on too long. Gayle Street was our fault. You got hurt because we didn't care enough to fight back."

"This was a triumph…I'm making a note here: Huge success…" The sweet electronic voice of a mostly-dead computer chimed in her mind: Santino was calling.

She opened the connection, but before she could greet him, she heard her partner shouting: "Where are you?!?"

"By the Pool. What's—"

"Southeast, near the World War II Memorial."

Rachel stood and threw her scans out. She didn't have to go far; a tidal wave of red was cresting as it rolled towards her.

"Oh hell," she said quietly. *"Santino? Tell me you're gone."*

"I'm safe. Zockinski's with me. We're joining up with the uniformed MPD, but we can't find Hill."

"I'll get him," she promised.

"Stay safe," Santino said before he hung up.

Beside her, Jamie was on his feet, his posture mimicking hers as they both looked towards the Memorial. "What's up?" he asked her. "Do you see something?"

"Jamie?" She tossed her Phyllis persona aside, as she moved her right hand under the back of her stained windbreaker to make sure she had ready access to her gun. "Get into the Pool and stay there until the danger's over."

An ugly orange scorn moved into his conversational colors: Jamie did not take kindly to being ordered around. He started to protest, and Rachel hit him with a full-on cyborg stare.

Jamie was knee-deep in the Pool before Rachel allowed him to look away.

When he recovered enough to glance up at her again, she gave him a quick wink, then walked into the crowd as the riot broke over her.

Elbows, torsos, shouting, red. She bobbed and weaved like a boxer who wouldn't throw a punch. No one cared about her, a small woman among thousands, as they pushed to reach the podium. As long as she kept her head together and stayed on her feet, she'd be fine.

Bodies flew past her, nearly crashing into her; once, Rachel used a man's bent knee as leverage to push herself up and over him to land on the far side. *Damn,* she thought, as she dropped lightly to the ground. *I didn't think that could happen outside of the movies.* "I don't know if that was you, or me, or both of us," she muttered to her implant as she dodged a group of men roaring like Scottish warriors, "but thanks for the save—"

There was a white-hot surge of pain in her lower back and she went down, face-first, the man who had hit her falling on top of her. Someone stepped on her calf, and she snarled as muscle twisted between rubber and hard-packed earth. Rachel pulled her hands under the shelter of her body as more feet beat past.

Never take out your gun, a little voice reminded her: it sounded an awful lot like Mulcahy's. *Never in public. Never, never...*

The man on top of her squirmed, his elbows gouging into her back as he tried to stand. He was knocked down once, twice, a third time—Rachel tipped her body so he rolled off of her, forcing him towards the stampeding feet. She didn't feel even slightly guilty as she turned him into her human shield: he was twice her size and could take the hits.

When she was finally free of his weight, she flipped over to face him. He was turtled up in a ball, all yellow terror and red pain. "Hey!" she shouted, then bashed her fist against the top of his head as hard as she could when he didn't respond. "Hey! Asshole! We stand up together or we don't stand up!"

He poked his head out, eyes wide. She grabbed his exposed shoulder with one hand and shouted at him to do the same: green comprehension finally dawned in his conversational colors, and he joined his strength to hers.

They made it to their knees, then pushed against each other until they were standing. She grabbed her former human shield by the front of his jacket, and pulled him back into the rush of bodies.

The crowd had thinned. They had been on the ground for thirty seconds at most, but it had been long enough for the densest parts of the crowd to move past them. Now, instead of fighting against a stampede, it was more like swimming upstream. Rachel threw her free hand—her gun hand—up to protect her face, and hauled the man behind her with the other. The signal from Hill's cell phone put him at thirty yards to the southeast, deep in the thick of things. There was no way to know what had finally started the riot (it could have been Hill himself, for all she knew), and it would take too long to reach him…

And then she was suddenly clear of the press of bodies, just long enough to see Hill with his back against a tree, his gun drawn, before she lost him in another surge.

Rachel reached beneath her windbreaker and drew her service weapon. Her imaginary Mulcahy started shouting again, but she boxed him back up. Coming to Hill's defense was a reason good enough to carry her through any argument. Behind her, the man she was towing stiffened and tried to pull away at the sight of her gun. Rachel gave him one last extra-hard tug to yank him the last few feet forward, and they were finally free.

They came out in a small clearing of trees in the shadow of the World War II Memorial. Hill pulsed red; he was bleeding into his eyes from a head wound, his gun trained on a man holding a woman against his chest.

Hostage situation, Rachel realized, noting the terror in the woman's colors, the hidden knife jammed against her lower ribs.

"Hey, Hill," she called. "Who's your friend?"

"Hey, Peng," he replied, his voice eerily calm. "Same question."

"Right." She turned to the man who had trampled her. "Sit down," she told him. "You're probably going into shock, and you definitely need medical attention." When he didn't react, she kicked one leg out from under him to put him on the ground, then pinned him down with one foot on his chest to keep him from squirming off.

"Smooth," Hill said.

"I try."

The man with the knife was yellow-orange, completely confused as to why the cop had started ignoring him to banter with a strange woman. "What the fuck?"

"Hang on, Chuckles, you'll get your turn," Rachel snapped. "Hill, what happened here?"

"Little bit of this and that. Some men don't like to be told to be nicer to their wives. By the time he realized I was MPD…"

"Little bit of escalation?"

"Little bit."

"He try and stab you before he saw your badge?"

"Little bit."

The adrenaline was starting to wear off, and Rachel's mind began to climb her way out of its tunnel vision. They had an audience, she realized, a huge audience, all rapt on the scene playing out in front of them.

With their phones out and recording it, of course.

Damn, she thought. Well, at least Mulcahy would have proof she had a legitimate reason to wave her gun around.

From across the Mall, a scream cut through the air. The man with the knife tensed, and the woman gasped as the edge pierced her skin. *Damn,* Rachel thought again. Bantering with Hill wasn't working: eighty percent of the time, an unplanned hostage situation could be resolved when the hostage-taker realized the cops were ordinary people doing their jobs. Sometimes she hated beating the odds.

"Put it down," Hill said to the hostage-taker. His tone was world-weary, but his colors never lost their red-tipped focus.

"Tired of repeating yourself?" she asked him.

"Little bit."

"Who the hell are you?" the man with the knife finally snapped.

"I'm Agent Rachel Peng, the OACET liaison to the MPD," she said, pitching her voice so it would carry. "My skill with a gun is abso-*fucking*-lutely legendary, so if you're stupid enough to think a hostage will protect you from me? Please, by all means, continue."

She swept her thumb around her neck and hauled out her badge on its chain, all bright golds and unmistakable eye-searing greens.

Across the clearing, Hill's surface colors blanched as Rachel outed herself.

Rachel shared his sudden surge of panic, but if she had read the crowd right (*oh God, please please **please** let me have read the crowd right!*), then they were the best friends she would ever have.

"Shoot him!"

The hostage-taker's head whipped around to see the speaker, but he couldn't spot them—others had taken up the chant.

"Yeah, shoot him!"

"Take him down!"

Just like that, the mob response was back. Rachel breathed a silent sigh of relief: they might not recognize her on sight, but they sure as hell remembered how she could shoot.

The man with the knife went pale yellow in shock and fear, and kicked his wife away from him. He turned towards the mob, brandishing the knife, threatening to cut his way past them. They pushed back, knocked him down, and swarmed over him.

"Oh crap," Rachel whispered. She hoped she wouldn't have to do that stupid movie thing where the hero shot into the air to bring the crowd to order: what went up always came down, and D.C. was so densely populated it might come down in someone's cranium.

Suddenly, Hill was there. He pushed one long arm down into the mob, and came out with the hostage-taker.

When they saw Hill lock the man in handcuffs, the deep reds of the mob began to fade, pushed out by self-satisfied blues. They had all come to the Mall in search of villains, and it didn't get more villainous than a man threatening his young wife. They had seen the cops bring him down. Justice was done. The mob was feeling pretty darned good about itself.

And they weren't leaving.

Great, Rachel growled to herself, wondering how she'd manage to scare them off now that her gun was back in its holster.

Hill solved the problem. "Thanks for your help," he told them. "Stick around. We'll need your names, addresses, witness statements…oh, and your phones. We'll keep them for a few weeks, so if you need any information off of them, get it now."

He turned towards Rachel, leaning down as if whispering something to her.

"Nicely done," she said, as the onlookers quickly melted away behind him.

"Thanks. Anyone left?"

"A few do-gooders, but their friends are dragging them away."

"Yippee."

Hill called Zockinski; Rachel remembered she was standing on a human being, and let him up on the condition that he would sit quietly on a nearby park bench until the EMTs arrived. He had gradually come to the realization that Rachel had saved his life, and by the time the ambulance pulled up, he was telling anyone who would listen about how he and the Agent had fought their way through the mob to rescue a damsel in distress. She was relieved to find her new friend didn't understand that she had used him, and as long as she kept her mouth shut, his version made the better story. She even signed a few autographs before the ambulance took him away.

The man with the knife went away, too. Hill booked the man over the phone, passed him off to a uniformed officer for the drive to the holding cell, and said he'd get to the paperwork after the events of the riot had time to shake themselves out.

When they were done and alone, the two of them staggered over to the World War II Memorial, and collapsed against a low concrete wall facing the fountain.

"Hungry?" Hill asked.

Starving. "No," she replied. She inspected her hands: the injuries on her right palm were no worse, and the cast had protected her left. She hadn't even remembered she was wearing the cast during the trampling and its aftermath. Jenny did quality work.

They didn't say anything for a few minutes. Then she asked, "Did you start it?"

"The riot?"

"Yeah."

His conversational colors were an exhausted grayish-orange, and these picked up a hint of yellow as he said, "Maybe."

"It looked like the crowd was rushing the podium."

"The podium was in the opposite direction of a black man with a gun."

Rachel laughed. There was no humor in it, but it was either laugh or cry, and laughing was close enough to let her ward off the imminent giggling. Hill, ever the stoic, sighed and stretched out to bask in the afternoon sun until she was done.

"That was a hell of a thing you did," he said, once she could breathe again. "How'd you know they wouldn't turn on you instead of him?"

"Calculated risk," she said. "Besides, if they had gone after me, you could have used that as a distraction to take Knifeman down."

Hill shrugged. "Fair enough."

After a few more minutes, he asked, "Did anyone die?"

She had been watching his colors move slowly through oranges and grays as he built up the courage to find out if he had accidentally killed anyone by starting the riot. "No," she assured him. "The news feeds say that there were several dozen major injuries, but nothing severe or critical. Broken bones, mostly."

Hill exhaled slowly as he sank into a relieved blue.

"Don't worry," she assured him. "It doesn't matter if you caused it or not. It would have happened anyway. They were looking for an excuse."

"Yeah."

More silence. The grays returned to Hill's conversational colors, but he didn't offer any reason why.

Sometimes Rachel wished Hill was more like Mako. His cousin never shut up, but getting the detective to talk was like dragging words out of a dead man. She finally gave up. "What are you thinking?"

"You remember Glazer?" Hill asked her, his thumb rubbing across the new bandage at his hairline. "What he said in that interrogation room, about how OACET was created?"

Rachel nodded. She cut Hill some slack for the stupid questions; he took time to build up steam.

"So you know government conspiracies exist."

"Personally. Intimately." Rachel replied. "The wool-pullings and backdoor shenanigans that they used for funding OACET make Watergate look like preschool kids on the playground."

"Say someone came to you and told you they were part of a government cover-up," Hill said. "Would you believe them?"

"Depends on the person," Rachel said. "If that person was someone like you? Yeah, I'd believe them."

Hill nodded. His conversational colors were motionless, uncertain oranges and yellows sitting on top of each other, her own turquoise core lacquered between them. Not a nice combination, all things considered.

He tapped a long index finger against the glass face of his watch.

Rachel waited.

"What do you know about Copper Green?" he finally asked.

"Patina or code name?"

Hill's lips twitched as he fought a grin; he was probably remembering her kitchen. "Code name."

"Assume I've been out of touch for a couple of years," Rachel said.

"Right," he said, still tapping that finger. "The story broke in early '04. Journalist named Seymour Hersh? He claimed the Pentagon and the CIA had a program in the Middle East, one which sanctioned torture."

"'Grab whom you must. Do what you want,'" Rachel said, remembering. Copper Green's motto stuck with you, like a virus in your cells.

"That's the one," Hill said. "Based on the idea that Afghanis don't respond to anything other than shame and pain. The Pentagon denied it, swore they wouldn't let a program like that exist."

"Of course not. We're the good guys."

"Right," he said, as his finger tap-tap-tapped and his yellows took on a dark gray film.

"But," she said, leaning over to pick up a small stone from the ground, "if they did have a program like that, somebody would have to do the grunt work. The real...hands-on shit."

Tap. Tap. Tap.

"I thought you said you were with the 7th."

"The 7th goes a lot of places," he said.

"Right." She whipped the stone out from her hip. It skipped twice before she lost its frequency in the spray of the fountain. "Maybe it's better if some of those places are forgotten."

"So I've heard," he said. The finger stopped tapping and his grays moved into black. "Mako doesn't talk about what they did to you guys."

He was lying, but Rachel let it pass: Hill was family. "That's another place that should be forgotten."

"How bad was it?"

Alienation. Brainwashing. Depression so dark you stared up at the sun until night fell forever— "Bad."

"That conspiracy theory you mentioned," Hill said.

"Hmm?" Rachel glanced up. It wasn't exactly a non sequitur, but he had been the one introducing topics which paired well with tinfoil hats.

"The one where Homeland stages an attack to keep its funding."

"Homeland's never been in danger of losing its funding," Rachel said. "Public support, maybe, but there's no way in hell they're going to lose their funding. Can you imagine if Homeland got hit with cutbacks, and there's another attack on the scale of 9-11? It would be told-ja-sos and finger-pointing of Orwellian proportions. The government'll gladly pay billions just to keep that from happening."

Hill nodded, and waited.

"I don't think we did this."

"No," he said. "*We* didn't. You and me? We got out."

"If this hadn't happened?" Rachel said, pointing at her head. "I would have stayed. I would have stayed until I died of old age and they gave me a monument at Arlington."

"You were CID," he said. "You didn't—"

"No," she cut him off. "Don't say I wasn't a real soldier and I can't understand. I saw more combat than almost any other woman over there. My unit was the clean-up crew for the shit you 'real' soldiers left behind."

He blinked at her. "I was going to ask if you'd still stay, even when you knew the brass was tripping you up."

"Oh." She took a breath to calm herself. *"That."*

It was a good question. Army CID had a long history of fighting with their commissioned officers: one of Rachel's jobs had been to solve crimes committed by soldiers, and one of the officers' jobs was to show that soldiers upheld the military code, and these two jobs came into conflict more often than Rachel had liked. Much of her time had been spent trying to find new and innovative ways to hold soldiers accountable for crimes that certain officers thought were best forgotten.

(She had lost more of these cases than she liked to admit, many of them swept aside and dismissed as casualties of war. *Not* forgotten, though—*never* forgotten! Like her ambition, the names of those victims were lurking at the back of her mind, waiting for the right moment. Her to-do list stretched for years in either direction.)

"Yeah, I'd have stayed," she said. "You know those people who say they were born to join the Army? That used to be me."

"Used to be."

"Yup. OACET got in the way. Still, I don't think we did this."

Hill said nothing, but his green core was lost within the black.

"I'm not saying we aren't capable of doing this," she said after a few awkward moments. "I just don't think we did. For the sake of argument, let's say the attack on Gayle Street was done by Homeland. So why is there evidence?"

Hill leaned back against the bench and looked at her, curious yellow peeking through the black.

"That's what bothers me," she said. "There's enough evidence to suggest we did this to ourselves."

"You're a cop. You know there's always evidence."

"Yeah. And each piece of evidence we find is usually part of a puzzle. Bombings especially: every single scrap of paper or piece of broken glass has to be put back together. Here, every time we find one piece, it goes right into its proper place." She thought back to Shawn, sitting on the floor of the medical lab and swiftly fitting the cardboard pieces together without knowing the final design. "I don't like how easy it's been to implicate our own people as the bad guys."

"Sometimes it's easy."

"No, it's almost always easy. It's almost always the asshole holding the gun, or the kids running away from the backpack full of pressure cookers. What did you tell me last August? It's almost always the boyfriend, the husband, or the ex."

"Or the junkie," he said. "Rage or money, almost a hundred percent of the time."

"Right," Rachel said. "And this wasn't about money, so, what? Rage? What would make Homeland so mad they'd blow up an entire street? Or what would make them so careless that they'd kill two cops, and then come back after we found the scene to erase it? I can't think of a single thing.

"Or," she said, as she turned that scenario around in her head. "What would cause someone to get so mad they'd blow up an entire street to get back at Homeland?"

"Loss," Hill said, and shrugged. "Loss, or being lied to."

"Human beings are fairly resilient to both of those," Rachel said with no small degree of certainty.

"Not always," Hill said, as his fingers went *tap, tap, tap.* "Sometimes, it gets to be too much."

She nodded, thinking again of Shawn.

"You ever think about what might happen if you snapped?" Hill asked. "Took what they gave you, and just let yourself... cut loose?"

Rachel reached out to the nearest Wi-Fi hub and gave it a light ping, then followed the connection through six laptops and a few dozen smart phones, across the phones to the nearest cell tower, down to the signaling station... *Wipe them out,* she thought. *Just a touch, just a thought, and all the circuits go crispy brown, and you can finally—**finally!**—escape from these stupid, screaming machines...* "Do I need to hide your rifle rounds?" she said, half-joking.

He didn't answer.

"Yeah," she sighed. "Doesn't everyone? It's the big bad fantasy we all carry around with us in our heads."

"Maybe someone wasn't happy with the fantasy. Maybe someone decided it was time to draw the line."

"Someone from Homeland, maybe?"

"Someone's who's lost too much. Or someone who was tired

of being lied to."

"Or both."

He nodded. "Or both."

EIGHTEEN

The thin leather clutch bumped against her hip. Rachel pressed it down with her hand to pin it against her side. She had pulled the tiny bag out of the back of her closet that morning, thinking that leaving her usual oversized purse at home would show she had put in the extra effort to dress up. Now, a quick scan of the restaurant told her she was underdressed. Excepting shoes, she was the only person in the room with a leather anything.

Oh well, too late now. Rachel tipped her chin up and swept through the front doors, smiling kindly at the maître d' as she passed him on her way to the bar. He smiled back at her, an ugly scornful orange hidden behind splendid orthodontics.

There was a certain simple irony to the fact that she was going on her first real date in months while the city was ready to burn. Rachel had called to see if they should cancel; Becca didn't want to. Instead, Becca insisted on confirming their reservation. She told Rachel everyone in her office was planning to go out that evening to send the message that they were not afraid, and it was likely the restaurant would be overbooked.

Becca had been right. About the overbooking, not the message—Rachel was pretty sure that terrorists or Homeland Security or an invading foreign army didn't really care if Washington D.C.'s upper class got to order the veal or not. The restaurant was packed.

Her date was early. Becca was nursing a drink and making small talk with a young man whose conversational colors put him as more than casually interested; her cool jade green core made a nice contrast against his surface colors of lusty red.

As a color, "jade green" was something of a misnomer. Rachel's maternal grandmother had once laid out a dozen pieces of jade stone on an old threadbare piece of cotton to prove to her how each was unique, ranging from white to pink to blue and nearly black, and had told her that a narrow definition would never give her the full sense of what things were, or what they could be. Even at the tender age of seven, Rachel had seen what her grandmother had meant, but she was also a child of Crayola and the name on the crayon was forever fixed in her mind. And, two decades later, "jade green" was how she defined the core of the beautiful Latina waiting for her at the bar.

Becca had a lovely spill of long brown hair, and she was not-so-subtly inspecting this for split ends as the businessman insisted on freshening her drink. She saw Rachel coming and straightened in her seat, her conversational colors brightening.

They kissed in the way of new friends, quick on the cheek; the businessman's lust pulsed. As Becca turned to order her a drink, Rachel gave him a long, dark glare. The businessman fumbled in his wallet and threw some cash on the bar, then scampered towards the door. She flipped her implant to reading mode and saw he had accidentally dropped a fifty; the bartender was about to have a good night.

"What did you say to him?" Becca asked.

Rachel blinked at her, pure innocence. "Not a word!"

The maître d' arrived to escort them to their table. There were linen napkins folded into pointy swans, and more knives than Rachel had expected. Multiple forks and spoons, those were a given, but when a restaurant offered more than one knife she began to get twitchy. They ordered wine, appetizers, and Rachel tried to ignore how Becca kept sneaking peeks at Rachel's chest over her menu in a curious yellow way.

After a few moments of small talk, Rachel finally had to pretend to notice. "What?"

"I don't want to be rude, but are you okay? Your hand's in a cast, and you look like you've lost fifteen pounds in the last week."

Oh. The cast spoke for itself, but this was the first time they had met somewhere fancy: Rachel was in a sleeveless dress which had left no room for her usual ballistic vest.

"It's work-related," Rachel said. "I usually have to wear some extra layers. And the cast isn't the nicest accessory, I admit."

"Ah." Becca wrapped her hands around her wine glass, her conversational colors going ever so slightly gray.

"We're still not talking about work?"

"We can. We *should.*" Becca said. "I just…I just don't want to."

"Bet you a dollar my job is worse than yours."

"My job's not bad! But…"

Becca was thoroughly gray now, intensely worried. This was probably the point right before her typical date stomped off, appalled. Rachel had to force a straight face; she had never been on this side of the conversation. It was a lovely change of pace.

"Prison?" Rachel asked.

Becca shook her head. "No."

"Dogfighting, cockfighting, bullfighting?"

"Investment banking."

Rachel laughed; she couldn't help herself. "That was my next guess."

Becca gave her a sharp glare, and her conversational colors flared a hot red. Rachel grinned back at her. God, how she loved fire.

"Okay," Becca took a deep breath. "Remember the subprime mortgage scandal in 2008?"

"The one that ruined the global economy?" Rachel lifted an eyebrow. "Yeah. I remember."

"Okay," Becca said. She looked down and toyed with the tablecloth. "Okay, I might have…had something to do with… that."

"The what? The mortgage scandal? I think a lot of people were involved in that."

"Yeah, well. Did you hear about Goldman Sachs? How they made a profit from betting on short-selling mortgages?"

Rachel ran a quick search through Wikipedia. "Yeah," she said slowly, mentally skimming the text as quickly as she could. "They knew the junk mortgages were bad and shorted the market."

"Yes." Becca nodded. "That was sort of…my idea."

Rachel felt her jaw drop.

"I was just a summer intern! I didn't think they'd take me seriously!" Becca insisted. "They held a cheap throwaway meeting with a Board member, one of those introductory seminars that's supposed to convince the kids they're a valued part of the organization. They told us to write up any proposals we had to advance the company. I…I might have suggested a bundling process involving high-risk mortgages."

"Oh my God," Rachel said. "You tanked the planet!"

"Not alone, but I definitely helped," Becca said, and then sighed. "Honestly, I did make a shitload of money."

"Did you keep it?"

"Ah…not all of it," Becca said as she reached for her wine. "I donated most of it. And I do a lot of pro bono work for a legal firm who helps recover bad mortgages for lower-income families. I'm trying to put it right, but I've got a lot of bad karma."

Rachel shook her head, chuckling. "This is hilarious."

"No!" Becca was indignant. "No, it's not! It's terrible! Do you realize how many people lost their jobs, their homes! I ruined *families!* People *killed* themselves over what I did!"

She fell silent, her colors sad and damp, with a trace of fierce red that was aimed directly at Rachel. Rachel put on her most sympathetic face, and the red faded.

"No, you're right," Rachel said. "The banking scandal? Not funny at all. I'm laughing because I'm usually the one giving the 'This is what I do for a living and hey where are you going?' speech."

"Sure."

In response, Rachel reached into the tiny clutch and took out her badge. She flipped its protective folio open, and the bright green and gold of the OACET seal gleamed in the low light of the room.

"You're a cop?" Becca smiled. "That's not so bad."

Rachel pushed the badge towards her. "Read the fine print."

Becca leaned forward, then snapped the badge off of the table for a closer look. Her colors bleached white in shock as she first stared at the badge, then up at Rachel, her mouth forming a small and perfect *o*.

"And this," Rachel said, "is usually when *my* dates end."

"You're a..."

"Cyborg," she sighed. "Or, in the language of past dates: *freak, machine, creature,* and the all-encompassing *one of those...*and they add a long pause for emphasis...*things*."

"Oh." Becca said quietly, then asked, "That's what happens? They call you names?"

"Well, one time I got a glass full of wine thrown in my face," Rachel amended. "She stormed out without saying a word.

"Stuck me with the bill, too," she added.

Becca snorted, hard. It was an odd sound, completely out of place coming from a beautiful woman perfectly at home in an expensive restaurant, and Rachel found herself laughing.

It took a few tense seconds, but Becca joined her.

"Heh," Rachel said, after the moment had passed. "Okay, that's the best full disclosure has ever gone."

"For me, too," Becca nodded. She was an uncertain yellow. "But...um..."

"You get one trick," Rachel said.

"What?"

"To prove I really am OACET."

"I believe you."

"No, you don't," Rachel said, shaking her head. "You won't believe until you have proof. That's just how this works. The easiest trick is you hold up some object, and I send that image straight to your phone. It'll be from my perspective, so you'll know it's from me. But there's a bunch of other ways, if you think I'm wearing a hidden camera or something."

"Oh." Sympathetic wine red bloomed through Becca's surface colors, swirling through the yellow. "You get a lot of shit, don't you?"

Rachel shrugged.

The waiter glided up to their table, tiny salads swimming in dressing on his tray. There was an unwelcome pause in the conversation as he pushed ground pepper; Rachel sent him running to the kitchen for bread to sop up the vinaigrette.

"So," Rachel said, "let's do this, let's get the image out of the way. Unless you want a text message instead? Or, you can pick another person in here at random and I'll make their phone ring…"

Becca shook out the cloth swan and draped the napkin across her lap. "Do you believe I'm a banker?"

"Hmm?" Rachel blinked; Becca had deviated from the usual script.

"Do you think I'm lying to you about what I do? Or about… what I did, back when I was just starting out?"

"No," Rachel said, catching on. Smiling.

"All right, then," Becca said, pushing the inedible salad aside. "Let me bore you with my fantasy football team."

They pointedly ignored all talk of work. It was slightly awkward between them, at first, but they soon settled into a pattern of jokes and complaining about family. By the time they had finished the main course, they were happily comparing overbearing Old Country grandmothers.

"Dessert?" Rachel asked.

Becca shook her head. "Not here, but do you have a few minutes? There's a bakery nearby that does some of the best assortment of ethnic pastries I've found. We can show each other what Grandma used to make."

Rachel shuddered. "You've obviously never had a traditional Chinese pastry. Most of them are a scary breed of jelly doughnuts."

"I *love* jelly doughnuts."

"Sugar was pretty expensive in China," Rachel said. "They did without in a lot of recipes—think Fig Newton without the flavor."

Becca gagged.

The check came and went, Becca's platinum card eating the

sum. The two women gathered up their coats and left, walking west towards the old warehouse district. Rachel kept her scans active; there were more people out tonight than was usual, and plenty of red in the street, but it wasn't worth breaking the evening.

"Tell me something," Becca said.

Yellow, but not questioning. Curious? "Tell you what?" Rachel asked.

"Anything. But it has to be something you wouldn't tell me until the tenth date."

"Huh?" Rachel laughed. "Shouldn't we save that for the tenth date?"

"Nothing's guaranteed," Becca said, and shrugged. "This question is my personality litmus test. Lets me know if the other person thinks we're compatible."

"Ah. I have one of those."

"When do I get to take it?"

"Right now. Professional wrestling: sport or entertainment?"

"Neither."

"You pass."

"Good," Becca said. She grinned and looped her hand through Rachel's. Her colors fluttered when her fingers brushed against Rachel's cast, and she loosened her grip. "Your turn."

"Hmm," Rachel murmured. "This doesn't seem fair. I asked a question; you want a story."

"Should have picked a different litmus test, then."

Rachel chuckled. She flipped off the emotional spectrum to keep herself honest, and ran through her Big List of Dangerous Topics until she found one that had nothing to do with OACET or her eyesight. "My dad took my mother's name."

"I figured that out already. Unless your dad was Chinese but born in Texas?"

"Nope. I think he's mostly Scottish."

"You think? You don't know?"

Rachel shook her head. "Mom got a visa to Texas A&M to study architecture. This was the early '80s, when Chinese students didn't leave the country, and Chinese women basically never went to college, period, so something else was going on there. They still won't tell me how my mom got to America, or why they got married, or why I've never met any family members on my dad's side."

"Suspicious."

"Very!"

"And you haven't tried to find out?"

"Of course I have," Rachel said. "They said I'd find out when they're dead."

"That's a terrible story. That's not even a story. That's..." Becca jabbed Rachel in the side with her thumb. "That's the *promise* of a story! That's even worse than not telling a story at all!"

Rachel held up her free hand, surrendering. "That's what we'd talk about on the tenth date."

Becca glared at her. "The implicit threat that I'd have to know you after your parents died to get the entire story?"

"Well," Rachel offered in a lilting sing-song, "maybe if you tell me something tenth date-y, then I'll give you a better one."

"Fine." Becca was quiet for a few moments.

Rachel flipped on the emotional spectrum for a quick peek; Becca's colors were a blend of Rachel's southwestern turquoise and an almost-anxious orange. *Uh-oh.*

"I've never dated someone for more than five months."

"What?" Rachel was shocked. "How old are you? Twenty-eight?"

"Twenty-seven, thank you. And my relationships tend to... They start strong and then fade out."

"Well," Rachel said. "I've heard you're never supposed to date someone who's more than thirty and who's never been in a long-term relationship. Twenty-seven is safe."

"Yeah," Becca said. She was grinning, but there was anxiety behind it. The yellows and oranges grew and began to bubble over into Rachel's turquoise. "Just so you know, though, I'm done with rushing into relationships. Move too fast, and it's over before it starts."

"You're right," Rachel said. "You're absolutely right. And this is an excellent tenth-date conversation, so I think we should wait until the tenth date to have it."

"Fair enough," the other woman said. Her grin lost its pinched edges and the soft pops of yellow-orange slowly began to fade. "Just so you know, I'm a bit of a control freak. It tends to put people off."

"Becca? My roommate has turned my entire house into an arboretum. I think I can cope."

The other woman laughed. She smelled of jasmine, and the sleeve of her blazer was soft raw silk against Rachel's forearm. Rachel cast around for a good tenth-date story. *Jade green.* "I think my maternal grandmother is gay."

"No! Really? The same grandmother you were telling me about over dinner? Your…um…Low-low?"

"Close. Lǎo lao."

"Why do you think she's gay? Did she tell you?"

"Oh God no! She's practically a caricature of the Chinese matriarch. Everything has to be *just! so!*" Rachel said, and jabbed at the air with her free hand. "My parents tell me she was furious when my mother emigrated to America, and nearly disowned her when she married my dad. And she loved me—I mean, she *had* to love me, she practically raised me once she moved in with us—but if I had suddenly turned into a full-blooded Chinese boy, she would have been totally okay with that.

"It was only after I came out to the family that she finally started to like me. After that, we used to stay up all night, talking."

"About girls?"

"Girls, boys, women, men, movies, music, religion, politics, China, America… It's weird to have known someone for almost your entire lifetime, but never, you know, have *known* them."

"Small reason to think she's gay."

Rachel nodded. "Yeah, but there's also some winking and nudging in the family. Her husband died awfully young, and she never remarried."

"That could be cultural. Or maybe she isn't the remarrying type."

"Could be," Rachel said. The other woman's hand was warm in her own, even through the cast. "I'll probably never know for sure. We're close, but there's family-close and then there's close-close."

They stopped talking long enough to run across a four-lane road. Rachel had been following their route through downtown D.C. on her stored copy of MPD's map of the city, and her instincts were starting to itch. They were wandering into an unsavory part of town, and the usual weight of her gun on her hip was conspicuously absent. Becca was oblivious in the way of the rich: this neighborhood might be tame enough in the day, but she didn't realize that most predators were nocturnal, and the riots had lured them out of their holes. It was a relief when they turned that last corner and arrived at the pastry shop.

Which was out of business, of course. The store was shuttered up, a handwritten note on a sheet of copy paper thanking customers for their loyal, but obviously insufficient, support.

"Damn," Becca swore. "Do you know how hard it is to find a good *ensaïmada* around here?"

"There's a…" Rachel said, then paused as she ran a quick search. "There's a bakery that does brioches a few blocks from here." The bakery was nearby, but was also located (by sheer coincidence, surely) on a casually gentrified street with more than a few afterhours clubs and pricey restaurants. The two of them would fit right in.

She and Becca fell back into their comfortable stroll, with Rachel casually steering them onto brightly-lit roads.

"Did she defend you when you came out?" Becca said as she picked up the thread of their previous conversation.

"Hmm? My grandmother? No! I mean, she didn't need to," Rachel said. "Coming out as being part of OACET was *way* harder on my family than coming out as a lesbian. I sort of vanished from their lives for five years, and then, hey guys! It's your daughter, the cyborg! I'm back, and…and I see you've remodeled my bedroom into the new kitchen. Yay, ranch house layout."

Becca laughed. "OACET wouldn't let you contact your own family? Why not?"

"Sorry, can't tell you." Rachel grinned at her. "That's an eleventh-date conversation."

"Give you time to make something up, you mean."

Rachel sighed and dropped Becca's hand. "Pick a streetlight."

"Hmm?"

"Pick a streetlight. Actually," Rachel corrected herself, "pick three of them, and point them out in order."

Becca gave her a wry smirk.

"Just do it," Rachel sighed.

The other woman pointed at the lamp directly above them.

Rachel glanced up, and the light popped off.

"Oh," Becca said.

"They've got solar sensors," Rachel explained. "I told this one the sun had come up."

The loss of one lamp made no difference to how Rachel saw the street, and shouldn't have affected the temperature one iota, but there was a chill in the night air that hadn't been there before. She released the lamp and the small dark pool they had been standing in vanished, but the chill hung around.

"Okay. Pick two more," Rachel said.

"I believe you," Becca said. "Why do you think I *don't* believe you?"

"Because…" Rachel flailed. "Because they don't believe me until they do, and that's when the date is over."

Becca found Rachel's hand again, and started walking. There was an awkward moment when Rachel's feet didn't realize they were supposed to follow, and then they tripped and fell back into step with Becca's.

They walked without speaking for the better part of a block, and then Becca said, "I'm sorry you've had problems, but those other women? They aren't me."

"Yeah," Rachel said. "I'm starting to get that. Why doesn't this bother you, by the way?"

"I don't know," Becca replied. "It's like watching someone freak out about their cell phone. It's sort of…overly dramatic.

"Certain people might," she added, "even think it was boring."

Rachel chuckled. "Okay," she said. "Point taken. I'm done."

"No, no, I'm sure it's very interesting how you can turn lights on and off. It's just that I've been doing it my entire life, so…"

"Shut up," Rachel said, bumping Becca's hip with her own.

They walked in comfortable conversation for another few blocks. The street was beginning to feel familiar; Rachel recognized the high-pitched chitter of the security cameras.

"Oh, hey," she said, stopping. "I know where we are."

The loft Santino had brought her to the week before was two streets over. Rachel pushed past her self-imposed limits and ran a cursory scan through the building. The lights were on upstairs, a single figure was bent over a worktable: Bell's conversational colors were a beam of intense blues and whites as she immersed herself in her work.

"Want to see what might be the most incredible place on the planet?" Rachel asked Becca.

"Big promise," Becca said, smiling.

"Statement of fact," Rachel told her. "It's a workshop, but not like dad's ol' trashheap in the corner of the garage. A bunch of kids built it."

"I don't know. My mother warned me about going into dark warehouses with strange cyborgs."

"Really? That must have been hell. I would have hated it if I were raised by a psychic."

"Come on," Becca laughed as she took Rachel's arm. "Show me the most incredible place on the planet."

They rode the rattling elevator up to the top floor, Becca swearing to commit revenge from beyond the grave with each jolt of the cables. Rachel was laughing as the cage swayed back and forth and bumped its way skyward, doing her damnedest to keep the panic off of her face when the elevator started bucking like a rodeo bull. When they reached the loft, Rachel folded the old safety cage in on itself, and they stepped into a pool of warm yellow light.

"Oh," Becca said, staring up at the door. "That is beautiful."

The skylight was a black hole in the ceiling, and with the sun down, the massive metal door was lit only by the clean light from the twinned gas lamps. Rachel flipped frequencies to try to see the door from Becca's perspective, but gave up and enjoyed the warm reds and blues flowing from the other woman instead.

"There's no knob," Becca said as she ran her fingertips over the words minted into the door's face.

"Watch this." Rachel guided Becca's hand until it lingered over *ENTER,* and the two of them pressed against the raised metal until they heard the click of the hidden mechanism. Instead of the door swinging open as it had before, they heard a sound like fluted birds coming from the other side.

As the chiming fell away, Bell's voice echoed through the hall. "Agent Peng?"

"Hey, Bell," she said, scanning the hallway. Whatever was carrying Bell's voice wasn't digital; she couldn't find the source until she followed the sound waves to a series of small holes cut into the lintel. "Can we come in?"

The metal door opened on silent hinges. Bell stood on the other side, skeptical in yellows. "Yeah, I guess. I wasn't planning on giving a tour tonight, though. I've got a project to finish."

"She's a potential donor," Rachel said, grinning at Becca.

"In that case…" Bell said, bowing and ushering them inside. "Welcome, friends, and enter."

The loft seemed larger at night. The computer lab at the far end of the room was illuminated from within, but the rest of the space was dark. Bell flipped a wall switch and the metal solar system began to glow; Rachel realized the planets were topless, their bodies hollowed out and fitted with hidden bulbs. Golden light filtered through their seams, causing the alchemists' workroom to come alive.

"Oh, this is going to cost me," Becca said as she wandered into the center of the loft, drinking in the space with her mouth open and eyes wide.

"Tour first," Bell laughed. "Money later, if ever."

The girl gave them a simplified version of the tour she had given to Rachel, skipping over the technical projects and stopping to linger on the art pieces. Becca's surface colors swept into happy blues and yellows as she took in the room: she began asking about the cost for custom work, and Bell's colors began to match Becca's as they blended into the same conversational patterns.

Rachel followed them, her scans wandering. Her dress fluttered in the warm air coming from the heavy industrial radiators. She and Becca tapped along in their low-slung pumps while Bell padded around in old sneakers, the girl making as much noise on the worn wood floors as a kitten. *No wonder Santino comes here,* she thought. Quiet, thoughtful, with enough hard edges to keep you on your toes. The loft felt like him.

She fell behind to inspect the progress Jake had made on his inlaid box. A quick, shallow scan of the box revealed the same hidden mechanisms as the door. She tapped a piece of polished maple with a fingernail, and the box unlatched itself and opened smoothly on secret hinges.

"Hey Bell?" she called. "Did Jake make your front door?"

"Yep," the girl replied from across the loft. "And the lights. He does art fabs, like I said."

Fabs are fabrications, she reminded herself. After their first visit to the loft, she and Santino had a lengthy discussion to help her learn the terms she needed to know to navigate this unfamiliar world. "Fabrications" was the generic catch-all term for the projects that Bell and her friends pursued. The whole place was a Fab Lab, a space where makers with diverse skills and interests could share tools and skills, collaborate if the mood struck them...

It was a little too fruity-utopia for Rachel's tastes, but she did appreciate the sentiment.

She meandered over to the windows on the east side of the loft, and paused. Resting in a quiet space in the corner was what could only be described as a kitchen sink giving birth to a copper octopus. The wild snarl of tubes was topped with a small canister about the size of a soda can, with a small digital display positioned on its side. The display was ticking away, the numbers climbing. She tracked the purpose of the timer: it counted the rotations of an impeller, spinning as water was pumped up from the sink and through the tubing.

*Oh…*Rachel thought, as the water tugged at her. *How beautiful.*

Water was her new poetry. It fascinated her: there was something about how it moved which tickled her brain on a primordial level. Sometimes when it got slow at work, she'd walk the four blocks up to the Southwest Duck Pond and pretend to read a book as she let her implant have its way. Hours could fly by as the two of them explored patterns within the movement of the water. She'd wake as the sun went down, coming aware as if pulling herself from deep meditation, her legs asleep but her mind refreshed and clean.

The copper octopus was spinning water through itself. Rachel followed its path, down and up, back, sideways… At the end, another soda can with a second impeller ticked away with its own digital count before the water poured out into the basin to start the process all over again.

"Oh, careful," Bell called out as she caught Rachel about to poke the uppermost canister with her finger. "That's one of our future moneymakers."

"What is it?" Rachel asked, trying not to shake her head as she broke the water's hold.

"It's…uh…" Bell put down the mandolin she had been showing to Becca, and came over to the octopus tank. "The short answer is it's a machine to measure pressure loss. How much do you know about hydrology?"

Rachel almost laughed. "Let's assume I know nothing."

"Okay," Bell said, her conversational colors glazing over

slightly in polite resignation. "Assume that water flows from Point A to Point B." The girl tapped the sink first, then the outlet where the water spilled back into the basin. "If a pipe is perfectly straight, there should be nothing to block the flow, right?"

Rachel nodded. Beside her, Becca was leaning over the octopus, her fingers knitted across her purse to keep it from clanging into the tubes.

"If you put something in the pipe, it'll slow down the flow," Bell continued, running her finger up the main straightaway of the copper tube. "Sometimes this is sediment which clogs the line, but it's just as likely to be a bend in the line itself." Her emerald green nails tapped the first kink, a knot which wrapped around itself like a bow. "Hydrologists, engineers? They've got to work out how to build bends into a water line and still get enough pressure to keep the water moving."

"So…" Becca said, pointing at the two canisters, "these are measuring water flow?"

"No," Bell said, grinning at her. "They've already got water pressure down to a science. What we're doing is testing whether we can make renewable energy from it."

Just when you thought you were used to nerd-speak… Rachel closed her eyes and tried not to sigh. "There are impellers in the soda cans," she said to Bell. "Are they generating power?"

Bell nodded. "Yes! Well, no. Not these. These are dummies with Arduinos to track overall rotations of the impellers at the beginning and end of the system. We're testing these to see if it's feasible to use water lines to generate power."

"Like a water wheel," Becca said, standing upright.

"Same principle," the girl said. "Water lines go everywhere, so there's untapped hydroelectric power everywhere. If we could figure out a way to harness that energy without impeding the flow…"

"Free renewable energy," Rachel said. She threw a scan into the building below them, running her mind along the existing water lines. Dozens within this one building, hundreds if she added those apartments to either side. Sinks and showers and toilets...*oh my.*

"Exactly!" Bell said. She sounded pleased, but Rachel spotted flecks of green in her conversational colors. "Well, not quite free. Not until we get a full-fledged wireless energy transmission system up and running. Until then, we'd have to hook each impeller array into the existing power grid, and that would probably cost more than it's worth. Right now, we're just getting the math right."

"You don't think it's going to work," Rachel said, finally placing those flecks of green as doubt.

Bell shrugged. "It's not my project. The guys who built this thing a couple of years ago don't think it'll work, either, since they're trying to break the laws of thermodynamics. It's sort of a..."

"A what?" Becca asked.

"...a pipe dream," Bell said, and then had to wait until the women stopped groaning. "But you don't learn what's possible if you don't experiment."

"If they do get it to work, this would be a marketable idea," Becca said. "Should you be talking about this to strangers?"

Bell shrugged. "We've already got patents on it," she said. "Besides, we're big believers that information should be free. Ideas don't grow in the dark."

That last line tripped off of Bell's tongue like a mantra, and the cop part of Rachel's brain flickered awake. "Who's 'we'?" Rachel asked her. "Whose name is on the patent?"

"Ours," Bell said, gesturing to the invisible spirits still at their workspaces throughout the room. "When we come up with something new, our patron pays to get the patent filed, but it's in our name.

"Don't worry, we've got a contract," Bell said, noting Becca's expression. "We're not stupid. Our arrangement is that he pays for all utilities and the rent on the loft, and if any of our patents start earning a return, he gets fifty percent."

Becca recoiled. "Fifty percent!"

"This place isn't cheap," Bell said defensively. "The entire top floor of a warehouse in the middle of the city? I'm sure it's, like, five thousand bucks a month or more. We wouldn't have this place if it weren't for him, so we're happy to let him think of us as an investment.

"And there's no guarantee any of our patents will ever pay out," Bell added. "So this arrangement is *totally* worth it to us. It's a privilege to be offered a free space here—it's the best maker space in the city. I was on the waiting list for over a year."

"Santino told me he has to rent his space," Rachel said.

Bell gave a little smug pink shrug. "You have to qualify if you want to stay here rent-free."

"I wish I had my checkbook on me," Becca said. "What you kids are doing here is fantastic. I'll have to mail in a donation."

"I take Visa and Mastercard," Bell said, pulling out her cell phone. "No Amex, though. I can't afford the service fees."

Rachel covered her mouth with a hand and walked away, snickering. She hadn't intended to bust Becca's budget, but she'd make it up to her by offering to buy dessert.

Over by the window, the octopus gurgled on.

On their way out, they took the stairs. These were joyously solid after their ride in the old cage-lift elevator, and the stairwell was no less beautiful. If the loft was the sky, the stairwell was the earth, and they walked down through layer after layer of painted continental crust. The paintings were richly detailed; at one point, Rachel had to flip frequencies to take in the fossil matrix of an ichthyosaur, and found the cinderblock wall had been chipped away to mimic the rise and fall of old bone. Each landing in the stairwell had its own theme, and Rachel paused on the third floor to peer at what lay beyond a fire door which sparkled like the center of a geode. She found the lower levels of the old warehouse had been converted into offices, a few white-collar professionals still burning the midnight oil in the spaces beyond. She wondered how they explained the stairwell—or that elevator!—to visiting clients.

"The things those kids are doing here..." Becca had stopped to inspect the handrail. It was shaped from fused lengths of sculpted stone, twisted yet smooth to the touch. Rachel had visited a cave on a school trip, years before, and the handrail reminded her of the time-polished nodes which lined the cave walls.

"I know, right? Bell says everybody in their community is pursuing their own ideal of beauty. I believe it."

"If they can get that renewable energy process to work, it'll be worth a fortune," Becca said. Rachel could practically hear the numbers crunching in Becca's head; Bell was right, everyone's definition of beauty was different. "I wonder if they'd take me on as an investor."

"Absolutely. I have the feeling that money is a huge problem for them," Rachel said. "The first time I met her, Bell said something that makes me think she had to drop out of college."

"A bright kid like her? That's a sin."

Rachel nodded. "Hope Blackwell gave her some money," she said. "And…?"

The other woman sighed. "I said I needed to see a proposal first. With an itemized list of expenses."

"That's sensible."

"You don't get to be rich by taking risks."

Rachel nearly fell down the stairs. She looked at Becca and tried to keep herself from laughing.

"Risks are how you get to be *insanely* rich," Becca added, slightly red with embarrassment.

"Well, I probably won't invest. I'll just buy art from the kids after they've finished making it," Rachel said. "The only one of them I've met who seems to have their act together is Bell, and she doesn't think that renewable energy process will ever work."

Becca shrugged. "I don't see why it wouldn't. We've already got something similar in place with water meters."

Rachel froze. "What?"

"You know, water meters? The things the city sticks on the side of your house to measure how much water you use? A displacement water meter works by measuring the volume of— Why are you looking at me like that?"

And then, to both of their surprise, Rachel kissed Becca squarely on the mouth.

"You are wonderful," she told Becca as she clasped the other woman by her shoulders. "You're smart and funny and I don't even mind your pathological insistence that fantasy football isn't *Dungeons & Dragons* for jocks. But right now, you should probably go home while I keep the country from coming apart."

NINETEEN

Television had done the Justice Department a valuable service: any schmuck now thought they could build a bomb using a bag of fertilizer and plans off of the Internet. This was a highly effective way to separate the crazies from the curious: both would download the plans, purchase the fertilizer, and then stare at the tiny crater they had made in their backyard. Those with a last lick of sense would do the math, shrug, and head inside to do something more productive with their time.

The crazies would figure they had done something wrong and try, try again. They would buy more fertilizer and up the payload. They'd visit cached files of *Inspire* and browse al-Qaeda's starter recipes (Simple jihad! Nothing but a pipe and nails required!), and test those at their leisure. When those failed to give a sufficient bang for their buck, they'd find people with similar interests, start going to meetings, talk about bigger and better explosions. "Bigger and better" required a little more kick than potassium nitrate and a trip to the hardware store, and they'd realize, all of a sudden, that bombs were more complex than what they saw on the weekly procedurals.

So they'd reach out through various contacts, friends of friends and the like, to find a supplier for the parts they needed to carry out their master plan. And, ninety-nine times out of a hundred, the friend of a friend just happened to be an undercover officer.

The Justice Department *adored* television.

Local law enforcement, on the other hand, couldn't stand television. Procedural cop shows had made their job that much harder. Not because it taught a criminal the right way to commit a crime, but because the police didn't need the extra hassle of explaining to a jury that no, bleach does not eliminate blood evidence and yes, murders can be committed without shedding incriminating DNA all over the body.

The wannabe criminal could, however, pick up some pointers along the way, which is why the gun in the storm drain had been driving Rachel absolutely batty. Anyone who had access to a television over the last thirty years knew you never tossed a gun in a storm drain, especially not a drain located a mere block away from your murder scene, and *especially* not when you were already on your way to a river to dump the bodies!

The power supply locked it all into place.

"Water meters?" Zockinski wasn't convinced.

"Yes!" Rachel was pacing across the wooden floor. Bell hadn't been happy that the MPD had invaded the loft, but Jason had shown up with pizza and all was forgiven: the girl was devouring slices as though her last meal had been at the diner. "When Phil gets here, he'll be able to walk you through the connections. The bottom line is, there's something in this very room that could power the arming device indefinitely."

The fire door on the other end of the loft opened. Santino came in, uncharacteristically unkempt in dirty jeans and a sweatshirt; when Rachel had called him, he had been digging in their garden.

"This better be good," he said, brushing scraps of metal off of one of the old slate-topped lab tables so he'd have a place to sit. "I was trying to get a tree in the ground."

"At eleven at night, in the middle of October?" Zockinski asked.

"Only time I've had to do it since Gayle Street," Santino said, yawning.

The floor started to shake and the windows rattled in their frames. Rachel glanced around in mild panic, noting that Jason was doing the same; they had both been stationed in OACET's West Coast office, and shared a learned caution for earthquakes. It was only when her scans hit upon the elevator grinding its way upwards that she stopped searching for a good place to take cover from flying glass.

"Why don't you guys fix that thing?" Rachel said to Bell, as she went to open the main door for Hill.

"Can't," Bell mumbled around a mouthful of pizza. "'s illegal. Haf to be licensed to r'pair an ele'tor."

There was a hard banging on the door; Hill wasn't in the mood for games. Rachel twisted a curved brass knob and the door swung open. Hill blinked as he saw the loft, the sides of his mouth twitching at the solar system above them, and then he noticed Rachel. The orange-yellow irritation in his conversational colors fell away in a rush of her southwestern turquoise and a very different sort of red.

"Oh, for fuck's sake," she muttered, dragging him into the loft with her good hand. "Yes, I'm wearing a dress. Go, go."

She followed him over to where Santino was setting up a rough staging area, and briefly toyed with the idea of retrieving her coat. *Screw it,* she decided. The loft was warm and she was comfortable: Hill would just have to deal with her legs.

"We good?" Hill asked the others. "It's getting late, and I don't like the streets tonight."

"Agent Netz," Zockinski told him. "He's the last one."

"Phil's stuck in traffic," Jason said. "There's some crazy accident off of the highway. He says he'll catch up when he gets here."

Rachel threw her mind towards Phil, and found him sitting in his car, drumming his fingers against the steering wheel, the sound of car horns blaring around him.

He felt her touch. *"What?"*

"Just checking."

"I'm fine," he said. He was still angry with her, and his emotions hummed across their link. She felt his anger hitch as something caught his eye.

"Phil?"

"Some assholes are trying to flip a sedan," he said. He pulled her into his perspective, and they watched as several younger men grabbed the bumpers of a parked car with a license plate that marked it as part of the D.C. government fleet. Before Phil

could get out to intervene, an MPD cruiser zipped to the curb, the officers waving the men off.

"Not good," Phil observed.

"Definitely not good. Am I'm overreacting if I ping the rest of Administration and have them put out an OACET-wide curfew?"

She felt Phil grin, as he said, *"Maybe a little."*

Rachel sighed. *"Just hurry. I noticed a lot of red out there."*

Phil nodded. *"I'll be there as soon as I can."*

When Phil broke their connection, Rachel took a moment to check on Becca. Over the past half-hour, the woman's cell phone had moved from the loft to a taxi to a condo complex in a swanky part of town. Rachel wondered if her new not-quite-girlfriend read to herself before bed.

She shifted her attention back to the loft. The men from the MPD were watching her, different hues of reds and orange flickering across Rachel's own southwestern turquoise. Jason, however, was deep in conversation with Bell. The girl was wearing a pair of Santino's optical display glasses, and was laughing in delight as Jason conjured a bower of digital roses for her.

Sorry, Phil, Rachel thought to herself. *You never had a chance.*

"Right." Rachel pulled one of the rolling blackboards over to her and swept the receipts covering it to the floor. She nodded at Jason, who turned orange-yellow in annoyance, but still went to find a piece of chalk. "Bell, maybe you should leave?"

"Are you telling or asking?"

"Telling."

"She can be trusted," Santino interrupted. "Besides, it'd be good to get an outsider's opinion on this clusterfuck."

"Okie-dokie," Rachel said. "All right, I've two good reasons for busting up your night. First? The formal investigation for Gayle Street is going nowhere. Second? Sturtevant doesn't want us to be part of the formal investigation, maybe for that very reason. Because honestly? I'm beginning to think Sturtevant's clairvoyant."

"Your point, Peng?" Zockinski was moving past irritation to anger.

"Hear me out, and then we're going to start looking for the bad guy in new places. Different places. I think a big part of the reason we haven't made any progress on the case is because we all—us, the MPD, Homeland, the general public—made the same basic assumptions.

"So," she said. "What's the one major part of Gayle Street that doesn't make sense?"

"That Homeland wants to block the investigation," Zockinski said.

"That Homeland is involved *at all*," Jason said from behind her, jotting down notes on the board.

"Bingo," she said. "Why?"

When they didn't answer, she did it for them. "Because you can't pull off something like Gayle Street with an entire government organization. A few guys *from* Homeland? Maybe as many as five or six of them could keep their shit together long enough to set Gayle Street up, and keep the secret after the fact, but there is no way an entire organization could do that."

"Rachel and I are already convinced that Homeland's not involved, so I'm playing devil's advocate here," Santino said. "What if a few guys from Homeland did cause this, and Knudson or someone else in Homeland's administration found out? That would explain why Homeland's been so…bureaucratic."

"Oh, I like that one," Zockinski said.

"I do too," Rachel said, "except for the evidence which suggests that Homeland's involved. Why would people who work for a government agency leave enough behind to show it was responsible for this type of crime? Hill?"

Hill usually responded to direct questions. "Because they'd want Homeland to be held responsible."

"*Held responsible*," she said. "Perfect. That's the perfect phrase. And if that's the case, then does it really matter who blew up Gayle Street?"

"Jason, can you write 'motive' up there? Draw a bunny beside it."

"Shut up, Zockinski," Rachel told him. "I'm getting to motive.

If you think about it, we don't have that many suspects. There's a foreign military or agency, there's our own military or agencies, there's fringe nutcases, and there's lone wolves. And lone wolves are usually fringe nutcases, so—"

"What about mercenaries?" Hill asked. "Business tycoon hires them to start a war?"

"Too complex," Rachel said. "Wars tend to start themselves. Revolutions, on the other hand…?"

"No," Zockinski stood and started pacing. "Too unpredictable. Nobody in their right mind would set up something like Gayle Street and count on it to start a revolution."

"You're right," Rachel said. "But he might, if he wanted to influence the public *just enough* to get them to put pressure on Congress. Like, say, before a big vote on military spending?"

There was a single beat in which the conversational colors of everyone in the room froze. Her partner stopped scraping dirt out from beneath his fingernails. "Oh *shit*," he said. "The coffee shop."

"Exactly." Rachel couldn't help but cross her arms and smile. "The murders in the coffee shop was the part of this that never fit. You've got an astonishingly clean terrorist event on one hand, and a clumsy-ass murder scene on the other. Why take the time and the effort to pull off the perfect crime if you have to follow it up with something so sloppy?

"That applies to everything after the coffee shop, too," Rachel said, as she used an old piece of tape to tack up a map of a section of the Potomac River, a bright blue circle ringing the spot where the officers' car had been located. "The dump site was off of a main road, in a popular boating area. Could you pick a worse place?

"And he chucked the gun down the storm drain," Rachel finished. "Less than a block from the site. Do we really think our guy is this stupid?"

Even Bell nodded at that, but Zockinski was still pushing back. "He could have panicked," he said. "He goes back to the coffee shop to retrieve the canister—"

"There was no evidence to suggest a canister was ever in that store," Rachel interrupted. "No scuff or drag marks in the dust, no scraps of pipe on the floor. Just a crimped gas line to suggest something had been removed. That's another thing—that's the *biggest* thing—why blow the store after the scene was discovered, and not before?

"Timing is everything in this case," Rachel said, making herself wipe the emotion from her voice. She needed the men to understand this next part, not sell them on it. "Who, what, where, and how...? The usual questions don't matter. *When* is the only real question, because Gayle Street was a major terrorist event in perpetual stasis."

Santino had already caught on; she watched as white-hot excitement started to pop within his colors. "Our guy could blow Gayle Street any time he wanted," he said. "Nobody's come forward who remembers any utility work being done over the last two years. Those canisters were put in place around the same time the gas lines were updated, when our guy was just another person in a utility uniform. The store owners assumed that any new equipment was part of the upgrade."

"Exactly. So, timeline again. Why did he decide to blow Gayle Street this week, and why did he decide to blow the coffee shop after we discovered the murder scene?"

When they didn't answer, she nodded. "Now flip those two questions around."

Hill snapped to his feet. "Because he wanted us to find the murder scene."

"Because?"

"Because nothing at the coffee shop pointed to Homeland."

Rachel was nearly dancing. "But...?"

Hill sighed. "But it did point to the military."

"Our guy was too smart," she said. "He outthought himself when he planned this scheme. He planted canisters that could be traced back to Homeland. He probably knew enough about forensics to realize that we'd be able to recreate the bombs, and he assumed no one would believe that Homeland would be behind it—nobody's stupid enough to use their own equipment! But he didn't know Homeland would block the investigation, or that the general public would jump at the chance to assume that Gayle Street was just one more destructive thing our own government did without expecting to get caught."

Hill walked over to Zockinski, their conversational colors rolling as they turned over the possibilities. Zockinski flipped through his notebook, and said, "Every piece of evidence taken out of the store implicated the military."

Rachel nodded. "We thought he waited until everyone was out of the store to blow it to keep from hurting the Forensics team. That's not true—he just needed to make sure most of the evidence was out of there. *Most*, not all...if the store was blown, it'd leave room for reasonable doubt if any evidence recovered didn't quite match up. And he ditched the gun where it'd be sure to be found, too."

"The public wanted Homeland to be the villain," she finished. "And we were so busy managing the fallout from that, we never asked who the *bomber* wanted as the villain."

"Jesus," Zockinski said. He looked up from his notepad. "If you're right, we've got a profile. A man with a grudge against the military. One who's got the skills to build a bomb, and the ability to work with commercial utility lines."

"I think we can narrow it down a little more," Rachel said. "Bell?"

The girl's head snapped up. "Agent Peng?"

Rachel took the chalk from Jason and sketched a circle smaller than the toe of her shoe on the blackboard. "Would your Arduinos fit in something this size?"

"You could get about two of them in there," Bell replied. "Maybe more, if you used small ones."

"And could these be locked to a signal or a frequency? Say, they could only be activated if someone unlocked them with a management code?"

"Yeah, we do it all the time with Arduinos," Bell replied. "I've seen them with RFID and Wi-Fi adaptors. I even built an Arduino cell phone a few years ago."

"So it's possible that he could have set the bombs up, and then left them there indefinitely."

"No. Even if they're just turned on once a day to synch, wireless interfaces need a ton of power. Once the power supply ran out, they'd be useless, and it'd—" Bell began, and then trailed off, her colors bleaching as she turned, almost against her will, towards the copper octopus in the back of the room. She looked back at Rachel, eyes wide.

Rachel nodded. "The key to this whole thing is the power supply," she said. "Once our guy figured that out, he could commit terrorism at his convenience.

"Bell?" she asked, trying to be gentle. "How many people have access to that hydrology project?"

"Agent Peng, we didn't—"

"How *many*, Bell?"

"It's like I told you," Bell said, nearly pleading. "We've got patents on this technology. The ideas are out there, and this loft? People are walking through it all of the time. I can't give you a list of who would have access. And it's not the world's most unique idea! Water wheels have been around for millennia!"

"Ones with a wireless Arduino interface?"

Bell was saved from having to answer by the sound of the fire door opening. A man with a chestnut brown core entered the loft. The girl brightened with recognition, and was out of her chair and running into the man's arms before he could close the door.

"Silver Bell?" He glanced over at the room full of strangers, his conversational colors twisting in bemusement as he took in the room full of strangers. "What's going on?"

"They think we blew up Gayle Street!" Bell said, her voice shaking.

"What?" The man's colors snapped into reds and oranges. "Who are you people? Do I need to call my lawyer?"

In Rachel's experience, people who asked for lawyers had a history of asking for lawyers. She gave him a thorough scan:

late middle-age, balding, pudgy, and rich. No one wore a suit that expensive to a warehouse in the middle of the night, not unless they wore a suit like that all of the time. The investor who owned the loft had just arrived.

The investor whose son was killed while serving in the military, her little internal voice reminded her.

Rachel considered this, and ran a diagnostic scan over the newcomer to be sure. *Nope.* His heart rate and blood pressure was through the roof after four flights of stairs; no way in hell he had moved two dead bodies, not without dropping dead himself.

Anybody with a warehouse full of strong, young artists-slash-heavy weapons manufacturers indebted to him is worth a closer look, whispered that little voice.

The newcomer's eyes bounced from face to face, finally landing on Zockinski as he decided the oldest member of their group must be the leader. "You," he said. "Explain yourself."

"Jacob Zockinski, Metropolitan Police. This is my partner, Matt Hill, and he's Raul Santino, also from the MPD."

Rachel half-hoped Jason would know to keep his mouth shut and let Zockinski paint the target on himself, but that wasn't how Jason worked. "Agents Atran and Peng," he said, before she could ping him. "Office of Adaptive and Complementary Enhancement Technologies."

"Agents. You brought more Agents, so… You're serious?" he asked Jason. "You think these *kids* are terrorists?"

This time, Rachel was able to shout in Jason's head before he could answer. What came out of it was a smooth, "We can't talk about an ongoing case."

"You obviously *have*," the man said, stressing the last word as he put a protective arm around Bell. "What did you tell Silver Bell?"

"I'm sorry," Jason said. "Who are you?"

The man's colors dipped from anger to scorn. "Terry Templeton," he said. "I own this building."

Santino's colors fell to a sickly bluish-gray; he hadn't recognized Templeton on sight. The detectives' colors jumped to money-green, then snapped into professional blues: Zockinski and Hill knew that if they weren't careful in how they handled Templeton, the backlash might put them out of a job.

And Jason started to burn red.

"*Careful,*" she warned him.

"*Another IT billionaire,*" Jason snapped through their link. "*Coincidence?*"

"*Until we know more? Yes. Let Zockinski deal with this. You and I can poke around later and see if he might be connected to Hanlon.*"

He felt her doubt at the idea, and shrugged it off: as far as Jason was concerned, anyone outside of OACET could be allied with Hanlon. But he did relent, his anger fading slightly as he let her talk him down.

Rachel shifted her attention back to Templeton. Zockinski was assuring him that, no, he did not need to call his lawyer, and no, they had neither a suspect, nor any evidence to incriminate any single member of the loft.

"We've learned that a component in the bomb might be similar to a device in the loft," Zockinski said, his professional blues wavering slightly at the edges as he realized he didn't know much more than that.

"What?!" Templeton's conversational colors of reds and oranges deepened.

"We're just here to do research," Santino spoke for the first time. His colors were weaving in and out of themselves as he weighed Templeton's involvement.

"Gayle Street's been keeping us busy," Hill added. "We're chasing every lead we can, even if it eats into our personal time." He nodded towards the others from the MPD.

Templeton followed Hill's eyes and noted the details: Jason and the detectives in jeans and casual jackets, Rachel in her fancy-restaurant finery, Santino covered in dirt... Templeton's colors started to move towards blue relief. "Fair enough," he admitted. "What can I do to help?"

"First off, can I ask why you're here? It's late, and you're a busy man."

Templeton's colors changed again. He had locked on to Zockinski's core of autumn orange, and this was centered within a deep business-suit charcoal. "I try to come down here every couple of weeks and check to see how the kids are doing," Templeton said. "There's a lot of people on the streets tonight, so it seemed a good night to drop in, maybe offer them a ride."

Bell beamed up at him, and he gave her a one-armed hug in return. Her smooth gray core was reflected in his colors, offset with a light money green.

The loft is an idea farm, Rachel realized. Bell and some of the other makers (Jake came to mind) weren't the sort of people who would thrive in a corporate structure. Templeton gave them equipment and resources and let them go nuts, and came along later to file the patents.

Rachel couldn't decide if she should be furious on Bell's behalf: college degree or not, there was no doubt that Templeton would have had offered the girl a job. It was Bell's decision to shuffle between free meals, but Templeton had cash to burn, and stipends had been invented for a reason.

"Now," Templeton said. "I'm calling my lawyer, and when he gets here, you can explain how my property might be connected to terrorism."

And then, as if speaking those words summoned the act itself, the building shook.

TWENTY

The explosions hadn't been close; the windows rattled, and some dust fell from the solar system overhead, but that seemed the worst of it, nothing more serious than what might happen if a truck crashed into a wall a block or two away. Then, the others jerked, traces of yellow-orange uncertainty blooming. Rachel had sometimes worried that she might accidentally out herself in the event of a sudden power failure, but she knew what had happened as soon as the others did: Bell's machines had stopped singing.

"Guys?" Santino asked.

"On it," Jason said. Rachel felt him touch the power lines and trace them from the building as he searched for the cause of the blackout.

She took a different route. While the others started calling around, Rachel hopped into the frequencies of the nearest police cars and listened to the radio chatter. She was the first one to hit on the problem. "Pepco says four of its transformers went out across the city," she said, as she repeated the back-and-forth between officers. "They've asked the MPD to check and see if it's just coincidence."

"Even with Pepco, that's an atypically high failure rate," Santino said, searching through the pile of coats for his old jacket.

"Nerd," Zockinski said, as he and Hill stood and joined him in rummaging through the pile.

Jason paused on his way to the door. He appraised Rachel with a critical eye. "Peng—"

"*I know,*" she said as she opened a link. *"Just keep Santino safe."*

Jason nodded, and followed the other men downstairs.

"All right," Rachel said in a bright and cheery voice. "Do you have any candles here?"

"Candles?" Bell's tone was almost as scornful as her conversational colors. "Please."

"I should head on out," Templeton said, as he watched Bell navigate the room by the light of her phone. "I need to get home to my family—"

"Actually," Rachel interrupted him, "I'm going to ask you to stay."

"Agent…Peng, is it? I'll drop Silver Bell off on my—"

"You can leave if you want, of course, but it's very likely the city's about to riot," she said. "I'd feel better if you weren't on the streets. And I'm definitely not about to let Bell outside until I know it's safe."

He grinned at her, as if the idea of a citywide riot was adorably old-fashioned. "I think I'll be fine."

As if on cue, the unmistakable sound of a gunshot cracked outside. Templeton's colors bleached themselves down to white, and he started towards the windows to see what was happening in the street.

She grabbed his arm. "Let's wait over here," she said, pulling him away from the glass.

There was a faint smell of gas, and the tail of a brass comet kindled into flame. The fire pulsed bright, then settled down to a steady glow as Bell adjusted the fuel supply. Rachel scanned the comet to learn why the flame traveled the length of the tail instead of shooting straight up, and found the comet's tail was lined with multiple jets.

Bell rejoined them. She had wrapped an old bed comforter around herself like a polyester cocoon. "Good?" she asked, pointing at the comet's tail.

"Great," Rachel said, and went to the second item on her mental checklist. She threw a scan downwards, passing through the office spaces on the lower floors. She had expected the building to be empty, but two people, a woman on the third floor and a man on the second, were still there.

"I'm going to do a sweep of the building," she said. "If I find anybody, I'd like to bring them up here, make sure everybody is in the same place.

"I'll be right back," she added. "I know it's tempting to see what's happening outside, but stay away from the windows."

"We will. Here," Bell said, handing her the phone.

"Thanks," Rachel said. She activated the phone for the light from its screen, and pretended to bump into a table on her way out for good measure.

Somehow, Rachel thought to herself as she clattered down the stairwell, *the ability to see in the dark does not make this place any less creepy.* She hadn't realized the building was as poorly insulated as it was; the heat was sucked straight into the night through the skylights and the elevator shaft. She had a better tolerance for cold than she used to—her new metabolism kept her body temperature ticking a few degrees higher than a normal person's—but the converted warehouse was already turning to ice as the heat escaped.

And then there were the rats. They scurried inside the walls and through the ceiling above, and, God help her, the damn things kept stopping to watch her through cracks in the plaster. It felt as though she was being circled by a school of small, fuzzy sharks.

She decided to start with the third floor: the man on the floor below them was sitting in his desk chair, but the woman was going through the motions of packing up her stuff to go home. Rachel walked down the hall, knocking on each door and shouting, "MPD! We're doing a building walkthrough. Please come out of your offices and we'll escort you to a safe location."

The woman's anxious oranges and frightened yellows shifted into relieved blues. Her office door opened. "Hey!" she shouted. "Over here!"

Rachel walked over, holding Bell's phone above her head to telegraph her location. "Agent Rachel Peng. I work with the MPD."

"Grace LaPonsie." She had a core of watered-down cinnamon and was wearing quite a lot of silk. The light from Bell's phone traced the edges of her face in green. "Are you here alone?"

"There are others in the loft," Rachel said, and started walking and shouting again.

LaPonsie chased after her. "The loft?" she asked. "You're with those... The artists?"

Rachel didn't have the strength to bother with the question. "We've set up a staging area," she replied. "There's light, heat, and pizza."

"You're a police officer?" LaPonsie asked, taking in Rachel's dress and elbow-high cast.

"I was off-duty when the power went out."

They reached the stairwell, and Rachel handed LaPonsie the phone. "Why are you here so late?" Rachel asked her.

"I'm an independent real estate agent," LaPonsie replied. "We never stop working."

"Really? Here?" Rachel could think of a hundred more appealing locations than the old warehouse. "I'd think that elevator alone would scare off your clients."

"I have more than one office," LaPonsie said quickly, her surface colors taking on the reds and anxious oranges of someone who realized she was saying something she shouldn't to a cop.

Rachel nodded and let the conversation drop. It was none of her business if LaPonsie had found herself a nice little tax dodge.

They descended to the second floor and Rachel resumed her knocking-and-shouting charade. Unlike LaPonsie, the man stayed rooted to his chair. His core color was a strangely medicinal shade of yellow, and Rachel realized she had seen him before, on that first day Santino had brought her to the loft. She scanned his wallet; the RFID tags in his credit cards identified him as Howard Les Rothbauer. When they reached his door, Rachel turned to LaPonsie and asked, "Do you smell cigarettes?"

"No?"

Rachel didn't, either, but it was easier to fake a mystery smell than admit she could see through walls.

"Hello?" She pounded on the door. "Sir? Sir, I know you're in there. This is the MPD. I'm here to take you to safety."

The explosion of reds and oranges from the other side of the wall was a stronger copy of LaPonsie's; apparently, every single person who rented an office in this building was scared of law enforcement.

A scurrying motion in the stairwell yanked her attention from the man on the other side of the door. She had kept her scans wide to make sure no one would come in and catch them off-guard. Instead, she spotted someone coming down from the loft: Templeton was trying to sneak out.

"Damn it," she muttered quietly. She thought about chasing Templeton down, but decided against it; if he wanted to behave like a child, he was old enough to accept the consequences. At least he hadn't taken Bell with him.

"What?"

"Nothing," Rachel said, then resumed banging on the door. "Sir, I know you're in there!"

After another fifteen seconds, LaPonsie said, "Officer Peng? I think it's empty."

Rachel ground her teeth together. "Yes," she said to LaPonsie. "I must have been imagining things.

"But if anyone *were* still in this room," she said, loudly, "they'd do well to stay put until the power comes back on, because there are *riots* in the *streets!*

"C'mon," she said to LaPonsie. "Let's go where it's warm."

The two of them went upstairs to the loft, where Bell was heating a copper bowl over a Bunsen burner.

"Oh my God," LaPonsie said, taking in the details of the makers' loft. Bell had opened the front door, and the gas lights from the hallway and the comet's tail softened the edges of the room.

"Beautiful, right?" It wasn't a question. Rachel gave LaPonsie a gentle push to get her moving again.

Bell was sitting on one of the lab tables, her face lit from below by the burner. "Hot chocolate?" she asked Rachel.

"Yes, please. Bell, this is Grace LaPonsie. She works downstairs." Rachel said, recovering her own coat from the wreck of a sofa. The temperature in the loft had dropped nearly ten degrees in the five minutes she had been gone. "I'll be right back. I need to make some calls."

She moved back into the stairwell. With luck, LaPonsie would assume the fire door had shut out all sounds; it would be a nice change to get through one night without giving the full "Yes, I'm Really A Cyborg" speech.

Santino's phone went straight to voicemail, so she pinged Jason. *"You guys okay?"*

"Getting rough down here," he replied, and let her see through his eyes. He was standing in front of a store with a broken window, the weight of something suspiciously like a baseball bat in his right hand. There was warmth running along the right side of his body; she realized the car beside him was burning.

"You guys in danger?"

She felt Jason roll his eyes. *"I'll call you back,"* he said, and broke their connection.

Fucker, she thought to herself. Still, Jason was fine, and he would have mentioned if any of the others were hurt. She considered going out-of-body to their location, maybe serving as an invisible advance scout to warn them of impending danger...

No. Only Jason would be able to see her, and he didn't need any more demands on his attention right now. She decided to ping Phil, and reached out—

—and couldn't find him.

"PHIL!" she shouted.

"WHAT?!" he shouted back.

"Oh Jesus, never do that again," she snapped.

"What? What did I do? No, never mind. I don't have time for this." She was suddenly standing in a stretch of black city streets, a woman and her three children in her arms as she fought against the crowd, trying to find an alcove or an alley or somewhere to get them out of the mob's way...

Rachel pulled herself out of Phil's body and ran a city map through their link. *"Take your next left,"* she told him. *"There's a church...St. Paul's Parish. It's big, it'll be open late for community events."*

"Thanks," he said, and vanished.

She spent a moment catching up with the collective. The others were divided into two groups. The chatty ones were those who were safe, off of the streets, hidden away in their homes or in stores or huddled together in the kitchen at the OACET mansion.

The silent ones were those who were deep in the chaos of downtown D.C. They were few in number, and all the more fascinating for it—Rachel and the others couldn't help but watch as Mulcahy broke apart a mob at Verizon Center with words alone, his wife standing beside him like his tiny bodyguard as he talked those clustered around him out of a riot. Across the city, Josh had swept through the streets and had converted dozens—hundreds!—of well-armed looters into a parade, singing and enjoying a carnival atmosphere straight out of Mardi Gras...

Rachel shook her head, bewildered. Somehow, Josh had even found *beads*.

There was nothing more she could do, so she returned to the loft. Inside, she found Bell and LaPonsie huddled under the comforter, sipping hot chocolate from cafeteria-style mugs. Bell pushed a third mug towards Rachel, the heat coming from it in a low red glow in the rapidly-cooling room, and she hopped up on the table to join the others.

It was a weird little slumber party, with the usual amount of secret-sharing. LaPonsie wasn't too thrown to learn that Rachel was OACET; she had heard that Agents hung out in the loft. (Judging by the cloud of relieved blue which had puffed off of her, LaPonsie would much rather associate with a cyborg than a police officer; Rachel wondered what the IRS might find if LaPonsie was anonymously fingered for an audit.)

She also learned that Bell wanted parents, badly. The girl wasn't an orphan, not in the technical definition of the word, but she had set out on her own the day she turned eighteen and had never looked back. Bell spoke of Templeton in the same reverent voice that some of Rachel's squadmates had used for certain ranking officers, a combination of hero worship and thinking they had finally found the replacement for the roughly person-shaped hole that had been cut into their psyche.

"Why did they make you stay?" Bell asked her.

"Hmm?" Rachel had been following Phil through the link. He had dropped the family off at the church, and had returned to the streets to help where he could.

"Santino and the guys. Why didn't you go with them?"

Rachel laughed. "Bell, do you like my dress?"

"I guess, but..."

"And my shoes? How about my pretty cast?"

"Oh," Bell said, her colors turning into sage greens.

"Yeah," Rachel said. "I even left my gun at home for the first time in...oh, I don't even remember. Right now, I'm about as physically intimidating as a soccer mom. If I were doing crowd control dressed like this, I'd cause more problems than I'd solve. I've got no problem holding down the fort until the big, strong men get back."

The windows shook as the concussion of another small explosion, much closer than before, rocked the building.

"That's not good," Rachel said as she jumped off of the table.

She walked over to the windows and took shelter behind a brick support column, pretending to peer around its corner as she ran a scan through the neighborhood. Jason and the others were a few blocks away, and safe: the MPD had arrived and had set up barricades, and her team had taken shelter in the back of a transport van. On a different street—one that dovetailed into the loft—a group of college-age men were flipping cars like pancakes; they were purple-blue and eager, all of them young and healthy and caught up in the invincibility of the mob. As she watched, two women lit a scrap of canvas in an old vodka bottle, and hurled it through a store window.

The women were laughing.

Rachel rested her head against the brick, and reminded herself it took all kinds.

She swept her scan down the street and found a second group moving towards the first. The men in this second group were older and running red.

"Bell?" she said, as softly as she could. "Kill the lights."

The girl caught Rachel's mood, and scrambled to obey. The comet's tail puffed twice before the gas was snuffed out, and the room dropped into black.

"Stay here," Rachel told them, as she grabbed a length of wrought iron from a nearby rack of materials. "I need to seal the building."

As the fire door closed behind her, she kicked off her heels and ripped open the toes of her nylons with the sharp edge of the iron bar; nylons provided decent insulation but shitty traction, and she rolled them up to her ankles so she could run silently down the stairs. When she reached the ground floor, Rachel slid one end of the iron bar through the door pull and braced the other against the wall; anyone committed to getting the door open would succeed, eventually, but the bar would give her enough time to run down from the loft with whatever weapon-like objects she could find.

The creaking of metal caught her attention, and she whipped her scans around to find the man from the third floor in the stairwell, climbing towards the loft. Rachel gave the iron bar one last tug to make sure it was square against the wall, and then sprinted up the stairs as quickly as she could.

He heard her coming; even in a grumbling old warehouse, he couldn't miss the sound of bare feet slapping against a linoleum floor.

"Hey," Rachel called out from two floors below him.

The man's colors took on a second overlay of yellow as his fear burst through. "Hello?!"

"Hey," Rachel said again. To her eyes, the man glowed as he tried to see the source of the voice in the dark. "Do you remember me? I'm with the MPD. I saw you when my partner brought me here to tour the loft."

"I don't, sorry," he said, his anxiety rising. "I can't even see your face."

"I took the elevator."

"*Oh!*" he said, his colors shifting. "You."

"Right." Rachel knew that would work; she'd be shocked if that elevator was used for ten trips a year.

"What's the MPD doing here? Did something happen?" he asked.

Rachel decided to give him an out. "Nothing's happened," she said. "The blackout's trapped me here, too. Did I miss you when I swept the building?"

"Yeah," he said quickly, the surface layer of yellows fading as he realized he didn't have to do anything except lie. "I'm Howard. Where is everyone?"

"The loft," she said. "Head on up. There's only three of us—four, now."

Rachel watched Howard's colors as he turned to walk upstairs. There was anxiety, reluctance, stress…these faded slightly as he went into the loft and found it ten degrees warmer than the rest of the building.

"Hello?" LaPonsie flashed orange-yellow until she caught sight of Rachel just behind the stranger.

"It's fine," she assured the woman. "This is Howard. He works downstairs."

"I wanted to sit out the riot and go home," Howard said, "but there… Was that an explosion a few minutes ago?"

"We think it was a car," Rachel said, as she scraped the bottom of each foot against the side of her leg before she put her shoes on. There was no way she was walking around the loft in bare feet; she had better things to do than discover a new form of tetanus.

Howard instinctively went to look out of the window before Rachel called him back, and the four of them were soon sitting around a lab table. Bell had fashioned a makeshift heater from the Bunsen burner and the ceramic insert from a slow cooker. She had turned the pot upside down over the burner, seating its base on four square chunks of carving marble to hide as much of the light from the flame as possible.

The heat radiating from the pot was practically magic, but Howard's arrival had broken their easy companionship. He seemed a nice enough guy; he said he was in construction, and there was a half-mention of a wife. But he kept checking his phone as if a good signal would come back before power was restored to the local cell towers, and he had little interest in talking.

Rachel wasn't helping; she was doing her best to ignore the small group as she kept her scans as wide as possible. She split her attention as much as she could, tracking anything moving in the direction of the loft. Near the limit of her range, smaller raiding parties of rioters were beginning to come together and form larger packs, growing bolder with each additional member. The largest of these were attacking moving cars and breaking store windows. So far, they had stayed off of the streets nearest to the loft, but as Rachel watched, a black Lexus tore through the nearest crowd—

"Oh shit," Rachel whispered.

The others stopped talking.

"Bell? Hypothetically speaking?"

"Yeah?"

"Did anybody ever get around to printing one of those plastic guns?"

TWENTY-ONE

The shriek of metal against metal caused them all to hunch over, hands slapped against their ears. Rachel scanned the street below: the driver of the Lexus had lost control, his car scraping the side of a parked van before careening over the curb and into a fire hydrant. She flipped a quick scan through the car: the air bag had gone off, and the driver was trying to swim against the fabric. The diagnostic autoscript chimed in her head, telling her in unpronounceable terms that he had suffered a moderate concussion, along with other injuries that the script couldn't attribute to the car crash.

She left the Lexus and pushed her scans outwards: the crowd was still several blocks away, but they were burning red and coming at a run.

"Agent Peng?" Bell asked. "What's wrong?

"Nothing, if the morons who worked in D.C. would bother to use public transport. Bell, I need you to trade shoes with me," Rachel said, kicking off her heels and sliding them across the table.

"What?" LaPonsie was starting to panic. "What's going on? Why do you need her shoes?"

Rachel took a breath, and spoke as calmly as she could. "The car that crashed? It's got a bunch of federal parking stickers on it, and this is a very bad night to be a government employee who can afford to own a luxury vehicle. I need her shoes because I need to go down there and rescue the driver, and there's no way I'm doing it in mine."

Bell pushed her old Converse sneakers across the table. Rachel tried to ignore the slightly sour smell coming from them; the sneakers were warm and damp, and had been beaten into shape around Bell's feet. The rubber creaked as Rachel put them on, as if in protest. She stood to check the fit: a size too small, but better she was wearing shoes too tight than trying to carry a full-grown man's weight in heels.

Rachel threw a quick scan through the loft, and abandoned the scan just as fast. There was too much junk—it would take too long to search it on her own. Instead, she took Bell by the shoulder and pulled her in close.

"Find me a weapon," Rachel said her. "Something sharp with a handle, and strong enough so it won't break."

Bell's colors were already pale, and these took on a fearful hue. She swallowed and nodded, and vanished into the dark of the loft.

Rachel pinged Jason. *"I need an ambulance and MPD at the warehouse. There's been an accident, and a mob is coming."*

"On our way," he replied.

She started ripping her nylons apart, removing them without removing them. She half-noticed Howard slide his chair closer towards hers, but she glanced up at him when she saw his core of yellow sheltering her own southwestern turquoise.

"No offense," Howard whispered, "but I should be the one to go downstairs. If things get rough—"

"No." Rachel cut him off, as she tore the mess of nylon off and tossed it aside. "If things get rough, the three of you are going to break into an office with a fire escape, and hide there until the MPD arrives. Unless the building catches fire, and then you jump out the window and run like hell."

"Ms. Peng—"

"Agent Peng," she corrected him. "And before that, it was Warrant Officer Peng, Army CID. So unless you've hauled a soldier out of a burning Humvee, I guarantee I'm more qualified to run this rescue mission than you are."

His conversational colors slowly changed, turning over themselves and losing the yellow of fear as these were replaced with an odd teal. She had seen that color several times before, but she had never been able to place it in her ontology.

"Iraq?" he asked.

"Afghanistan."

Bell returned, her arms full of long, rattling objects. "Here," the girl said, kneeling so she could let the rods fall safely from her arms onto the floor.

One rolled towards Rachel. She stopped it with her foot and bent to pick it up. It was nearly three feet long; more than half of it was wood, a rock-hard walnut with grooves sized for larger hands, but it was tipped with a thick wedge of metal sharpened to a flattened point. She ran a cautious fingernail over the edge, and came back with half a manicure; the blade was sharper than a razor. "What are these?" she asked Bell.

"Extra-long chisels for wood turning," Bell replied. "Jake gets them from a guy he knows in England."

"Nice," Rachel said, swinging her chisel in front of her to test its balance. She felt like a knight with a new sword.

Howard knelt and picked up a second chisel.

"You coming?" she asked him.

He nodded, his yellows wrapping around her southwestern turquoise as if to protect it. That might cause problems; she'd have fought him on it, but it would have taken time that the man in the Lexus didn't have. Besides, two people could drag a man to safety faster than she could alone.

"Bell?"

The girl's head jerked up.

"I've called OACET. Jason's a few minutes away. Lock the doors, stay away from the windows, and don't open them until he gets here."

With that, she and Howard pounded downstairs.

By the time they reached the ground floor, she could feel the fury seething from the mob. They were still a block away, but closing fast. The iron bar she had used to seal the door was still in place; Rachel bashed the end of the bar with the handle of her chisel, knocking it away, and she and Howard were out.

The city was screaming. Sirens, near and far, split the air. There were gunshots, and other sounds she couldn't place, and the drone of helicopters as they circled overhead.

Behind her, Howard whispered a prayer. His colors fell to reds and grays and sickly yellows, a mix of everything wrong with the night—anger, misery, terror, guilt—twisting like a tornado.

Rachel grabbed him by the arm and pulled him after her.

The man in the Lexus had managed to open the door. That was as much as he could do for himself; he was bleeding from an ear, and unable to stand due to a badly broken leg. When Rachel and Howard reached the car, the man coughed, and tried to shut the door.

"Agent Peng, MPD," she said. "We're here to help." With that, she wrapped her good hand across his back, stuffed her shoulder in his armpit, and hauled him out of the car. Howard pushed himself under the man's other arm, and the three of them staggered as quickly as they could towards the warehouse.

"Thanks, thank you…" The man's voice was weak, and his head rolled as if he couldn't hold it steady. "'m Frank. Frank Bolden, from Homeland…"

"That's nice," Rachel replied. She had already run the E-ZPass on his windshield to get his name, and the parking passes on his car to learn where he worked. She had been amazed to learn that a bureaucrat from Homeland had not only survived what must have been a hell of a beating, but had also managed to escape an angry mob. Ten points for Homeland.

Bolden's busted leg slowed them down. He was dragging it, unable to pick it up; his foot kept knocking against Howard's knees, tripping him up as they ran. When Bolden lost consciousness, Rachel saw Howard drop his chisel as he struggled to keep his balance against the dead weight in his arms. She shifted as much of Bolden's weight to her as she could bear, forcing them to pick up the pace—

They had almost made it back to the warehouse when the mob turned the corner.

"C'mon," Rachel grunted. "Hurry!"

If they were lucky—if they were *really* lucky—Bolden's car would function as a decoy. Its lights were on, the engine still running, and pressurized water was starting to jet from the cracked fire hydrant. It might be enough to hold the mob's attention long enough for the three of them to disappear into the warehouse.

The three of them reached the side street, and Rachel kicked the door open at the same moment an angry shout rose up from the mob.

Caught! shouted her lizard brain. *Leave them! Run!*

She told her lizard brain to go fuck itself, and heaved Bolden into the lobby. The iron bar was where she had left it: she snatched it off of the ground and wedged it back into position.

"Get him into the elevator," she whispered to Howard. The leading edge of the mob had reached the door and were shaking it to see if it would open. "My guys are on their way. We can close the doors and get it stuck between floors until help arrives."

Howard didn't move. Rachel took a moment to check his colors: they were still the same swirling mix of reds, oranges, and grays...

She wanted to punch him for freezing up on her when she needed him, but she made herself take his nearest hand in both of hers. "Howard?" she said. "We have to hold this room—not for long, I promise! Just a few minutes. Can you keep it together?"

He didn't see her. "I didn't know it would be like this."

This time she slapped him. "Howard!"

He still didn't move, but now he noticed her, his colors shifting to let her see her southwestern turquoise caught in the edges of his internal storm.

"Right," she muttered. She abandoned Howard and Bolden, and turned her attention back to the door. The iron bar was holding, but there was a crack of night sky starting to appear between the door and its steel jamb. Rachel scanned the other side of the wall, and found knives, guns, even Howard's abandoned chisel, all held in the hands of people who burned blood-red.

"I didn't know it would be like this!" Howard said again,

much louder this time.

"I'm sorry you thought your first mob experience would be all kittens and rainbows!" she snarled. Jason's signal put her team at a block away and closing fast, and they still might not get there in time.

Rachel grabbed the door pull with both hands, put one leg on either side of the door, and threw her entire body into holding the door closed. The thermoplastic cast provided astonishingly good traction; she had the fleeting idea that she should start wearing one full-time.

Then the iron bar bent, just enough, and the muzzle of a gun appeared in the opening.

She didn't move; she *couldn't*. If she did, the door would open and that'd be it, game over, man! So she hung there with both feet off of the ground, in borrowed sneakers and a party dress, the familiar comfort of her ballistics vest lying on her bathroom floor at home—

I can't believe I'm about to die because of date night, she thought, as the black eye of the gun found her.

There was a sudden impact along her left shoulder as she crashed into the wall, and she felt something in her left hand break when it was too slow in letting go of the handle. These were nothing compared to the pain from the kick; Howard must have had some martial arts training back in the day, as the perfect side kick he drove into her ribs knocked her clean across the room.

She landed on her face. That didn't keep her from seeing the door fly open, Howard ramming her chisel into the stomach of the man with the gun, the man coughing, aiming, firing...

Howard's twisting colors turned blue-black, and then were snuffed out like a candle.

"Rachel!"

She heard Santino shouting her name from ages away, felt Jason wrap himself around her pain in the link and draw as much from her as he could hold. It was enough; her good hand found the iron bar and she launched herself forward, swinging.

She held the breach.

It could have been seconds, or hours, or days, but she knew nothing except the sound of iron on meat until she heard: "Peng! *Peng!* **Stand down, Peng!**"

The adrenaline haze lifted. She saw Hill standing in front of her, hard in Army greens. She scanned the area; Bolden in the corner, still unconscious but alive. Outside, the mob, hurting, broken, running from her and the MPD. And Howard—

"Oh *God!*" It was both a prayer and a sob; she dropped the iron bar and staggered over to Howard's body.

He had been shot at close range in the neck. It wasn't pretty, and it had been instantly fatal; her diagnostic autoscript reported spinal cord damage.

Behind her, Santino's colors faded to gray grief. "Rachel—"

"He saved my life," she heard herself say. "I was about to... There was a gun pointed right at me, and he knocked me out of the way—"

"Come on," Santino said. "Don't...just don't." He took her away from Howard's body and guided her to the stairwell.

Jason was waiting for her. She collapsed into his arms and he pulled her close, wrapping his hands around hers to share in her confusion and grief.

"We need to get you back to the mansion," he told her. *"You're hurt."*

"I need to give a statement. I need... Someone has to do damage control." For the first time she could remember, she didn't feel the need to laugh and let off stress. She just felt numb.

"It's chaos out there. No one has to know we're OACET—it'll be a lost detail," he said, touching the side of her face. She thought he was trying to comfort her, until she realized he was wiping Howard's blood off of her skin.

"Peng?"

Zockinski was kneeling in front of her. She pulled out of Jason's sense of self to focus on him; Jason sighed in relief as she took the pain back. She stood and dusted off her coat as best she could, and fell into parade rest. Her ribs were screaming. "Need a statement?" she asked Zockinski.

He nodded. She ran through everything that had happened since he left the loft, and spent the most time on Howard's decision to follow her downstairs, how he had helped her rescue Bolden from his wrecked car, how he had panicked, and then...

"He sacrificed himself to save me," Rachel told him. Except for her voice, the shabby lobby was silent; even the EMTs loading Bolden on a stretcher were hanging on her every word. "There is no doubt in my mind that he knew what he was doing when he kicked me out of the way."

She heard a small sob from above, and sent a scan into the stairwell. Bell and LaPonsie were on the second-floor landing, both of them standing with their backs to the wall to hide what was left of Howard from their line of sight. LaPonsie was weeping.

"All right," Zockinski said quietly. "Peng, you're done for tonight. You're a wreck."

She took stock of herself, and found Zockinski was right: there was Howard's blood, of course, but there was another layer of blood drying over his. For the first time, she noticed the walls and floor near the door were covered in fluids and tissue—she didn't often allow herself to cut loose, but when she did, she left her mark.

"I want to be there when you notify his next of kin," she said, letting herself sit back down on the stairs. Jason took a deep breath, reached out for her hand, and went red as part of her pain moved into him. "He mentioned a wife."

Zockinski moved towards Howard's body; Hill turned green and stepped outside before his partner started searching for Howard's wallet.

"Here we go," Zockinski said. "Howard L. Rothbauer from Leonardtown, Maryland. Wow. Guy had a hell of a commute..."

Zockinski kept talking, but Rachel couldn't hear him. There was nothing in her mind but poor Howard's name—

Rothbauer.

That name hadn't meant anything, before. Howard had been

just another faceless nobody. *A clue isn't a clue when it doesn't have a context*, she heard herself think—

And then there was Jason. He called out to her, tried to find her through her shock, *shouting!* Slapping her through the link as hard as he could.

She barely noticed.

Rothbauer.

"Jason?" Rachel heard herself ask. *"I need you to drive me to the hospital."*

TWENTY-TWO

Texas was always on her radar. When she had been overseas, she seized on every mention of Texas, those little conversational connections which kept her memories of home where they belonged. One piece of information she had picked up along the way was that soldiers who were badly burned were sent to the USAISR Burn Center at San Antonio. It didn't matter what branch of the military you were in; if you were a veteran and a burn victim, you went straight to Texas for treatment.

The exception was burn victims who also had traumatic brain injury. Then you went to Walter Reed.

No, not *that* one. The defrocked Walter Reed Army Medical Center had been closed a few years ago. Repurpose the historic buildings under different names, raze the modern ones to the ground, and it might be easier to forget the scandal, maybe, how the men and women who had served and come back broken were shoved into a vermin-infested hellhole. It had been replaced by the Walter Reed National Military Medical Center, a multipurpose medical complex which spilled over into area hospitals and clinics.

One of these housed soldiers who would never recover.

She had expected some sort of resistance at the door, but she was covered in blood and had a military record besides: she had no problem talking her way past the receptionists, telling them as long as she and Agent Atran were at Walter Reed to receive medical treatment for their heroic roles in the D.C. riots, they might as well pay a fast after-hours visit to a friend.

They got off of the elevator at the sixth floor. Anyone watching would have assumed they were a couple: Rachel was past the point where Jason could pull pain from her via the link alone, and they had resorted to skin contact. Holding hands was easiest, although it meant she had to concentrate to tell her feet apart from Jason's, and he kept shaking his head to clear it as her perceptions blurred his sight.

The rooms were small and close. Private rooms for each soldier: as Jenny had said, they were entering the post-antibiotic era. It was more convenient to put soldiers in shoeboxes designed to minimize exposure than to treat multiple infections after the fact.

She peered into each room as they walked the length of the hallway. The bodies in the beds lacked conversational colors— even those thin bubbles which had glided over the tops of the patients in the ICU was gone.

They stopped at the door of one of the last rooms on the hall. Jason peered through the window at the man lying on the bed, and gasped.

She didn't try to see the man's features (*what's left of them*, that horrible part of herself whispered), or dwell on how the pieces of his head were held together by a flexible sheet of plastic. She peered past these to check his colors. There was no prismatic soap bubble here, either. His surface colors were red, thick red…*pain-red.* Rachel went deeper, to try to see his core, and stopped when she realized that he was pain-red through and through.

She squeezed her eyes tight. It didn't help: the old boy in the bed still pulsed red.

How much pain, she wondered, *do you have to be in before it eats away your soul? How long does that pain have to last before it's the only thing left of you?*

Rachel took a step back, and flipped frequencies, searching. The chicken-wire window in front of her was coated in a collection of skin cells and oils. Squalene, sebum, a few other biological secretions she recognized but didn't know by name. The imprint was mostly round, and was just about six inches above where her forehead would be if she pressed it against the glass while watching the living-dead figure on the other side. The metal sill below was covered in a film of fingerprints and more secretions, many of which looked like burst rings, like water balloons dropped from a height.

"We're sorry for your loss," she whispered.

Jason's arms went around her, and she let him hold her while she cried.

"How did you know?" he asked when she finally pulled away.

She wiped her eyes with the back of her bad hand. *"I didn't. Not until after his father took a bullet for me. But I should have known when Howard walked into the loft—if you've never been there before, you can't help but stop and stare. Howard didn't even bother to look around."*

They had gone through Howard Rothbauer's records on the drive to the hospital. Howard had said he was in construction, but that was an oversimplification: he had managed a laundry list of contracting projects, including utilities installation and maintenance. His company hadn't worked on the Gayle Street update, but he would have known how to blend the canisters into the upgraded systems without raising suspicion.

"What do you know about Pat Tillman?" Rachel asked.

"The football player? The one who gave up his career when he volunteered to go to Iraq?"

She nodded. *"You know how he died?"*

"Friendly fire, right?"

"Yeah. Our own guys took him down," she said. *"Nobody's sure why, and there was a huge internal cover-up to keep the details out of the press. But—"*

She turned her scans back to the shape on the bed. *"Tillman's death turned into a huge scandal because he was famous. But the same thing happened to a lot of other soldiers. Close combat can get...messy.*

"This guy is famous, too," she told Jason, tapping softly on the glass. *"Not to the general public, like Tillman, but everyone in the Army's Criminal Investigation Command knows Keith Rothbauer's name. He was at the Second Battle of Fallujah, and his unit was pinned down by heavy fire in Operation Phantom Fury. He got hit by a white phosphorus round."*

"*What's that do?*"

Rachel paused. "*Melts the skin.*"

"Oh Jesus," Jason breathed aloud, glancing at the shape in the bed on the other side of the glass.

"Yeah," she sighed, then returned to their link. "*Thing is, our side was the only one with WP rounds. And our side tried to deny using them as part of our offensive munitions.*"

"*That's bad,*" Jason said.

"*No,*" Rachel said, shaking her head. "*Phosphorus burns on American soldiers are a problem. Bad is when an American soldier with phosphorus burns is shot and left to die on the side of a road in Iraq. Very, **very** bad is when the Iraqi physician who saved his life turns him back over to the United States, and the bullets that physician took out of the soldier's body are American munitions.*"

"*A mercy shooting?*"

"*That's the kindest answer. Could have been mercy, could have been mutiny. Or anything, really—war's mindless. If there was any proof of a cause, we'll never know about it. There was a massive cover-up. Evidence was lost, members of Rothbauer's unit were stationed overseas before they could testify. Nobody was held responsible. The CID in Iraq were furious. They wanted accountability for one of our own who was used up and thrown away like garbage. They fought like demons to try to get to the truth, but...*

"*It's not like the movies.*" Her mental voice was sad and quiet. "*The worst crimes usually aren't resolved. Our commanding officers made a lot of promises to find out who was responsible, but nothing ever happened. The brass tried to wait us out, but the CID didn't let it go. At the end of the day, they sent Rothbauer back to the States, with the promise he'd get the best medical care available.*"

"*Did they ever admit what happened to him?*"

"*No. But the CID has kept his story alive. His, and hundreds like his.*"

Jason was shocked. "*This happened to **hundreds** of soldiers?*"

"*Same basic story, plenty of changes to the setting, characters, plot... If it had just been Rothbauer, we probably could have gotten the Army to move, but with so many who were hurt, or raped, or killed... I personally worked a dozen cases like his. Public pressure works best when it's focused on one cause. There were just too many causes, too many victims.*

"*But we did get them to stop lying to us,*" she said, and now she was pretty sure she wasn't talking to Jason any more. "*It's not perfect—they still send us off to die—but now they have to tell us why. If we keep at it, if we keep pushing back, we'll hold them accountable for things like this, too.*

"*That's why we remember Rothbauer's name,*" she finished, her mental voice soft.

"*You told his father you used to be CID.*" It wasn't a question: Jason had figured out why Howard Rothbauer had taken a bullet for her.

"Yeah," she sighed. "*He must have known how we fought for his son. When we were trapped in the stairwell, he kept saying he didn't know it would 'be like this.' I thought he meant he had never expected a riot to be as bad as it was. I didn't realize he was saying he was responsible for it.*"

They watched Rothbauer's chest rise and fall with the aid of the ventilator.

After a few moments, Jason asked, "*What do we do?*"

She reached out through her implant to caress the IV morphine drip running into the vein on Rothbauer's arm.

"*No!*" Jason was still holding her hand, and his panic leapt within her. "*Don't!*"

Rachel gently pulled his mind into her perspective. "*Look at him*" she told Jason. She focused her attention on the shape on the bed, and brought the other Agent into the emotional spectrum. "*You see that red? You see how he's nothing but red? That's all pain,*" she explained. "*There's no soul left in him. No identity. No sense of self. He's never coming back, and what's left of him is suffering.*"

"*This isn't your decision to make.*"

"This isn't something to decide," she said. *"This is what's right."*

"This is what's right to you," Jason said. *"But our faces are on the security feed. If he dies through spontaneous equipment failure, they'll come after OACET."*

Fuck, she thought.

Jason heard her, and his anxiety eased as she took her mind away from the morphine dispenser. He looked back at the soldier on the bed, and his conversational colors wove in and out of themselves as he weighed the options.

"Not while we're here," he decided. *"And not for at least a month, until they can't connect us to it."*

She laughed, sharp and cruel. *"Your idea of mercy sucks."*

He was still sharing her perspective, and he closed his eyes so he could see Rothbauer. *"I know."*

After a moment, he asked, "What do we do now?"

Rachel didn't answer him.

"Rachel?"

"It was a good plan, if you think about it," she said. The numbness she had felt since the stairwell was fading as the shock wore off, and it was getting harder to ignore the pain. She wanted to go to the mansion and sleep within a cocoon of the collective for the next decade. *"Sort of a...a subverted form of false flag terrorism."*

"Yeah," Jason sighed. *"Make the public think the government staged an attack on its own people to justify its budget."*

"And the public would demand greater transparency and oversight within the military," Rachel finished. *"Rothbauer could rationalize Gayle Street as the cost of the greater good.*

"Oh God," she said aloud, and started giggling at last. "He would have gotten away with it, too, if it weren't for those darned national security scandals!"

The giggling was unsustainable; her ribs throbbed with each breath. Even with Jason carrying half of the load, it hurt too much. The fit burned itself out almost immediately, and she slumped against the wall.

"So," she asked him. *"What **do** we do?"*

And then Jason's eyes went wide and his colors went white, and she knew he understood why she had brought him. Not Santino, who could reason his way through any ethical quagmire and still come out on the side of a passive good. And definitely not Phil, who didn't quite understand that this was a world in which blood was a commodity, and not always a precious one.

"Oh, Rachel—" he whispered aloud.

He started to pull his hand away, but she dug her fingers into his and pulled him close. "Do we let this happen?" she asked him, as quietly as she could, and out of the link to make sure no one else in the collective might hear. "It won't come back on OACET—no one else will ever know how we put the pieces together.

"And maybe things need to change. You saw those riots! The country can't go on this way without breaking. Maybe it would be better to have a small break now and let some of the pressure escape, instead of allowing it to build so it explodes. Good things could happen. Legislation could be written," she said, and then placed her hand against the window to Rothbauer's room. "People might finally be held accountable."

"Why are you asking me? You don't even like me!"

"Because I know you can keep a secret," she whispered back. "And this isn't a black or white question. It's a decision, but it's too big for one person to make, and you're the only other Agent who's part of this who knows that the ends can sometimes justify the means."

She watched an ugly rainbow weave itself together within his conversational colors. Anxiety and anger, panic, fear...and excitement. Finally, Jason shook himself. "No."

"Why not?" she whispered back.

"Because if I agreed to let this happen, it'd be to make Congress pay for what they did to us."

"That's a pretty good reason."

"That's a *shit* reason!" Jason snapped. "Rothbauer's dad might have been doing it for revenge, too, but he was also doing it to avenge his son. If we're going to let the country burn itself down, it should be for better reasons than to scratch our itch."

"Okay," she said, and let Jason pull his hand out of hers. The full measure of pain rushed back into her; she grabbed the window sill to keep herself on her feet.

"That's it?" Jason asked, his colors an angry yellow-orange. "Just...okay?"

Rachel shrugged. "That's what I was thinking, too, but I needed to hear it from you."

She turned her back on Rothbauer and walked away, Jason stumbling after.

They had almost finished the hour-long drive back to the mansion before he said anything. "There's no guarantee."

"Hmm?" She had shut down the emotional spectrum once they left the hospital, and Jason couldn't drive while nursing phantom pain. With emotions off and their link closed, Jason had turned into a mystery.

"I came up with a better reason."

Rachel kept the grin off of her face. "Which is?"

"If we did let it happen—let the country blow off steam, that is—there's no guarantee the right people would go down. The fallout would be random."

"Well, yeah." Rachel was surprised it had taken him this long to think it through. "That's what war is."

His head snapped towards her, and she didn't need any cyborg tricks to feel the fresh wave of disgust as it rolled off of him.

"Jason," she said, as she sighed aloud. "You realize you and I are already at war, right?"

"With each other?"

"No, idiot. OACET is at war. It's us versus them. Mulcahy thinks it'll get better if we keep working at it. I don't know about that. He might be right—I hope he's right!—but if he is, it'll be a long time before we stop fighting.

"I do know everything we do now is tactical. Strategic. Because if we fuck up, they'll pull us down. Do you agree?"

"Yeah."

"What are your limits on what you'd do to keep us safe?"

He didn't answer, but the lines of his face and body softened.

"We don't need to fight Rothbauer's war for him," Rachel said. "We could let it go until it burns itself out. And after that, we could probably turn what he did to our advantage, maybe discover that one critical piece of evidence that no one else found—"

"He died in front of you, so it'd be plausible if you started digging into his history."

"Exactly," she said. "We'd be heroes. OACET put the pieces together and discovered who was responsible for Gayle Street when nobody else could."

"But?"

"But I'd rather not fight more than one war at once," she admitted. "OACET's already working with limited resources, and all of our existing plans hinge on knowing who the key players are. Tactically, it's safer to turn Rothbauer in, and use him to prove that Homeland wasn't responsible. What happened on Gayle Street was home-grown domestic terrorism, plain and simple."

"Yeah," Jason sighed, as he turned onto the mansion's front driveway. "You ever think you'd get to this point in life? Plotting whether or not to go through with a minor *coup d'état*?"

"Honestly? Yes," she said. "But I thought I'd have been appointed Secretary of Defense first."

He stared at her. "You're kidding, right?"

"Mostly. Suppressing Rothbauer's involvement and letting the riots burn themselves out might not work, anyhow. I'll bet our team is probably already done sifting through Rothbauer's office, and if I know Santino, he's already found what he needs to wrap this mess up."

"Not what I meant," Jason said. When she smiled at him, he shook his head and sighed.

"Can you brief Administration?" she asked him. "I'm really starting to hurt. Where I fall, that's where I shall be buried."

"What?"

"It's from Robin Hood, sort of...the arrow and the grave?" Jason stared at her blankly. "Never mind," she said. "Just tell them about the connection between Gayle Street and Rothbauer once I pass out. And call Santino? Our team needs the same information."

He nodded.

The front gates were locked, but swung open before either she or Jason could ping them; someone was waiting for them.

Many someones, actually: Rachel felt a large number of the collective standing by the curve of the driveway. When the car stopped, she stepped out and into Josh's arms.

"If you hug me right now, I will shoot you," she warned him.

"I know," he assured her.

The others surrounded her and took the pain away. She flipped on the emotional spectrum to see if they could bear it, and found herself immersed within that same odd teal.

Oh, she realized, as her heart broke a little. *Teal means family.*

They waited for Jason, and then they all went down to the skull cellar together.

The medical lab was filled to capacity. Jenny Davies and the other physicians were scrambling to keep up with the damage; even Hope Blackwell was there, stitching up a long gash on an Agent's arm. Every member of OACET who had been involved in the riots seemed to have been injured in some way or another. These injuries were mostly minor, but four out of the five hospital beds in the back were occupied, and Rachel had a sneaking suspicion she knew why that fifth bed was still empty.

Jenny glided up, all professional whites, and assessed Rachel with a hawk's eye. *"Three cracked ribs, internal bruising, distal radius and metacarpal fractures... Good, I can finally put you in a proper cast.*

"Take a shower," Jenny said to her. *"Josh, Jason, go with her, and make sure you scrub the blood out of her hair. I'm not treating her like this."*

The three of them made their way to the community bathroom. Phil was already there, half-dressed and with bruises down the left side of his body.

"What happened to you?" she asked.

"You should see the other Buick," he replied, and came over to help her out of her jacket.

The back of his knuckles brushed against her bare arm, and she felt love, belonging, relief... The tension Rachel hadn't known she was carrying vanished as she learned the sourness between them was gone.

The four of them stripped and showered. It might have been somewhat awkward for Rachel if Josh hadn't been there: as he was, and as he had recently gone to Aspen with seven members of the U.S. women's ski team, it was easy for her to get lost in his stories instead of letting her prudish nature fret itself sick. By the time he got to the part about his underwear and the wild elk, she was clean, dry, and the shared pain from Rachel's laughter had them all begging Josh to stop.

They raided the community closet, and shuffled back to the medical lab in ill-fitting clothes. Rachel was wearing an old t-shirt of Mako's, and the hem hit at her knees. When they reached the lab, Jenny pointed wordlessly at the empty hospital bed in the back room. The men helped Rachel into the bed, Josh gave her a kiss on her forehead, and they finally let her rest.

She flipped off the visual spectrum, and let herself float within the warmth of the collective.

Clean sheets and family, she thought. *Is there anything better?*

"Not that I've found," replied Patrick Mulcahy.

She jumped as she turned visuals back on: Mulcahy was looming over her.

"Shit! Sorry," she said, and tried to stand.

He put a heavy hand on her shoulder. *"Don't,"* he said. *"I just came by to thank you."*

She didn't need the emotional spectrum to know that was a white lie; he was multitasking, his own fresh bandages hidden under his shirt.

"Thank me?" she asked, surprised he already knew: Jason

must have flown through the debriefing.

"Do you know who you rescued?"

"Res—Oh, right. Bolden, the Lexus dude."

"You mean, Deputy Assistant Director Franklin P. Bolden, from the Department of Homeland Security."

She couldn't keep herself from chuckling. A Deputy Assistant Director was almost as high up the bureaucratic food chain as it got. *"I did not plan that,"* she promised.

"I know. If you had, I'd be giving you a bonus," he said. She flipped emotions on, and saw he was smiling.

"Out." Jenny Davies appeared, brandishing a pair of medical shears at Mulcahy.

"Jenny—"

"Patrick? Tonight, she's my patient. Out."

Mulcahy nodded. *"Heal fast, Penguin,"* he said to Rachel, and turned to leave.

"Oh, Mulcahy?" Rachel called. "I also solved the Gayle Street bombings. Jason has the details."

He didn't bother to turn back as he left the room, but she saw him cover his mouth with a hand as he turned a vivid purple, and dropped out of the link so the others wouldn't feel him roar with astonished silent laughter.

Jenny sighed. *"Did you really learn what happened on Gayle Street?"*

"Yeah," Rachel replied. "I think so. I feel like there's something I missed, but it'll come."

"Tell me what happened."

She did. The horror of what the Rothbauers had endured had been locked away in the back of her mind since she and Jason arrived at the mansion, and it came flooding out in the telling. While she spoke, Jenny poked and prodded, cutting off the old thermoplastic cast to set Rachel's wrist and rewrap it in cotton, and coaxing her out of Mako's comfy shirt to tape up her ribs. The only time Jenny faltered in her work was when Rachel mentioned the extent of Keith Rothbauer's phosphorus burns, and Jenny's professional whites gave way to a nauseated green.

When Rachel reached the end, she realized she was fading, her head rolling down as she tried to stay awake. "Not exactly a bedtime story," she said to Jenny. "I think it's time for you to dope me up so I can go offline."

"Adrenaline crash," Jenny said, pulling the sheets over Rachel's new hospital gown. *"And I'm not doping you. Activate the biofeedback autoscript, and tell the timer it needs to keep you under for eight hours. It'll knock you out, but you'll stay online so we can manage your pain."*

She was too tired to argue, but not to barter. "If the autoscript doesn't work, then can I get some drugs?"

"Yes, Rachel. If the autoscript doesn't work, I promise I will personally dope you into oblivion."

"Good," Rachel said, and summoned her newest script. "Ready?" she asked Jenny. Her eyes were already heavy.

"One last thing," Jenny said, brushing Rachel's short hair behind her ear with the back of her fingers. The familiar sense of Jenny's love and strength crossed into her, and she heard Jenny ask, *"You said you were nearly shot?"*

"Yeah?" Rachel replied, holding the autoscript lightly within her mind.

"You didn't run."

It took Rachel a moment, and then she understood. *"Yeah,"* she said, smiling, as the autoscript carried her away.

TWENTY-THREE

She awoke a few hours after dawn, her good hand clasped firmly in Shawn's. The room was dark, the only light coming from the low glow of the wine fridge and from the tiny reading light dangling over Shawn's head. If she'd had her old eyesight, she might not have even noticed that Shawn was wearing an old football jersey but was completely naked from the waist down.

Shawn must have felt her wake; he leaned back and gave her a wide grin. Combined with the reading light bobbing around on its suspension wire, the grin gave Shawn an eerie similarity to an anglerfish.

"Hello, Shawn," she said.

"Hello, Rachel! I'm supposed to tell Jenny when you wake up!"

"Thank you," she said. The cotton wrapping on her left hand had been swallowed up by an old-fashioned plaster behemoth of a cast. There was writing on it: Rachel flipped frequencies to read *STOP FUCKING AROUND!!!* in thick block letters an inch tall. At the foot of her bed was a canvas sling the right size and shape to cover the cast: Jenny had finally found a way to immobilize Rachel's hand while she was at work.

The room was quiet, the Agents occupying the other four beds still asleep. She flipped the emotional spectrum on. Shawn's silver minnows were swimming in a red sea; she ran the diagnostic script on him to learn where he had been hurt, but the script came back clean. Rachel traced the source of the red through his colors and found it was flooding into him through their clasped hands, and realized that for the first time since Howard Rothbauer had kicked her, she felt no pain.

"Oh, Shawn, I'm sorry," she said, as she tried to pull away. "You don't have to do that for me."

He wouldn't let her take her hand back. "Rachel?" he said, with all of the seriousness of a five-year-old about to deliver the punchline to a joke.

"Yes?"

"Shut up."

She grinned; there was a stripe of Josh's core of tattoo blue within Shawn's conversational colors. She wondered how long it had taken Josh to coach Shawn before he got the timing right.

"Rachel?" Shawn said again. He was inspecting their joined hands as if they held secrets. "I never forgot what pain felt like. Is it good?"

"Sometimes. It can keep us from making decisions that might hurt us."

Either Shawn had asked the wrong question, or she had given the wrong answer; his colors tipped over themselves like pills in a bottle. She was saved from additional Shawn-management by a quiet knock on the divider separating the ICU from the rest of the medical suite.

"Hey, Jenny," she sent to the woman on the other side of the divider. *"You and Santino can come on in."*

Her partner entered, with Jenny in tow. He was carrying a manila folder.

Rachel ran a scan through it; not text, a photograph... *Oh.* "You get any sleep?" she asked him in a low voice, pointing at the folder.

"No," he replied. "I'll sleep when this is over. You ready to go?"

"What?" Jenny whispered, her mood twisting and turning stabbing-sharp. "No. She needs to stay here for one day, minimum, and then I *might* let you take her home."

"A man died for me, Jenny. I'm going to see this through to the end." Rachel gestured for Santino to pass her a nearby bathrobe; he did not need to see her stagger to the community bathroom with her ass hanging out of a hospital gown. "I'll come right back as soon as it's over, and you can finally chain me to the bed."

"We're just going to First District Station," Santino promised Jenny.

Jenny's colors glazed in resignation. "Police station, then right back here," she said. "No vest, no gun, no movement faster than a walk."

"Agreed," Rachel promised. She wrestled her good hand away from Shawn's, and gasped as the full weight of her pain settled back in her ribs. Jenny didn't have to worry about her running through the halls; she could barely stand up.

When she returned from the bathroom, her hair wet from a soapless shower, and wearing someone else's emergency suit and shoes, Jenny and Shawn had gone. Santino was waiting, a plastic grocery bag dangling from an arm. He helped her into the sling, and they left the warmth of the medical lab behind them.

They took the route through the mansion with the fewest stairs, and Santino passed her the grocery bag while he went to get the car. She opened it and found a bottle of water, a cold tuna sandwich, and a small slip of folded paper containing two codeine pills. "Bless you, Jenny Davies," Rachel muttered, ripping apart the cellophane wrapping. By the time Santino drove up, the sandwich and the pills were gone, and Rachel was feeling nearly near-human again.

The drive back to the city was like a dream; nobody was on the roads. "Tell me what happened," she said.

"I don't remember much of the riot," he admitted. "Everything seemed fine, at the beginning. We were talking, they were listening. Then, someone broke a window and they completely flipped their shit. The only reason they didn't trample us flat is because last night? The MPD were the good guys. I never want to be in that situation when the MPD are the bad guys."

Rachel nodded. "Amen."

"Once we got backup, we were fine. The uniforms started to funnel the crowd into parks, try to keep them off of the street… Sometimes it worked, sometimes it didn't."

"Fire hoses?"

"Yeah." Santino winced. "Along with pepper spray and rubber bullets. Didn't you read the reports?"

She had browsed the news feeds while she was in the shower, but it was somehow more authentic to hear it from Santino. "Sixteen dead, hundreds injured."

"And the fires, and so much property damage it'll take days to add up. Did you hear that the blackout was caused by teenagers?"

"What?"

"Bunch of stupid-ass kids figured out a way to blow transformers. They managed to coordinate the blowouts across the city. It'll be days before the grid is stable again. Once we round them up, the DA wants to charge them with multiple counts of constructive manslaughter and try them as adults."

"Good," she said, and meant it. She pointed at the manila folder on the dashboard. "How did you find this?"

"We checked the local support groups. All of the community centers were open late, in case people needed shelter from the riots. Howard Rothbauer moved from Arizona to Maryland about three years ago, to be closer to his son, and we knew when the canisters were installed, so that gave us a timeline. The rest of it was just a bunch of volunteers going through old security footage.

"It's ironic," he said, a little bit of humor sneaking into his grays. "We never would have found proof this fast, if it weren't for the riots."

"How did you know?"

"That woman? Grace LaPonsie? She stuck around while we went through Rothbauer's office. Good thing, too. She was surprised to learn Rothbauer paid his rent biweekly, when she and everyone she knew in the building paid each quarter."

"Oh, now that's clever."

"Right? So, how did *you* know?"

"I didn't. Not until you showed up with the photo." She pressed her hand against her taped ribs, testing if the codeine was still going strong. It was, and she chanced a deep breath before adding, "I just couldn't bring myself to think the guy who let himself take a bullet for me was a hundred percent evil."

Santino let her out at the main door of First District Station. The front steps still clung to their heritage as an elementary school; she felt as though she were skipping class as she waited for Santino to find a parking space.

When he rejoined her, they walked through halls filled with officers shining in bright, cheery yellow. The dark mood that had hung over the building was gone: Gayle Street had been solved—not just closed, but *solved!*—by their own people. She and Santino all but got a standing ovation as they made their way towards the meeting rooms.

"What exactly did you boys do after I went to the mansion?" she whispered.

"Once Jason called us, we ripped apart everything Howard Rothbauer owned. We couldn't find anything to tie him to the bombings, but we did find a pair of gloves with McElroy's blood on them," he whispered back. "It's circumstantial at best, but…"

She sighed. "But it's not like you have to convince a jury."

"Yeah." He paused, and she caught some mild orange irritation seeping into his conversational colors. "You should have told me about Rothbauer before you left."

"I wasn't sure until I saw his son," she told him. "And after I did, I wasn't sure how to handle it."

Santino blinked down at her: she saw her own turquoise core, along with Zia's violet, Phil's silver-light, and all the others, moving and twisting within his conversational colors, and all of which existed on a separate plane from the professional blues of the MPD.

She nodded.

"I don't like that," he told her, feigning a smile as he waved to a passing friend.

"Please let me know when my options get easy," she said. "Honestly, I don't know if I'll be able to recognize that if it happens."

They reached the Annex, a room furnished with several

chairs, a stainless-steel table, and a television mounted next to a small one-way mirror set in the wall. On the other side of the one-way mirror was a deliciously posh meeting room, a comfortable space designed for four people to relax with fresh coffee in the leather club chairs. The meeting room had deep pile carpeting, mahogany wainscoting, and low bookshelves nestled under antique oil paintings. There was even a cappuccino machine in the corner.

Santino assured her that Washington's elite expected such treatment, but she wasn't convinced; even if she weren't a cop, she would have heard the trap snap shut the instant she stepped into that room.

She and Santino were the first to arrive, and she headed straight for a chair in the corner. Codeine or not, she had reached her limit on standing upright.

A few minutes later, they were joined by Zockinski. He was dressed in his nicest suit, his colors popping in happy purples and bright yellows. There was a strong streak of gray exhaustion underneath those; he hadn't slept and was running on caffeine. "Nice job last night, Peng," he said, as he hung his suit coat by the door. "C'mere so I can give you a hug."

She shot him a one-fingered salute with her good hand.

"Really, how're you doing?" Zockinski sat across from her, spread out across the metal table.

"Broken ribs, broken wrist, broken…whatever the bones inside the hands are called."

"Metacarpals."

"Thank you, Santino. Broken those."

Zockinski snorted. "I believe it. When we showed up, you had a serious Valkyrie thing going. The EMTs took eight men to the hospital because of you."

"No, they took eight men went to the hospital because those men wanted to hurt me," she said. "Clear cause-and-effect relationship, in my opinion."

"No argument here. Hey," Zockinski said, "you know how you wanted to be there when we notified Howard Rothbauer's next of kin?" When she nodded, he said, "There isn't any. That wife he mentioned? She committed suicide not long before he moved to Maryland."

"God, this keeps getting sadder," she said. "He was talking about her as if she was still alive."

"The people we've been able to locate—his coworkers, old neighbors—they all mentioned he had a breakdown after his wife died. What happened to his son was bad enough, but he couldn't take losing both of them. So, yeah, the last few years? His life was misery."

"What's the final death toll for Gayle Street?" she asked.

"Fifty-eight," Santino said. "About triple that in injuries."

"Right," she said, slumping over to rest her chin on her good hand. "Good luck reconciling those two tragedies. I know I can't do it."

The door opened again, and a reporter who was friendly with OACET entered, followed by Jonathan Dunstan and Josh Glassman. Dunstan's colors were mainly gray and had been whipped flat, while Josh's were light and gleeful; the Agent had taken Dunstan aside for a friendly pre-meeting chat.

"Morning, folks," Josh said. "This is Kathleen Patterson, from the *Washington Post*, and you all know Dunstan. They're up-to-date on the events of last night, and are eager to start writing, but I've managed to convince them that a brief tour of First District Station will be worth their time."

Nice, Rachel thought. It wasn't exactly illegal for the MPD to invite the media to watch an interview, but the liability skyrocketed. Josh, on the other hand, was neither MPD nor affiliated with the Gayle Street investigation, and everyone could pretend he just happened to bring the reporters to the right place at the right time.

Patterson's conversational colors were churning. Whatever Josh had promised Patterson had gotten her worked up in the worst way, and...and Rachel decided to leave the rest of that thought alone.

On the other side of the one-way glass, Sturtevant and Hill

had entered the executives' meeting room. Hill carefully positioned a manila folder that was a twin to Santino's on the coffee table. Then the two of them began to fluff and dust; the meeting room was kept under lock and key until it was needed, the brass well aware that the beat cops and detectives would turn it into a lounge the first chance they got. Rachel watched through the wall as Hill got the cappuccino machine heated up, and took some porcelain mugs out of a storage cupboard.

The mugs *matched*.

Rachel shook her head in disbelief. If she ever walked into a room in a police station and saw a matching set of coffee mugs, she would never stop running.

"Okay, people," Josh said. "Here we go."

The television flared to life as Terry Templeton and a second man entered the meeting room. The hidden microphones picked up Sturtevant's warm welcome, but that didn't go past his skin; to Rachel, Sturtevant showed the same reds and blacks that he had worn that first day on Gayle Street.

The monotony of the first ten minutes of the interview was to be expected, as Sturtevant and Hill asked the right questions to put Templeton and his lawyer at ease. *Of course* Templeton had to come down to the station, and provide some information about Howard Rothbauer. *Of course* they all knew this was a waste of time. *Of course* they knew that Templeton had never met Howard Rothbauer, ever. It was all bad luck and coincidence, and they all just needed to clear the air.

Oh, and one more thing...

Hill casually moved his hand from his porcelain mug to the manila folder, and flipped the cover open.

Rachel watched as Templeton instinctively glanced down at the photograph. His conversational colors closed in on themselves, as though he had shut his eyes.

"The support group was supposed to be confidential," he said.

"The group was," Hill said. "The community center where it was held? Not so much."

"It was years ago. I didn't think they'd still have the footage."

Templeton's colors were shifting towards purple, as if there were humor in the situation. Beside him, his lawyer was open-mouthed in shock as he realized what the photograph might mean.

Terry Templeton and Howard Rothbauer, standing together. Talking.

Hill slid the first photograph to the side, and there was another beneath it, nearly identical to the first save for the men's winter clothes.

"Digital storage," Sturtevant said. "Cheap and plentiful. There's no good reason to delete security files any more. Seems like the kind of thing someone like you should know."

Templeton sighed, and his colors locked themselves down. It was a common enough visual phenomenon within the MPD's Interrogation wing, where those who knew they were caught stopped talking. "Please direct all questions to Mr. Hunter," he said, gesturing towards his lawyer.

"I need to call my office." The lawyer's voice was almost a squeak.

Hill smiled like a viper. "Don't bother," he said. "Your client thinks he already knows how this'll end. He's sure that Rothbauer left nothing to incriminate him, since there's nothing to tie the two of them together except some old photographs and some rent checks.

"Good move on the rent checks, by the way," Hill said to Templeton. "Rothbauer drops his check in the building's mail slot every other week, and you slide his receipt under his door. No cell phones, no email, nothing to connect you to each other. Hell, you even cut out the post office, just in case."

On the other side of the wall, Rachel stifled a chuckle. She loved watching Hill work.

"So, rent checks and receipts to exchange notes," Hill said. "You probably destroyed the notes and the envelopes, but we found all of Rothbauer's receipts in a file. Taxes, you know. Nobody wants an audit. Forensics has those, in case you were wondering. They're testing those to see if there was any transfer left behind from the notes.

"There's close to forty receipts in that file," Hill said, leaning towards Templeton. "Are you a betting man? 'Cause the odds aren't good for you, but you never know. You might still get out of this."

"We're done here," the attorney said, standing. He had recovered from the shock of learning Templeton was involved in Gayle Street, and his instincts had kicked in. Fight or flight? Yes, please.

"No," Sturtevant said. "We're not. Did you know your client has been trying to branch into defense contracting?"

Templeton's colors bleached white.

Rachel sighed and slumped back in her chair as the final piece of the puzzle dropped into place. *Rage and money,* she thought. *It's always rage or money, or both. And two men, but each of them was acting alone...*

How did we manage to get it all right and wrong at the same time?

The attorney sat back down, revulsion clear within his colors. That same sickly orange-green was reflected in the colors of every other person within the two rooms, save Templeton's.

"This is what we think went down," Hill said. "Your son is killed in Iraq. You're mourning, you bump into Rothbauer at the support group, and for a while you're just two angry dads. Then one of you—probably Rothbauer, since he's got no closure—starts talking about payback. No, not just payback. He wants payback with a purpose. And you? You're a smart guy, and you've just filed a patent for one of your makers, and since Rothbauer's in construction, you've got this idea that's so crazy it Just. Might. Work.

"At the beginning, it was all talk, right?" Hill said, watching Templeton for signs he was hitting close to home. Templeton didn't so much as twitch, but Rachel saw his fear, his stress and anxiety... There was even a large measure of shame, and this grew as Hill kept moving through his version of events. "The thing about this bomb you built? *It never had to go off.* For a while, it was the ultimate form of walk-and-talk therapy. The two of you did something secret. Something *empowering*. And once it was done? You could forget it existed and get on with your lives."

"But you couldn't, could you? It *itched*. All of this power, right there, waiting... You could win yourself the world, if you got the timing right.

"Did Rothbauer know why you started pushing him to set Gayle Street off?" Hill asked. "Or did he still think you wanted justice for your sons? From what we've learned about him, it seems like he'd be pissed if he found out you'd profit from the bombing.

"See, Congress and the military are about to throw down over budget," Hill explained to Templeton's attorney. "There's a big problem with the current state of the military, where it's become so institutionalized it might as well be a force of nature. Certain people—politicians, defense contractors, traditionalist officers... you get the idea—these people *love* their tanks and battleships. Problem is, we don't fight tank-and-battleship wars these days. Congress and the military both say they need to align how the military spends its money with these new wars, but that's like changing the course of a river."

"Which can be done," Sturtevant added. "But you either need a million years, or dynamite."

"Blow Gayle Street, convince the public the military is behind it, then make sure the public turns against the military," Hill said. "And there's the excuse needed to gut the existing system and make major reforms.

"One of those being a major shift from a military-industrial complex to a military-digital complex," Sturtevant said. "With Templeton Industries poised to provide the hardware for everything from drones to new surveillance devices."

"We need more time to find your lobbyists," Hill said to Templeton. "When we find them, they'll probably have plenty of interesting things to say about what you've promised you can deliver."

"One thing I don't understand," Sturtevant said. "How did you convince Rothbauer to kill my officers? I know why; I don't think I'll ever understand how."

"Am I under arrest?" Templeton asked.

Sturtevant and Hill said nothing.

Templeton finished his coffee, stood, and walked out of the room.

No one followed him except for Rachel, who sent her mind down the hallway after him. Templeton was staggering on weak legs towards the entrance. She rather hoped he'd have a heart attack and drop dead on the spot, but no such luck; Templeton left the building and vanished into the autumn sunlight.

"I didn't know." The attorney was all but pleading with Sturtevant and Hill. "I swear, I didn't know!"

Rachel pulled herself back into the Annex, and felt Josh reach out and snap off the television. The attorney's voice cut out in mid-protest. The other Agent turned Dunstan and Patterson, and said, "I hope you both enjoyed your tour of First District Station."

"Very much so. Thank you, Agent Glassman," Patterson said. They were her first words since she had arrived, and her voice was as warm and rich as expensive chocolate. Patterson nodded at the others, and left.

Dunstan seemed rooted in place. He was staring through the one-way glass, his colors weighing OACET's greens and golds against a complicated, tangled mess of emotions.

Josh tapped Dunstan on the shoulder. "Would you like to continue our conversation?"

Dunstan didn't reply, but he let Josh steer him away. The Agent tipped his head over his shoulder, and shot Rachel a wink as the door closed behind them.

"Remind me to never, ever get on OACET's bad side," Santino said.

"What did I miss?" Zockinski asked.

"There's not enough evidence to go after Templeton," Rachel said. "There never will be—he used Rothbauer to keep his own hands clean."

"That part I knew," Zockinski said. "And how those reporters can go digging where we can't."

"Well, Dunstan's got a decision to make," Rachel said. "He can use this tip to help him break the biggest story of his career, and owe OACET forever, or he can let it slide and stay allied to Hanlon."

"It's nice and all, telling Dunstan he'd benefit from ditching Hanlon and siding with OACET, but it's better to prove it," Santino finished for her.

There was a tapping on the one-way glass. Hill stood there with one eyebrow raised. Zockinski walked over and knocked out a quick "Shave and a Haircut", and his partner vanished. A moment later, the doorknob rattled, and Sturtevant and Hill entered the Annex.

"That went better than I had hoped," Sturtevant said to the room.

"The meeting, or the entire Gayle Street investigation?" Rachel asked.

He ignored her. "As of now, your jobs have changed," he said to the room at large. To Zockinski and Hill, he added, "Officially, you're still Detectives, but you're no longer with Homicide."

"Sir! We—"

"In case I wasn't clear, Zockinski, this is a promotion, not a punishment, with titles, duties, and wages to be adjusted accordingly. Santino, same for you. Congratulations." Sturtevant paused. "Agent Peng, I wish I could reward you, but…"

"I know," she assured him. "I'm good, but thanks."

"Sir?" Zockinski asked, angry in reds at losing Homicide. "Why?"

"Because this is going to keep happening," Santino said.

Sturtevant pointed at him.

"Sir?" Zockinski wasn't going down without a fight. "With all due respect, Gayle Street was a once-in-a-lifetime event."

"Probably," Sturtevant said. "But tell me this: could it happen again? If you can promise me the bombs aren't already out there, I'll take back the raise and the promotion."

"Hey now—"

"Did you ever think you'd be working with a cyborg?" Sturtevant asked Zockinski. "Or involved in a case as completely off the rails as Gayle Street, or Glazer before that? Hell, fifteen years ago, I wouldn't have believed a fucking smartphone could even exist, and now I can't live without one. We've got to get ahead of new problems—we're going to adapt *before* change kicks us in the ass! Not after.

"The next time?" Sturtevant said, pressing a hand against the closed door. "We *will* be ready. They don't get to rip our city apart and walk away free. Not again. Never again.

"The four of you are all going to increase your training, your education—yes, Zockinski, the city will pay for it—and your experience in whatever ways you see necessary. Santino? Draw up a curriculum. I want it on my desk tomorrow morning.

"Do I think this bullshit cartoon supervillainy will happen all of the time? No. We're going to handle the tech crimes that show up every day, the ones that fall through the cracks in our usual methods. But if something like Gayle Street does happen again, we'll be ready."

And with that, Sturtevant left the room and slammed the door behind him.

There was a moment of stunned silence while the four of them processed what Sturtevant had said. Rachel was the first to shake herself out of it. "He must have been preparing for this since OACET went public. Maybe before."

"Man plays a mean game of chess," Santino said.

TWENTY-FOUR

A sign had been taped over what was left of the elevator, a heavy black **CONDEMNED** notice printed on top of a poorly photocopied seal of the city.

They took the stairs.

The mural was ruined, the journey from the center of the earth to the crown of the sky spray-painted over in bloody threats. At the top, the fire door had been staved in, its steel face cratered by multiple blows. It was no longer capable of closing, the handle and latch pounded until they had failed. Plastic police tape had been roped across the gap. Rachel started to weave her way through the tape; Santino reached over her and ripped the whole thing down, then used his shoulder to bash the door wide open.

"Vandalism" was such a tame word. The officer on the other end of the phone had used it a couple of times when he let them know the loft had been broken into—vandalized, actually—but no one had been there so no harm done.

That was a matter of opinion.

The loft had been turned into a landfill. The massive front door had been ruined by heat and pressure, and groaned inward on a single surviving hinge. The solar system was gone, pieces of frayed wire twisted over the empty space where each planet had hung. The small projects, those personal works which had dotted each desktop, had been smashed beyond recognition.

Someone had taken a sledgehammer to the clean room's glass walls. The room was silent; there was no happy hum. Bell's equipment lay dead on the floor.

All of that beauty, gone.

She swept her foot through the nearest pile, and the soft glint of mother-of-pearl caught her scans. Rachel ignored her aching ribs and knelt, gently brushing aside the debris until she found what had once been a piece of a wooden box. She flipped her implant off and cradled the scrap in her good hand.

When she turned her implant back on, she found Santino leaning against the only upright table in the room, staring at the pile of glass where fragments of his and Zia's equations could be seen, twined around each other to the end.

"This wasn't our fault," she said.

"I know," he replied. His voice was flat in the air.

"These kids were—*are*—good people. They got used by someone who wasn't."

"I know."

It had been a week since Templeton had walked out of First District Station. They had learned he had left the country for a vacation in Morocco, claiming he needed to distance himself from Washington until those terrible unfounded rumors about his role in the Gayle Street tragedy had died down. Morocco didn't have an extradition treaty with the United States.

The repercussions of an American citizen bombing his own capital were starting to emerge. The rage-smashing of the loft was but one outcome; some of the pundits had already declared Howard Rothbauer to be the perfect example of why domestic surveillance needed to be increased. When the objection was made that Rothbauer's actions couldn't have been prevented via traditional monitoring methods? Well, the pundits said, maybe this was proof that domestic surveillance needed to be applied using different strategies. More *innovative* strategies.

This last week had been one of those times when she was glad OACET had decided to go public.

Santino bent over and picked up a piece of glass. He turned it over in his palm, uncaring of the edges.

"I'll call Hope Blackwell," Rachel offered. "She's got more money than she knows what to do with. I bet she'll be happy to rebuild this place."

"It won't be the same," Santino said.

"I know." The makers could rebuild, but the spirit that had

defined the loft—that unbreakable optimism, the drive to create, to *improve*—might never return. "But it's worth trying."

He nodded, but the grays within his conversational colors didn't change.

She went to find a broom.

Her ribs throbbed as she cleaned, one-handed, but it could have been worse. After Templeton's interrogation, Jenny had used the biofeedback autoscript to keep Rachel under sedation for three days. (Not three days straight, mind. Jenny had allowed Rachel to wake up every six hours for food, fluids, and a trip to the bathroom. Towards the end, Rachel had felt so well-rested she could have fought a tiger during those breaks.) By the time Jenny finally let Rachel leave, her ribs and wrist had taken on that dull ache she associated with month-old injuries. There was no longer any doubt that Agents healed faster than normals. They just didn't heal fast enough that Rachel could talk Jenny into removing the cast.

It was several minutes before Rachel had cleared a space large enough to turn a second table upright. Santino, who had been watching her clean without realizing it, moved to help. When the table was standing, they both climbed on top, sitting within the small sanctuary she had made.

Rachel ran the thumb of her good hand over the edge of the table. The slate had chipped along one corner, but the table was otherwise undamaged; she took a large measure of comfort from that.

"We can rebuild," she promised him. "We can always rebuild."

"Do you know about Italy and Operation Gladio?" Santino's voice was still flat and lifeless.

The name sounded familiar, like a lecture that had droned on in the background of a class spent daydreaming. "Some of it," she said, as she ran the term through Google.

"It's the end of World War Two. Everyone hates the Nazis, right? But now the Nazis are gone and everyone's scared of Communists. NATO decides the best way to deal with the Red Menace is to embed a bunch of covert government operatives and paramilitary groups within different European countries. Back when it started, the plan was that if the Soviets tried to come to power, NATO would already have an infrastructure in place to deal with it.

"But what actually happened," Santino continued in that same dead voice, "was that NATO entrenched their forces, gave them a doctrine to protect the country, and then basically left them unsupervised except for the annual meeting with a CIA spook and his suitcase full of money. So? The longer the NATO embeds hung around, the more they assimilated into domestic politics, or were subverted through infiltration. In some countries—Italy, especially—whenever it was time for a vote or a political decision, someone would conduct a large-scale attack. Shootings. Assassinations. Bombings.

"The Soviets had almost nothing to do with these attacks. Most of them were done to motivate public support. After a while, it was common for someone...say, a right-wing organization, to bomb another right-wing organization, and then blame the left, or vice-versa.

"Italy got the worst of this—the country was stuck in internal conflict for decades, because each time the government was supposed to decide something significant, there'd be another shooting or bombing. It got so bad, the Italians called it the Years of Lead."

"I'd heard Operation Gladio was overblown. Almost a conspiracy theory," Rachel said.

"My dad's parents lived through it," Santino replied. "They believe what they believe."

"What are you saying?" Rachel asked him. The loft was cold; the broken windows funneled the November wind inside in dusty gusts. She was in her heaviest coat and starting to shiver. "If we don't learn from history, we're doomed to repeat it?"

"Are you kidding? Nobody ever learns from history." Santino gave a bitter laugh. "History's just an after-action report to show where we fucked up."

"How did it end?" she asked.

"The Years of Lead? You already read its Wikipedia page."

"No," she lied. "I'd rather hear it from you."

He gave a raw chuckle; he wasn't fooled. "Revolution, of course. Same way it always happens…the middle class got fed up and finally snapped."

He paused. "I don't know if we should make the effort to rebuild."

"Of course we should."

"Why? Does it matter if we do? I mean, does it really matter if we're already on the path where everything's going to be torn down anyhow? This case, and the one from last August?" Santino asked. "Our two big cases, Rachel. Our *only* two big cases so far? Both of them were frame jobs. Neither of them should have happened, but we've got no trust left."

"Learned response," she said, turning the piece of wood over and over again in her hand. She thought of her conversation with Jason, whispering aloud so the collective wouldn't hear them, Keith Rothbauer's body lying on the bed… "Every time we do put our trust in someone, we get fucked."

"Not always," he said. "Almost never, really, if you think about it. We just remember those few times when we did get fucked, and that's how we react. You're right: it's a learned response. We've turned ourselves into dogs who cringe every time we see a rolled-up magazine."

He stopped talking. Outside, the angry sound of traffic rose and fell with the wind.

"We can't live like this," he finally said.

"I know."

"We can't let ourselves be *used* like this. This lack of trust? *Anyone* can manipulate us—it's death by a thousand imagined cuts."

"Sturtevant thinks it's only going to get worse," she said, and then realized something important. "But Mulcahy thinks it'll get better. Those're two of the smartest guys we know, and they put us together for a reason. They know we can still turn this around."

"Maybe."

"Hey," she said, bumping his shoulder with her own. "We'll get through this."

He didn't answer for a moment, and stared at where the copper octopus had once nestled in its sink. When he did reply, she almost couldn't hear him. "I know we can't just lie down and do nothing," he said softly. "But do you ever get tired of knowing that everything we do—or make, or *think!*—can be twisted to make a bad situation worse?"

"All the damn time."

"Call Hope," he said. His voice had come alive again, but now it was shaking with hard red fury. "Tell her if she wants to pay to rebuild the loft, I'll do what I can to bring the others back."

He jumped off of the table, and walked away to see what he could salvage from the pile of glass.

Rachel left him to mourn.

She went downstairs and sat on the same landing where Bell and LaPonsie had hidden from the sight of Rothbauer's body. A light scan of the floor showed the MPD's cleaning service had been thorough; the only blood left was what had seeped between the cracks in the old linoleum floor.

She had told herself that Rothbauer didn't realize what he was doing when had he kicked her out of the way, but that thought didn't quite fit. Suicide by sacrifice was more likely, with Rothbauer driven past the point where he could justify the outcomes of Gayle Street with what had happened to his son.

Or maybe he had finally realized he'd been used, and thought he had one last chance to put it right.

She'd never know.

She did know she was tired of living like a beaten dog. Of thinking of everyone outside of OACET as enemies. Too scared to fully trust herself, to take a chance...

To make a change.

And in the back of her mind was Sturtevant, shaking hands with Mulcahy while saying, *"We get very few opportunities in life to do lasting good."*

It had been more than a week, but the crumpled business card was still in the pocket of her purse. She flattened the thick cardstock by rubbing it flat against the edge of the stairs, then ran her thumb along the embossed letters and the little bumps beneath it. She felt each number as she placed the call.

"Visual Cybernetics, Incorporated. Dr. Gillion's office. How may we help you?"

"Other way around," she said. *"I'm Agent Peng, with the Office of Adaptive and Complementary Enhancement Technologies. You guys might want to clear your schedule."*

Acknowledgements and Apologies

Maker Space was supposed to be a completely different novel than the one you've just read. *Digital Divide,* the first book in the Rachel Peng series, was released on April 2nd, 2013. It was my first long work of fiction and I was ready to drop. I figured I'd take a few months off, maybe write some recreational stuff to shake up my thinking, and then get to work on *Maker Space.* Two weeks later, I was on the phone with my sister, the two of us panicking because we didn't know if our mother had kept to her tradition of watching the Boston Marathon from the finish line.

This new version of *Maker Space* came from the institutional shakeups caused by the Boston Marathon bombings. I strongly recommend Brian Castner's article for *Wired*, "The Exclusive Inside Story of the Boston Bomb Squad's Defining Day," in which he describes how none of the traditional search-and-response methods used by the Boston Police Department applied to the Tsarnaev brothers and their backpacks full of pressure cookers. Castner paints a picture of how one of the world's best response teams found themselves in a scenario in which their training and their established methods were not only inadequate, but if used, could have allowed a bad situation to become much, much worse.

The ingenuity and imagination of the maker community is astonishing. They've been portrayed in this book as an artists' community of younger adults, but in reality, makers come from all walks of life. In terms of access to new technologies, there has never been a better time to be a maker (or a law enforcement officer, for that matter). In terms of how these technologies can be put to use? We've always had a history of twisting words and purpose to suit our own ends. As Rachel said, it's a brave new world, and we're all trying to find our way.

For myself, I need to thank my husband, Brown, for being there with me as we find our way together.

As always, thanks also goes to Fuzz, Gary, Tiff, Joris, Greg, and Elizabeth for fighting through the rough drafts. To Joie, Elissa, Erin, and Jonathan, who lent their names to this book. And to Danny, my copyeditor. We may never agree on hyphenated adjectives, my friend, but you have the patience of a saint.

Rose Loughran of *Red Moon Rising* provided the fantastic cover art.

Finally, *Maker Space* is set in a larger fictional universe. Patrick Mulcahy's story is free to all readers and is in graphic novel form at agirlandherfed.com. You can find updates on current projects and novels at kbspangler.com and agirlandherfed.com. Thanks for reading!